TEMPLAR SILKS

TEMPLAR SILKS

ELIZABETH CHADWICK

sphere

SPHERE

First published in Great Britain in 2018 by Sphere

A CIP catalogue record for this book is available from the British Library.

ISBN 978-0-7515-6497-6
C format ISBN 978-0-7515-7208-7

Typeset in Baskerville MT by Palimpsest Book Production Limited,
Falkirk, Stirlingshire
Printed and bound in Great Britain by Clays Ltd, St Ives plc

Papers used by Sphere are from well-managed forests
and other responsible sources.

Sphere
An imprint of
Little, Brown Book Group
Carmelite House
50 Victoria Embankment
London EC4Y 0DZ

An Hachette UK Company

www.hachette.co.uk

www.littlebrown.co.uk

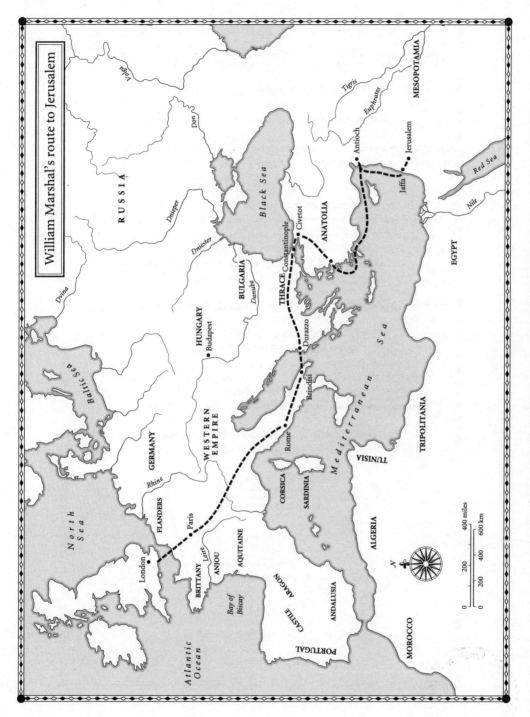

William Marshal's route to Jerusalem

RUSSIA

Volga

Dvina

Don

Dnieper

Dniester

Danube

Black Sea

Baltic Sea

North Sea

Rhine

GERMANY

FLANDERS

Paris

London

Atlantic Ocean

BRITTANY

Loire

ANJOU

AQUITAINE

Bay of Biscay

ARAGON

CASTILE

PORTUGAL

ANDALUSIA

MOROCCO

ALGERIA

TUNISIA

TRIPOLITANIA

CORSICA

SARDINIA

Rome

WESTERN EMPIRE

HUNGARY

Budapest

BULGARIA

THRACE

Constantinople

Civetot

Durazzo

Brindisi

Mediterranean Sea

ANATOLIA

Antioch

Jerusalem

Jaffa

Tigris

Euphrates

MESOPOTAMIA

EGYPT

Nile

Red Sea

N

200   400 miles

200   400   600 km
0

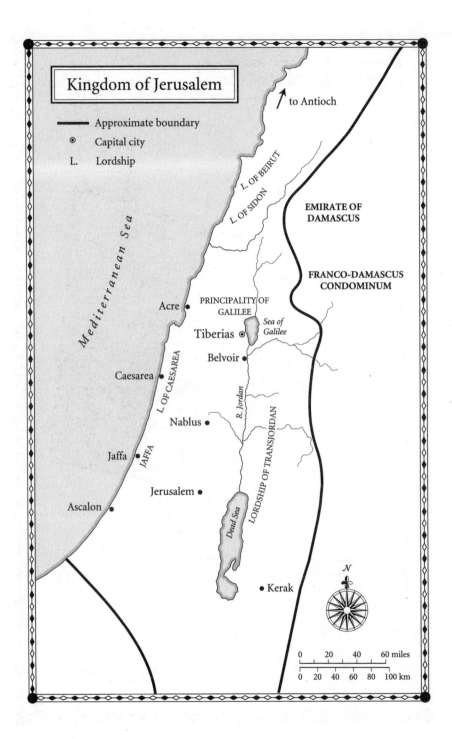

Kingdom of Jerusalem

—— Approximate boundary
⊙ Capital city
L. Lordship

to Antioch

Mediterranean Sea

L. OF BEIRUT
L. OF SIDON

EMIRATE OF
DAMASCUS

FRANCO-DAMASCUS
CONDOMINUM

Acre ●

PRINCIPALITY OF
GALILEE

Tiberias ⊙

Sea of
Galilee

Belvoir ●

Caesarea ●

L. OF CAESAREA

Nablus ●

R. Jordan

LORDSHIP OF TRANSJORDAN

Jaffa ●

JAFFA

Jerusalem ●

Ascalon ●

Dead Sea

● Kerak

𝒩

| 0 | 20 | 40 | 60 miles |
| 0 | 20 | 40 | 60 | 80 | 100 km |

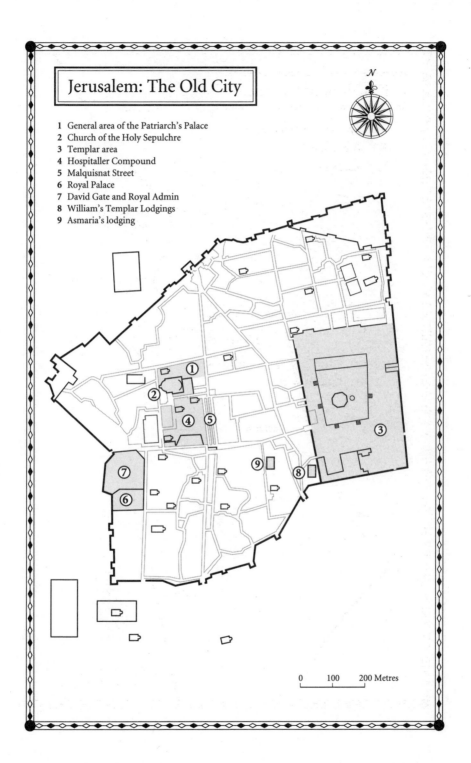

Jerusalem: The Old City

1 General area of the Patriarch's Palace
2 Church of the Holy Sepulchre
3 Templar area
4 Hospitaller Compound
5 Malquisnat Street
6 Royal Palace
7 David Gate and Royal Admin
8 William's Templar Lodgings
9 Asmaria's lodging

N

0   100   200 Metres

1

Manor of Caversham, near Reading, Berkshire
– home to William Marshal, Regent of England –
April 1219

'It will not be long now.'

William moved his head on the pillow in response to the voice, but he could not tell if the words came from his mind, from the spiritual realm of dreams and visions that kept him constant company now, or whether someone in the room had spoken aloud. He frequently had the sensation of being asleep even while he was awake and the struggle to return to full awareness took longer with each passing day.

A fresh breeze carried the green scents of spring to him through the open window. Sunlight warmed the triple arches of stone from stippled grey to pale gold, and flowed across the bed, enriching the plain brown blanket and touching his mottled hand in benediction. Gazing at the frieze running around the top of the wall, depicting his scarlet lion device interspersed with Isabelle's red chevrons on gold, he thought how short a lifetime was in God's great scheme. There was so much still to do, but his ability to accomplish it was over and others must now take the reins. His destiny lay elsewhere.

The door opened and a sturdy man in his middle years entered the chamber. After murmuring a swift word to William's Templar almoner, Brother Geoffrey, he advanced to the bedside. 'Sire, you sent for me?'

William exerted his will to focus on his visitor. Jean D'Earley had joined his household as a squire more than thirty years ago, and as he grew to knighthood and lordship had become a close friend and confidant. Even so there were things he did not know.

William indicated the flagon on the table beside his bed. 'A drink if you will, Jean.'

Eyes filled with concern, Jean poured clear spring water into William's cup. 'Have you eaten today, sire?'

Had he? Food meant little to him now – ironic when his nickname had once been 'Gasteviande', meaning that he would devour everything in sight and still seek more. What an appetite he had possessed, not just for food, but for the full, joyous feast of life. 'The Countess brought me a dish of sops in milk earlier,' he replied. The sustenance of infants, the elderly and the dying. He had only eaten it to placate Isabelle.

He concentrated on keeping his hand steady as he raised the cup to his lips. Two years ago, at seventy, that same hand had possessed the strength to swing a sword and cleave a path through the press of battle. Troubadours sang that he had been as 'swift as an eagle' and as 'ravenous as a lion'. Perhaps he had, although he suspected they were exaggerating in hopes of a good fee.

He took a few sips to moisten his throat. 'I want you to do something for me. I would not ask this of any other man.'

'Willingly, sire,' Jean replied earnestly. 'Consider it already done.'

William gave a mordant smile. Half a lifetime ago his own lord had spoken similar words to him on his deathbed and he had agreed, never knowing what it would cost him. He returned the cup to Jean. 'Your loyalty is wholehearted.'

'It is to the death, sire.'

William laughed, and then caught his breath in pain. 'Yes,' he wheezed. 'But not yours, not yet I hope.'

He gestured for his visitor to plump the pillows and help him sit upright. Jean's pummelling disturbed the dried lavender sprigs in the stuffing and filled the air with a clean, astringent scent.

'What would you have me do, sire?'

William chased the sunlight across the covers with his hand. 'I want you to go to Wales, to Striguil, and I want you to ask Stephen for the two pieces of silk I entrusted to his care after I returned from Jerusalem.'

Jean's dark eyebrows rose toward his thatch of silver hair.

'Yes,' William said. 'Half a lifetime and grace I did not expect to have. I need you to take letters to our men on the Marches too, but your priority is the silks, and you must bring them to me without delay.' He saw dismay fill Jean's eyes as he recognised the significance of the request. It was so difficult giving the news of finality to a friend who did not want to believe the inevitable even when confronted with the evidence.

'Of course. I will leave immediately, sire. But what if . . .' Jean broke off, rubbing his neck.

William reached out and gripped Jean's forearm as firmly as he could. 'Do as I say, my boy, and I will be here when you return – I promise. I have never broken a promise to you, have I?'

'No, sire, you have not.' Jean swallowed. 'I would not break a promise to you either. I swear I shall return as swiftly as I can.'

William looked toward the light streaming through the open window. 'The weather is set fair and the roads will be firm.' He gave a semblance of his old smile. 'I would go with you, but since that is impossible, I shall accompany you in spirit. God speed your way.'

Jean performed a deep bow, pressed his hand to his heart as he straightened and then briskly left the room, his step filled with pride and purpose.

Weak and worn out, William subsided against the pillows. He gazed at the arches of blue sky through the window, felt a light breeze stroke his face and remembered distant April days when he had competed in the tourneys with the elation of youth, taking ransoms beyond count and winning every prize. He had ridden in the entourages of kings and queens, life pounding through him with the speed and strength of a galloping horse. All that physical power and vigour was now a faint imprint within his dying body, yet the memories remained as vivid and rich, as joyous and painful as the moment of their creation.

The fresh air from the open window carried to him the sound of grooms shouting to one another as they saddled Jean's palfrey and prepared his pack-horse. If the weather held and there were no delays on the road, his errand would take him less than a fortnight. So little time, yet leading to all the time in the world. An eternity.

Closing his eyes, William sent his mind down tunnels of memory, until he came to the moment on a warm summer's evening that had led him inexorably to those two lengths of silk cloth.

It had begun at a shrine in the Limousin, and he had been intent on robbery.

Martel, the Limousin, June 1183

The small silver coin flashed as it spun through a bar of dusty sunlight before tumbling into the afternoon shadow and landing with a soft clink on the table between William and his young lord.

Henry – Harry to his intimates – eldest son of the King of England gestured at the fallen coin. 'There,' he said. 'All that stands between us and destitution.' He wore his customary smile, but his blue eyes were quenched of humour. 'No money to pay the troops, provide for the horses or feed our bellies.' He tossed his flat purse onto the table to emphasise the point.

William said nothing. The only way out of this morass was for Harry to sue for terms with his father with whom they were at war, something he would never do because most of this fight was about Harry not having the landed power to rule his own life and being dependent on his sire for funds.

They had foraged the surrounding countryside and villages, taking tribute by various often underhand methods of persuasion until that particular larder was bare. Having already sold and pawned their most valuable possessions, a second round of scrimping and tallying was not going to raise anywhere near the hundred marks required. Next week it would be a further hundred. They were cornered and facing pressure from their own mercenaries who were demanding their wages with threats.

Despite Harry's theatrical gesture with the penny, a few baubles still remained from his plundering of the tomb of St Martial a few months since – a jewelled cross, gilt candlesticks, and sundry items of altar dressing – but they were held in final reserve, to be stashed in his palfrey's saddlebags if he had to run.

Harry picked up the coin and flicked it again, light to shadow. 'I suppose we shall have to pay a visit to Rocamadour and request another loan from the Church,' he said casually. 'They have plenty of money up there and they are not doing anything with it, are they?'

The penny bounced off the table and disappeared into the thick layer of rushes strewing the floor. Resentment and challenge lurked beneath the nonchalance.

'Sire, I would counsel against it.' William began to feel uneasy. He had not been present at the raid on St Martial, and had no desire to become involved in pillaging a shrine as holy as Rocamadour.

'Hah, all the silver and gold that the Church has amassed does nothing but drape their chapels, gawked at by peasants and gloated over by priests. God understands I will repay him. Have I not taken the cross in His name?' Harry gestured to the two strips of silk stitched to the breast of his mantle.

'Would it not be better to renew peace talks with your father?'

William's words elicited a contemptuous snort. 'All he will do is pay my debts and tell me to behave myself in future without giving me the courtesy of listening. Hah! Perhaps I really should go to Jerusalem. That would whiten the old goat's beard!' Harry waved an impatient hand. 'I will do what I must – unless of course you have another idea, one that does not include my father?' He shot an imperative glance at William, throwing the onus onto him; making it his fault that they were in this situation.

William grimaced. The truth was that they had the stark choice between stripping the altars of Rocamadour to pay their debts, or face becoming the victims of their own mercenaries, who would deal with him harshly, because he was the paymaster, the interface between them and Harry, who could at least be ransomed back to his father. Nevertheless, he tried one more time, for God's wrath was not just of the moment, but eternal. 'Sire, I still say you should not do this.'

'I will decide what I should and should not do,' Harry snapped. 'Does any man dare to question my dear brother Richard? Am I less than him? Do you think Richard and his mercenaries would hesitate to take whatever they needed? Christ, he's been stripping Aquitaine like a butcher fleshing a corpse for the last ten years!' He jerked to his feet. 'See to it with the men, and keep them in order. Tell them they shall have their pay. Ah Christ, my guts!' Abruptly, one hand on his belly, the other flinging a gesture of dismissal, he hastened to the alcove housing the latrine shaft.

William left the room, filled with deep misgiving, knowing he was trapped. He had sworn his oath to stand by his young lord through thick and thin, and if that included the path to hell then he was bound on that same journey, defending and protecting Harry every bitter, fiery step of the way.

Crossing the courtyard, he was aware of the mercenary soldiers watching his progress with feral eyes. Sancho, one of the captains, had been crouching over a dice game in the dust but he rose now and intercepted William's path, folding his arms and pushing one foot forward to draw attention to the sword hilt resting on his hip. 'I trust you have good news for me, messire Marshal?'

'You will be paid,' William answered shortly. 'You have my word.'

'And I trust your word.' A hard grin parted the mercenary's full black beard. 'But the question is when?'

'By tomorrow night, I promise.'

'I'll tell the lads then.' Sancho inclined his head and sauntered back to his game.

William walked on, keeping his stride loose and his hands open while his thoughts spun in tight decreasing circles.

'Here, you'll be needing this. Get dressed and make ready to ride.' William tossed a padded tunic to his brother Ancel, who sat on the edge of his pallet, pushing sleep-tangled hair out of his eyes. The ties on his shirt hung open and his sturdy legs were bare save for his short under-breeches.

'It's still the middle of the night,' he groaned, squinting against the lantern light.

'It's an hour before dawn.'

'Where are we going?' Ancel fumbled for his hose.

'To arrange some funds – make haste.'

'About time. There's only soup bones in the larder and we're wagering with tent pegs at dice. Is it a long ride?'

'To Rocamadour.'

Ancel ceased dressing and his eyes widened. 'Rocamadour?'

'Yes,' William snapped, 'Rocamadour.' He lifted a satchel from a wall hook and slung it across Ancel's bed. 'You'll be needing this for the booty.'

Ancel stared at him in horror. 'It is a sin,' he said hoarsely. 'God will surely punish us!'

'It's a loan and will be returned with interest paid.'

'Yes, on our souls.' Ancel shook his head. 'We'll pay in hell – I'm not going.'

'Yes, you are. We have no choice, unless you know where we can find enough money to pay the mercenaries before the next sunset. If not, we might as well cut our own throats now and have done.'

Ancel pressed his lips together, his expression mutinous.

William eyed his sleep-tousled younger brother with exasperation. He had taken Ancel into his tourney entourage four years ago, and then into military service with Harry. Ancel was a strange mingling of opposites – innocent and knowing, dextrous and clumsy, often foolish yet possessing a core of truthful wisdom. An asset and a liability.

'We'll be damned for this,' Ancel repeated.

William bit his tongue. The only way to deal with his brother when he got into this repetitive pattern was to ignore him. He might sulk but he would do as he was bidden, even if it was with dagger looks and dragging heels. He could ride at the back, which would suit everyone. Someone would have to guard the horses and keep lookout anyway.

'Make haste,' William said tersely. 'Do not keep our lord waiting.'

Outside the troops were gathering in the hazy pre-dawn light. Amid grunts and spitting and snatches of uneasy laughter, they exchanged furtive looks, their mood one of defiant bravado tinged with apprehension.

Eustace, William's squire, was buckling the leathers on William's powerful bay.

'Is it true, sire?' he asked, as William grasped the reins and swung into the saddle. 'We are going to raid Rocamadour?'

William rolled his eyes. 'Not you as well! It is not for you to question. Keep your head down and mind your duties – understood?'

'Yes, sire.' Eustace dropped his gaze, surreptitiously crossing himself in the shadows, but William noted the gesture with irritation born of suppressing the desire to do the same himself.

Harry emerged from the lodging, donning a small felt cap. Unlike his knights whom he had bidden wear their mail, he was robed in his court finery – an embroidered tunic, a cloak edged with gold braid, and a fine red belt punched with silver studs – items held back when other personal embellishments had been sold to feed horses and men.

He gave William a fixed smile as he set his foot in the stirrup. 'Well, what are we waiting for? Let us ride to Rocamadour and secure ourselves a loan.'

As the troop lined up to depart, Ancel emerged from the lodging, his mouth narrow and grim. Without looking at anyone he tossed the satchel over his chestnut's withers and mounted up.

William gave him a hard look but let the moment pass. At least he had not had to drag him out by the scruff, and for now he had more pressing matters to worry about.

* * *

9

The shrine of St Amadour embraced sheer cliffs towering four hundred feet above the silver gleam of the River Alzou. Gilded in early morning light the chapels built into the rock face of the gorge seemed to shine like holy beacons against the new sky. William clenched his jaw and strove to ignore his misgiving and his fear of God. He dared not let a single chink of doubt show because it would take just one glimmer for the men to notice and react. Several were already on the verge of bolting like frightened horses.

Harry had resolved his own dilemma of conscience by declaring that the treasure was only a loan and that as the son of a king and a future benefactor of the shrine, he was entitled to borrow its contents. Even a fool could see he was justified. His father had had him crowned heir to England when he was just fifteen years old, and he had armoured himself in his royalty, using the dazzle of his easy charm as a shield.

A handful of soldiers guarded the entrance to the walled town leading up to the shrine but Harry and William had planned for that and had divided the troop. The dozen mercenaries they had brought with them from Martel were hidden well back out of sight. Riding up to the gate, Harry's only escort was his personal guard.

Smiling to light up the world, Harry announced that he had come to worship at the shrine, promising that he intended no harm, only reverence and esteem. 'I have been sorely troubled.' He placed his hand over his heart, his expression contrite and his eyes enormous with innocence. 'A dream told me to seek guidance and comfort here from St Amadour and the Blessed Virgin.'

The guards conferred and became two more victims of Harry's devastating charm as they took the decision to open the gate and admit him. From there it was easy. In a few practised moves William and the other knights disarmed the soldiers and tied them firmly to a hitching post. Three swift blasts on the hunting horn summoned the mercenaries. 'Remember, no bloodshed,' Harry warned. 'I want no stain of death upon this enterprise.'

Leaving the mercenaries and the squires to defend the gate, Harry and his knights made their way swiftly along the narrow street to the steep staircase leading to the shrine with its candlesticks and plate, its gold and gems and relics including the famed sword Durendal that had once belonged to the hero Roland.

Pilgrims fled in terror before the glint of mail and the threat of swords. Tense and alert, William expected to meet resistance where the stairs led to the terrace of the Virgin's chapel, but no alarm sounded. A solitary grey-bearded guard was present to keep the pilgrims in order, but he had been taking a piss in a corner and was still rearranging his garments as the raiders arrived.

'Stand aside, and no harm will come to you,' William said.

The guard spread his hands in surrender and was immediately disarmed and tied up. Two monks who had been inside the chapel rushed to secure the wrought-iron grille in front of the shrine, but William was faster, striding forward to thrust his mail-encased shoulder through the gap and force the brothers aside.

'Fetch your abbot,' Harry ordered. 'Tell him that King Henry desires to speak with him urgently.'

The monks bolted, robes flapping around their sandals. Half a dozen pilgrims huddled before the altar and William ordered them out, and watched them flee because it was easier than facing the mother of God and wondering what his own mother would say if she could see him now.

Harry approached the altar, with affected nonchalance. 'Leave these.' He indicated the statue of the Virgin with the Christ child sitting on her lap, and beside it a jewel-encrusted reliquary that housed a scrap of her robe. 'Take everything else.' He picked up a silver-gilt candlestick and admired the filigree decoration around the base. 'We'll definitely have this – my father presented this to them the year I was crowned. That chalice too.' He indicated a golden cup studded with gemstones.

Tight-lipped, William slammed back the lid of a chest standing against the wall, venting his pent-up fear and revulsion on the furniture. Priceless silk vestments encrusted with gems and embroidery shone in deliquescent folds of emerald and sapphire together with smocked linens as white as sea foam – garments intended for use on feast days and at times of high religious significance, but misappropriated now as bundles for bearing away plunder.

William issued curt orders and the men began stuffing the rich contents of the shrine into the vestments as if their haste would conceal their actions from the eyes of God. William directed operations and kept watch, detaching himself from the terrible desecration, knowing if he thought about the enormity of the sin they were committing, he would be overwhelmed.

Ancel worked in the background, scooping jewels and plate into the satchel while casting dagger glances at William, who eventually faced him out with a glare so steely that his brother dropped his gaze and turned away.

Their damnable work done, the shrine of Our Lady of Rocamadour stood bare of all adornment save for the ancient, blackened carving of the Virgin herself, her expression inscrutable in the light from the shrine lamp burning upon her stripped altar. Rape; it was rape. His belly crawling with nausea, William brusquely ordered the men back to the gate.

Alone, he finally faced the statue, and in the faint red glow fell to his knees and bowed his head. 'Holy Mother, everything will be restored, I promise,' he vowed. 'My lord has great need . . . I beseech you to have mercy and to forgive us our trespasses.'

The shrine was silent. The flicker of ruby light deepened the shadows and edged his mind with visions of hell, as far removed from redemption as the sky was from the bowels of the earth. Rising to his feet, he turned abruptly and followed the knights, forcing himself not to run.

The monks had gathered in a huddle of hand-wringing reproach to bear witness to the plundering of their shrine. Their abbot,

Gerard D'Escorailles, was an old man, but still strong enough to be forthright and do battle by condemnation.

'It is a great and mortal sin you commit in desecrating this holy place, and God sees all and rewards accordingly!' his voice rang out, filled with fire. 'Take warning for your soul; your kingship will not protect you from God's wrath. The weight of your sin will drag you down to hell!'

'But you can afford to give generously to poor pilgrims,' Harry replied, smiling. 'I am under oath to visit the tomb of Christ in Jerusalem; surely you would not deny me your donation?'

Abbot Gerard's white beard quivered. 'You commit blasphemy! Are you intending to rob the Sepulchre too and claim you do it in the name of Christ?'

Harry's smile remained, albeit fixed and brittle. He held out to Abbot Gerard a sealed parchment, written by his scribe before he set out. 'Here is my solemn promise that I will make good on our borrowing.'

The abbot struck it aside. 'Such a document is worthless when you thieve the belongings of God to pay for war and wreak misery upon righteous folk with your hell-bound men!' His gaze flicked with contempt over the gathered knights. 'What you steal can never be replaced like for like, for it will be scattered far and wide.'

'You have my oath that you will be recompensed.' Harry's expression was stiff with irritation. 'I would say five-fold but that smacks of usury and we all know how much the Church abhors that sin, don't we?'

'God is not mocked,' the abbot warned, his tone flat and hard. 'When you weigh that gold, you weigh it against your mortal soul. I shall pray for you, but in vain I fear. You are marked for hell.'

Harry flushed. Leaning forward, he tucked the scroll under the old man's rope belt. 'Until my return,' he said, and pivoting on his heel, swept out.

Following on the tail of his young lord's cloak, William felt the hostility of the monks and pilgrims boring into his spine, and beyond that, he sensed the heavy hand of God and the condemnation of the Virgin shaming his soul for eternity.

That evening, at their lodging, Harry gave William the task of dividing the spoils among the mercenaries. William did so efficiently, his blank expression concealing just how sullied he felt. Like Judas selling Christ.

Now Harry was solvent, the wine flowed freely, washing down chicken simmered in cumin, and coneys cooked in almond milk. A suckling pig once destined for Abbot Gerard's dinner table was served up with forcemeat and preserved apples and everyone dined until their bellies were as tight as drums. They all drank far too much, trying to smother with merriment and over-indulgence the memory of what they had done at Rocamadour.

William's reward for his part in the robbery was a pouch of jewels – sapphires, rubies and rock crystals gouged with a knife-point from the altar panels of the shrine. Tied against his hip, the little leather bag felt like a heavy sack of sins as he went about his duties. Yet he had to eat, to feed his horses and support the knights who depended on him for sustenance; as their leader, he could not be seen as weak or squeamish.

Amid the heaps of plunder was the sword Durendal that had once belonged to the great hero Roland who had died defending the Pass at Roncesvalles against the Saracens. Everyone knew the story. An intricate pattern of gold interlace decorated the hilt and the grip was fashioned from overlapping bands of rose-coloured leather. The sword had been thrust into a crevice in the wall and then chained to a ring hammered into the rock, but that had not prevented it from being appropriated.

'Blade's as blunt as a peasant's wits,' Harry said, examining it with a critical eye. 'Not been sharpened in years. The monks do not know how to care for such things. It probably isn't the real sword of Roland anyway. If it really belonged to him, it was meant to be wielded by a warrior, not left to rust on an altar.'

'Indeed, sire, but it is perhaps not the best way to obtain weaponry.'

Harry cocked his brow at William. 'Do I sense you are about to deliver me another lecture, Marshal?'

'Only that we should trim our expenditure,' William replied. 'Shrines such as Rocamadour are few and far between and do not replenish as swiftly as the men require payment.'

'Yes, yes.' Harry waved the sword and light flashed on the hilt. 'We'll discuss it tomorrow.'

'Sire.'

In desperate need of fresh air, William went outside to check that those who had drawn the short straws for guard duty were in their place and that the horses were properly bedded down for the night. Once he was certain all was in order, he paused by the trough in the stable yard to splash his face before uttering a soft groan and pressing the heels of his hands to his eyes. The enormity of what they had done was like a black tree growing up through his body and stretching its branches into every part of his soul. This was with him for eternity, this dishonour with God. Lowering his hands, he braced them on the stone sides of the trough and gazed at the moon's distorted reflection shimmering in the water, while in his mind's eye he saw the flames of hell reflected back at him through his own darkly transparent image. Eventually he stood upright, drew himself together, and returned inside.

Harry was playing dice, wagering with coins from the plunder, the sword resting across his lap.

William skirted the game and climbed the stairs to his chamber. The room was in darkness save for a sliver of moonlight piercing the shutters. From Ancel's pallet came the saw of ragged, distressed breathing. William fetched the lantern from the wall niche outside the room and, lifting it above the bed, saw his brother on his knees, his body shuddering with dry sobs and his fists clenched at his breast.

'Ancel?'

Ancel turned, his face contorted with fear bordering on terror. 'I dreamed I was being roasted alive by demons,' he wept. 'They drove their pitchforks through my guts and twisted them on their tines, and the Virgin of Rocamadour looked on and cursed me for what she had seen me do.'

Ice crawled up William's spine. 'It was no more than a nightmare,' he said curtly. 'Harry will make amends – it will all be returned.'

'You expect me to believe that when it has all been apportioned out? We'll never be forgiven for this and you know it! I should never have left home to follow you to the tourneys.' Ancel turned his back on William and lay down, curling into a foetal position.

'Ancel . . .' William opened his hands, then let them fall to his sides. His brother did not understand what it was like to have a position of command and make decisions for the good of all. Ancel loved to wear the glory and parade in finery, but had no grasp of the underlying realities. Others had to make those hard choices and then be damned.

William sighed, heeled about and returned to the dice game. Harry's place on the bench was empty.

'Latrine,' said Robert of London, nodding in the direction of a low doorway. 'Too much feast after famine.' A woman leaned over to refill his cup and he ran his hand over her hip and snatched a kiss.

Harry returned a moment later, rubbing his stomach and grimacing, but resumed his place at the table. 'Sit, Marshal, and play hazard,' he said. 'Have some wine.' He handed William an ornate rock crystal flagon from the spoils of their raid.

William took his place at Harry's side, poured the drink, and knew as Harry shook the dice and cast them that every man sitting at this board tonight was damned.

William paused on the threshold of Harry's chamber and braced himself. He did not need to ask the frightened servants how his lord had spent the night because he had heard the disturbance and the stifled cries of pain. Harry had been sick for several days and his condition was steadily worsening. Any food he ate was either vomited back up, or voided from his bowels faster than he could reach the latrine. William had seen the bloody flux often enough to know its consequences. Some survived; many did not.

He had told the men that Harry was recovering well, but had seen the doubt and disbelief in their eyes, and although he maintained an optimistic demeanour in their presence, beneath the façade he was sick with fear.

Entering the chamber, he inhaled the stench of vomit and faeces, and fought valiantly not to retch as he came face to face with a servant holding a bowl of bloody brown liquid.

'Get rid of that,' William ordered in a constricted voice, 'and see to it that the King has clean linen.'

The servant covered the bowl with a cloth. 'We have changed the sheets twice already, messire . . .'

'Then change them again.'

'The laundress has gone to fetch clean ones.'

The man departed and William advanced to the bed and sat down at Harry's side. 'How are you today, sire? Better I trust?' He noticed with dismay how sunken Harry's features were, the moisture sucked out of him, cleaving skin to bone. His lips were dry and drawn back from his teeth and there was no saliva in his mouth. William glanced over his shoulder at Harry's fearful attendants and shot them a warning look.

The laundress arrived with bed linen fresh from the drying ground and smelling of sunlight. Harry had to be eased out of bed while his sheets were changed. Pale and gasping, gritting his teeth, he hunched on a stool, clinging to William for support. 'If demons exist,' he panted, 'then they have set their talons into my entrails and are ripping them to shreds. I am shitting my life-blood into a slop bowl.' He sent William a desperate look.

'It is because of Rocamadour and the other shrines; that is what they are saying, isn't it? That this is punishment for my sin?'

'Sire, no one says anything.'

'Yes, they do, and they think it . . . and they are right.' Harry swallowed, the sound a dry click. 'I am bound for hell.'

William's own mouth was parched. 'No, sire . . . I do not believe that.'

Harry's face twisted. 'You do, and so do I. Do not sell me false comfort, Marshal, and betray me now.' He gripped William's sleeve, digging in as a spasm tore through him. 'You have been at my back since I was a youth, and steadfast in your loyalty.'

'Always, sire.' William's eyes stung with remorse and pity. Harry's royal parents had entrusted him with the position of protector and mentor to their eldest son and he had failed on all counts. 'And I shall not leave you now.' Others were already doing so – the vermin who always hung around on the peripheries of armies to pick up the crumbs and had a survival instinct to move on before the cupboard was bare.

'I do intend to return all I took from the shrines of St Martial and Rocamadour.' Harry's grip was like a vice on William's sleeve. 'You know that.'

'Yes, sire,' William answered. In a way, it was true, but intent and deed were not always the same thing with Harry.

The young man's face contorted as another spasm seized his gut. 'I need you to help me make amends, because I cannot make them myself.'

William was still trying to persuade himself against all the evidence that Harry would live and the words numbed him because they forced him to face the truth. 'If it is within my power, then I shall do it, sire.'

'Marshal, I do not want to burn in hell and I surely will without prayers and intercession.' Gasping, Harry struggled to speak, and William helped him to take a few small sips of watered wine.

18

'I . . . I want you to go to Jerusalem and lay my cloak on the tomb of Christ at the Holy Sepulchre.'

William stared at him.

'Promise me . . .' Harry's sunken eyes filled with fear and pleading. 'Do not abandon me in this. If you ever loved me, do this for me.'

'I promise, sire, willingly,' William answered immediately, concealing his shock. He set his hand over Harry's, feeling the bones jutting beneath the skin. 'But I hope you will make that vow yourself in Jerusalem.'

'No,' Harry whispered. 'This is God's judgement on me for my sins . . . This is the end – I shall not leave this room save on a bier.'

It was over. On the tenth hour of the tenth day of June, surrounded by his disbelieving and frightened knights, Henry the Young King, eldest son of the King of England and Duke of Normandy, died in suffering, lying on a bed of ashes on the floor of his chamber in Martel, a rope around his neck in token of his penitence and a simple wooden cross clutched in his hands. He was just twenty-eight years old but looked a hundred.

William stooped and gently removed the large sapphire ring from Harry's index finger, then kissed the back of his master's limp, cold hand. Harry's father had refused to come to Martel, convinced that the summons was a ruse of war and fearing assassination; however, he had sent the ring as a compromise and at least it was proof that a bond of sorts still existed between father and son, although now it would have to be returned to Henry with news of tragedy.

During his final lucid moments, Harry had again begged William to go to Jerusalem and lay his cloak at the Sepulchre, and William had repeated his promise in public before the weeping knights and clergy, gathered around the deathbed. Harry had been his charge in life and he had failed him. He had an even greater onus to protect him in death from the fires of hell, and if possible, which William was not sure it was, to atone for their sins and receive not only God's forgiveness but also the Virgin's.

Retiring to snatch an hour's sleep before dawn, William discovered Ancel on his knees, praying before a lighted candle and a small wooden cross. His brother had been absent when William had sworn to go to Jerusalem, because someone still had to be on guard duty and Ancel had volunteered.

Without looking round, Ancel said in a raw voice, 'All the things we robbed from Rocamadour . . . People came to that place and prayed over them for succour and intercession or gave them in gratitude for prayers answered. Now, because of us, they are tainted – all their power has been stolen. They were of no use to our young lord in his illness; perhaps they even brought about his end. Many will say he got what he deserved.' He drew a shaken breath and looked at William with glassy eyes. 'And if that is the case for him, then what will God's punishment be for us? We shall surely burn in hell.'

William sat down heavily on Ancel's mattress and put his head in his hands.

'I don't know what truth is any more,' Ancel said raggedly. 'I looked up to you because I thought you knew what it was, but after Rocamadour I no longer have that trust. All men die, and I do not want to suffer for eternity, which is surely what will happen.'

William looked up with an exhausted sigh. 'You are right. I will not make excuses. I came to tell you that before he died Harry entrusted me with his cloak. He asked me to take it to Jerusalem and lay it upon the tomb of Christ to atone for his sins so that he, and all of us, might pray for absolution from the crimes we committed through necessity. I know you only rode to Rocamadour because I forced you. I acknowledge my blame. Now I ask you to accompany me to Jerusalem and atone for what we have done. I will understand if you refuse.'

Ancel's eyes widened, the whites glistening in the lantern light. 'To Jerusalem?'

'Yes. And Eustace and as many of the others as wish to make the journey. I do not know if we will achieve our goal, or return, but better to die trying than to live with the sin.'

Ancel's throat worked. And then he gasped and put his face in his hands and tearing sobs shook his frame.

William set a tentative hand on his shoulder. 'So, what do you think?'

Ancel turned and pressed his head into William's breast, and when he spoke, his voice was thick with tears. 'Of course I will go with you – you could not stop me!'

'We will make it right, I promise,' William vowed, his own throat tight with emotion, adding with bleak determination, 'And I shall keep that promise with my life if I must.'

3

Tower of Rouen, July 1183

Ancel held the reins of William's powerful sorrel warhorse Bezant. 'I still say you are mad. Why would you give up your best horse to the King – your two best horses in fact?' He indicated William's second destrier, Bezant's younger half-brother Cuivre, who was being tended by Eustace.

William struggled with his patience. They had been over this several times already, but to Ancel, an opinion, once made, was set in stone. 'I have told you why. I will not risk these animals on a vast journey like this, and I know the King will accept nothing less in exchange for funds.' Besides which, William had a personal need to sacrifice, to do penance and purge himself. Giving up his best horses would help to balance the scales.

'The lords who rode to free Jerusalem long ago took their warhorses,' Ancel objected.

'And lost them along the way. Do you truly think any man arrived in Jerusalem on the destrier he rode from home?'

Ancel opened his mouth, ready with another argument, but William cut him off with a sharp look and departed to his audience with the King.

He had already spoken to Henry of his son's death – a painful interview conducted in the royal campaign tent in the Limousin. Henry's grief had been deep and raw but concealed under a surface of rigid control. Now that Harry had been buried in Rouen Cathedral, it was time for another audience. William was not relishing the prospect, but he was prepared and stoical.

He was ushered into the King's chamber which bustled with officials, scribes and clerics, lords, servants and messengers – all the many cogs, small and large, that turned the wheels of the most dynamic court in Christendom. The man responsible for the manipulation of all these cogs was slumped in his cushioned chair, one hand cupping his beard of grey-salted auburn. His expression was flat, and for a king with a legendary reputation for never a moment's stillness, this dull, world-weary pose was a startling departure. But then yesterday he had buried his eldest son.

William knelt before Henry and bowed his head. Henry said nothing for a long time, allowed the silence to gather weight in the space between them. When eventually he spoke, his voice had the grittiness of sifted ashes. 'So, you come to me, and I have to wonder why you should do so, and why I should want to set eyes on you ever again.'

'Sire, you are my liege lord, where else would I go?' William replied.

'You did not think that when you were biting my back, did you?' Henry sat up and leaned a little forward, his neck hunching into his shoulders. 'Why should I accept you in my court? Why should I not have you thrown out, or flung in prison?'

William's hair rose at the nape of his neck. It would be so easy for Henry to make him a scapegoat for his grief. 'Sire, you appointed me to the position of marshal to your son and I served him to the best of my ability through thick and thin. No more was within my power – would that it had been.'

Henry fell silent again. Flicking a glance, William saw that the King was fidgeting with the sapphire ring that Harry had worn as he lay dying. William had returned it to Henry at their last meeting and now Henry was examining it, pulling it off his finger, pushing it back, lost in thought.

William drew breath and spoke before the silence became impenetrable, 'Sire, in his last days your son asked me to take his cloak to Jerusalem to lie on the tomb of Christ and pray for absolution and I vowed to do so. I intend to fulfil that oath to the utmost of my life – nothing shall prevent me, save my own death.'

Henry shot him a sour look. 'That notion at least has merit, and perhaps it is best if you are gone from my sight for a while. When are you leaving?'

William cleared his throat. 'As soon as possible, with those of my men who choose to accompany me. I must go to England first and make my farewells and arrange funds.'

Henry said nothing, and William did not know whether to remain kneeling or back out of his presence. Another swift glance revealed that the King's jaw was trembling.

'Is that why you have come to me?' Henry choked out at last. 'For funds? Have you not got plenty of your own after what you have been doing with my son? Hah, you surprise me, Marshal!'

William took the blow willingly, but it was still like a knife slicing the scab off a recent wound and all the memories came pouring out of the gash, all the shame and bitter remorse of what had been done at Rocamadour. He had already been forced to petition the King to pay Harry's mercenaries their due wages. William had promised them that they would be paid and Henry had seen to it and settled his dead son's debts, but grudgingly, and he blamed William.

'Sire, I have brought you my two best horses – I thought you might keep them until I return.'

Henry's expression sharpened, and his energy changed, becoming brisk and business-like. 'You have them with you?'

'Yes, sire, in the courtyard.'

'Show me. After all, I don't want you saddling me with nags, do I?'

William took another underhand blow. He had never in his life owned a nag. As a royal marshal, he knew horses better than anyone, including the King.

Henry gathered his cloak, and as he stood up, the sapphire ring slipped from his finger and bounced away, tinkling across the floor tiles. Both men stared and again a short, terrible silence ensued before Henry turned away and, leaving the jewel where it lay, strode from the room. William followed him, experiencing a sense of desolation, for the dropping of the ring emphasised to him the non-presence of the Young King in the world and how final it was.

Henry stamped into the courtyard where the two warhorses waited, groomed and glossy, swishing their tails against the flies and tossing their heads. He studied the powerful golden sorrel and his darker bronze brother with a shrewd eye. 'How old?' he demanded.

'Bezant is seven and Cuivre six,' William replied. He knew Henry would accept the horses. He would stable them at someone else's expense and use them as breeding stallions during William's absence. Plenty of fine foals would be sired in that time.

Henry assessed the horses like an experienced Smithfield trader, running his hands over their muscles and down their legs, all the time making faces as if he were looking at inferior goods. Eventually he stood straight and delivered his verdict. 'For the love I bore my dear son I will take these animals and care for them while you are gone, and I will pay you a hundred pounds for the pair of them to defray your expenses. Should God spare you to return, you may come to me and redeem them for a promise to repay that sum.'

Beside William, Ancel choked with indignation, and William warned him with a swift nudge. 'Sire,' he responded, bowing deeply, 'it is my honour to accept with gratitude.'

Henry gave him a calculating look, assessing his sincerity, but William felt that they had returned to familiar waters, even if the sea was still rough.

'Let it be done,' Henry said. 'I will have letters made out for you to take to the papal court in Rome and also to my cousin

King Baldwin in Jerusalem.' Giving a brusque nod to conclude their business, and rubbing his hands as though washing them, he left without a backward look.

'I cannot believe you agreed to give him these horses for a hundred pounds!' Ancel protested, aggrieved. 'They are easily worth twice as much!'

'Would you have had me refuse him or resort to haggling?' William snapped. 'His son is dead and I was responsible for looking after him – for keeping him alive, and I failed. I knew full well he would not give me what those destriers are worth, but a hundred pounds will see us a long way on the road and our mounts will be well cared for. Others will give us funds and supplies and I have money held at the Temple. We shall not be destitute – and even if we were, I would go barefoot in my breeches to Jerusalem to fulfil this mission.'

Ancel glowered, but held his peace. William took Bezant from him, rubbed the destrier's white blaze and fed him some dried dates purloined from the royal stores. He had spent numerous hours training this horse and a deep bond of trust and cooperation existed between them, but he would not risk him on the journey. He made his farewell to Cuivre too before handing both animals to Henry's grooms. Watching as they were led away, he was sad, for even if he did return and ride them again, it would never be in the joyous tumult of the tourneys and jousts he had once shared with his young lord. That time was gone for ever.

4

Manor of Caversham, April 1219

Beyond the quiet tranquillity of his sickroom a perfect spring morning sported a handful of fluffy clouds against a clear blue sky. The light was so strong that it dazzled William's eyes and, walking beside his litter, Isabelle gently adjusted the brim of his hat to shade his face before taking his hand in hers. In Jerusalem he had looked into sunlight much stronger than this, but his eyes were attuned these days to the softness of shadows.

Usually people came to his bedside, but today he had felt well enough to attend mass in his chapel of St Mary. His marriage to Isabelle had given him the financial means to embellish and enrich this place as was the Virgin's due. He had sworn his oath to her at Rocamadour, and he had kept it here, at Caversham.

He was dressed as the Earl of Pembroke to attend the service, his emaciated body clad in a tunic of green cendal and a fur-lined cloak with clasps of gold. There were rings on his fingers for the first time in weeks, although Isabelle had had to wrap the shanks with her sewing thread because they were so loose. His physician had thought it unwise for him to make even this short journey, that it would weaken him, but William had ignored his advice. He was not going to recover. What did it matter if he died a day sooner? He would at least be stronger spiritually.

He would do as he had always done when at Caversham, even in extremity because Caversham was his home. The place where he had always been able to remove his belt, put his feet up on a footstool and enjoy moments of private comfort with his family.

A child in his lap, a dog at his feet. Isabelle smiling at him across the firelight. Isabelle lying in their bed, a pale shoulder gleaming through her heavy golden hair. This would be one of the last times that he came to the altar in his living body, and he was determined with all of his formidable will to see it through.

The knights bore William through the chapel door into the sacred space, and the light changed, becoming not of sun, but of hundreds of slender beeswax candles illuminating the jewelled figure of the Virgin seated upon her throne with the Christ child on her knee, and a heavenly crown upon her head. Incense perfumed the air and mingled with the candle haze creating a soft golden glow before her image. William begged silent forgiveness that he could no longer prostrate himself before her as was her due. Yet he felt enormous gratitude for the grace of entering her presence while he still had breath in his body. He would serve her now with his prayers, and again very soon in spirit, when the moment came to leave his earthly cladding behind.

5

Temple Church, Holborn, July 1183

It was raining in London, a summer downpour that dimpled the surface of the Thames and shadowed the water with the hues of a dull sword. William had crossed the bridge from the Southwark side with his small entourage and they had immediately been engulfed by the ripe smells of the wet city, a perfume so robust and complex that it raised the hairs on his nape, simultaneously attracting and repelling. Ordure and excrement, the brackish, muddy waft of the river shore at low tide. Smoke from cooking fires, the smell of people, wet wood and stone. As they turned from the river and into the butchers' quarter the meaty stench of offal struck them like a bloody smack in the face, thankfully not as powerful as it would have been in full heat. The rain also kept the flies at bay.

Their horses splashed in the muck swilling down the overflowing gutters until eventually they came to Ludgate and passed beyond the city walls into the suburbs where the scent changed to that of gardens, drenched and green. The dwellings no longer hugged each other like fighting drunkards, but were spacious with prosperity. Apart from occasional glances William paid scant heed to his surroundings, keeping his head down and his thoughts to himself. Unable to share his burdens with anyone in his entourage, they had grown heavier by the day. He did not suffer nightmares like Ancel; what need when he was living them every waking moment? He knew of only one person who might help him, but whether he would want to when he heard the tale was another matter.

Eventually they came to Holborn and turned in at an open gateway guarded by two serjeants wearing dark robes. Beyond a courtyard, stables and a packed jumble of timber and stone buildings, the tubby rotunda of the church of the Knights Templar was just about visible.

'Wait here,' William commanded his entourage, indicating an open-sided shelter built against a wall. Ancel started to follow him, but William ordered him to stay with the others and take charge. 'I need to see Aimery alone.'

Ancel scowled but did not argue and William left, entering the crowded maze of buildings. As a boy, he had occasionally visited the Templar complex when his father was working at the Exchequer. He had even attended services here, but the church had vastly outgrown its original foundation and its buildings were now cramped together as though squeezed by a giant hand. A new church was being built on land near the river just over half a mile away, but was not yet ready for consecration.

William paused beside a small pink marble fountain and dipped the chained cup to take a drink. A horse was being shod at the smithy and a hammer rang out in solid rhythmic strokes that beat inside his skull. Making horse shoes was one of the first adult skills he had learned, although he had still been a child at the time. His muscles still held the memory of the effort it had taken, and he could recall the pride in his father's eyes when he struck true, and the stinging red of the sparks on his arms.

With an abrupt motion, he replaced the cup and approached a doorway where two Templar knights stood guard.

'I am William the Marshal, formerly in the service of the Young King, God rest his soul. I have urgent business with Aimery de Saint Maur.'

'Brother Aimery is at his devotions,' one replied, eyeing him with speculation. 'Wait for him in the warming room and we will send a squire to tell him you are here.'

William nodded his thanks and, swallowing his desperation,

went where they directed. He could not bear to wait, yet he must. Sitting down on a bench, he clasped his hands and bent his head, feeling shivery and sick. These last few weeks had been like trying to keep everything together in a threadbare sack where holes kept appearing and he knew it was just a matter of time until his whole life fell out and ruined on the floor, leaving him holding an insubstantial rag that had once been his honour.

'Gwim?'

He looked up into the twinkling blue eyes of Aimery de St Maur and the holes in the sack increased in size as he heard that name from his childhood. No one ever called him Gwim except for Ancel and Aimery. The Templar's ruddy complexion glowed with cheerful good nature and although his brown hair was cropped and tidy, it still had that irrepressible boyhood curl. He wore the white robe of the order, a red cross stitched over his heart, and gripped a decorated staff in his right hand.

'What are you doing here – although you are very welcome and it is good to see you!' The smile of greeting died on Aimery's lips and his gaze filled with compassion and concern. 'We heard the terrible news about the King's son. What a tragedy. That poor young man and his parents. We have prayed daily for his soul – it must be a terrible grief to you. Were you with him?'

'Yes . . .' William swallowed. 'Yes, I was.' He pinched the bridge of his nose between forefinger and thumb. 'Aimery . . . I have come to . . .' He paused to steady himself. 'I need your counsel. You have been my best and truest friend since we were young.'

'Of course.' Aimery immediately leaned his staff against the wall and sat down. 'You know I will help if I can.'

'Well then . . .' William squeezed his eyes shut. 'It is all my fault.' He forced his words through the constriction in his chest. 'I should have found a way to stop him from robbing the shrine at Rocamadour. I broke my sacred oath to keep him safe and now Harry is dead and damned, as am I and those I led into

31

damnation through my orders. How will God ever forgive us for what we did?'

Full of consternation, Aimery set his arm around William's shoulders. 'Come now, God always forgives the penitent sinner. Many have committed far worse than you and found salvation. There is always hope.'

'I am not sure there is,' William said wretchedly. 'I might as well die in battle and let God do with me as He wills.' The holes in the sack merged into one and all the things he had been holding back, the vile, murky layers like the mud and detritus at the bottom of a river, came pouring out in an overwhelming deluge of grief, remorse and shame.

Aimery held him fast, gripping him tightly, rocking him a little as he wept. 'Hush now Gwim,' he said after a while. 'It is fitting to grieve, but it is done. God created you for a purpose and you should look up and follow it with vigour. You are my friend and an honourable soul whatever has happened. Do not think less of yourself.' He shook William and his voice grew firm with authority. 'You have too much to accomplish on your path to wallow in self-recrimination. Do you hear me?'

William drew a shuddering breath and cuffed his face. 'I want you to hear my confession, Aimery. That is why I am here, so that you will know everything – and then perhaps you will not feel the same as you do now.'

Aimery was quiet for a moment, patting William's shoulder, and then he said tenderly, 'Nothing will change, because I know your heart and I am not that easily driven away. I shall most certainly hear your confession if that is what you wish, although it is for God to receive. But I am glad you have come to me for succour.' He rose and extended his hand. 'Come, we will go and pray together.'

William rose unsteadily to his feet. He still felt ashamed and unworthy but they enabled him to move forward rather than remain stuck in a terrible limbo.

* * *

Later, Aimery joined William and his men to eat in the visitors' guest house on the edge of the crowded Templar precincts.

He clapped Ancel heartily between the shoulder blades as they took their seats around a scrubbed trestle table. 'William's little brother, but not so little now,' he said with a grin. 'A fully fledged knight and your own man. When last we met you were barely a squire.'

Ancel puffed out his chest and smiled, although the expression did not reach his eyes. 'I have learned a great deal.' He shot a glance at William. 'More than I ever imagined before I left England. Now here I am, bound for Jerusalem.'

The food was simple but plentiful – fresh loaves, a large pot of fish stew, and wine of Bordeaux to wash it down. Aimery blessed and broke the bread and everyone set to with a will. William had had no appetite for weeks, but was now ravenous with a need to fill the tender hollow inside him that had been scoured by his recent outpouring and confession.

'You were gone a long time,' Ancel remarked to William as they ate. He gazed curiously between him and Aimery. 'We wondered where you were.'

'We had much to discuss,' Aimery replied smoothly, sparing a grateful William the need to reply. 'A pilgrimage is a serious undertaking, and you have a sacred mission to fulfil. Whichever route you take involves peril. You must gather as much knowledge as you can before setting out. You will need funds, places to stay, and guidance on your road.' Dipping his bread in his stew, Aimery turned to William. 'I assume you are not going by sea?'

William grimaced. He harboured a deep aversion to sea crossings. Apart from always being sick, the awareness that a flimsy layer of wood, the skill of the crew and God's grace was all that lay between him and fathoms of dark water terrified him. Even crossing from Normandy to England on a calm summer's day was an ordeal. 'Only where we must. We shall go by way of

Rome. I have letters for the papal court. We shall cross to Durazzo at Brindisi and then take the road to Constantinople.'

Aimery looked sharply at William. 'That is a most difficult and dangerous route.'

'Perhaps, but the hardship will nourish our souls,' William said stubbornly. 'My young lord often spoke of the wonders of Constantinople and he desired to see it just as his mother did on her own pilgrimage when she was queen of France. I shall honour his wish and pray to the Virgin in the great church there.'

Aimery frowned at first, but eventually nodded, although he was clearly concerned. 'Ever since Emperor Manuel died there has been great hostility to Christians who are not of the Greek Church. Last year the Pisan and Genoan merchants in the city were massacred as well as many others not of the Greek religion. I have heard that attempts are now being made to conciliate and it may be that you can foster peace and test the lie of the land – but you should be on your guard.'

'I intend to be,' William said and folded his arms across his chest. Nothing would change his mind, for it was a dead man's wish and the more difficult the path the better for his soul.

Aimery rubbed his chin. 'I shall arrange letters of commendation to present at the Templar preceptories along the way, and other refuges where pilgrims are sheltered and made welcome. He drew a considering breath. 'We have two worthy brothers here who are travelling to Jerusalem and who would gladly accompany you and offer protection. I can vouch for their abilities; indeed, if they were with you, I would worry a great deal less about your survival.' He gave William a meaningful look. 'It is a Templar's foremost duty to protect pilgrims and it will reassure me to know you are travelling in their company. I would see you return from your mission so that we may share company on many more occasions.'

'I would hope for that too,' William said.

'Then I shall send for them when we have finished our meal,' Aimery replied, and touched the red cross over his heart.

Augustine de Labaro was a personable young knight, tall and lithe with flashing dark eyes and a white grin. He was familiar with the roads between England and Rome, for he often conducted business between the Templars and the papal court.'

'Augustine will organise the hostels and supplies for you as far as Rome,' Aimery said, 'and deal with all fiscal matters arising.'

Augustine inclined his head. 'It is safer to travel in a group and I shall be glad to accompany yours. Messire Marshal, your reputation in the tourneys and on the battlefield is legendary.'

William did not want to think about his reputation. What good was glory if it was corrupted? 'That part of my life is over,' he replied, although he bowed a courteous acknowledgement. 'My duty is to seek absolution for my young lord and lay his cloak on our redeemer's tomb.'

'Amen,' Aimery said, 'but your skills will still stand you in good stead on the road and in Outremer itself.'

The second Templar was an older man, wide in the body, powerful, with thick silver hair, cut short and bristling like a terrier's. Onri de Civray knew Jerusalem well and was returning there after a mission to England. His attitude was solid, pragmatic and composed. 'I shall gladly do what I can to help.' He fixed each man in turn with a shrewd stare. 'Brother Augustine is your man for the letters of safe conduct and such, but you will find me competent in dealing with practicalities on the road. We are both well travelled and know our business.'

William received the impression that Onri de Civray was assessing them and deciding whether they too knew their business or were going to be a liability.

The older Templar stretched out his legs and accepted a cup of wine. 'It is two years since I was last in Outremer but I will tell you what I know, although the situation changes from day to day.'

William's eyes were heavy; he was tired, but no longer sick and desperate. Tonight, he would sleep well, but was still able to absorb what Onri was telling them. He already knew that Baldwin the young King of Jerusalem was suffering from leprosy although it had not prevented him from ruling effectively and he had won several victories against the Saracens. However, the news emerging from Jerusalem was that his health was failing and he could no longer pursue with vigour the course required of a king in a beset territory.

'King Baldwin must name his successor,' Onri said, 'although for now he still holds the reins of power – more by iron will than anything else.'

'Who might he choose?' William asked as Ancel refilled their cups.

'Well, that is the difficulty,' Onri said. 'Many factions are quarrelling over the succession and there is no one with sufficient strength to unite the kingdom. I tell you this so you will know what you face when you get there. If you arrive bearing letters from King Henry, then all factions will put their attention on you and it is well to be prepared before you walk into a lions' den.'

Onri paused to drink from his refreshed cup and then settled once again into his stride. 'Raymond of Tripoli is a strong and steady pair of hands – he acted as regent during King Baldwin's minority but he has many enemies. The Ibelin brothers Badouin and Balian are his staunch allies, as is Bohemond Prince of Antioch. They are the best hope for stability in the kingdom, but they face many obstacles. King Baldwin's heir is his sister Sybilla's son, but he is still a small child and his father died before he was born. His mother has married again, to a Poitevan newcomer, Guy de Lusignan. As the child's stepfather, he is potentially the consort and guardian of the future ruler of Jerusalem, but there is no love lost between him and Raymond of Tripoli.'

At the mention of Guy de Lusignan, William stiffened. 'I knew de Lusignan had gone to Outremer, but I had not realised he had done so well for himself.'

'You know him?' Onri sent a keen look in William's direction, and also glanced at Ancel, who was sitting upright.

'De Lusignan and his accursed family murdered my uncle Patrick in front of my eyes when I was a young knight,' William said, with remembered anger and pain. 'Guy speared him in the back while he was unarmed. The Lusignans took me prisoner at that battle and treated me worse than a dog. If Queen Alienor had not intervened and paid my ransom, they would have killed me. Guy went to Outremer after he was banished by King Henry, but from what you tell me, he seems to have landed on his feet.'

'Indeed he has,' Onri said, 'and you had best be careful, because in the Kingdom of Jerusalem he is a powerful man on the road to the throne, and has even more powerful allies in Reynald of Châtillon lord of Kerak, and Heraclius the Patriarch of Jerusalem.'

William was dismayed. He had expected never to see Guy de Lusignan again and now it appeared that their paths were likely to cross in Jerusalem where Guy was in a position to do him great harm should he choose.

'The power lies with his wife, Sybilla,' Onri continued. 'She is the player on the chess board. De Lusignan is both her pawn and her knight; he does her bidding, and that does not sit well with many.' Onri looked around the gathering. 'In Outremer, the male lines often fail in the heat and it is the girl babies and the women who survive and spin their policies behind closed doors.' A note of disapproval entered his voice. 'Even the Patriarch has a concubine of such influence that she is known as "Madame la Patriarchess".'

William was not surprised. Great Churchmen often had mistresses, and he knew how the politics of the bedchamber played their part in ruling countries. 'And the Templars and Hospitallers? Who do they support?'

Onri withdrew a little. 'They stand on neutral ground. There is a widespread hope that a king of Christendom will journey to rule the throne of Jerusalem in due course.'

William raised his brows. King Henry was closely related to the royal house of Jerusalem; his grandsire had once sat on the throne and the young leper king was his kin. But he could not envisage Henry abandoning his many political concerns at home to travel there even if he had sworn to take the cross. He did not speak. Onri had been here for two years and must know the lie of the land.

William realised he had much to think about and a great deal more to learn as they prepared for their journey.

6

Manor of Caversham, April 1219

William woke from his doze to a bright, sun-flooded morning. He had made his confession to his chaplain, Roger, earlier and been shriven, lest this day should be his last, although he felt in his heart that it was not time for God to take him yet. The pain came and went and for the moment it was bearable. They gave him poppy in syrup to dull the sharpest pangs, but he insisted on small amounts, for he wanted to balance his critical faculties against his discomfort. How long since he sent Jean for the shrouds? He was not sure; his sense of time had detached from its anchor and swept him far out on an undulating sea where night and day, sea and shore and horizon blended as one.

The door opened and his eldest son entered, ushering five children before him. The look he sent his father held question, and concern, but also a sparkle of amusement. 'How are you today, my father?' Will enquired. 'Well enough to receive visitors?'

William found a smile. He had no stamina and knew he would tire soon, but he was comfortable enough and ready for a little diversion. 'Come.' He beckoned to the group of wide-eyed youngsters. 'Let me see you.'

The children came to kneel at his bedside. His own two youngest, Ancel aged twelve and Joanna ten, and with them his three grandchildren belonging to his eldest daughter Mahelt: Roger was twelve like Ancel, Hugh was nine, and their little sister Isabel was six. The future of his dynasty was spreading its branches like a great oak tree, and he was sad that he would not live to see these fine acorns become adults.

Will gestured for them to stand up. 'They have some entertainment for your chamber since you cannot join us in the hall,' he said.

'I would welcome that.' William's heart warmed. Amid all the concern for his spiritual well-being, he was still ready to take pleasure in brief snatches of the world.

The children linked hands and performed a carol-dance, Hugh singing the words in a pure, clear voice that brought a lump to William's throat.

Each child then performed a small turn. Roger and Ancel put on a wrestling display, not all of which William could see from the bed as they rolled around on the floor, but which they greatly enjoyed, emerging red and sweating from their endeavours. Hugh, more studious, read a psalm from the book he had brought with him, and the girls performed another dance that involved much waving about of silk ribbons. By the time they had finished, William had dozed off again. Through his sleep he was aware of whispered conversations, a soft tinkle, a fairy touch on his hand, and the rumble of Will's voice telling the children that their father and grandfather was tired but would speak to them later and had enjoyed their entertainments greatly.

When William roused, the children had gone, the sun had moved to another quadrant of his pillow and Will was talking quietly to one of his attendants. The children had left small gifts at his bedside. A toy wooden knight on a horse with an iron jousting lance, a soft doll wearing a blue gown, a silver harness bell on a worn leather strap, and a square of exquisite embroidery upon which perched a rosewater sweetmeat.

Noticing that he was awake, Will ceased his conversation and joined him. 'They tired you out,' he said.

William smiled. 'It takes nothing to tire me these days. Even keeping my eyes open exhausts me. I enjoyed their company and I am glad you brought them. What are these gifts?'

'Ah.' Will chuckled. 'The bell is because they thought you might want to ring it if you needed something and could not speak, and also a bell is a prayerful thing. The knight is to remember your prowess. Isabel left you one of her dolls for comfort and company.' He gave his father an amused, sidelong look. 'She sleeps with hers at night and thinks you should have the same succour.'

William grunted with amusement.

'The sweetmeat is from all of them that you might taste it and have pleasure.'

A sudden tearful sharpness stung William's eyes, all the more powerful for how unexpected it was. He had first tasted these rosewater confections in Jerusalem, fed to him under a jewelled dome by a laughing woman, her lustrous black hair sweeping his naked shoulders as she leaned over him, teasing him, snatching small bites and sweet kisses as she moved upon him and he moved within her. Long ago, long before Isabelle, long before any of his children had been born. His love for Isabelle was a powerful enduring thing, strong and deep as the ocean, but Jerusalem had been a walk through fire to a new forging and he had not emerged unscathed. 'I am supposed to be detaching from worldly things,' he said ruefully, 'but it would be good to taste it one last time.'

Will knelt to him like a squire in formality at the high table and presented the confection on its embroidered cloth. William was touched by the gesture. He fumbled the piece into his fingers, raised it to his lips, and as he bit down, the delicate flavour of rose mingled with the pure sweetness of sugar burst delightfully on his tongue and in his memory. But even as he chewed, his appetite waned. He craved the taste but it was so difficult to swallow and his body was unable to deal with the physical process of assuaging hunger even while his mind yearned for the experience.

'Enough,' he said having managed a third of the square. 'I shall save the rest for another time. It was well thought of.'

'I am glad to hear there will be another time,' Will said as he gently wrapped the cloth around the remains and put it on a shelf in the wall cupboard at the side of the bed.

'Indeed. I want you to share more of these at my funeral feast.'

'It shall be done.' Will's face clouded. 'I shall miss you,' he said quietly.

William lifted one eyebrow. 'I am not gone quite yet.'

'But you will go, and I shall miss you. For all my life, you have been a solid rock in my awareness.' Will swallowed. 'I love you for that steadfastness even though a solid rock can be infuriating and will not move from your path no matter how much you push against it. With familiarity, you come to love it, and it is part of you.'

William smiled ruefully. He and Will had often not seen eye to eye. At times they had been on opposing sides during the turmoil that had riven the country in the reign of King John not of blessed memory. That they had not drawn swords against each other during that time was close to a miracle. 'I loved you always, and that love is unchanging and it is with you always – even when I am gone. I remember your hand curled around my finger when you were a newborn and it was all that mattered in the world. You will never know how much.'

A muscle flickered in Will's jaw and he would have looked away, but William locked his own stare upon his son's in firmness and truth. For just a little longer he could be that rock.

Will's throat worked. 'I cannot bear for you not to be there.'

'You have no choice but to bear it as you must,' William replied. 'I can do nothing about it and neither can you, and that makes it very simple indeed.'

7

Rouen, late July 1183

The perfume of honeysuckle drifted across the lodging house garden, intermingling with gauzy layers of smoke from the fire pit around which the men had gathered to drink wine, eat bread and toast cubes of meat glazed in honey and spices. The light was pinkish-tawny in the west with the final tints of sunset. It was their last evening before setting out to Jerusalem and the long days were still upon them. For the first few weeks of their expected four-month journey they would be able to take advantage of those hours and, if the weather was fair, travel long distances.

Gazing around the small band of men who would be his fellow pilgrims and travelling companions, William wondered how this pilgrimage would change them and if they would survive to bring home tales to one day tell to sons and daughters.

This morning they had attended a prayer service in the cathedral and to the chant of 'Kyrie Eleison' and the reciting of the Pater Noster had taken up their satchels and staffs and received the Pilgrim's Blessing from the Archbishop, together with the presentation to each man of a small wooden cross. And then they had honoured the tomb of their dear, dead young lord, and made their solemn vow to fulfil his final wish.

Robert of London was one of the Young King's knights with whom William had tourneyed in his carefree days. A family neighbour from Wiltshire, he was a strong fighter, quiet and steady, although better at following orders than using his initiative. Tall, broad-shouldered Guyon de Culturo had a cheerful nature and was always ready with a jest or a practical joke. Guillaume Waleran was fair-haired, slender as a whip and unbelievably fast with a dagger. Geoffrey FitzRobert, a curly-haired freckle-faced knight, possessed excellent practical skills when it came to improvisation and repair. His quick hands could mend anything and he was adept at bandaging wounds and dealing with the horses.

The two Templar knights Augustine de Labaro and Onri de Civray had mostly kept their own counsel, but were not unfriendly and William hoped to become better acquainted as they travelled. A handful of squires and servants brought the company up to twelve in all, including his own squire Eustace who was serving both himself and Ancel.

William's gaze lingered on his brother who was sizzling a chunk of lamb in the coals at the side of the fire pit. He could clearly remember the day Ancel was born – himself a small boy, tiptoeing into his mother's chamber to be shown the tiny swaddled baby snuffling in her arms amid relief and thanksgiving in the family that both mother and child were safe. He had loved Ancel from that moment, even if exasperation and annoyance frequently overlaid the fixed emotion. They were very different beings, even if Ancel had striven to close that gap from the moment he could walk and talk, following William around, emulating him, wanting to be him despite the gulf separating their skills and personalities.

That bawling baby, that child who had dogged his footsteps was now a full adult, not overly tall, but stocky and strong. He had their mother's wavy brunette hair and dark hazel eyes filled with a wide innocence that was usually true, but occasionally feigned.

Ancel met his gaze across the fire and for a moment the brothers were as one, like a mirror and shimmering reflection, before they disengaged. Nothing was said; the atmosphere was full between them without words and the talking was over. Tomorrow the journey would begin and test their mettle to the full measure.

*   *   *

In the pre-dawn twilight, the pilgrim party walked through the dewy coolness from their lodging to the great cathedral of Notre Dame, there to pay their respects at the Young King's tomb and offer up final prayers asking for the strength to achieve their goal. The church was dedicated to Our Lady and each man devoted special prayers to her, prostrating themselves and begging her mercy and forgiveness for their sins.

Filled with determination, William knelt at Harry's tomb. The effigy had yet to be carved and the place was marked by a plain stone slab covered by a pall of purple silk. A sheathed sword lay upon it, the hilt pointing toward the head of the tomb, and the tip to Harry's feet – although Durendal had been returned to Rocamadour. A gilded sword belt spiralled around the scabbard, and a pair of golden spurs glinted at the side. There was a crown too, encrusted with rubies, pearls and sapphires. William had been present on the day the Bishop of London had set the diadem upon his young lord's brow and made him a shadow-king in his own father's lifetime. Now it decorated his tomb; but all the worldly trappings of kingship were worthless frippery when it came to the soul.

Lighted candles haloed the tomb as though it were the shrine of a saint, which was ironic after Rocamadour. Claims had been made that Harry, in death, had effected miraculous cures upon the sick. William wanted to believe such stories were true, and his young lord safe in heaven, but the heat from those candles might also be a portent of the fires of hell.

Producing Harry's cloak, William laid it over the riches covering the slab. The candles fluttered and then steadied as the garment settled. 'Sire,' William said. 'Today I leave for Jerusalem with my companions to lay your cloak at Christ's tomb as you charged me and as I have so sworn. My prayers for your soul shall mark every step I take and I shall do my utmost to pay your debt to God and atone for my own sins. Amen.' He crossed himself, rose to his feet, and lit another candle to join the hundreds shining around the tomb. The others emulated his gesture, all making the sign of the cross and bowing their heads. When the final respect had been paid, William lifted the cloak from the tomb, folded it in its wrappings and placed it in its satchel.

The pre-dawn twilight had yielded to the dewy green of a summer sunrise. As he left the cathedral, William felt as he had sometimes done when stepping onto the tourney field where powerful opponents were ranged against him and he knew the fight would be a tough challenge but he intended to acquit himself with honour.

Gathering his companions around him, he cleared his throat and looked at their mingled expressions of anxiety, eagerness and anticipation. 'It is strange to think that this is an ordinary morning, one we could see at any point in our lives at this time of year. But it is momentous too, because we will be changed from the instant we take the first step of however many we must travel to bring our young lord's cloak and our sinning selves to atonement in Jerusalem. We will face dangers, challenges and trials, but our faith and courage will carry us through. I am confident in all of you as my friends and my companions and I trust in God's mercy to penitent sinners that he will be with us on our journey, and permit us to reach our destination. Amen.'

The 'Amen' was repeated around the companions. And then Robert of London broke away to mount one of the two horses pulling the cart carrying their equipment. Later they would sell the cart and change to pack beasts, but this served for now. William turned to one of the two palfreys he was bringing on the journey, intending to ride them on alternate days. Both were sturdy, steady beasts with good wind and a comfortable stride.

A small crowd of well-wishers had gathered to bid the pilgrim party Godspeed, although few from the court, William noted. King Henry was absent governing his far-flung realm and Queen Alienor was a prisoner in England. To William it was like the final mark ending an era. His youth was gone. If Harry had been here, there would have been toasts and laughter, minstrels and largesse, and an array of clergy in glittering robes; but without him, the farewell was subdued.

A few men from the Young King's household had turned up to bid farewell, among them William's good friend Baldwin de Bethune. 'We shall hold a feast of celebration and remembrance for our Young King when you return,' he promised, embracing William. With a flourish he produced an embossed leather box of the kind that would normally have been used to transport a crown, but today held a dozen small meat pies wrapped in a cloth and still warm from the oven.

'Godspeed, Gasteviande,' said Baldwin with a grinning reference to William's youthful nickname. 'Do not eat them all at once.'

William laughed and shook his head, for Baldwin always knew how to lighten a situation. 'I shall try my best but I make no promises.'

He swung into the saddle and the company turned in a jingle of harness and rumble of wheels to face the open road. Children dashed alongside the group, crying out for alms, and William threw a fistful of silver that he had reserved for that purpose, flashing and spinning, reminding him of the coin Harry had tossed at Martel before issuing the order to raid Rocamadour. The children dived on the money shouting, jostling, and William picked up the pace. The cries of the youngsters followed the men like the tail end of a banner.

The town dogs pursued them for a while too, but gradually that ceased except for a single scrawny tan mongrel that trotted along at William's side, nose twitching at the scent of the pies. Taking pity, Ancel tossed the dog some dried sausage from his own pouch.

'You should not feed it,' William admonished. 'You will attract all manner of waifs and strays.'

Ancel shrugged. 'Then we are alike you and I,' he said with

a twisted smile and glanced at Eustace whom William had plucked from obscurity into his service between one tourney and the next. Ancel too owed his position to William's influence and largesse. 'You never know how useful they might be – they could save your life one day!'

William found a smile from somewhere and his heart lightened a little. 'Well then, I sincerely hope to find out before this journey ends – and he is your responsibility.'

Ancel acknowledged William's words with a sarcastic flourish.

During the four weeks of steady travelling it took to reach Rome, the company gradually became more closely knit as they adjusted to the daily routine of the journey and grew to know each other. Passing through towns and villages, folk waved them on their way when they saw the crosses on their cloaks and often donated gifts of food and drink, and offered lodging. Sometimes the men spent the night in pilgrim hostels, sometimes in castles, abbeys and preceptories, where they were made honoured guests in return for news. If caught between such havens, they would pitch tents, build a fire and camp under the stars. The weather was fine, the grazing was good, and their progress swift.

Ancel's stray dog acted as a unifying presence among them. He slept curled up against Ancel's neck at night and by day either trotted alongside his horse, rode on the prow of his saddle, ears pricked, or dozed in the cart. Robert of London had wanted to call him Fleabag, but Ancel declared that since he had chosen to walk the same path as them, he was God's creature and should be called Pilgrim. The name had stuck and the dog had swiftly learned to respond to it, especially when lured by a chunk of dried sausage.

Ancel fashioned a collar from an old piece of rein and groomed him every evening so that gradually he became less of a fleabag. Geoffrey FitzRobert made him a leather ball stuffed with wool and the dog quickly learned to play the game of retrieve and drop.

One evening, Pilgrim lay down on his back beside William, forepaws folded over, ears cocked.

'He wants you to scratch his belly,' Ancel said.

William rolled his eyes. 'I know perfectly well what he wants.'

'Well then.'

Despite himself, William obliged and the dog wriggled, changing angle, pedalling his legs in bliss. William relaxed and however reluctantly had to laugh, and felt healed to do so.

Another day they stopped by a waterfall cascading into a pool, to take refuge until the burning summer heat lost some of its ferocity. The water was crystal clear and icy from mountain streams and the halt provided a fine opportunity for a spot of laundry. Amid much splashing and bawdy jests about washer-women, the men bashed their shirts and braies on the boulders at the side of the pool and then spread the linen to dry. Pilgrim swam for sticks, and in between climbed out onto the rocks and shook himself over the nearest person.

Several small caves dimpled the sides of the waterfall, draped with ferny overhangs. The echoes they produced were stupendous and the men sat in the cool green hollows sheltering from the heat, legs dangling over the edge as they sang and shouted to each other, using the resonances as an instrument. For the first time since before Rocamadour, William felt happiness glimmer within reach and raised his voice, full, rich and powerful, in a psalm to the glory of God. The Templars, who had never heard him sing, gazed in wondering astonishment.

'You have a fine voice, messire,' Augustine said. 'I wish I was so gifted.'

'It has always been my joy to sing,' William replied. 'But I was not sure God wanted to hear my voice any more.'

'God always wants to hear the voice of His child,' Onri said with quiet gravity.

The Templar's bare chest revealed a curved purple welt along his ribs. William had noticed it earlier and said nothing, but

Ancel was less circumspect. 'How did you come by that injury, sire?' he asked.

Onri touched the scar. 'Turkish blade. We were attacked north of Nablus. A band of them came at us while we were escorting a pilgrim caravan. We drove them off in the end but not before they had killed two of our number and injured many more. I was saved by the skill of a Saracen chirurgeon working in the great Hospital in Jerusalem.'

Ancel's gaze widened. 'A Saracen chirurgeon? Did you trust him?'

'He was the most skilled man there,' Onri replied. 'The wound was putrid and my life hung in the balance. The Hospitallers trusted him enough to employ him, and that was sufficient recommendation for me.' He gave Ancel a penetrating stare. 'All is not as it seems in Outremer. Look once, and then look again. It is like a wheel. More than one spoke leads to the truth at the centre, and what is true at one turn will be upside down within a moment.'

Ancel chewed his lip. 'But the Saracens are our enemies.'

Onri shrugged. 'Some are, some are not, but you must decide for yourself who to trust. You will discover many who call themselves Christians have different ways about them and may be hostile, especially to newcomers. It is not only a different place, but a different world, and you must learn their ways if you are to survive.'

'Then I shall trust no one,' Ancel said and put his arms around the dog, receiving a series of enthusiastic licks in response.

William assimilated Onri's words and then said, 'Perhaps you will teach us how best to fight to counter these kinds of blades.'

'Indeed, it will be my pleasure,' Onri replied, 'although not all Saracen swords are curved. Many are straight like our own, and the best of Damascus have edges so sharp they can cut a silk veil in two and shave a man's beard to bare skin.'

Leaving the pool, he went to his baggage, returning with a curved sword sheathed in a plain leather scabbard. The hilt was decorated with an intricate geometric design and the pommel was set with a dull red stone. 'This is the weapon that wounded me. I keep it as a reminder of what it is capable of.' He handed it around for everyone to examine. 'You are all experienced warriors, well practised. You know that half the battle lies in out-thinking and outmanoeuvring your opponent. In taking a superior tactical position. It is not how swiftly you move, it is how quickly you think.' He tapped his temple.

There were nods all round. William noted the gleam in Onri's eyes and felt an answering spark. 'Will you show us?'

Onri dipped his head and William sent Eustace to fetch his sword from his pack. He had fought sword against the Saracen shamshir before, but as a novelty at a tourney. He and Harry had sparred with one out of curiosity, taking turns, but it had not been a discipline either of them had pursued.

Eustace returned from the cart with William's sword and shield while Onri had a small round Saracen buckler brought from his own baggage.

William studied the way Onri positioned his feet for the terrain always had to be taken into account.

'Come at me,' Onri said. 'Remember that on the ground, even if you think you are light and swift, your enemy will be lighter and swifter still, and you will not see the cut coming.'

William attacked and Onri parried and hooked the Saracen shamshir under William's shield. 'It is like the beak of a vulture,' Onri said, moving back, 'and it will tear out your entrails and stop your heart in the time it takes you to step forward into the blow. Again.'

Onri proceeded to show William the ways of the Saracen blade, although it was but a short demonstration of the basic technique – how to be aware of the devices and tricks that differed from a straight sword and how to react and counter-attack.

Onri practised with the others, too; as usual Ancel was the

slowest learner, clearly signalling his responses when he attacked and defended, and constantly being caught out by the probes and feints of the curved blade. William watched impassively and was not overly dismayed. Ancel was a thoroughly competent and trust-worthy swordsman who could hold his place in any line and fight his corner well, but it took him a long time to learn. Once he had absorbed a technique by constant drilling and repetition it stayed with him for ever, never losing its edge, but what William could grasp in a day took Ancel a week.

Red-faced and dogged but increasingly flustered and ashamed, Ancel wanted to continue the fight, but it was time to cool off in the pool again before donning their now clean, dry clothes and riding on.

'It will come with practice,' William told Ancel as they dressed. He nudged his shoulder supportively. 'We both know that.'

Ancel shrugged moodily, but William let it go, knowing that he would come around if left to his own devices.

That night, under the white ball of the moon, the pilgrim group camped on the outskirts of a small village. Eustace cooked a stew with two fowl purchased from a farm along the way, seasoned with onions, herbs and garlic. They had bread too – the remnants of loaves doled out at yesterday's pilgrim hostel, hard but edible once soaked in the stew.

'What will we do after we reach Jerusalem?' Ancel asked, scraping his bowl so clean that it only required a quick polish on his cuff. Pilgrim lay at his feet, crunching a chicken bone held upright between his forepaws. 'After we have laid the cloak and fulfilled our duty, are we to turn around and come straight home?' As usual he had recovered from his sulk as they rode along, and was back to his customary self.

William shook his head. 'We can decide that later. We do not know what we will find and there are places other than Jerusalem in Outremer to visit and worship. If we arrive in time to celebrate the Nativity, then we should stay until Easter to mark Christ's rising from the dead. There will be many opportunities for employment given the skills we possess, and we have our introductions to the court.'

Ancel nodded but still looked pensive.

William was conscious of his brother's need to know what was around every corner, but could not give him that assurance when he did not know himself. Each new day along their route brought fresh challenges; indeed, he was very aware that they might not reach their destination at all.

'And our souls will be cleansed and we will find forgiveness.'

'Yes.'

'I need to know that,' Ancel said almost forlornly.

Roughly pulling him close, William kissed his forehead. 'In Jerusalem all sins are forgiven, and in the meantime all we can do is travel in hope.' As he spoke he realised he had found that glimmer of hope during their weeks on the road, even if it was a delicate light that could easily be extinguished. He had to believe because the alternative glow brought him straight to the flames of hell.

Under a grey wash of moonlight, William took the cloak satchel and, quietly leaving the camp, walked down the track to the simple village church, dedicated to the Virgin – one of the reasons he had stopped here for tonight. The wooden door creaked open and, stooping under the arch, William bowed and crossed himself before entering the nave. The only light came from moonbeams slanting through the windows which were plain, unlike those of the great cathedrals and wealthy churches of towns and abbeys with their stained-glass jewels. Yet the corbels on the pillars were exquisitely chiselled with foliate designs and over the altar was painted a vivid portrayal of the crucifixion on the left, and Mary's ascent to heaven on the right. On the altar itself stood a cross of silver gilt, a garnet at its centre like a perfect drop of blood, and beside it a statue of the Virgin with the Christ child in her lap, lovingly carved, the paint softened into richness by the dim light of the hanging lamp.

William took the cloak from the satchel and spread it before the statue, and prostrating himself, prayed. He and his men had paused at many churches and shrines along their road, marking each place as a sacred point on their journey like jewels on a robe – Chartres, Tours, Vézelay, William had been careful never to make a parade of the cloak in public because it was his sacred charge and he knew some folk viewed it as a relic itself and might not be above appropriating it for their own purposes. However, in moments alone like this, he could tap into a deeper well of spirituality and open out the cloak, which to him had almost become the disembodied representation of his young lord.

The hours passed and the moon climbed the sky, shining down as clear as winter daylight upon William's spread-eagled form as he prayed, asking forgiveness and mercy for the sins he and his young lord had committed. Even in the midst of his devotion, a thin strand of awareness held him to his surroundings and alerted him to the faint squeak of the door hinges and a soft footfall. In haste but without panic, William eased to his knees, crossed himself to honour the Virgin, and began carefully folding the cloak.

Onri quietly joined him, going down on one knee in the moon-light, crossing himself and venerating the altar. 'I saw you leave the camp.' He glanced at the folded cloak.

'And you deemed it necessary to follow me?'

'You were gone a long time,' Onri said. 'You might say it is none of my business, but I am a monk as well as a warrior and Aimery bade me look to your well-being.'

William fastened the cover around the cloak. 'I know Aimery has my best interests at heart, but I am not in need.'

Onri inclined his head. 'Then forgive me for intruding on your prayers, and I hope you found what you sought.'

William crossed himself, reverenced the Virgin once more and turned to leave. 'Enough that I can sleep.'

Onri followed him. 'Brother Aimery thinks very highly of you,' he said as they stepped outside into the blue-grey half-light.

William shrugged. 'I do not understand why, save that he has a good heart and we have known each other since we were children.'

Onri clasped his hands behind his back. 'Brother Aimery recognises the potential in men – it is his particular skill. As you say, he has a good heart, and when he focuses on someone and goes out of his way to help him, then I pay attention.'

William said nothing. He was not at all certain that Aimery's judgement was sound in his case and perhaps owed too much to childhood loyalties.

'Have you ever considered becoming a Templar?' Onri asked as they returned along the track.

William shook his head. 'I am not deserving of the white mantle.'

'But if you were to become worthy in time through prayer and deed?'

Frowning, William wondered what lay behind Onri's question. Recruitment into the order? The Templars were always seeking knights with competent fighting or administrative abilities to join them. His family had had connections with the Templars since he was a boy. His father had granted his manor at Rockley to them and William himself had received his own religious instruction from his father's almoner who had been one of their order. He admired the military organisation, the discipline and devotion of the men who took the vows, but he had never thought beyond that to his own future. 'Perhaps,' he said, hedging his reply. 'I do not know my road beyond the one to Jerusalem. Until that is accomplished, all else must bide.'

Onri accepted the response with composure. 'If ever you should consider taking vows, I know Aimery would speak for you, as would I – but I understand that for now you have other duties and responsibilities to discharge.' Onri lightly touched William's arm before moving off to his bedroll.

William lay down and gazed at the sky, thinking about what Onri had said. He truly did not know his road beyond Jerusalem, although he had vowed to many people that he would return if he was able. But what then? King Henry had said he would give him a position at court but Henry's promises were fickle and Queen Alienor could only give him limited assistance because she was her husband's prisoner. However, to commit himself to the Templars would be an irrevocable step, cutting him off from ordinary life; from his family, his siblings, nieces and nephews. He would never have heirs. One day he might walk away from all those worldly concerns and desires, but for now it was too great a step, and he was not worthy in his own eyes to fulfil such a calling.

Of course, a man might join the Templars in a temporary way and dedicate himself to their service for a set amount of time without taking vows – as many did in fulfilment of penance. He acknowledged that Onri probably knew exactly what he was doing in planting an idea following a moment of deep spiritual contemplation when the soil was at its most fertile.

Placing the cloak against his pillow, William turned his shoulder to the sky and closed his eyes. Fertile perhaps, but not ready to be sown.

8

Manor of Caversham, April 1219

William studied his vassal and knight Henry FitzGerold whose turn it was to sit in vigil at his bedside. It was night and all the shutters were closed, and the lamps in the room gave off a soft golden light. Henry had just given William a drink of water and was frowning pensively.

'Is there something wrong?' William asked as he took small sips from the cup, striving to hold it steady from a stubborn sense of independence.

'No, sire, save that I am grieved to see you so unwell.'

William gave a humourless smile. 'Well only my death will change that, and then I shall not be sick any more.'

'Sire, you should not say that,' Henry replied, looking uncomfortable.

'Why?' William asked forthrightly. 'There is always hope, Henry, but in me now, it is the hope of release from earthly bonds.'

Henry lowered his gaze. 'We do not want to lose you, sire. In truth, I am a little troubled but I do not wish to burden you.'

Henry's words emphasised to William how often his men had brought their difficulties to him and sought his advice. Soon he would not be there for them save as a memory, and he experienced a pang of guilt. 'Come, what is your trouble?' he asked. 'I will not be able to counsel you for much longer, but for now I shall do my best.'

Henry looked troubled. 'A priest said to me in church that no man will find salvation on any account unless he returns all that he has taken in his lifetime.' He screwed up his face. 'I would not bother you, but I am worried for your soul.'

William had not thought he had the energy to feel irritation and anger any more, but the emotions surged through his body like wine from the dregs of the barrel, red and silty. Although Henry had not said which priest, he knew full well it would be one of the household clerks or chaplains, probably Philip, who despite pleading poverty was overly bothered about ways of making money and gaining approval from his peers.

'Churchmen always give us to believe that no man will find salvation on any account unless he goes from the world naked,' William said. 'They shave us too closely while not shaving themselves. If because I have taken the ransoms of five hundred knights in tourneys and kept their arms, their horses and all their equipment the door of heaven is closed in my face, there is nothing I can do about it. What matters more is penitence in the heart and a wish to atone for one's sins. Men of the Church might push me, but I have reached my sticking point on this score. Either their argument is false, which I believe, or else no man may find salvation.'

Henry reddened. 'Without a doubt, you are right. I should not have listened, and I should not have let him go unchallenged.'

'I can tell you from a lifetime's experience that the interests of the Church are closely connected to Saint Silver and Saint Gold. If I cannot enter through the gates of heaven, then that leaves the Pope without a chance.' He gave a rusty chuckle. 'If I do not let it trouble me, then you must not let it trouble you. Only listen to those men of the Church whom you trust to have your best interests at heart – and God's – and that is not the same as their interests and the interests of the Church.' He fixed Henry with a firm stare. 'Do I make myself clear?'

'Entirely, sire.'

'Then all is well,' William said, and closed his eyes.

9

Rome, August 1183

William and his men arrived in Rome at the end of August after a month on the road. The octogenarian Pope Lucius was not in residence, but had retired to Verona, incapable of dealing with the sharp knives of politics in the city.

William and his company found lodgings in a hostel not far from the Lateran Palace, although Onri and Augustine made their own accommodation at the Templar preceptory on the Aventine Hill. Although the papal court had mostly moved to Verona, a nucleus remained in Rome to whom William delivered Henry's letters. Indeed, although the Pope had absented himself, a new Vatican palace was under construction and churches and palaces were springing up within the city faster than mushrooms in humid autumn weather. A hundred years ago, Rome had been sacked by the Norman adventurer Robert Guiscard, but since then the rebuilding and embellishment had continued apace.

William and his company stayed in the city for three days, resting themselves and their mounts, replenishing supplies, obtaining money and safe conducts using the documentation from the Temple Church in London, and securing the all-important indulgences, forgiving sins, for which Rome was renowned for being especially generous.

The men visited the churches, wondering at the apse mosaics of St Clemente and the marble fittings of the quire and the frescoes of Santa Maria Antiqua. Everywhere work of striking beauty dazzled William's eyes, executed in gold and gilt, with glass and marble tesserae. The great cathedrals of England and France had nothing to match the splendour of Rome.

He drank in the magnificence, not just for himself but for Harry too, using his own eyes to see for Harry and include him in the experience by proxy. He laid the cloak before the altars in the churches where he prayed, seeking atonement for their sins. St Peter's and St Paul's, St Lorenzo, St Giovanni in Laterano, St Mary of the Crib, St Mary Cosmedin.

On the last day, William took the opportunity to view the older, pagan edifices of the city because he knew Harry would have been fascinated. With Ancel in tow, William visited the Colosseum and the Forum, the temples and unknown walled structures, walking around the tumbled, weed-choked stones of a past mighty civilisation, eyes wide to absorb as much as he could but knowing he could never do more than garner a general impression in the time allotted.

Pausing in a shady courtyard to take a respite from the baking heat, the brothers came upon the statue of a woman with hands raised to her tumbling hair, a wisp of stone cloth flowing diagonally over her body, leaving little to the imagination. Vestiges of flesh colour lingered in the elbow crevices and along her jawline. The cloth wisp had once been bright blue.

'Do you remember the statue we had in the courtyard at Hamstead?' Ancel asked. 'A naked man with his right arm raised?'

William chuckled. 'Yes; he'd lost his hand, so we had to guess what he had been holding. Mama thought a bunch of grapes.' He folded his arms. 'During the war, our father raided a merchant train bound for Winchester, and it was among the spoils. The Bishop was a keen collector of pagan statuary. Do you know what happened to it?'

Ancel shrugged. 'Our father sold it while you were away training in Normandy. He said the silver it fetched could be put to better use than having it hang around gathering pigeon shit. The last straw for him was when our sisters dressed it up in tunic and hose and put a garland on its head – although I think he was secretly amused.'

William grinned at the image Ancel had conjured. Their father had been a pragmatic man who had never suffered fools gladly, but he had possessed a biting, sarcastic wit.

'I wonder what he would have thought of Rome,' Ancel mused.

'He would have had no time for the bureaucracy or the statues, but he'd have been interested in the defences – and he'd have appreciated the brothels.'

'Yes,' Ancel said. 'That's what I thought – especially the brothels.'

On their last night in Rome, William and his men, except for the Templars and their serjeant who were at the preceptory, dined together at an eating house near their lodging. They raised toasts to the Young King, remembering the times when life was sweet and unburdened by bitter grief, when they had followed the tourney circuit, jousting by day and carousing by night, care-free and unfettered.

The women of the establishment offered services beyond the provision of food and wine. William was reminded of the cook shops and bath houses in Southwark across the Thames from London where such comforts could be procured; indeed, the Bishop of Winchester was the landlord of several of those establishments and one of his statues had graced the garden of the most exclusive one.

A woman with honey-brown plaits and hazel eyes sat down beside William and, taking his hand in hers, traced her forefinger over the lines on his palm. 'They say you can read a person's road in life by the maps written here,' she said in passable French.

William eyed her with amusement. 'Do they now? And what does mine tell you?'

She smiled, revealing crooked front teeth. 'I could not say, because such reading is not Christian, but your hand is strong, and you are a man with fine tastes.' She lazily wandered her finger up and down his palm, sending a surge to other parts of his body. It was a long way to Jerusalem and only the Templars were under a vow of chastity. Fornication was a minor sin compared to the reason for their pilgrimage. If a bishop could endorse a brothel, then a knight could be entertained in one.

He let the woman take his hand and lead him to a curtained-off chamber, dimly lit by a hanging lamp. The bed cover was clean; he had seen far worse in military camps, on the tourney circuit, and sometimes at court. The woman was pleasing and professional – enough that he gave her an extra coin when their business was concluded. She told him her name was Magdalena. 'A fitting name for my profession, no?'

'Perhaps, but it has its own grace,' he replied, and bowed to her as if she was a lady of high estate.

'Pray for me in Jerusalem,' she said.

Going outside, he leaned against the wall. The night was clear and stars sparkled to eternity across a moonless sky. His body felt heavy and earth-bound, but calm.

The door opened and Ancel emerged, buckling his belt, sleeking his hair. 'Eustace will be a while,' he said. 'He's going for second helpings.'

William shook his head and grinned. 'He always does say extra prayers at the shrines of such ladies when he gets the opportunity.'

'What was yours like?'

'She asked me to pray for her, and I said I would.' He did not reciprocate the question because he did not want to know. 'Are you ready for the morrow?'

Ancel nodded pensively.

'We should reach Brindisi in just over a week if the roads are good.'

'And then into unknown territory.'

William shared Ancel's tension but concealed it. 'With God's help, we will get there. If there is danger, we are united and that makes us strong.'

One by one the others emerged, laughing, joking, looking a little sheepish, but smug too. Eustace was the last to leave, still tucking himself inside his braies, his smile as wide as a half-moon.

'I trust everything was to your satisfaction?' William asked with amusement.

'Oh yes, sire,' Eustace replied with a beatific grin. 'It's almost as good as the Swan in Southwark.' He tugged his tunic straight.

The others rounded on him, slapping his back, calling him a randy young dog, and Eustace puffed out his chest and played to their joshing. William let them have their moment; it would stand them in good stead for their journey. A good leader knew when to have discipline and when to slacken the rein.

10

The Adriatic Sea, September 1183

Eight days of brisk travelling brought them to the port of Brindisi on the shores of the Adriatic Sea, there to procure a vessel to transport them across to Durazz in order to pick up the old Roman road, the Via Egnatia, which would bring them to Constantinople.

William loathed sea crossings, but they had been an unfortunate necessity for much of his life as he traversed the Narrow Sea between England and Normandy in all seasons and weathers at the whim of royalty. The voyage was less than thirty miles at its narrowest point, but the winds, like the King, were unpredictable and could whip up a storm out of nowhere.

The crossing from Brindisi to Durazzo took a little under a day's sail using two galleys to ship the men and horses across the blue Adriatic. They departed with the afternoon's high tide, gulls wheeling and screaming over the red sails of their ships, and the breeze sufficiently brisk that the crew did not have to break out the oars. William gripped the mast and clenched his jaw as the coastline receded. Already his gut was rolling with each forward surge of their vessel. It did not matter that the weather was fair and the waves gentle folds under the keel. Indeed, he would rather have had a strong wind behind them to make his purgatory shorter, even if one of the virtues of pilgrimage was supposed to be suffering.

Ancel, capable of tripping over his own shadow on land, was totally at home on the sea, graceful almost. He adapted to the roll of the ship, emulating the sailors, and was as nimble on deck as they were. He sang cheerful snatches of song and delighted in the strong breeze through his hair as Brindisi vanished from sight. Passing William, he patted him on the shoulder with sympathetic encouragement in which there lurked a hint of smug superiority.

The wind dropped as the sun set and the crew broke out the oars. Night fell and a fine sea mist crept over the water, enveloping the galleys in veils of grey cobweb. The galleys blew horns to each other to stay in contact and lit bright lanterns on prow and stern. As the lights glimmered intermittently through the cloud, Ancel took his turn at the horn blowing, for he had a fine pair of lungs and was eager to the task.

To William it was like sailing off the edge of the world. They really were leaving all they had known behind. When they made landfall at dawn, presuming that the crew had navigated well, they would be stepping ashore on new territory and all the old certainties would either be gone or worthless. In many ways it would be like starting afresh, which was a reason for optimism, but he was apprehensive. The next leg of their journey was almost seven hundred miles to Constantinople and who knew if they would reach it and what they would find there.

The mist was still thick at first light, but dissipated in time for William and his men to see the port of Durazzo rising on their flank, the buildings gilded in morning sunlight. The breeze had strengthened with the dawn and the crew had shipped oars and were relying on the sail to weave them into port.

Ancel came to stand at William's side and gazed out over the water at the approaching harbour. 'I told you all would be well.' He leaned against William, arms folded. 'I hope there is somewhere we can break our fast on more than just stale bread. I'm starving.'

William merely grimaced. He would be much happier thinking about food once he had solid ground underfoot.

* * *

65

The Via Egnatia stretched out before William's party in a rough track of worn cobbles, woven with grass and moss. Built by the Romans as one of the great arteries of their empire, their influence could still be seen along the way in ruined temples open to the sky, in markers erected as inscribed pillars, and even in the occasional tombstone that had been reused to slab the road.

Despite occasional rough patches and moments of bad weather, William and his men often covered distances of more than thirty miles a day and William hoped to reach Constantinople by early October. They slept in shelters and hostels built close to the road and their safe conducts and letters of pilgrimage still held good in the towns and monasteries where they sought accommodation and where they were generally welcomed and asked for news.

Sometimes they encountered other travellers – merchants, fellow pilgrims, messengers on the road – and they journeyed with them for a while, enjoying the increased safety in numbers. News and stories were exchanged and useful information traded. William learned of a good smithy where they had the horses reshod, and spent the night sheltered in good, sweet straw.

They paused to pray and give alms at the shrines and churches along the way, especially those dedicated to the Virgin, but as they drew nearer to Constantinople, the welcomes and the hospitality grew noticeably less enthusiastic. Folk watched them pass in silence and no longer ran out to offer them small parcels of food, or direct them onto the best paths. When they entered villages, people let their dogs run loose to snap at their heels. Ancel had to keep Pilgrim on his saddle and leash him, from which vantage point the little dog bristled and growled his own threats at his canine adversaries.

In some of the larger places the notes of recommendation were still proving their worth, and their pilgrim garb was respected, as were the swords, but William was becoming increasingly uneasy. They were too far along their road to retrace their steps to

Brindisi, and it was unwise to chance a sea voyage from one of the Marmara ports at this time of year. Besides, he had sworn to visit Constantinople on Harry's behalf, and to venerate the Virgin at the great church of Hagia Sophia, third only in the world to the Holy Sepulchre, and St Peter's in Rome.

One day at noon they stopped at a wayside spring where the water spouted from a carved head with an open mouth. 'We should camp here for the night,' Ancel said as they ate the last of yesterday's dates and bread. 'The horses need to rest.'

William knew Ancel meant that he needed to rest. He had been querulous and difficult all day. 'That would be a waste,' he replied. 'We still have several hours of travelling left and we need to keep up the pace.'

'One day will not make much difference,' Ancel objected.

'But one day becomes two and then three, and then a week. This good weather will not hold for ever, and we should make the most of it.'

A muscle flexed in Ancel's cheek. 'I have the belly gripes.'

'We are not going to stop because you have gut ache,' William snapped.

They set out again but after less than a mile Ancel leaned over his horse's withers and vomited. William glanced at him in irritation laced with concern. After what had happened to Harry he was on edge, and his anxiety increased when Ancel had to dismount from his horse to void his bowels, groaning loudly and making a parade of his ailment, ensuring that everyone knew what straits he was in.

Ancel had to stop several more times as they rode on to either vomit or squat at the roadside and William watched him, feeling grim and a little afraid. He had hoped to push on to the safety of their next official shelter, but Ancel's condition and the constant stops had slowed them so much that he knew they would not reach that security by nightfall.

In the end, William called a halt and made camp, deciding to ride on in the morning. Ancel had stopped puking and voiding, much to everyone's relief, but he was weak and fractious. He lay down under a blanket while the men set up the camp around him, putting up tents and picketing the horses, lighting the fire and rummaging out their meagre food supplies. No one had much of anything because they had expected to eat at their next stop and replenish supplies.

William was walking past Ancel's hunched form when Ancel deliberately stuck out his foot to trip him up. William stumbled, righted himself, and then stooped to his brother. 'Do not try my patience further,' he said with quiet but forceful scorn. 'You may be ill, but that is no excuse. Be a man.'

Ancel shrugged over onto his other side. Suppressing the urge to kick him, William walked away.

Eustace got the fire going with his usual brisk efficiency and saw to the horses, including Ancel's. After prayers led by the Templars, the men sat down to more stale bread and cheese, and the last of the dates. A single flask of sour wine did the rounds, and after that they made do with water.

Augustine and Onri played a board game with counters, wagering tent pegs on the outcome. William set about mending a piece of harness and the others busied themselves with similar tasks, exchanging desultory conversation.

William thought about the road they had travelled and the road yet to come. By his reckoning, they were about halfway to Jerusalem. They had done well thus far, but the new territory was a constant challenge and the further they rode, the more difficult it became. But then the greater the trial, the more valuable the penance.

After a while, Ancel shambled over to the fire, a blanket round his shoulders. 'I should not have done that,' he said by way of apology as he sat down.

'No, you should not.' William offered him his cup. 'Are you feeling better?'

'A little.' Ancel took a tentative sip. 'When it began, I thought . . .' He shrugged. 'You know . . .' He gestured.

William nodded. They all feared the bloody flux, not just because it was a terrible way to die, but because if it happened, it would be evidence of God's wrath. 'Yes, but since it isn't, we can press on tomorrow at first light. Here, make yourself useful. Your hand is more dextrous than mine.' He handed Ancel the harness he had been repairing. Ancel might be clumsy in his larger movements, but his deftness with fine things was that of a craftsman. No one could sharpen a sword like Ancel either – a surprising talent, and one for which he was cherished.

Ancel took the piece and set about the repair with efficiency. Watching him, William was filled with a mingling of love and exasperation for his awkward brother with all his flaws and gifts. From an uneasy beginning, the silence settled into companionship and William curled his arm around Ancel and gave him an impromptu embrace. 'You try me sorely at times,' he said, 'but I love you – never doubt it.'

Ancel pushed him off but gave him a crooked smile. 'You try me also,' he said, 'but I forgive you.' And he ducked under William's playful cuff.

The next day, they came to the castle where William had intended to spend the previous night. Studying its walls, looming over the road, he was partly relieved but also apprehensive because he was uncertain of their welcome. They needed supplies and decent sleep and the horses had to be fed and rested, but who knew if they were friend or foe? Riding between the dwellings clustered below the castle, he was acutely aware of the stares from the locals, wary at best, and occasionally hostile.

Once at the gates, William gathered himself. He would not show his unease to the men, although he knew they must feel it too.

The porter on duty, grizzled and elderly but not infirm, regarded the visitors through a grille in the door. William presented him with the parchment of safe conduct and their map, and Augustine, who spoke a little of the language as well as fluent Latin, told him that they were pilgrims seeking shelter on their way to Jerusalem. The old man grunted and shuffled away, leaving them standing in the drizzle.

Eventually he returned, unbarred the door, and beckoned them to enter, then further directed them by means of gestures to a stable area to tether their horses and provide them with fodder. A cleric arrived as they were at this task and addressed the Templars in Latin with several flourishes and gestures.

'He says we are welcome to stay and claim hospitality,' Onri said, 'and he requests that we attend his master who desires to speak with us and seek news of our journey.'

Leaving the company's squires and servants to see to the horses and guard their goods, William and his knights followed the cleric into a tower and up some stairs to a spacious chamber on the upper floor where the master of the castle had recently sat down to dine. He was perhaps forty years old, his beard still dark at the sides with a stripe of silver between lower lip and chin. He was holding William's notes of safe conduct and proof of pilgrimage in his hands and now studied his guests from intelligent dark eyes.

'Pilgrims,' he said in accented but passable French, 'you are welcome to my hospitality for the night.' He gestured to his board where a servant was setting out more cups and dishes. 'My name is Barnabas o Sofos, and I trod the pilgrim road to Jerusalem myself many years ago. Please, sit.'

Thanking him, they took their places, and he continued to study them shrewdly.

'Of late fewer people pass through here, both pilgrims and merchants,' he said as wine and bread arrived together with a large dish of fragrant mutton stew. 'It is to be expected after the trouble. Those whose allegiance is to Rome are right to be cautious.

For me, such things matter little except where they affect my trade and prosperity. I would advise you to be very careful. In Constantinople, the Emperor is building a new Latin church to make restitution for last year's happenings, but many still harbour grudges, and as you well know, thieves and criminals abound in all great cities.'

'Our sole intention is to worship Christ and find swift, safe passage to the next stage of our journey,' William said. 'Be assured we shall take your advice to heart.'

'I have friends in the city,' Barnabas said. 'I shall write you a note of introduction.'

'Thank you, sire.' William inclined his head and their host gravely responded. No more was said about the recent massacre in Constantinople, although it remained like a block of rough stone in everyone's awareness.

As pilgrims, their duty in return for hospitality was to relay the news they had garnered along the way, and to speak of their own world and life. William was circumspect about the cloak, but gladly told tales of the Angevin court and the tourney field, and as he spoke the atmosphere warmed and grew convivial. He recounted the occasion when he had got his head stuck inside his helmet and had had to lay his head down on an anvil and let a blacksmith prise off the armour with his tools.

'And when I finally drew a breath of fresh air, it wasn't so fresh after all because it was laden with the smell of fish,' he said with a chuckle. 'I had won the prize of the day and it was a huge pike on a platter. They had been looking for me all over and by the time they arrived at the smithy, the fish was not looking quite as fresh as when they hooked it from the pond!'

The tales continued, spilling over each other, entertaining reminiscences from each man. Home was far away and they derived pleasure and comfort from the recounting. Their host greatly enjoyed the tales too and added several of his own as the wine sank in the flagons and more was brought.

After a while, Ancel rose and went outside. Noticing him leave, William thought at first he had gone to relieve himself, but the moment stretched out and he did not return. It was time anyway to retire, and after a last round of stories, William thanked their host, gathered his men, and took his leave.

He found Ancel in the stables, tending to his horse while Pilgrim snuffled about in the straw, hunting for rats.

'Why did you leave?' William asked.

Ancel ran his hand down his horse's shoulder. 'It was all the talk of what we did before, and knowing that it's only memories now. That it can never be again.'

'That is true, but it is still part of who we are, and better to take joy in the good memories than be sad that they exist. Besides, tales serve a practical purpose, to entertain one's host. That is what guests do to earn their bed and board.'

Ancel nodded, but continued to frown. 'And what of memories that are not so joyful? What purpose do they serve?'

'Learning I suppose,' William said eventually. 'And the wisdom to see a way through, so that mistakes are not repeated.'

Ancel made a wry face. 'Amen to that.'

'All memories should be cherished. Will you shun the ones made on this journey? They will be a part of you, whether you will it or not.'

Ancel screwed up his face. 'Now you terrify me, brother.'

William had almost terrified himself with that last statement. Grasping Ancel's shoulder, he gave it a gentle shake. 'Come, enough of that. We should get some proper sleep. We have a long road tomorrow.'

11

Manor of Caversham, April 1219

'Sire?'

William struggled to drag air into his congested lungs. He was suffocating, being drawn into the abyss, but he fought with all his will, refusing to relinquish his grip on mortal life because he was not yet ready for it to be the end.

'Sire!' The voice came again, urgent but without panic, and he latched onto it like a drowning man to a rope. A warm, dry hand clasped his own. 'Sire, you are dreaming.'

William surfaced with a jerk and a dry inhalation to find Henry FitzGerold standing over him. Breathing was like trying to draw air through a thick cloth, and his chest shuddered with the effort. A fit of coughing wracked his body and wordlessly he gestured for Henry to prop him up against the pillows and bolsters while he battled to breathe. The pain was deep, like knives unmaking him.

'Shall I send for a physician, sire?'

William waved a negation. The coughing fit gradually eased and he was able to draw air into his lungs, although it was still not enough. Henry offered him a drink and he took a few small sips from the cup, and felt half of it trickle down his chin.

'Bad dream,' he croaked.

Henry dabbed him with a napkin. 'Would you like the comfort of a priest, sire?'

William shook his head. 'I shall be all right.' It was no more than dealing with a pile of excrement blocking his path.

He gazed down at his forearm, lying outside the covers – crêpey skin and wasted muscle. The faintest white scar ran up the under-side of his wrist almost to his elbow, and was crossed by three others, two near his wrist and one further up. A mark, barely visible, and more so to him than others, but he could still recall the shock, the pain – and the humiliation.

It had been many years since he had endured that particular nightmare, but it had been one of the testing moments of his life. Men returned from the East, their pouches and saddlebags stuffed with mementos. He had done so himself – ampoules of water from the River Jordan, an olive wood cross from the Garden of Gethsemane, and his own silk burial shrouds. This particular souvenir, scored into his flesh, he would wish on no man, and was one of several souvenirs he would rather not own, but the only way to deal with them was to lay them to rest.

'Sire – what is it?' Henry asked. 'Are you in pain?'

William gave him a bleak smile. 'I have been in better comfort, Henry, but it is nothing a physician or priest can heal. I shall be all right by and by. Bring more light if you will.'

Henry hastened to light more candles and hung an extra lamp above William's bed, forcing the shadows to retreat, although they lingered in the corners, dark and deep. William glanced at them and then focused on the little wooden knight that his grandson had left at his bedside. The knight's lance bore an embroidered copy of William's lion banner, and the candle flame turned the wood to gold.

'What was your dream about, sire? If it is not presumptuous to ask.'

William dropped his gaze to his arm again and sighed. 'It is not presumptuous, Henry, but I do not know if I can tell you. I have had this ever since my pilgrimage to Outremer – ever since Constantinople.' He hesitated. Only those who were with him and had shared the experience would understand – perhaps. Most of them were grave-dust now, and he would soon join them. 'I said it was a dream, Henry, but that is not true. It was and is a memory.'

12

The Via Egnatia near Constantinople, October 1183

Augustine folded his arms and shook his head. 'I cannot do this.' He faced William with mutiny in his dark eyes. 'When I took my vows, I undertook to wear the apparel of my order whatever the consequences.'

'Consequences for whom?' William retorted, standing his ground. 'You are endangering everyone here. You and Onri cannot ride into Constantinople garbed as Templars. You have seen the increasing hostility and we cannot fight off everyone.'

For the last two days Onri and Augustine had been concealing their Templar garb under borrowed cloaks, but it could not continue. Glimpses of their robes still showed through. Augustine in particular would throw his off when they were alone on the path but sometimes they would round a corner and come upon other travellers and it would be too late for concealment.

Augustine shook his head, a stubborn set to his lips. 'It is against my vows.'

'You have a choice.' William refused to soften. 'Either change your garb or ride alone.'

Onri patted Augustine on the shoulder. 'We are doing God's will in seeing this party safely to Jerusalem,' he said gruffly. 'We have been so entrusted, you know this. We can make it right later. It is only for a few days. If you are to go into a temple of money changers, then you must look like a money changer too – even if you are not one.'

Augustine looked even more disgusted, but eventually yielded under duress and then went aside to pray.

'He is proud and the order is his family and his belonging,' Onri said to William. 'You are asking a great deal of him – of us.'

'I understand that,' William replied. 'I would not ask it were it not necessary.'

Onri gave him an assessing look and then with a brusque nod went to talk to Augustine. William raided his clothing pack and found a tunic for Augustine, who matched him in height and build. Guyon provided similar for Onri, and the Templars changed garments, Onri stoical and Augustine grim. Their tell-tale Templar robes were turned inside out and folded at the bottom of the baggage sacks, and the party set off again.

Approaching the great walled city of Constantinople, the road widened, but William and his party advanced no more swiftly than before because it was now a busy thoroughfare and they had become part of a huge shoal swimming upstream. For a while they travelled behind a flock of sheep, their noses assaulted by the ammoniac stink of the animals and their vision one of dung-clagged rear-ends. The sound of baaing and clonking bells made it impossible to hold a conversation. Once past the sheep and the wary but at least not hostile herders, they had to negotiate a cart piled with cages full of squawking poultry, and then another one pungent with ripe cheeses. There were travellers on foot, baskets strapped to their backs, pack ponies bearing sacks of onions, donkeys laden to the ground with bushes of kindling. All the world, it seemed, was coming to Constantinople, the great consumer, in order to trade. Augustine muttered something under his breath about the whore of Babylon and Onri silenced him with a look.

Two miles before they reached the city, William paused at a roadside stream and instructed everyone to spruce themselves up. 'We should look like men of quality when we arrive,' he said as he wrapped clean bindings of dark green linen round his legs and secured the ends neatly with ornate silver tags. 'If we are to have respect then we must seem worthy of respect.' He washed his face and hands, combed his hair, and attended to his harness and baggage, making sure all was clean, neatly latched and secure. From his saddlebag he took their pilgrim documents, and a map that the lord Barnabas had given to him with details of a house of shelter in Constantinople where they would find fodder for the horses and lodging for themselves.

They approached a trinket stall on the dusty road leading up to the great gate of golden stone that terminated the 670 miles of the Via Egnatia. The proprietor wore a tunic of green silk with blue sleeve linings. Every finger was adorned by a gold ring and a white turban covered his head, the end draping forward over his left shoulder. A boy sat on a stool at the back of the stall, carefully threading blue beads of lapis lazuli onto a length of string.

The trader had been paring his nails with a small knife and watching people pass by but his glance sharpened as William's troop approached and his dark eyes flicked over them, assessing.

Eustace pointed to a string of gold coins on the stall, linked by rows of delicate chain. 'Do you think they are real?'

'Probably common brass,' Guillaume Waleran said scornfully.

The seller sheathed his little knife with a forceful motion. 'Come!' he called out in heavily accented French, and beckoned. 'Come and see! My goods are genuine and valuable! Fine rings and brooches and pendants!' He flashed a smile and indicated his wares with a theatrical gesture. 'All the riches of the Frankincense Road!'

William gestured for the men to draw rein and, dismounting, approached the stallholder because at least he spoke French and could direct him to where they needed to go – and was prepared to be friendly, in the interests of trade if nothing else. If his information cost William a purchase, it was a small price to pay.

He looked at the strings of beads, the gold coins that were probably not gold at all as his men had already speculated, the dangling earrings that women wore in this region that would be considered scandalous in England. Heavy bracelets, wide and cuffed. Queen Alienor had a pair of them, but hers were studded with gems, while these, he suspected, were glass and paste.

'Perhaps you would like to try one of these fine and valuable rings?' The trader plucked one from a wooden dowel and thrust it under William's nose. It was a sort of seal ring, marked with the three-barred cross of the Orthodox Christian Church unlike the Latin single cross.

'Your rings are fine indeed,' William said diplomatically, 'but I was thinking of something more like this.' He indicated a small icon of the Virgin and child painted in deep blue and gold.

'Ah,' said the man. 'You are discerning.' His tone became more conversational. He directed the boy to leave his beads and deal with another customer. 'Where have you come from to our city?'

'From England,' William replied, thinking that it was the most diplomatic thing to say. He remembered his father telling him that the Emperor of Constantinople had once employed English huscarls in his guard. 'We are making a pilgrimage to Jerusalem, but wish to pay our respects at your shrines on our way.'

'Ah.' The man nodded and fingered his scarf. 'I have met people from your country before many times.' He swept his gaze over William's waiting entourage. 'Do you have somewhere to lodge?'

William unfolded the piece of parchment Barnabas had given him and showed it to the man, together with the map made for him in England. 'We have been bidden to find the house of Andreas the scribe near the Western Gate.'

'Ah.' The trader took the parchment from him and scratched the side of his nose. 'That is a long way into the city and you will need a guide to show you, for you will never find it otherwise.' He studied the documents a moment longer before returning them to William, flicking his gaze around the men as he did so. 'I can arrange a guide for you if you wish.'

William eyed him with wary interest.

The trader shrugged and gave a rueful half-smile. 'There have been many difficulties since last year and business has suffered. Fewer people come to the city now, especially from the lands of the Farangi, and we desire to restore goodwill between us.' He signed to the boy who had finished dealing with the other customer. 'My brother's house is not far. Mikael will send word to him to offer you hospitality and he will have someone take you where you wish to go.'

'How do we know we can trust him?' Ancel demanded, scowling when William turned to consult with the men.

'We don't,' William replied, 'but we have to decide whether to take our chance with him or with the city and its denizens.' He glanced at the sky. 'We are losing the light and we have to make a choice.'

Ancel shook his head, which was no less than William expected given his brother's distrust of every situation. 'He will fleece us.'

'I will make sure he does not,' William replied. 'Of course, he will seek payment, but we are accomplished bargainers ourselves.'

Eventually, despite Ancel's misgiving, they agreed by a majority to accept the stallholder's offer, and with a smile the man addressed the boy in rapid Greek, tweaked his ear for good measure and sent him off at a run.

William and his men stared around with wondering eyes as the boy, who had returned swiftly from delivering his message, led them through the fabled streets of Constantinople. The golden city, land of fabulous wealth where it was said that even the poor wore silk. Where the buildings were of polished marble and the air was scented with spices. A most holy city of gold and mosaic, and yet also a city that had a reputation for possessing a foul

79

underbelly beneath its glittering scales – a place of dark deeds, murder and corruption.

The boy led them past houses and buildings, some in good repair and others neglected and in ruination with weeds growing through the cracks. There were areas that spoke of recent fire and destruction. Empty dwellings with broken doors and smoke-blackened walls told their unsettling tale of the previous year's unrest.

The boy's gaze was alert, indifferent and inured as he guided them through numerous thoroughfares and alleyways that grew progressively darker and narrower. Pungent cooking smells alternated with those of sewage and rot. William's nape started to prickle and he considered drawing his sword, but even as the thought occurred to him the boy stopped before a set of heavy wooden gates that were open to reveal a decent-sized courtyard and a dwelling house beyond it with a green door and arched windows. Chickens pecked about in the yard. A tawny mastiff that had been lying near the wall lunged to its feet and strained at its chain, baring its teeth and uttering deep warning growls. From his perch on Ancel's saddle Pilgrim retaliated, stiff-legged, while Ancel kept a tight grip on his collar. 'I do not like it here,' he said.

Two women were setting out a meal on a trestle table in the yard. One seemed to be a maid, and the other was a young woman of higher rank with her hair bound up in a kerchief. She wore a close-fitting red gown that showed a gentle roll of flesh at her belly. Large gold earrings swung from her earlobes.

A man came hurrying from around the back of the house and hastened to greet them with a wide smile, teeth bared. 'Welcome to the home of Theo!' he declared, spreading his hands in a benevolent gesture. He was grey-bearded and small but looked taller because he was plump. His French was thicker than his brother's but passable. 'I promise you will be well looked after until your guide arrives. This is my son-in-law Cimon, and my daughter Irene.' He indicated the woman and a tall, thin man with bushy eyebrows and protruding teeth who had emerged from the house to place a jug of wine on the board. The latter gave a stiff nod and retreated, his sandals flapping against the hard skin of his heels.

William thanked Theo. Once the horses had been tethered and tended, he and his men sat down around the table. The women brought out a basket of bread and bowls of thick vegetable stew, a layer of green olive oil floating on top. They worked quickly, without looking at the men and with eyes downcast, then returned to the house.

Their host, Theo, joined them, and although he did not eat, he drank a cup of the rough red wine. His toothy smile flashed again. 'You have travelled far to make this pilgrimage, and you are indeed brave to come here.'

'It is part of our pilgrimage.' William was on edge. Their host was amenable, but the atmosphere held a strange tension.

'And your eventual destination is Jerusalem?' Theo lifted his cup and drank, but kept his eyes on them, assessing.

'That is so. To pray at the Sepulchre and atone for our sins.'

Their host stroked wine from his moustache. 'You must have faced many difficulties along the way, but I can see that you are men of quality.'

'All men are the same on pilgrimage,' William said. 'We are here to ask Christ's forgiveness for our sins and make atonement. We support no faction.'

Theo nodded. 'You came down the old Roman road from Durazzo? I went there when I was a young man.'

'Yes, that was our route.'

'So, you crossed from one of the Sicilian ports?'

'Brindisi,' William replied, unsure if these questions were just the general currency demanded of strangers or whether a greater agenda was at work.

Theo was nodding as if calculating to himself. 'And before that Rome, may I guess?'

'That was our route,' William said, a little brusquely.

'You do not like to travel by sea?'

William shook his head. 'Only when we must. The road is part of our greater penance, and I am not a good sea-farer.'

'That is the unfortunate lot of some men.' Theo rose and excused himself. William glanced at the sun which was low in the sky and his sense of unease increased. A few minutes later Theo returned, rubbing his hands and looking chagrined. 'I am sorry; the man I had hoped to be your guide is not at home. It will soon be dark and you should not venture through Constantinople at night even with an escort. Like any city, it is dangerous after dark, and considering the troubles of last year it would be doubly unwise. You are welcome to stay here in the courtyard tonight. My gates are strong and no one will harm you. In the morning, my son-in-law will take you where you need to go.'

William was reluctant but they had no choice because everything Theo said was true. The women came with more bread and wine and they were left to pitch their shelters against the wall, using hay from his store for insulation and bedding.

'We should never have come here,' Ancel muttered as Eustace lit the wicks in the dimples of the cresset lamp on the table. 'I do not trust him, I do not trust any of them.'

'We cannot go wandering through the streets of Constantinople in the dark,' William said. 'It is far bigger than London; even in daylight we would struggle to find our way without help, and I doubt that will be forthcoming. Better to leave at first light.'

Ancel curled his lip. 'And if we are all murdered in our sleep?'

'We take it in turns to keep watch, the same as we have done all along the route, and we show that we are on our mettle. Onri and Augustine shall take the first watch. Then me and you and Eustace, then Rob, Guillaume, Guyon and Geoffrey.'

Ancel received the decision with a tight mouth but went to lie down.

William stayed awake a while longer, going to check the horses and equipment before retiring. He glanced toward the house, but the door remained barred and whatever was happening within, all was quiet. Heaving a pensive sigh, he sat down on his mattress of stuffed straw. Ancel lay with his cloak drawn up to his shoulders and Pilgrim curled up nose to tail above his head like a rust-coloured hat. A tent mallet lay close to his hand, ready to seize in a moment, and as William passed, Ancel half opened his eyes, revealing that even at rest he was alert.

Lying down, William placed his sword near his own right hand and acknowledged that they had begun the most dangerous phase of their journey. They could have travelled by sea, but that held its own dangers and discomforts including the vagaries of the weather at this time of year and the threat from pirates, and taking the sea route would have meant leaving out many holy places from their itinerary and would have weakened the impact of their atonement and acquisition of indulgences. Harry had always wanted to see the great church of Hagia Sophia, of which his mother had often spoken. But it was very different hearing people at home tell tales of Constantinople to being here and seeing the looks in men's eyes, even when they smiled. Perhaps Ancel was right and he was wrong. He could only pray to God and the Holy Virgin to spare their lives and deliver them safely.

As the roosters of Constantinople crowed to herald the dawn and the sunrise kindled the sky, they were all still alive and nothing beyond their own tension had troubled the night. The woman and the maid brought them bowls of fresh warm milk and bread, but went swiftly about their business and were gone. The great gate remained locked while the men ate and drank, but as they were seeing to the horses, the son-in-law emerged with a bunch of keys in his hand and opened it. He did not greet them beyond a brusque nod, and when William tried to ask him a question, he, like the women, hurried back into the house. The boy from the stall who had guided them here came out and scampered out of the gate at a run.

'If no one is going to talk to us, then it seems we shall have to find our own way,' William said. 'If we head eastwards, we can find the wall and follow it down.'

He was putting a small handful of coins on the table to pay their hosts when the door opened again and Theo emerged. 'If I may speak with you, sire, for a moment,' he said to William, and indicated the house. 'I have a matter with which you can help me in return for the hospitality you have received. Cimon will show you the way now it is light. Do you have your map with you?'

William nodded.

'Good, bring it, there is something I wish to show you.'

William signalled his men to wait and, map in hand, entered the house.

Theo closed the door and gestured for William to sit down at a trestle table. The room was comfortably furnished with colourful hangings on the walls and rugs on the floor, both sheepskin and woven. An icon of a saint stood in a wall niche, surrounded by candles.

'May I see your map?'

William passed it to Theo, expecting him to explain the directions to him. His daughter entered the room, cloth in hand, and began to clean the ironwork on the door.

Theo unfolded the map and studied it from top to bottom, his lower lip pursed, and then nodded to himself before looking at William with hard eyes. 'I know you are not simple pilgrims,' he said coldly. 'I know you are here spying for our enemies in Rome and the lands belonging to Sicily.'

William stared at him in astonishment. The accusation took him so much by surprise that he was speechless.

'You came through those places on your road here; do not tell me you are common pilgrims.' Theo tossed the map on the table.

William shook his head in disbelief. 'Indeed, we are on a pilgrimage exactly as we have told you. If we were spying, we would not be calling attention to ourselves: we would travel by stealthier means and you would not know we were here. We came by way of Rome and Apulia for spiritual and diplomatic reasons that have nothing to do with our route through Constantinople.'

'Do not lie to me,' Theo returned. 'I can see straight through your ploy. You think you will receive more respect if you come dressed as men of means, but I know you for the papal spies you are. You will tell me who your contacts are in the city or it will not go well for you.'

William's stomach lurched as he realised this man suspected them of espionage and was clearly more than an ordinary merchant. But how could he give him what he did not have? 'You are mistaken.' He pushed to his feet. 'We have nothing but letters of safe conduct and lists of places to lodge.'

'If you say so,' Theo said, 'but until you tell me what I need to know, you cannot leave.'

'I have told you, we have no information.' His heart slamming in his chest, William started for the door, and found it barred. As he gripped the handle, the son-in-law appeared from another room accompanied by two burly servants wielding clubs, knives stuck through their belts. William placed his back to the door, and prepared to sell his life dearly.

The woman had left the room but now returned, swirling something around her head, and by the time he had realised it was a fishing net she had cast it over him and the men were upon him, striking and beating. 'Run!' he bellowed desperately through the door to his men. 'It's a trap!' He hoped to God they would hear him, but it was his last coherent thought for some time as he was kicked and beaten half insensible, bound and gagged, and pushed down some steps into a dusty cellar. Above him a trap door slammed and he was left in utter darkness.

*　　*　　*

William lay at the foot of the stairs, concussed, winded, and furious with himself. He should have trusted his instinct and left yesterday, even if it meant wandering the streets. Now it might all end here with his vow unfulfilled, his men scattered, murdered or sold into slavery, and the sacred charge of the Young King's cloak lost for ever; his mission yet another failure to add to his tally and drag him down to hell. He should have listened to Ancel.

The room was pitch black but his vision was full of dull-coloured flashes. Pain fisted through his body from the blows rained on him. For a while he lay still, his cheek pressed against the gritty floor as a fine trickle of blood ran down his cheek. Dear God, it could not end like this. He would not allow it to happen. He forced himself to sit up, and, placing his back against the wall, pushed himself to his feet. His hands were tightly bound with no leeway for movement and struggling only served to swell his flesh and make the bonds dig more deeply.

Shouting was pointless because there was no one to hear. Groping around with his feet in the darkness he found the steps leading to the trap door and stumbled up them to the top. His head bumped wood, but there was no means of lifting the trap from the inside, and although he strained his ears, he could hear nothing.

Cautiously he groped his way back down the stairs and walked around the cellar, keeping his back to the wall, finding out that the underground room was ten paces long and six paces wide. Venturing out into what he judged to be the middle of the room, he discovered it empty – no furniture, no bed, no slop bucket. Just the dirt floor. Sick, dizzy, his head pounding, he found the stairs again and sank down at their foot.

Hours passed, he did not know how many as he drifted in and out of awareness and over and again he called himself a fool. When eventually his mind returned to a semblance of clarity, his nausea had turned to hunger, his mouth was dry and his bladder full.

Suddenly the trap door was flung open and because he had been shut in total darkness the light dazzled his eyes and he had to look away, squinting. The burly men who had thrown him in here came down the stairs, treading heavily, followed by Theo, licking his lips as though his tongue was a strop, sharpening his teeth. A sheathed dagger hung from his belt. William's heart kicked in his chest and began to pound because he was trussed up like a sacrificial animal and unable to defend himself.

One of the men hung a lamp from a fixture on the roof, casting light around the cellar, which was indeed a bare room, and then stood at the side with his companion, arms folded. An ominous reddish-brown stain splattered the wall behind him.

'Now then,' Theo said, removing the gag from William's mouth, 'let us see if time for reflection has sharpened your memory. Just tell me what I want to know and I will let you go free. If not . . . well, things might not turn out so well.' He unsheathed the knife. 'Tell me who you were going to contact in the city. What messages were you passing?'

William coughed and Theo ordered a guard to give him a drink from a jug he had brought down with him. William took several gulps, but then Theo snatched the jug and splashed the rest of it in William's face.

'What have you done with my men?' William demanded, spluttering.

'I have done nothing with them – yet. They are waiting for you, but if you do not give me the right answers then I shall send them into slavery. Do not say I cannot do that, because I can. You have no jurisdiction here and you are at my mercy – should I choose to have any. Now tell me what information you were passing and to whom.'

William said a little desperately, 'I have told you. All we have are directions to hostels where we will be given food and lodging and letters of safe conduct. I cannot tell you what I do not know. Our only business is pilgrimage.'

'Indeed?' Theo set the knife against William's throat and applied pressure with the blade until William felt the steel bite and the blood start to trickle. 'Tell me, or you shall die.'

'Then I shall die because I do not know,' William reiterated, his heart pounding with fear. 'I am telling you the truth. I read neither Latin nor Greek. All maps and safe conducts were given to me in good faith and are nothing more than directions to meals and lodging. We have no interest in anything else.'

Theo licked his teeth again. 'Yet you say you come from Rome and then Apulia, and you dress as men of noble rank, so I know that you are lying.' He made a second, slightly deeper cut. 'Your contact was Andreas, wasn't it?'

'I do not know anyone called Andreas. I do not know anyone in Constantinople – nor do I wish to!'

Theo made another cut. 'I say to you again, was it Andreas?'

William closed his eyes and swallowed. 'We stopped at a castle – I couldn't tell you its name, but the lord gave us directions to someone who would give us shelter here of his Christian charity. We are not spies.'

Theo bared his teeth. 'I know you are concealing things; I know your kind. You are here for a purpose and I will find out what it is.'

'Only to worship on our way to Jerusalem,' William replied wearily.

Theo glared at him, but removed the knife and stepped back. 'We shall see, but know that I do not believe you, and that your life hangs in the balance. You will tell me the truth before I am done.'

He went back up the steps and his henchmen followed, the last one giving William a vigorous kick in the ribs as he departed.

Once more William was left alone in the dark and silence. He could feel blood trickling down his neck and a thin stinging pain from the cuts inflicted. His need to piss was so great that he had to let his bladder go and flood his braies and hose in a hot deluge of shame and humiliation. Tears oozed from beneath his lids and like his released urine came because he could no longer control them.

He remembered the golden times he had spent on the tourney circuits of France and Flanders, living a charmed life, showered with adulation, the darling of crowd and court alike. A supreme royal champion at the height of his prowess with the world at his feet. Now Fortune's wheel had tipped him off the pinnacle and into the filthy mill race at the bottom. He was detritus, tied up in a cellar in Constantinople, beaten, abused, lying in his own piss while God alone knew what was happening to his companions.

Several more hours passed in darkness and William's thirst increased, for he had taken no more than a few swallows from the jug before Theo's henchman had emptied it in his face. At last the door opened again and the guards returned, this time escorting Theo's daughter, who held a jug in one hand and a bowl and spoon in the other. The men stopped at the foot of the stairs to guard the exit and she knelt in front of William. The piss had dried on him, but he was aware of the smell, like the corner of a hall the morning after the men had been drinking.

The woman kept her head lowered but flicked him a glance from almond-shaped dark eyes filled with fear. 'You should give my father what he wants,' she whispered. 'He will kill you if you do not.' She held the jug to his lips so he could drink. William strove not to gulp, making a conscious effort to mind his manners because women were the peacemakers; the ones who brokered the deals behind closed doors, and brought softness into the world – she was his only glimmer of hope. Her hands were clean but smelled faintly of onion and garlic and the neckline of her gown gaped as she leaned forward, affording him a glimpse of her cleavage, and the milky scent of a breast-feeding woman.

'I cannot give him what I do not have,' he replied, and drank again.

She looked over her shoulder at the guards. 'But you must

give him something. We know you have come from Rome, and it is obvious you are not ordinary pilgrims.'

'Then why treat us as your enemies?' William answered. 'It might benefit you greatly to let us go on our way. Perhaps you should ask what our business is with Jerusalem, not Rome.'

Her gaze sharpened and he detected a glint of calculation in her eyes. She set the jug to one side and began to feed him some kind of pottage from the bowl. Perhaps she had been sent to see if a female approach would encourage him to talk. Well then, why not?

'Then what is your business in Jerusalem?' she enquired in a gentle voice.

'To pray at the Holy Sepulchre for the soul of the man who was my lord,' he answered. 'He was a king's son and on his deathbed he entreated me to do so, and to pray for him at the great church of St Sophia in Constantinople. I vowed to him that I would do so or die in the attempt. And if this is to be my own death then so be it. I prayed for his soul in Rome and we took ship in Brindisi. That is what we were doing in those places – my duty to my lord and to a family I have long served.' He gave a broken laugh. 'Many told me I was foolish to come this way. I should have listened to them.'

'Do you have a woman at home?' she asked after a moment.

He shook his head. 'No, but I have sisters. I would like them and my nieces and nephews to know what has become of me should God wish me to die here.'

She finished feeding him and stood up. 'I am sorry,' she said, 'so sorry.' She made a sign to the guards and started back up the stairs. Again William received a kick in the ribs and the door slammed down, leaving him in darkness. Curling up, drawing his knees to his chest, he closed his eyes. At least they had fed him. At least he was still alive.

He had fallen into a restless doze when the trap door slammed back again. This time he was dragged to his feet and upstairs into the room. His legs would barely hold him up and he stumbled forward before being pushed to his knees. However, he was not afraid that he was about to die. The cellar with its blood-stained walls was the killing place.

Theo was there again with his smile and his knife, but uncertainty flickered in his face now. 'Andreas has been arrested and is being interrogated,' he said with a sneer. 'Soon we shall know everything.'

William said nothing. He hoped that the man Andreas, as unwitting a victim as himself, would survive whatever questioning they put to him.

A muscle flexed in Theo's cheek. 'You can make things easier on yourself by telling us what you know. What is the point of suffering when you do not need to?'

'I have nothing to conceal and I know nothing,' William replied wearily by rote now. 'I only ask you to return me to my men and let us be on our way.'

The woman stood on tip-toe and whispered in her father's ear. He listened, his face twitching with impatience.

'You told my daughter that you serve a king, and indeed of your quality there is no doubt.' His lip curled. 'But even quality can be overcome.'

William nodded. 'A king who is dead, brought down by sickness in his youth and prime, and my duty is to pray for him at the tomb of Christ. That is the vow I took. I was a knight of his household, a man sworn to guard him, but I could not protect him from death. This is my last service to my lord; I have no interest in anything else. I am no spy.'

A baby's wail filled the room and the woman went to a basket-work cradle, lifted out a swaddled infant, sat on a stool and put the infant to her breast. She spoke in rapid Greek to her father. His reply was a terse command and a chopping motion before turning back to William.

A loud knock shook the door and one of the male servants

went to open it. After a muttered conversation with whoever stood outside, Theo was summoned. Then more discussion and some sharp exchanges. The merchant returned to the room clutching a piece of parchment, his beard bristling.

'Well,' he said to William, 'it seems I have no further use for you, underling of a king.' He fingered the knife, and William tensed. 'You may return to your friends, but from this day forth you are a marked man.' He nodded to his henchmen. 'Hold him.'

They seized William and pinned him down, even though he fought and lashed out with what strength he had. They held his left arm to the floor and pushed up his sleeve. Theo took the knife and with focused deliberation cut a vertical line from wrist to elbow in a single narrow stripe and then made three horizontal slashes, marking William with the emblem of the Greek cross. The sensation burned his flesh like white fire, and he gritted his teeth against the shock and the pain.

'Now,' said Theo, his eyes glittering with hatred, 'you bear the mark of the true faith. Let this be a lesson to you and to all with whom you associate and who would come through here, spreading their slime of lies.' He stuffed the map back inside William's tunic.

His daughter put down the baby and brought a cloth to staunch the blood running down William's arm, and then bound the wound, flicking William looks of sympathy and warning.

The henchmen dragged him to his feet and bundled him out of the door into the courtyard. Theo followed and indicated to his son-in-law that he should sever William's bonds, which he did with a few short chops of his knife blade, nicking him further in the process, before shoving him to his knees.

William struggled to his feet and stood swaying and blinking in the light. There was no sign of his men. The mastiff growled and lunged on its chain. 'Be on your way.' Theo gave him a shove. 'If I see you again, I shall not be so lenient. And know too that you are being watched.'

The servants marched William to the gate and pushed him out into the alleyway, and then the door was shut and barred behind him. He stared numbly around, lost in the midst of a dark nightmare. He had no money, no safe conduct – but perhaps he was well rid of that considering what it had brought him – and only the soiled and stinking clothes in which he stood. He had expected to end his life in that cellar with its rust-stained walls. Now his horizon had widened to the gutter in the street and he was in just as much danger as before. His arm was throbbing, so was his head, and he had a raging thirst. He had no idea where his men were, or how to start looking for them.

He took one step and then another. His vision swam and he had to hold on to the wall. Behind him the gate opened again and he tensed, thinking that they were going to murder him beyond their premises. However, it was the woman who emerged, a water skin in one hand, a cloth bundle of food in the other and his cloak over her arm. 'Quickly, take these.' She looked hastily over her shoulder. His knife was there too, and his belt.

'Why are you helping me?' William demanded.

'Because there has been too much bloodshed already and I will not have yours on my hands. And also for the sake of your sister. When you spoke of her, I believed you.' She looked anxiously over her shoulder again. 'He let you go because he thinks you are spying for Rome and that if he has you followed, you will lead him to bigger fish.'

William snorted. 'Then he will have to follow me all the way to King Baldwin in Jerusalem, and it will not be worth his while because I know nothing and have nothing – or I might just lie down here and die.'

'That shall be as it is. You are warned and I can do no more.' She indicated his wounded arm. 'The last one who came through here, he killed, and he may yet do the same to you. I hope you reach Jerusalem. Turn right and then right again and you will come to a wider road. Follow it away from the sun and you will reach the sea wall.' Turning around, she went back through the gates and he heard the bolt ram shut.

He unstoppered the water skin, took a sniff, and then a dubious swallow. The taste of leather filled his mouth but nothing worse, and he took several deep gulps before donning the cloak and following her directions with faltering steps. On the second right turn he came to another alley, darker than the one before, but with a tunnel of light at the end. Two men stood inside a narrow doorway, pulled back a little, concealing themselves. William fumbled for his dagger, knowing this was the end if they chose to set on him.

'Sire? My lord? It is you! I knew you were still in there!'

William stared at Eustace and Geoffrey FitzRobert as both men fell to their knees in the filthy alleyway, and thought it the finest sight he had ever seen. 'Get up, you fools!' he said, his voice almost cracking. 'That's the last thing you should be doing, but by God I am glad to see you!'

Eustace stood up, tears glittering in his eyes, his features beard-shadowed and gaunt. 'Praise God! We've been keeping watch for three days now!'

'Three days?' So that's how long it had been. He pulled Eustace into a fervent embrace, the same with Geoffrey, but swiftly released them, knowing the terrible danger they were still in. 'Where are the rest of you?'

'Waiting near the basilica,' Geoffrey said. 'It is the best we could do. We have joined some travellers who were friendly disposed toward us.'

Sweet relief swept through William that his men had come to no harm, and it almost buckled his knees. 'We should not stay here.' Stepping into the alley, he stumbled, but thrust himself upright by force of will spurred on by the knowledge of danger.

As they made their way through the narrow passageways and entered more open ground, William told Eustace and Geoffrey what had happened to him. 'They are part of a spy network, but for which faction I do not know. Perhaps the Emperor, perhaps one of his rivals. The one named Theo said they would be watching us closely. They think we are carrying secret messages from Rome to undermine them.'

'That brat of theirs has been shadowing us,' said Eustace with a sneer of distaste. 'I caught him yesterday and told him I would cut off his ears if I saw him again. I don't know if he understood me, but if we are being followed it is no longer by him.'

'I have no doubt someone else will have taken his place,' William said. 'We must leave this place as soon as we have made our prayers.' Assailed by nausea and dizziness, he slowed his pace. 'What happened to you when they seized me?'

'They told us you had important personal business to conduct with Theo and that you would be some while and we should leave and come back later,' Geoffrey said. 'We were reluctant to go, but knew how dangerous it would be to create a disturbance, so we left, but kept watch. They barred the gates and when we demanded to see you Theo told us through the door grille that you had left by another way and continued on your own and had ordered us to do the same. They even invited Ancel and Robert into the house to search for you, to prove you were not there, and then told us to go before they called down the Emperor's soldiers on us. We knew you hadn't left, unless they had murdered you, so we found this place, made our camp and kept watch.'

'I was in the cellar,' William said hoarsely. 'Trussed up like a chicken for the pot. I never heard you, but nothing would have emerged from that place – unless they wished it to. It was a room full of hidden screams.' He shuddered and stopped for a moment, squeezing his eyes shut.

'Sire?'

He took a drink from the water skin. His flesh was crawling as if being walked over by ants. 'Is the cloak safe?'

Eustace nodded. 'Yes, sire, Ancel has it, and we still have the

95

horses and most of our supplies. We spoke among ourselves and if you had . . . if we had not seen you again, we were going to continue to Jerusalem so that our young lord's cloak would get there even if we were down to the last man.'

William swallowed and blinked moisture from his eyes. 'I was a fool,' he said roughly. 'I thought I had their measure and I thought I knew all the perils of men's trickery and evil deeds, but not so.'

Geoffrey noticed the blood seeping through the bandage on William's arm. 'What have they done to you, sire?'

'Nothing. A scratch.' William hid his arm behind his back. 'It does not matter now.'

Entering broader thoroughfares with better light, they passed street sellers shouting their wares. The smell of hot oil, garlic and spices wafted from braziers over which street vendors were griddling slashed silver fish. There were stalls selling flat breads and hot vegetable stews glistening with oil. William's stomach growled with hunger, but he felt sick too and almost retched.

Eustace, with his strong sense of direction, led them through the twisting entrails of the city. William gained glimpses of towers and porticoes of polished marble, of churches, curved and domed; mosaics and statues, and beyond them dark alleyways leading back into the city's bowels. He tasted sick fear, knowing how easily they could all be swallowed up again.

The route seemed to go on for ever and William's feet began to drag and trip, and his pace slowed. Geoffrey offered him his arm to lean on and he was tempted to take it, but pride kept him upright and in his own control and he pushed himself onward. Eustace led them down another alley that opened out into a space where a building had once stood, now a heap of rubble and charred timbers tendrilled with weeds. People had taken advantage of the open ground to set up ramshackle tents and were sitting around fires, and among these groups, William saw the rest of the men.

Ancel leaped to his feet, his face crumpling with an agonised expression of joy and grief. 'Gwim!' He rushed at William, flung his arms around his neck, and burst into tears. 'Dear Christ, I thought you were dead!' His voice tore. 'I thought we would never see you again!'

William returned the embrace and felt Ancel's shudders almost as his own. 'You can see I am not,' he said in a choked voice. Pilgrim was jumping up at him, licking his hands, snuffling and thrusting at his sleeve. 'You were wrong on both counts, for which I am overjoyed.'

'What happened to you?'

'I will tell you later.' William slumped down on the ground as all the strength left his legs. 'But all of the hostels on our itinerary are compromised.' He looked round at his companions who were staring at him with equal measures of shock and joy. 'We must make our way as best we can and be on our guard. They believe we are bearing messages from Rome and Apulia that oppose their rulers – we are in grave danger.'

Eustace handed him a cup of wine laced with sugar.

'I told you we should never have come here,' Ancel said with bitter satisfaction. 'We should have sailed direct from Brindisi.'

William drank the wine, and as it burned down his gullet it gave him strength. 'Hindsight is a wondrous thing, brother,' he snapped. 'Eustace says you still have the cloak?'

'Yes . . .' Pursing his lips, Ancel nodded to the familiar bundle among the baggage.

'Then first thing on the morrow we shall take it to the great basilica and pray, and then we must leave.' The role of leader settled over him again, and through his exhaustion he welcomed the familiar comfort of the burden. To be under his own control and not in the power of others.

Ancel gestured to William's arm as Geoffrey FitzRobert bound and anointed it. 'What happened?'

Feeling smirched and embarrassed, William kept the wound

97

turned away from Ancel's curiosity. 'They cut me because I had nothing to tell them, and they wanted to mark me with their symbol to show their power.'

'Bastards,' Ancel muttered.

'It is nothing.' It was like being a branded felon.

'It will soon heal,' Geoffrey said as he finished bandaging the wound.

William pulled his shirt over it and stood up, feeling defensive and uncomfortable. Onri was eyeing him with mistrust that only served to increase his chagrin.

The great church of St Sophia was older and greater than St Peter's in Rome and entering through its doors was like being engulfed in an enormous reliquary, the lofty interior of its dome covered in golden mosaic, arched with light. Everything shimmered and dazzled. Gold and jewels, crosses and candelabra, the heady smoke trails of sacred incense thickening the air like gauze floating toward heaven and dusting the light. Seated in majesty in the dome of the apse, the Virgin Mary with the infant Jesus on her lap gazed out over all. Her right hand was on the Christ child's shoulder and it seemed to William that she was looking down at him with calm and critical evaluation.

Overwhelmed by the opulence and beauty he fell to his senses and fear. The glorious interior of the church and the horror of what he had endured at the hands of some of the city's denizens was a contrast beyond comprehension. His injured arm throbbing to the beat of his heart, he struggled to make sense of God and wondered if he was still being punished for Rocamadour even though he was doing his utmost to make it right. Perhaps indeed he was being tested and had to prove his mettle. Beneath the Virgin's stare he still felt unworthy of forgiveness, but even more determined to prove himself. He had been spared, and that was cause for hope.

* * *

Ancel ceased spooning broth into his mouth and glowered at William. 'I don't trust him, Gwim, he's a shark. We would be mad to cross the water on that thing!'

William swallowed his exasperation. Ever since first light he and Augustine had been at the waterside, striving to find someone willing to bear them across the Arm of St George to the trading port on the other side. The prices the boat owners were asking were extortionate, and deliberately so he suspected. They had been met with hostility and indifference from every person, save for one man in a threadbare tunic with a vesselbark that reflected its owner's state of dress. His price was ridiculous for what he was offering and normally William would not have contemplated such a transaction, but he was desperate to leave this place. If God really did want to forgive him, then let Him show it now and let him survive.

Ancel waved his arm. 'Look at all the fine ships moored here, all clean and seaworthy. Why can't we cross on one of those?'

'Do you think I have not tried?' William snapped. 'If you can get one of them to take us across then be welcome. If not, then hold your tongue.'

Ancel continued to scowl. 'You would trust all our lives to him and those battered planks?'

'I trust all our lives to God,' William said tightly. 'The crossing is less than a mile and the weather is calm. I would not do this unless I had to – you know I hate the sea, but I will not stay in this place another night.'

Ancel cast his bowl aside. 'I wonder what our mother would say if she knew you were putting us all in line to drown. If you expect me to sail on that thing with you, then you are mistaken. I shall go my own way!'

William grimaced at Ancel's tirade, but took it as a positive sign. At least matters were returning to normal if Ancel could harangue him like this, although bringing their mother into the conversation revealed how agitated his brother was, since she was always saved for William's greatest transgressions. 'As you wish, but first you must find someone willing to take you, and then you have to be able to pay their fee. However much you think Augustine and I have been shirking our efforts, you will not find it easy.'

'Money is not much use if you do not reach the other side.'

'I intend to get us all across this water, or that man will die for it.' He nodded at the boat owner, who was making ready to load his rickety vessel with their goods.

Ancel clenched his jaw.

Through his exasperation, William felt a thread of compassion and even love for Ancel. He knew it wasn't about the crossing because Ancel was not afraid of water. It was because of what had happened earlier, and now they were facing another transition from something bad toward something potentially worse. It was the child crying for his mother and his home. But their mother was in her grave, and the only way home lay across this stretch of water and by way of a leap of faith.

Ancel strode off for a dozen paces and then stopped, rubbing the back of his neck. William left him to it and turned back to organising their crossing. No one spoke, for all were accustomed to Ancel's ways. However, Geoffrey FitzRobert, ever the peacemaker, followed him and clapped his shoulder on his way to load his own baggage.

They had to make two journeys. William clambered aboard the boat with Geoffrey, Robert and Eustace, and called to Ancel.

'No,' Ancel said. 'No, William.'

'Does your courage baulk? If I can do this, then so can you.' William leaned closer to him, in his turn bringing a parent to bear: 'What would our father say?'

'Christ, he would call you a mad bastard!'

'But he would take his chance – he always did, and he always knew the odds, and that when the advantage outweighs the disadvantage you seize it.'

'He also lost an eye and nearly got you hanged.'

'But he survived to beget you, and I am here now, so he defeated the odds.' William beckoned again.

Ancel cursed through his teeth and thrust out his arm like a blow, but at the last moment he seized William's hand. 'May you be damned if we sink.'

William gave him a brusque nod. 'Accepted.'

They had to take it in turns to bail water from between the leaking planks with buckets, two men either side, sluicing for all they were worth. Standing with the soles of his feet in sea-water, Ancel gripping him fiercely, William fought his fear and fixed his gaze on the buildings lining the other side of the Arm of St George. By the time they reached mid-channel he had acquired some sort of equilibrium. They had not sunk yet; the water level in the craft had stayed the same, and nothing could be worse than being bound in that cellar with a knife at his throat. Nothing.

The sun had moved an hour in the sky as they disembarked on the far shore. William's gut had barely had time to churn, and as he stepped onto dry land he was euphoric not only at having survived, but triumphed. He gave Ancel a brief, hard hug.

'There now,' he said, 'what do you say?'

Ancel shrugged, still grumpy. 'You took a risk and got away with it,' he replied. 'Fortune was with you. I still think you were wrong.' He stalked off to see to the unloading of their baggage, releasing his tension with sweeping gestures and loud commands. Had there been someone to fight, he would have swung his fists.

The boat owner returned to ferry the second part of their contingent across, and by the time he returned Ancel had recovered some of his equilibrium, and although he had not apologised he was making himself useful and had stopped flinging himself about.

It was nearing dusk so they pitched camp with other travellers and traders journeying to or from Constantinople. A troop of performers returning from a wedding invited them to a meal of stewed lentils and bread. Sitting among them, experiencing the goodwill of strangers, joining in the laughter and making exchanges using gestures and different broken languages, William began to feel better, although his injured arm was still throbbing like a brand.

A woman rose to dance around her fire to the music of drum and flute, her thin leather slippers turning in the dust, bells tinkling at her ankles, skirts flaring. William had encountered such entertainments before at tourneys. Sometimes the women would dance in the tents, collecting coins and offering services that went beyond the turn of a nimble ankle around the fire.

William withdrew a little from the light, although there was still enough to see by, and unbandaged his arm to examine his wound. The cuts were red and sore, a little puffy at the edges, but did not appear to be festering. Glancing up, he realised that Onri was watching him with a taut expression on his face.

'That is a very pretty cross you have there,' the Templar said, his tone cool, almost hostile.

William covered the marks and drew down his shirt sleeve. 'I was not glad to receive it I can assure you,' he replied curtly because he was ashamed and Onri clearly suspected him of some kind of dishonourable dealing, or thought him not up to the mark. William recognised the Templar's anger because he had anger of his own that could either act as a strengthening glue or bog them down in recrimination and bring them to ruin.

Standing up, he left the fire and went to check on the horses which were being guarded by Eustace and the Templar's squire. And then, exhausted, he said his prayers, rolled himself in his cloak and lay down.

The woman was still dancing and the laughter and music spoke of a world that had once been familiar and friendly, but now was alien and hostile. Ancel was playing dice with Geoffrey, Guillaume and Guyon. Onri had joined Augustine and was talking quietly to him, one hand on his shoulder, and Robert was darning his hose.

William closed his eyes and the music and laughter faded away. He awoke suddenly to the sight of the errand boy from the trinket stall who stood in front of him, pointing to him and calling out over his shoulder. He was seized and tied up, his wrists bound with cords, and when he looked round the camp, all of his men had been grabbed too and trussed like hogs ready for the slaughterer's knife. Theo stood watching in his silk robe and turban, licking his lips. The trinket seller was there and Theo's tall son-in-law and the henchmen with their clubs. The woman too, her doe eyes sorrowful, but a knife bare in her hand. 'I am sorry,' she said. 'So sorry.' And turned to cut Ancel's throat.

'No!' William roared, and fought his bonds, striving to win free before it was too late. He could see Ancel's eyes, huge with terror.

'Gwim, no!'

He managed to loosen an arm from the ties and punched upwards, striking flesh, and the surge of pain from his cut arm jerked him awake and bolted him upright.

Ancel was struggling up from the ground, touching a bloody lip. 'It's all right, Gwim,' he panted, looking at the red smudge on the back of his hand. 'You were dreaming – a nightmare.'

William bowed his head, dry sobs shuddering from the centre of his chest.

Ancel regained his balance. 'I know what it's like,' he said, and briefly squeezed William's shoulder before disappearing into the darkness, returning a moment later with a cup of wine. 'Here.'

William took a few swallows, although he felt sick and the wine tasted of tar and grease. Ancel was watching him with the same wide eyes as in his dream, but without the terror in them.

'What did you see?' Ancel asked.

'Nothing I want to repeat.' William shuddered. 'It is like having bad guts after a suspect meal, that is all.'

'You never share things,' Ancel said reproachfully.

'You would not want to have the sharing of this, I promise you.'

Ancel touched his bruised lip. 'I already have, and I do not suppose it will be the last time you'll punch me in the face.'

William could not tell if it was a weak jest or a pessimistic expectation. 'I am glad you are here with me.'

'How much would you miss me?'

'Like a tooth – and take that as a compliment.'

A single voice rose in song on the cool night breeze, clear and holy. The dancers and revellers had gone to their beds, and this psalm, an Alleluia, came from their own fire, from Augustine. Its strength was like the blade of a clean, pure sword and it brought a lump to William's throat.

Ancel pinched the inner corners of his eyes between finger and thumb. 'He could make angels weep. If it helps you to pray, I will kneel with you.'

William nodded, recognising the rare fragility of a moment when they were at one with each other. He was grateful to Ancel, for being there, for waking him up, and for staying at his side.

Together the brothers knelt in prayer and William asked God to look on them with mercy and guide their road from now on. He would trust to the map of his instinct, not man. Twelve days' journey would bring them to Smyrna, a passage to Antioch and the relative safety of Latin Christian lands.

13

Manor of Caversham, April 1219

'So they believed you were a spy, sire?' Henry FitzGerold leaned forward on his stool like a rapt child in thrall to a story teller.

William looked down at his arm. It was a miracle that they had survived Constantinople and the road through Anatolia, so in that way God had answered his prayers. 'They thought we were carrying messages from Rome to their allies, and that our letters of safe conduct and lists of hostels would lead them to people they could arrest and question. We were flies trapped on a spider's web.' He raised his gaze to Henry's. 'I learned a great deal from that part of the journey and I never trusted the same after that. We had been on our guard, but it wasn't enough. The courts of England and Aquitaine were nurseries for small children compared with the scorpion nests we found in Outremer.' He grimaced at the dark residue of the memory. 'It was the terror of my life, even though men think I have never been afraid.'

Henry raised his brows. 'I do not think I have ever seen you afraid, sire.'

'Because I never show it to my men. What would it do to their morale to see fear in their leader's eyes as he sent them into battle? Some things are only between me and my saviour.' He turned his arm so that the scar was no longer uppermost. 'Besides, what is the worst that can happen? To lose a life? What is that?'

Henry mulled William's words, his expression contemplative. 'You said they followed you?'

'Yes.' Even now William shivered at the memory. 'It took us

two weeks to reach the coast and we were in danger every step of the way, whatever choice we made. We could shelter in the fortresses controlled by the Greeks and risk arrest, or we could take our chance in the open and become the victim of robbers. Indeed, those fortresses often guarded the road so closely that we had no choice but to pay the dues demanded and roll the dice.' He gave a grim smile. 'But bonds were forged on that road that would never have been tied in gentler lands. We learned about ourselves and how hard we could stand at need.'

14

Anatolia, October 1183

William and his men had come to the dour fortress walls at dusk under the charcoal sky of an autumn storm. They were in desperate need of shelter and rest, but knew they might not emerge from the maw of that place alive, and end up as corpses thrown into the rocky gloom of the ditch beneath the entrance bridge.

Granted entry, their weapons had been confiscated and they had been given sleeping room in a shelter built against the castle wall. They had been able to buy fodder for the horses and hot onion stew for themselves but once again William was taken aside and questioned, this time by the castle commander. William answered him squarely that they were pilgrims, passing through to the port of Smyrna to take ship for Jerusalem. The commander was an experienced, pragmatic soldier and of the opinion that extra fighting men within the keep added to its security and he sent William back to his men with the promise of provisions for their journey and a note of safe conduct to take on down the line. William was dubious about that, but reasoned that even if they had been followed from Constantinople, this recommendation was not connected and was probably as safe as matters could be along this route.

Nevertheless, the men set a watch and kept their weapons close to hand.

William took the second watch with Onri, deliberately pairing himself with the Templar. The two knights of Christ had continued to disguise their calling, although Augustine was becoming increasingly disgruntled about the matter and Onri had been dour and suspicious ever since Constantinople. Just now he was eyeing William narrowly following his return from speaking with the commander.

William's leg binding had come loose and he stooped to rewind it. The silence drew out. Onri stirred their fire to life with a long branch and put on some water to heat to make a tisane. William wrapped the linen firmly over his hose and then paused to look at Onri. 'I know you are angry with me. In God's name, I am angry with myself for our scrape in Constantinople. It was my fault, I admit it, but I have done my best to set it right. I try to learn from my mistakes.'

Onri said nothing, his expression tense.

'It is over now and we must continue as best we can. Your business and Augustine's is to protect this party on its journey, and I shall expect it in future, as God is my witness.'

Onri looked almost startled at William's direct confrontation. He rose and fetched two cups from his baggage. 'And I vow we shall do so. I too am angry with myself that we were not more vigilant after we had sworn to keep you safe.'

'Then let no more be said about this business and let it not fester. It is finished.'

To mark the point, William secured the clasp on his leg binding. Onri filled the cups from the cauldron and they toasted each other, and held their peace.

They departed the next day as soon as the gates opened, determined to push on. The safe conduct stood them in good stead for their second night on the road. The third one they camped with a family of shepherds who were wary but willing to exchange dried meat, bread and cheese for a handful of coins, and to provide blankets of pungent sheepskins for extra warmth, since the weather had taken a cold turn.

On the fourth day they came to another fortress, ruinous and uninhabited, with tumbled walls, holes in the roof and weeds sprouting from the mortar. Pigeons were nesting in various recesses and droppings and feathers smothered the floor. The sound of their wings echoed like handclaps. A pile of ashes, smudged and cold, darkened the floor in the middle of the courtyard. Old chicken bones, dry and porous, littered the grey flakes. Even Pilgrim turned up his nose at them after a sniff and cocked his leg.

William gave orders to make camp and set about delegating tasks to the men. Ancel and Eustace went to reconnoitre and find firewood, while the Templar's squire saw to the horses.

'Who do you think dwelt here?' Augustine asked, looking round, hands on hips. 'And why did they leave?'

William shrugged. 'We have seen many ancient remains on our road. Things have their time and then that time passes.' Although he spoke philosophically, he noted that the ruins were not ancient, but of buildings more recent.

'Sire . . .'

He turned at the soft warning in Guyon de Culturo's voice.

'Ambush,' Guyon mouthed, his sword drawn. 'Three men creeping up using the rocks as cover – probably more.'

William's heart began to pound. Drawing his own sword, he issued swift commands to the men in the courtyard. Three would not attack a dozen; there must be more. His thoughts flew to Ancel and Eustace who had gone to gather firewood and were only armed with their knives.

Leaving the courtyard, he followed Guyon outside. The knight pointed to the rocks where he had seen the men, but there was no sign of them now. William sidestepped softly toward a ruined building that had once been a storeshed or stable.

He heard voices, low-pitched and guttural in a language he did not know, and signalled Guyon to stay in to the shadow of the wall. Pressing his spine against the stone, he reached the edge of the wall, peered round, and saw Ancel and Eustace being menaced by men with drawn knives.

'I don't understand what you want!' Ancel was saying, his voice sharp with fear.

The man hissed the question at him again in a foreign tongue and pressed the point of his knife against Ancel's ribs.

William whirled round the corner and attacked from the side, taking one of the robbers off guard and bringing him down with a swift killing chop of his sword. Another sprang at him from a different direction, a long knife poised to strike, but Ancel stepped sideways across his path and punched him in the face. As his head snapped back Ancel seized his wrist, grappled the knife from him and slashed him down; Eustace finished him.

William tossed Ancel the first man's sword and the brothers fought side by side and back to back, defending each other against the next surge of attack that proved there were definitely more than three. Steel flashed and darted. William had been wearing his padded tunic for warmth and he was glad of it. A savage rip from a knife disgorged layers of woollen stuffing. He rammed the hilt of his sword into the cheek of his attacker and then pivoted to hack at another man, side-striking him and thrusting him off balance.

Yelling, Onri and Augustine burst into the knot of men around the outbuilding, unravelling it on the instant and tipping the balance. The last two raiders took to their heels in the gathering dusk, scrambling over rocks and bushes to make their escape, and William sharply called back those of his men who would have given chase in the fire of battle.

'Leave them,' he commanded. 'You would become their prey – as you probably still are.' He stooped to wipe his sword on the tunic of one of the dead men. 'There may be more, who knows how many.' He looked round. 'Is anyone injured?'

The wounds were mostly minor cuts and bruises. Robert of London had a rapidly swelling black eye and the Templar squire had lost a tooth and one side of his mouth more resembled trodden grapes than lips, but he would survive.

'We should not stay here,' William said. 'They may return with reinforcements and we cannot be found here. There's a moon tonight. We shall ride by that and sleep when we are safe.'

Returning to their horses, sweat cooling on their bodies, making them shiver, they saddled up and rode out, using the last of the light to push on for another couple of miles. Between sunset and moonrise, William halted the group by a stream to take a brief respite and eat the rest of the cheese, meat and hard bread provided by the shepherds, but as soon as the moon was high enough to cast weak blue light over the terrain they set out again, picking their way but still moving forward, every man wearing his armour.

They had not been travelling long when they heard sounds behind them. The scrape of a hoof on rock, the jingle of a bit. The moon was brighter now, but it only served to darken the shadows and who knew what might emerge from them? Yet they dared not increase their pace and risk foundering their horses in this grey half-light.

They came to a rock formation rising above the track and William considered dismounting and concealing themselves among the boulders to create an ambush of their own, but that too had its drawbacks when they did not know how many were following and he decided against it, reasoning that their pursuers would be cautious here for that very reason and their party might gain a little time.

Behind them a war-cry ululated, echoing off the rock formation, and William realised with dismay how close their enemy was. Trying to discern original cries from ricochets, he estimated those on their tail were probably twice their own number. It would be a bloody fight, perhaps the last of their lives.

William reined his horse about to face the way they had come. Let God decide as he willed. Either they would survive or they would die, as so many others had died on the pilgrim road. His only regret was not fulfilling his duty, and going to his maker with a stained, unshriven soul.

The cries swept over them like an advancing wind before a thunderstorm and William roared the battle-cry that had carried all before it on the tourney field, the rallying call that had once belonged to his young lord: '*Dex aie le Roi Henri, Dex aie le Mareschal!*' The others caught up the cry and shouted with him, calling on God and the strength of their arms to help them in their moment of need.

Shadows moved in the moonlight – horses, men with swords drawn, ring mail glinting.

A sudden ripple shuddered the ground as though an animal had shaken itself. Small boulders bounced off the rock formation and struck the narrow path. The horses plunged and skittered, and William pulled his reins in tight. The shaking increased in intensity and a chunk of rock split from the top of the outcrop and crashed onto the path bringing more stone and debris with it, bouncing, smashing, burying the first of their pursuers under a pile of rubble and striking down the man behind. Powdered stone rose like smoke in the moonlight as the earth growled.

'Ride on!' William commanded, and offered up his thanks to God, who had indeed sent His aid, if not in the way William had been expecting. He urged his horse onward down the track. The earth gave another weak shudder and was still. Glancing back over his shoulder, William saw that the path behind had been obliterated. Their enemy might find a way around, but with at least two of their number dead under the rock fall, and a detour to be made, pursuit was much less likely.

For the rest of the night they rode on, twice having to make short detours themselves where the quake had blocked the path. As dawn streaked the sky they happened upon a wayside shrine dedicated to the Virgin, and here they dismounted to pray and give thanks for their deliverance.

Everyone was exhausted, but too full of wonder and tension to sleep. The horses had carried them all night and needed to rest, but they rode on a short distance from the shrine and arrived at a village where freshly baked bread was being sold from a communal oven. William and his men bought loaves to break their fast and negotiated with the head man for fodder and an open barn in which they and the horses could rest for a few hours. The villagers were wary but not hostile and brought them bowls of lentil and chickpea stew. One of the village men, Agnos, had worked on a Genoese trading ship and had a smattering of several languages so was able to translate between William and the villagers. He sat down to talk while they ate and William asked if the earth tremor had caused much damage in the village.

Agnos shook his head and made a tilting motion with the palm of his hand. 'We are used to it. A few years ago, a great one brought down the castle and killed many people.' He pointed to the road by which they had come. 'No one lives there now.'

William nodded, the puzzle solved as to why the place was ruined. 'But it is still used?'

Agnos twisted his lips. 'By robbers and brigands. We chase them off when they venture down here but always they cause destruction first.'

William told him about their own fight and the rock fall during the tremor. 'I do not think they will bother you again for a while.'

Agnos flashed a grin and repeated William's story to the other villagers, which prompted more gifts of food for their journey and praise that they had fought the brigands off and killed some of their number.

William questioned Agnos about the road ahead and he offered to act as a guide the rest of the way in return for a fee. 'It now will be good to see the sea again and escape for a few days.'

'Was there a reason you came back to the village instead of working on the sea?' William asked.

The spark left the young man's eyes and his expression grew

sombre. 'I was in Constantinople when my ship's master died in the slaughter,' he said. 'I escaped but only because God was with me and I managed to hide and make my way to safety at night. They would have taken me and either killed me for a spy or carved my arm with a cross and sold me into slavery, although I am one of their own.'

William drew a swift breath and involuntarily touched his arm, where his shirt sleeve and a light bandage now covered his own wound. 'We had a narrow escape ourselves. There is still turmoil in the city and great hostility to foreigners.'

Agnos gave a cynical shrug. 'They will make a treaty with Venice though. My master told me that the day before he died. He said they would bring one trading city down in favour of the other and make their profit. I earned good money on the ships, but I would never return to that occupation now.'

The next morning William and his men saddled their horses and packed their supplies, rearranging the burdens so that Agnos could ride one of the sumpters. And then they were on their way again, bound for the port of Smyrna, there to take ship for the port of Jaffa and from there to Jerusalem, the centre of the world and city of redemption.

15

Manor of Caversham, April 1219

It had been raining earlier. English rain, cold and soft. The rain that grew the sweetness of grass and opened the petals on the dog rose blossoms. Now it had stopped and the window was open, wafting in the fresh scent of drenched grass, and he could hear the blackbird's evening warbles. This was the last time he would ever see this season and he felt a pang of wistful regret.

'I have said Compline prayers in the chapel for your well-being and your soul,' said his chaplain Nicholas, placing his warm, firm hand over William's. He was a kindly man, with twinkling brown eyes and greying hair winging his temples and curling round his ears. 'I came to see how you are faring.'

'Well enough for a dying man,' William said wryly, 'and I am glad for your visit. I have been thinking on my pilgrimage to Outremer.'

'Then I hope you are finding comfort in your memories, sirc.'

William smiled a little. 'Not all are comfortable, but they are instructive and enlightening. When I returned, I stowed them away and did not look at them again, but now it is time to make my peace with those that are still difficult, and to draw sustenance from the uplifting ones.'

'I shall never see the Holy City,' Nicholas said sadly, 'but I bless all those who have done so in my stead.'

William looked toward the window. The sky was clear teal in the summer dusk. 'It was a place that took my heart when I arrived, and when I left, a part of it stayed behind.' He fell silent for a long time. 'Eventually I found other meaning to patch the tear, but I must make my peace with that too before I die.'

16

The Vicinity of Jerusalem, November 1183

A few stars still hung in the clear pre-dawn sky, but there was enough light to see by. William donned the shirt he had washed the previous night and spread across the thorn bushes to dry, wondering if Christ's crown had been made from those same thorns. The linen smelled clean, if a little dusty. Having attended to his undergarments, he put on his tunic and brushed it down with his palm. The creases from the saddlebag would drop out as they rode. Eustace fussed around him, tugging and tweaking like a chamber maid until everything was level and in order. Yesterday evening he had trimmed William's hair and beard to make him respectable when he entered the city of God.

Augustine was polishing his sword fittings. The Templar robes he had donned the moment they embarked from Smyrna were spotless. The same for Onri, who was adjusting the fastening on his white mantle.

Everyone was travel-worn, thin and hardened from the arduous journey, but buoyed up by the knowledge that today, at last, they would set eyes on Jerusalem. Two days ago they had sailed into the harbour at Jaffa. Only forty miles had then lain between them and Jerusalem and they had covered almost thirty of them yesterday.

Other pilgrims on the same road had gathered to camp for the night and prepare themselves for entering the city, but William and his men had climbed further away from the road in order to have solitude for contemplation. For the last time, they had erected their shelters and lit a fire to sit around while they ate bread and olives – their final night as comrades who had been through so much to come this far. No words were spoken beyond prayers. No dice were produced, and no one jested or indulged in horseplay. A sense of united companionship bonded the group in an atmosphere of reverence tinged with awe. They had almost reached the heart of Christendom. They had set their feet in the very dust that Jesus Christ himself had trodden, and every footstep was wondrous.

The sun rose in the east, lighting the direction they must take for their first glimpse of Jerusalem. Eustace set out bread and cheese to break their fast, and a flask of wine they had bought in Jaffa. No one was hungry but they forced down a few mouthfuls to sustain themselves while they exchanged glances that said far more than words. This was an ending and a beginning. Many times they had despaired of reaching their goal, and it was unsettling that it was so close now. There was an unreasoning fear that it would be snatched away from them before they could taste it.

William went to the horse he had purchased in Jaffa, for they had sold their other mounts in Smyrna. Eustace had groomed Chazur until his liver-chestnut hide shone like dark bronze. He was a handsome horse with a distinctive white blaze and a flash of speed. William had bought him from a homeward-bound pilgrim. He rubbed the horse's nose and offered him a dried date on the palm of his hand, then checked the harness again to make sure all was in order, no loose straps or ties. He had no intention of riding into Jerusalem because that would show overweening pride, but he did desire his accoutrements to be of the highest standard.

He gathered his men together, bade them kneel, and asked Onri to say a prayer. Following the final amen, they rose as one, crossed themselves and set out to join the well-worn path crowded with other pilgrims. William held his head high, feeling holy but humble, as if he was walking down the long nave of a church with Jerusalem at its heart, the altar and the treasure.

The path wound through the dusty Judaean hills to the summit of the hill known as Montjoye because it granted travellers their first glimpse of the outskirts and approach to the city. A Premonstratensian monastery stood on the site and here too was the tomb of the prophet Samuel. William's heart was alight and a tender, tight sensation filled his chest. He had envisioned this many times both from his imagination, and in pictures conjured for him by others who had been here. Now those dreams and images were blending with the reality of seeing with his own eyes. He had to raise his hand and smudge away tears.

Dismounting, falling to his knees, he gave thanks to God for letting him come this far and prayed to be allowed to live long enough to reach the final sanctuary of the Holy Sepulchre. Everyone else was kneeling too – weeping and praying, overcome at the first sight of the Holy City, centre of the world, source of their striving. Ancel threw his arms around William's neck and cried, and William embraced him in a tight bearhug.

'I never thought . . .' Ancel swallowed. 'What I mean is that I never dared to think we would come this far. I couldn't let myself believe lest it didn't happen.'

'If we had not succeeded then it would have been God's will, and who knows what He has in store for us?' William hugged Ancel again and then laid his arm along his shoulder so that they stood side by side, fixing Jerusalem in their vision.

Four miles from Montjoye, approaching ever closer to the city walls, a sudden flurry disturbed the road behind them and loud cries rang out. 'Make way, make way for the Princess of Jerusalem and the Count of Jaffa!'

Looking over his shoulder, William saw soldiers, bright silk surcoats covering their mail, pushing their horses through the dusty stream of pilgrims, forging a path for a covered litter borne by four powerful attendants wearing livery of blue and gold. Everyone was forced to the side of the road to let the procession through, and as the litter passed William, a small hand parted the curtains. A little boy peered out at the pilgrims. He had blond hair, blue eyes and the milk-white skin of a child protected from the sun and accustomed to an indoor life. Jewels and rich embroidery encrusted his crimson silk tunic and even the tight sleeve of his undergown sparkled with gold thread. A woman's voice, low-pitched, came from within the litter, and another hand appeared, elegant and long-fingered, to draw the child back inside. Before she tugged the curtain closed, William caught the glint of a long earring. Women in Normandy did not wear such jewellery, but no well-born lady of Outremer considered her toilet complete without them.

The litter moved on. Behind and to the left a nobleman rode a white Arabian stallion, the harness decorated with tassels and gold sunburst pendants. A blue cap banded with gems sat at a rakish angle on his head and his hair flowed from beneath it in long, fair waves. A wiry beard of darker gold emphasised his firm jawline.

A jolt shot through William as he recognised Guy de Lusignan, once a rebellious vassal of Queen Alienor's, and in another lifetime responsible for the ambush and murder of his uncle, Patrick of Salisbury. Now, through his marriage to Sybilla, sister of King Baldwin, he was close to the throne and acting regent for his ailing royal brother-in-law. William had always expected Guy to go to perdition in Outremer, but instead he had climbed Fortune's wheel in a most spectacular manner. He had known he would encounter the man at some point, but had not expected it to be quite so soon.

Guy barely glanced at the pilgrims as he rode past on his high-stepping horse, and William hoped he would go unnoticed, but then Guy saw the Templars Onri and Augustine and his interest in them brought his gaze to William at their side. A brief look of astonishment flicked across his face before he schooled his expression to neutrality. Reining around, he rode over to William, uncaring of the pilgrims his mount shouldered out of the way.

'Marshal, I never thought to see you here,' he said.

'My thoughts the same,' William replied, and inclined his head. Guy's tight hose were patterned with tawny lions, drawing attention to his well-muscled legs.

'What are you doing?'

'Making a pilgrimage – sire.' It stuck in William's throat to address Guy by that title, but it was potentially dangerous not to do so.

Guy nodded curtly. 'Yes, we had heard your master was dead.' His voice curled around the words.

'I am here to lay my lord's cloak at the Sepulchre.'

'Then God speed your quest.' His light blue eyes were as sharp as glass. 'How long are you intending to stay?'

'I do not know,' William answered warily. 'It depends on many things, but long enough to recover from our journey.'

Guy flicked an imaginary speck from his cloak. 'Then I wish you a swift recuperation.' He turned his mount and rode on to join the litter, light twinkling on his gilded spurs. The curtain parted again and Guy leaned down to speak to the occupants before glancing back at William.

'You should have a care when you visit court,' Onri warned. 'The Count of Jaffa has many influential connections.'

William grimaced. He could have done without this encounter, for now he had been marked by a man who was in a position to make his life difficult. 'I shall trust in God,' he said. 'He has brought me this far.'

De Lusignan's entourage had raised a cloud of dust that stung the eyes and put grit between the teeth of those left in their wake. William made a determined effort to cast Guy from his mind. This was about the climax of his pilgrimage, about the Young King's cloak and fulfilling a vow. Sacrosanct. He was not about to let such a man rob the moment of its holiness.

Within a mile the walls of Jerusalem rose in full view, and the Gate of the Tower of David, the heavy stones gilded in sunlight. Trinket sellers lined the road, touting their wares, and William noted them with a flicker of anxiety, and kept on walking. A blind beggar, his legs twisted and deformed, held out a cracked bowl and begged alms in the name of Jesus Christ. William sought into the pouch beneath his tunic, found a coin, and tossed it in the bowl.

Guards stood on duty at the gates, observing all who came and went through the gap, and kept the throng moving like a vast herd of cattle. A prod here, a poke there. Merchants and traders entering the city had to draw aside to a trestle and pay their dues in order to sell their wares. The air was pungent, dusty and filled with so much noise that William could barely hear himself think. Jerusalem might be the holiest city on earth, and it was daunting and wonderful to know he was walking in Christ's very footsteps, but in a practical way it was still like any other city and he had to concentrate on not bumping into people around him, many gaping in wonder and exultation, like him and his entourage eager to reach their goal after so long on the road but uncertain of which way to go.

Languages darted at him in a wild melange. He saw men with crimped black hair and faces as dark as ebony wood. A water seller, the bulging skins of his trade hanging over the pack saddle of a tiny donkey. Native Christians with tawny complexions; fair-haired men from northern climes with ruddy faces; almond-eyed silk merchants from the land of Zin; and everyone clumped in their own groups yet mixing and mingling as they made their way through the streets and went about their business. Everywhere was colour and light and life. Even the dull tones of the newcomers' garments stood out because they were such a contrast to the bolder hues worn by the residents.

Onri, familiar with the city, took the lead to guide them through the narrow streets. From the Gate of David they had to turn eastwards, skirting the palace complex and the great tower, bustling with soldiers and officials. They walked up a street bordered by a large rectangular reservoir and then past a massive building of many arches that Onri told them was the great Hospital belonging to the Knights of St John. Shortly beyond that another turn brought them onto a thoroughfare lined with stallholders doing a brisk business selling palms and small wooden crosses, rushwork prayer mats and bundle upon bundle of candles, lamps and oil. William had his own candles, brought from England and blessed by the Archbishop of Canterbury, but some of his men hurried to make purchases. William waited, although his jaws were tight with strain and he was trembling with the effort of containing the emotions churning inside him. Onri noticed, and put his hand firmly on William's shoulder. 'Not long now,' he said. 'Have courage.'

Candles obtained, another fifty paces brought them to the paved area in front of the church of the Holy Sepulchre itself with its embellished arches and its great double doorway. Even here there was a market with yet more candle sellers. Swallowing, William handed Chazur's reins to Eustace and took Harry's cloak from its protective wrapping, his fingers clumsy. He was here, at the heart of Christendom, where Jesus had been crucified for their sins and had risen again in triumph to give man, unworthy as he was, eternal life and redemption. He was awed, unworthy, and overwhelmed. And although his burning goal had been to arrive at this place, he hesitated to enter the church and fulfil his undertaking, afraid that even now God would strike him down within sight of his goal, and he would deserve the blow.

'All is well,' Onri said, his voice filled with quiet command. 'Go and fulfil your duty.'

William exhaled, walked forward to the hallowed portals and entered the dark, incense-permeated church with its numerous chapels and altars. The next breath he drew was filled with the sanctity of God's shrine.

The rotunda was ablaze with the light of lamps and candles reflecting from jewelled and burnished surfaces. Chequered mosaic pavements gleamed in the lamplight like the inside of a seashell and smoke rose in ethereal veils from burning chips of incense, unfolding the scent of heaven. Ripple upon ripple of heat-shimmer from a thousand small flames blurred his vision to a sea of silver and gold, brimming with gems. He could hear voices chanting and he was lost in the glorious susurration. Trembling, he tightened his fingers on the fabric of the cloak. 'Sire,' he whispered. 'Sire, I have done as you asked and fulfilled your vow.'

At the centre of the rotunda stood the Sepulchre itself, housing the tomb where Christ had lain between his death and resurrection. The walls of the edicule were clad in panels of beaten silver as was the cupola rising about the central part of the tomb. The roof of the cupola shone with segmented sheets of polished bronze and upon its pinnacle stood a jewelled and gilded cross surmounted by a golden dove. William's eyes stretched wide to take in these marvels, but the task surpassed him and all he absorbed was an impression of glory beyond mortal comprehension and a wonder too great for his heart.

The line of pilgrims in front of him shuffled forward, waiting their turn to enter the most sacred place in Christendom, accessed through a small chapel and then a dark archway into a chamber beyond that was a concentration of the outer chamber. The walls gleamed with mosaic, and the tomb itself where Christ's linen-wrapped body had lain was overlaid by a slab of polished marble.

Dropping to his knees, William laid the cloak upon it, entreating God and Jesus Christ to have mercy on Harry's soul. 'He transgressed against you, but deeply regretted it, and he desires to atone for his sins, as I do for mine. He was a good man and would have proven himself had he lived. I implore you to forgive his sins and accept him into your presence and have mercy on his soul, and on mine, if it pleases you.' William swallowed against the tight, hard knot in his throat and focused his attention on the head of the slab where Jesus's own head had lain. Tears streamed down his face and the knot unravelled, and he sobbed for the loss of his lord and the ending of his own young manhood. All the remorse, all the guilt and sorrow, all the stored-up bitterness flowed from him as he relinquished his burden. Part of the deluge was gratitude and awe that he should be in this place and in a position to beg God's mercy for Harry and for himself, although he had no expectation of the latter.

At last, the storm passed through him. Exhausted, wrung out, he staggered from the tomb and took the cloak to the Stone of Unction where Jesus had been prepared for His burial. William spread the cloak upon the stone to absorb the spiritual essence of Christ's precious blood, and bowed his head in further, quieter prayer.

One by one his men joined him after they had taken their turn to visit the Sepulchre, say their prayers and make their peace. A dark-clad Augustinian monk arrived to speak with them and William told him who they were and why they were here.

'This is the cloak of an earthly king,' William said. 'The eldest son of King Henry of England, and one who in dying asked nothing but God's mercy on his soul. Had he not passed from this earth, then he would have come in person to beg mercy for his soul. He was not spared to do so and I have continued the task, undeserving though I am.'

The monk listened carefully before going to fetch a more senior associate who questioned William closely about the Young King and then with solemn respect took the cloak and folded it carefully.

'It is yours to do with as you will,' William said, 'but I ask you to treat it with proper reverence and ceremony. I was entrusted with its keeping on my young lord's deathbed, and it has been soaked in prayers and blessings from the churches throughout the long miles of our journey. All I ask is that you give me the cross from the breast and a small piece from the hem so that I may return it as proof to his father.'

'It shall be done, I promise you,' the monk said gravely. 'And we shall accord the cloak a place of reverence.' He bowed to William and his men, and departed into another part of the church. William suppressed the urge to follow him and snatch the cloak back into his own keeping. Having been its custodian through so many dangers and experiences, it was like giving up a part of himself, and it was the final physical connection to Harry.

Another monk guided William and his men to the great pilgrim Hospital adjoining the Sepulchre which they had seen on their way to the church. Administered by the brothers of the Knights Hospitaller it was not only an infirmary for the sick, but provided temporary refuge and shelter for weary pilgrims. Augustine and Onri parted company with the group, for they had to report to their own quarters on the Temple Mount; however, they promised to return to make an accounting of the moneys William had lodged with the order and settle the costs of the journey. The Templars had also agreed to house the party's horses in their extensive stable complex and to find William and his companions a house to rent for the duration of their stay in Jerusalem.

While arranging his pallet in the pilgrims' hostel and tidying his baggage, William was still reeling – poured out to the dregs like an empty pitcher waiting to be replenished. The others were similarly affected. No one spoke of their experience, but each man went away to be silent, to pray and to reflect on his own. William felt as though a layer had been stripped from his skin so that everything was sensitive and keen – or perhaps new. The morning's dawn had been a moment of anticipation before a fresh start. Now in the late afternoon with the sun setting and the candles gleaming in the niches of the hostel walls, he and his companions had completed their walk through fire and were forever changed.

William and his men spent the next several days sleeping, eating, recuperating and visiting the holy places of Jerusalem. They returned to the Sepulchre and spent time in prayer and contemplation at the numerous altars within the church until they were familiar with all of them. The Chapel of Adam, the Prison of Christ. Calvary, the Altar of the Holy Blood where Christ's blood had flowed through a rift in the rock, and which was now commemorated by a hollow in the rock over which a lamp was kept perpetually alight. The chapel of Mary of the Sorrow, and the place where Jesus ascended to heaven. William prayed for hours at all of them, and presented all the small gifts and items he had been asked to bring to the Sepulchre by friends, family and well-wishers.

Exploring the various streets and markets that made up the quarters of the Holy City, they bought food in Malquisnet Street where all the pilgrims congregated to eat. Vulgarly known as the Street of Bad Cookery, some of the dishes on offer deserved that reputation, but others excelled. William found a stall that sold bread as thick as the palm of his hand, fragrant and hot, piled with a spicy mutton and raisin stew. Another boasted fresh fish, seared on a hot griddle, scattered with herbs and drizzled with lemon juice. The knights bought lengths of chopped sugar cane and chewed them to extract the sweetness as they walked, and marvelled at all manner of exotic fruits and spices, including the elongated yellow fruits of paradise with their creamy sweet centres. Fare from home was available too, cooked by settlers catering to the pilgrim palate, and Ancel and Eustace often ate at a stall where the Norman proprietors cooked proper pottages and hearty pork and bacon stews.

Everyone visited a bath house on the second day in order to thoroughly cleanse and prepare themselves for entering noble society. Any dreams harboured of accommodating lady bath attendants such as those in Southwark and Rome were swiftly dissipated by the muscular men, towels knotted at their waists, who scrubbed and pummelled William and his knights until their flesh was scoured and glowing. The clothes they had worn for travel were picked over and those worth keeping were laundered and repaired; the worst were turned into rags, and the men bought new garments more suited to their environment. Onri was their guide, showing them the best stalls to purchase goods, and pointing out those that were better avoided.

Walking with Onri, William passed a group of thin-legged, dark-haired children playing a ball game and yelling to each other and he smiled. That at least was a familiar sight in every place he had ever been. A beggar was curled against the wall of a street corner, his eyes sunken and cheekbones sharp. His left leg ended at the knee and his hose was tied around the stump, crusted with blood and stains. Suppressing a shudder, William dropped a coin into his cracked wooden bowl. Beggars too were a ubiquitous sight in cities. The man thanked him in the German tongue. William had quickly discovered that while the court spoke French, the language of the settlers ranged far and wide.

Two women accompanied by their maids passed the men near the bath house. The former, clad in numerous layers of gossamer silk, shot the knights bold glances, whispering behind their hands. William heard an exchange of suggestive laughter and his senses were assaulted by a waft of exotic perfume.

Onri quickened his pace, his complexion flushing. 'The Holy City is not always holy,' he muttered. 'You will find many temptations here.'

William thought that he might just be interested in those temptations. He had already discovered the sinful joy of the sticky rose-flavoured sweetmeats that melted on the tongue and could be bought from a little stall on Malquisnet Street, and was pondering how to bring a supply back with him to England. He would not mind unwrapping those women too. However, glancing at Onri's set expression, he maintained a grave countenance since he knew he was supposed to be serious and prayerful. And indeed it was miraculous that he was walking where Christ had once walked; that he was at the centre of the bible stories he had learned sitting at the priest's feet as a child.

'Have you decided how long you intend to stay?' Onri asked on the fifth morning when William was checking up on Chazur and the other horses in the stables beneath the Temple Mount. He had been astonished at the sheer size of the underground complex – it was said that it could hold three thousand horses when full, and the stalls stretched for ever under the vaulted roof. There were nowhere near that many stabled here, even given the fact that each Templar knight was supposed to have three mounts: the place was three quarters empty. There were dwellings here for the grooms and alcoves that were used for storing fodder and tack.

'I am not certain,' William replied, 'but at least until we have celebrated Easter at the Sepulchre. We need to replenish our resources and I have to seek audience of King Baldwin and deliver the letters from King Henry.'

'I have spoken to my superiors and there is a dwelling they are willing to rent to you and your men for the duration of your stay – or until you find other accommodation to suit. We can arrange a price that will not beggar you and that you can repay in part in training and horse management while you are here.'

William raised his brows and Onri gave a half-smile. 'Your reputation goes before you. I expect your services will be greatly in demand. I can show you the house now if you wish.'

'Yes, indeed,' William said with alacrity.

Giving Chazur a final pat, he left with Onri to walk a short distance from the Templar gate to some dwelling houses on the western edge of the Mount. At the second door along, Onri produced a key. Etched into the stonework at the side of the door was a shield carved with a large letter T.

'This is our mark,' Onri said. 'Elsewhere you will see others that belong to the Hospitallers and the Convent of St Anne. These are used by Templar associates and secular knights in need of lodging at the Grand Master's discretion.' He admitted William to a room smelling of dusty stone, with a ribbed, barrel-vaulted ceiling. A small fire pit occupied the centre of the room – enough for cooking and keeping warm if the night turned cold. There were hooks in the wall for making partitions between living and sleeping quarters. Several niches and shelves cut into the rock afforded space for belongings and lamps. In the corner a trap door opened on steps down to an underground storage room, with two more sleeping spaces rather like tomb shelves at the side of the walls. William declined to inspect it beyond a cursory glance. He was wary of cellars after Constantinople. 'It is small for all of you,' Onri said, 'but it is somewhere to sleep and shelter. Do you think this will suit your needs?'

William considered the room, hands on hips. After the perils of their journey, this small, cavern-like building in the holiest city on earth was almost a palace. 'It will indeed, and I thank you for the offer.'

'There is no need since it is to our mutual benefit.' Onri went to a bench carved into a side wall and sat down, folding his arms. Someone had left a brass lamp on the shelf and the hanging chain twinkled in the light from the half-open door. 'I have learned much since last I saw you. There are things you should know before you attend the King.'

William eyed him sharply.

'King Baldwin's condition continues to deteriorate and no one knows how much longer he can continue to rule,' Onri explained. 'His will is strong but his body is failing. He is much worse than when I went to England and I am shocked to see the change in him. He can barely use his hands and feet at all now.'

'I am sorry to hear that.' William knew that King Baldwin suffered from leprosy, but was uncertain what he would find when he did enter his presence.

'The succession must be decided and the High Court has been convened to discuss the matter.' Onri looked sidelong at William.

'That was why Guy de Lusignan and his entourage were on the road. The crown of Jerusalem is chosen not inherited, although it tends to stay within the ruling family and de Lusignan has been the acting regent until now.'

William remembered the small boy he had seen peeping out from the curtains of the litter. That was indeed a precarious future for the Kingdom of Jerusalem. Even more so with Guy steering the ship. 'Until now?' he repeated.

'The court is to discuss whether he should continue as regent,' Onri said. 'Many oppose him, and of late the King has bent his ear to their complaints.'

William was not surprised. His only astonishment was that anyone would think de Lusignan capable of ruling in the first place. Although perhaps as an unknown, his charm had initially masked his shortcomings.

'The King wished to retire to the coast for the sake of his health and asked de Lusignan to exchange his lands in Tyre for estates in Jerusalem,' Onri said. 'But as well as fresh sea breezes, Tyre is also extremely wealthy. De Lusignan would rather keep his lands than please the King. Many think him arrogant and foolish. The barons complain that de Lusignan is untrustworthy – that he has poor judgement politically and in battle. There have been incidents that do not instil confidence.'

'He is a strong fighter,' William replied. 'Some would say he is courageous. I would say he has the blood lust of a lion and his judgement is flawed. He does not think of the consequences of his actions, or if he does, then he only sees the ground in front of him, not the horizon. And the mistakes are never his own fault.'

'That accords with what others say, but his wife loves him dearly, and she is a power to be reckoned with since she is the King's sister and mother of the future king. She will fight for what she desires, and what she desires is Guy de Lusignan no matter his failing – and she is not without allies.'

'So, what's to be done?'

Onri shrugged. 'Half the court is absent. The King's half-sister Isabelle is wedding Humphrey of Toron at Kerak, and many are there as guests, including the Patriarch. It will be at least two weeks before they return. It remains to be seen whether the King uses their absence to push through a decision or wait.' Onri rubbed his chin. 'There is another option to the succession of course.'

William looked at him.

'The King intends sending a deputation to seek aid from the rest of Christendom. He will ask for money and soldiers, equipment, horses, but ideally a ruler to take his place. He plans to send the Grand Masters of the Templars and Hospitallers and the Patriarch to the courts of Spain, France and England.'

'Indeed?' William raised his brows.

'We are under threat as never before,' Onri said. 'The Saracens have a great general, Saladin. In the past we have held him off, and he has troubles of his own, but Jerusalem is his goal and he is dangerous. We need someone who will unite us all and face him down. That person is not Guy de Lusignan. This mission will demand the princes of Europe to rouse themselves and come to our aid – perhaps King Henry himself, or Philippe of France.'

William said nothing. He could not envisage either man abandoning the reins of his personal kingdom in order to rule Jerusalem, settling among unfamiliar factions that were not beholden to him. Especially Henry, even though he had sworn to take the cross and had the necessary funds. He suspected Onri thought so too, but was not going to say so. Whatever happened, the situation was fraught with difficulty.

The palace of the kings of Jerusalem stood on the western side of the city a short walk from William's new lodging. An arched portico gave entrance to a building with a gabled roof. On the south side stood a small domed tower and on the north a taller

132

one, toothed with crenellations, from which flew the blue and gold banner of the Kingdom of Jerusalem.

Armed knights stood guard at the entrance, and when William showed his letters bearing the seal of England he was directed into a vestibule where he explained who he was to an official wearing the blue silk livery of the King. The man was all for taking the letters away with him, but William held onto them because they were his only authority. 'My liege lord the King of England bade me present these to his cousin the King of Jerusalem personally, and as I am his servant, so I must act.'

The official looked William up and down as if he were a dubious horse trader trying to sell him a nag and claim it was a destrier. William returned an implacable stare. He had experienced such petty officials before at King Henry's court and knew their ways. This one would doubtless like to dismiss him out of hand, but dared not while he had a letter with the seal of the King of England dangling from it on red silk cords.

'You will wait,' the official commanded, and stalked off in the direction of the domed building.

William loosened his shoulders and forced himself to relax. 'Remember that we are knights of the English royal household,' he told Ancel, Robert and Geoffrey who had accompanied him. 'We are servants of a king. We must bend the knee and give proper obeisance, but we are knights of the English Royal household. Do not fidget or show anxiety. It is our right to be here.'

'That toady did not look as if he thought so,' Ancel muttered. He fidgeted with his belt, adjusting the buckle.

'Since when has such opinion counted?' William replied with scorn. 'The summons will come and we shall make the best of it.'

They occupied the waiting time by observing the toing and froing of members of the court, robed in their colourful, exotic fashions. Heavy wafts of musk and balm assaulted their noses as people passed. There was more protocol than at the English court, more exaggerated compliments, flourishes and hand gestures. However, the expressions were often the same. The wariness, the sidelong looks, the visual daggers, sometimes sheathed, sometimes not. William studied the flamboyance with interest and absorbed the nuances.

'They think we are uncouth peasants, don't they?' Ancel muttered.

'I do not know what they think,' William replied, but secretly thought that Ancel was right. At home they had been handsome silver fish swimming in their own sea; now they were no more than minnows, to be pecked at by the bigger fish in an alien ocean.

Eventually the official returned and beckoned William with a crook of his forefinger, but held up his other hand to prevent the others from accompanying him, indicating they should stay where they were.

Ancel scowled but pressed his lips tightly together and held his peace. With Geoffrey and Robert, he went to sit on a bench at the side of the room where other attendants were awaiting their own lords.

The official took William to another doorway and brought him through into an ante chamber leading into a large barrel-vaulted hall in which many of the people William had seen flit through the vestibule were in attendance, bright as fields of flowers. Several other men were gathered in the ante chamber waiting to be presented to the King and the official strutted before them like a cockerel, instructing them on appropriate behaviour and etiquette.

'You are to go on your knees before the King and keep your head bowed. Only look when you are bidden, and if he does not choose to bid you, then keep your eyes on the ground. You will present your petition when told, and await his pleasure.'

It was a process not unlike that of the English court but with more flourishes and William understood the procedure but was impatient with the posturing because it was all so much frippery.

He watched the supplicant before him go forward, reach a certain point, kneel, and inch forward on his knees with bowed head. He presented the gift of a roll of silk cloth, which an official took and placed at the side of the throne with a murmur to the man sitting there. The King leaned forward to speak to the petitioner. From this distance and angle, William could see little of King Baldwin beyond a figure in pale silk robes. He made occasional gestures with a gloved hand, but a draped cloth prevented a direct glimpse of his face. His courtiers surrounded him like the wide fan of a peacock's tail. A small fair-haired child sat on a stool at his side, hands folded, and William recognised him from the litter on the Jaffa road.

After a brief exchange of words, the supplicant bowed and backed from the room, and then it was William's turn.

He stepped into the hall and walked across the glinting marble and mosaic floor until he reached a cross pattern in the tiles where he dropped to his knees, bowed his head and made his obeisance. The attendant took the amethyst ring that King Henry had given William to present to Baldwin, and placed it with the other gifts beside the throne. The letters were shown to Baldwin and he gestured for the attendant to break the seals and read them to him. At his side, the little boy swung his legs and gazed around.

'Look up,' Baldwin commanded, and William raised his head.

King Baldwin was just twenty-two years old, but William would never have known it from the ravaged features. The cheeks, jaw and mouth were a landscape of swollen lumps, pustules and lesions; one eye was chalky and blind. A faint smell emanated from him, febrile, unpleasant, but masked a little by incense and rose perfume. He was garbed in voluminous pale silk robes embroidered with gold thread. Padded, bejewelled gloves covered both hands and a coif of lighter fabric draped his shoulders and head, topped by a silk cap adorned with gems and pearls. A gold hook fastened a veil to the side of the cap, but he had now thrown it back to expose his face. His air was one of command, courage and defiance. Here was someone prepared to hold his ground whatever the odds.

William's father had been badly disfigured when burning lead from a church roof had dripped on him and burned out an eye, and William was able to regard Baldwin with composure. He had cause to know that a physically damaged man could have a steelier will than a whole one.

Despite being almost blind, the young King possessed an intent focus. William could feel himself being scrutinised like a gem in a jeweller's workshop.

Baldwin indicated with his gloved right hand that William should come forward and kneel on the embroidered cushion positioned on one of the dais steps.

William did as he was bidden, setting aside the unease he felt at being so close to a leper, yet one who was royalty. It was a strange juxtaposition. Lepers were shunned by society but therefore closest to God. And the King was God's anointed, the sovereign of all, yet who dared to share his bread? The child watched him, his own pale skin unblemished and pure.

William could feel the peacock fan of courtiers watching him with speculation. Not entirely hostile, but not welcoming either. He knew none of them, but they were clearly men of high importance. At least Guy de Lusignan was not among the gathering, although he must be in the palace somewhere.

'So, you were the Marshal to the son of my cousin King Henry?' Baldwin asked.

'Yes, sire, may God rest my young lord's soul.'

'Amen.' Baldwin continued to study him. 'I am sorry to learn of the loss of such a Prince of Christendom. I hear that because of this you have been left without a position in your homeland and are here to seek your fortune instead.'

Behind his courtier's façade, William was astonished, wondering just what Henry had said in his letter, but he swiftly reasoned that Henry had no cause to vilify him when he was taking his son's cloak to Jerusalem. Queen Alienor had written a letter of recommendation too and he knew that one to be positive. Baldwin had said 'I hear' which suggested verbal sources, and he knew immediately from whom they came.

'If that is the case then be sure you make a good impression, because we shall be watching you with interest,' Baldwin continued.

William bowed his head. 'Sire, I undertook this pilgrimage at the behest of my master to lay his cloak at Christ's tomb, to pray for his soul and to atone for my sins and his. The King and Queen expect me to return to them in due course when I have completed my prayers and penances.'

'Do they indeed?' The tone of Baldwin's voice was tepid and formal. 'It is my understanding that you caused much trouble throughout King Henry's lands while other men were more righteously employed.'

William said nothing but felt all eyes trained on him, including the innocent blue ones of the child.

Baldwin sat up straighter and one of the courtiers moved to adjust the cushions at his spine. When he spoke again, his voice had a slight slur. 'A reputation for causing trouble and scandal at court follows you – I am told you were banished at one time for inappropriate behaviour and that you played an instrumental part in robbing a shrine sacred to Christ's mother in order to pay mercenaries engaged in rebellion against the King of England.'

When put in such terms, William's reputation sounded utterly sordid.

Baldwin continued to study him hard, forcing him to the point. 'What do you have to say to this? How do you reply?'

William raised his head and said directly but without challenge in a clear, calm voice loud enough for all to hear, 'I will leave it to you, sire, to decide on my character by what you see, and I will conduct myself as I have always done with utmost trust in God and loyalty to whomsoever I give my oath of service. And that loyalty is pledged unto death and shall remain so.'

Baldwin rubbed his right glove against his thigh. 'You speak well. You remind us that a man should always be judged by his deeds and not by the rumours that surround him. How long will you stay?'

'Sire, I am sworn to return to my lord King Henry, but not yet.'

'And you have an entourage to maintain?'

'Sire, I have five trained knights under my banner and three squires who know their weapons.'

Baldwin's ruined mouth curved in what might have been a smile as he considered William's reply. 'You are dismissed, but return today after Compline, and we shall talk further.'

His audience at an end, William bowed from Baldwin's presence and returned to Ancel, Robert and Geoffrey. 'He wishes to talk more,' William said. 'I have to return at Compline.' He considered how much to tell them. 'He said he knew about our past, but most of his awareness seems to have come from the Lusignans.'

'If that is the case we are finished,' Ancel said morosely. 'We might as well just mount our horses now and ride home.'

William shook his head. 'He is no fool this King of Jerusalem. Even if he is ravaged by leprosy, his mind is as keen as a blade. Anyone who underestimates him or takes him as a weakling misjudges him. He wanted to know if I had an entourage to maintain, and I believe he will employ us if all goes well.'

'What about de Lusignan?'

'What about him?' William shrugged. 'He was not present. I have no doubt he will make our path difficult, but he has his own troubles for all that he is wed to the King's sister.'

'What kind of troubles?' Geoffrey asked.

'The same as ours – those of an outsider,' William said. 'Those of an upstart. But since he has been here longer, and knows the territory, he is more able to deal it out to others.'

He was turning toward the arch that led to the street when the little boy from the audience room skipped across his path, slashing the air with a toy sword as he fought imaginary foes. A nurse was hurrying to catch up with him while holding a rosy-cheeked baby in her arms, fair hair peeping from under its cap.

Following more sedately came a tall, elegant woman robed in golden-red silk. Earrings of tiered pearls gleamed beneath her gossamer veil. Several women followed in her wake, all richly clad, but none to outshine her. Realising the lady's identity, William knelt and bowed his head as he had done to Baldwin and shot a swift glance from beneath his brows that sent Ancel, Robert and Geoffrey to their knees also.

She skimmed them a look, and beckoned them to stand. Another, older woman joined her, her hair drawn back and up beneath a full wimple, pulling her flesh taut to her bones. She was thin, almost to the point of emaciation, and her coral-coloured gown lent false colour to her complexion. Although she was clearly unwell, the resemblance between the women made William think they were mother and daughter.

'You were on the road into Jerusalem a few days ago,' the younger one said.

William bowed. 'Yes, madam. I remember seeing your litter and the young Prince looking out.'

'You know who I am?'

'Madam, you are the King's noble sister, the Princess Sybilla, Countess of Jaffa.'

She lifted one eyebrow. 'My husband tells me that he knows you.'

William met her eyes; they were a light green, clear and shrewd. 'That is so, madam, but from another life – for both of us.'

She gave him a calculating look, not quite hostile, but with that potential lurking at the edges. 'Then have a care how you conduct yourself at court for this is the life you have now, not what it was, and my husband is a powerful man and acts in the King's name, and mine.'

'Madam, that is foremost in my mind,' William replied smoothly.

'Then keep it so, messire Marshal, and you shall do well.' She swept on, the hem of her gown whispering over the tiled floor.

The older woman paused before following the Countess. 'A word of advice,' she said. 'Do not make an enemy of the Princess and keep out of her husband's way if you would prosper here. My son needs strong knights in Outremer and it would be a pity not to employ you.' She encompassed all four men with an assessing look from faded green eyes that had perhaps once been as beautiful as her daughter's and then walked on.

'Ah, Agnes of Courtenay,' Onri said with a knowing look when William came to check on the horses at the Templar stables before going to the meeting with the King at Compline and told him of his encounter. 'Mother of the King and the Princess Sybilla, and grandmother of the heir to the throne. You will hear rumours of her enjoyment of strong, handsome men, including the Patriarch Heraclius. Some say it is through her influence he gained that position. Others will tell you that the King's leprosy is a punishment on her for her carnal sins.'

Having served Queen Alienor, William knew how such virulent rumours were apt to grow and spread, and how wrong they could be. Queen Alienor had always appreciated the young, lithe squires who served her court, and the handsome men to whom she handed largesse and sponsorship at her table, himself included, but only in the way she might look at a fine horse parading in the courtyard or a beautiful ring. Mostly it was about power and patronage. 'I have learned not to give credence to rumours. In truth, the lady looked frail to me and unwell. It is easy to tilt at the reputations of women of rank.'

Onri stooped to lift and clean out his horse's hoof. 'I am telling you what is said because you asked and because you need to know for your own preservation. I am no peddler of gossip.' The scraping tool grated on horn.

'Indeed,' William reassured him swiftly, knowing Onri's touchiness on the matter of honour.

'Trust to your own instincts,' Onri continued. 'I do not think the Lady Agnes will help you, but if you do not make her your enemy it will be of benefit.'

William brushed Chazur's flanks and rump, making the dark bronze coat gleam. He was still in awe of the size of these great underground Templar stables. A man could disappear in here for days.

'The court is driven by factions, many of them from the distaff side,' Onri said. 'The King's sister and mother are highly influential, especially Sybilla, but the King has the strongest will of all because he must. Guy de Lusignan knows how to bow and flourish but he is . . .' Onri frowned, seeking a comparison. 'He is like a fire made of dry kindling. He burns hotter than you can bear and dazzles your eyes, but he will not warm you for long. The Countess is devoted to him, and she will choose his welfare at every turn – even above that of the Kingdom of Jerusalem.'

'And what of the King?'

'You have seen the state of the King,' Onri said sombrely. 'Without a miracle, his days are numbered, and who then will step up to the throne?'

Two men approached down the walkway between the stalls, deep in conversation, and Onri immediately knelt and bowed his head. William swiftly and prudently followed his example.

The leading Templar bade them rise and signed the cross over them.

'Grand Master, my lord seneschal, this is the knight I mentioned to you,' Onri said. 'This is William the Marshal from England, who served King Henry's son.'

The knight who had signed the cross and whom Onri had

addressed as Grand Master was grey-bearded and elderly, but still tall and upright. He had intelligent dark eyes, fierce and haughty, and a long, thin nose with a patrician bump in the middle. Arnold de Torroja was a Spanish Templar who had worn the mantle of Grand Master of the order for a little over two years. His companion, the seneschal, Gerard de Ridefort, was younger with grey-salted brown hair and heavy brows shadowing narrow grey eyes.

'Your reputation goes before you, messire Marshal,' Grand Master de Torroja said in a firm, resonant voice without a quiver of age.

William inclined his head. 'So I understand, my lords, although I hope to prove myself as I stand and not through the tales of others.'

De Torroja's lips curved without warmth. 'I am sure you will do so. Brother Onri and Brother Augustine speak well of you, but as you say, you are here to prove yourself in person, not by reputations bestowed by others. We shall talk again.' The two senior Templars moved on to look at some new horses that had just arrived.

William exchanged glances with Onri. 'I appear to be on trial,' he said ruefully.

'Because no one knows your mettle yet and they have only heard tales about you from those who are not your friends. If the Grand Master wishes to speak further with you, it can only be to the good. With all this talk of a deputation to France and England, you might prove very useful.'

William gave a humourless smile. 'I suppose I can count that as Fortune's favour.'

Onri scratched his mount's neck. 'Men of your calibre are always welcome in our order – if they have the inclination to take vows.'

William wiped his hands on a linen rag. 'I know you would not say such words unless you considered me worthy, but I am not ready for such an undertaking. I have too many sins to atone for and I have a promise to keep to the King and Queen of England before I am free to consider my future.'

'But you will keep it for later perhaps?' Onri gave him a keen look. 'Do not dismiss it out of hand.'

The court assembly at Compline was informal. Although the King had bidden him attend, William, as a newcomer, was of no great consequence, and thus he sat with lesser men away from the dais. However, it was a chance to meet and talk with others and William made the most of the opportunity by being amenable and gregarious.

Later, once the meal had finished and men gathered to talk in groups, William made his way into the presence of Bohemond lord of Antioch who stood talking to the barons Raymond of Tripoli and Badouin lord of Ramlah, all of whom had been part of the peacock fan surrounding Baldwin that afternoon.

King Baldwin himself sat over a chess board in a window embrasure with his sister Sybilla, but the moves were being played out in vigorous, low-voiced conversation rather than with the gaming pieces, the Countess making her point with rapid gestures of her elegant fingers.

Bohemond regarded William with a shrewd eye and curiosity as if contemplating some new type of creature that had washed up on his personal beach. 'I was sorry to hear of the loss of my cousin – truly sorry. Even though I did not know him personally, we still heard of him in Outremer. News reaches us slowly here and through many more filters but it always arrives eventually – even if it is sometimes changed.' He spoke with a slight speech impediment. It had earned him the name of Bohemond the Stutterer in certain circles, although never to his face. He was Queen Alienor's cousin and there was a look of Harry about his eyes and his jawline, edged by a dark blond beard.

'It was a great loss, sire.'

'And you come on pilgrimage on his behalf?'

'And my own, sire, to atone for our sins.'

Bohemond stroked his chin. 'We saw you speaking with the King today. You acquitted yourself well in a difficult situation.'

'I merely gave an honest accounting, sire.'

'Well that is more than most men do,' said Raymond of Tripoli darkly.

'How fares King Henry himself?' Bohemond enquired. 'We know he is sworn to take the cross. Do you think he will find his way to Jerusalem? For certain we could use his skills.'

William was rescued from answering by a sudden flurry at the end of the room as Guy de Lusignan entered, attended by several of Sybilla's knights. The atmosphere changed immediately and men drew into themselves.

'Ah,' said Bohemond lightly, 'our illustrious consort and regent of the kingdom. Is he not magnificent?' He looked at William with a mischievous glint in his eyes. 'A veritable lion, no?'

William said nothing. He was not going to voice an opinion until he better knew these men and the dynamics of the court.

Guy made an elaborate, almost sarcastic flourish to Bohemond and his group, who returned the acknowledgement with pointed courtesy. Guy's gaze fixed on William and noted the company he was keeping and then he sauntered over to his wife in the embrasure and stood behind her, placing his hands possessively on her shoulders before leaning round to kiss her cheek, his gesture both proprietorial and affectionate, sending a message to all present of their union, their marital harmony and his masculine ownership.

She raised her hand to take his in reciprocation and smiled up at him, before focusing again on her game.

William observed the interplay with interest.

'It would seem that the Count of Jaffa and his wife are keen to demonstrate their affection for each other this evening,' Bohemond said.

Raymond of Tripoli snorted in contempt. 'Given the circumstances what do you expect?'

William looked between the men. Although standing with them, he was an outsider of lesser rank, and asking what circumstances would be inappropriate.

'How well did you know Guy de Lusignan when you were in Poitou?' Bohemond enquired.

'I was his family's hostage for a few weeks after they murdered my uncle and took me prisoner,' William replied. 'I had to share his company, but it was not from choice.'

Bohemond looked thoughtful. 'We should talk more. We mean you well, but I can see you are a prudent man, and that is all to the good in Outremer.' Removing a gold ring from his little finger, he presented it to William. 'Come to my dwelling before I return to Antioch. I may have a project for you, or patronage I can send your way.'

William bowed and accepted the ring with gratitude, taking it as a mark of approval, if not yet patronage. It was always useful to have several irons in the forge, as he had learned from his time at the Angevin court. Raymond of Tripoli gave him a meaningful nod too, although clearly reserving his judgement.

The Countess of Jaffa rose from the chess board and Guy took her place. William noted the move with interest. In giving up her place, Sybilla was demonstrating that she and her husband were a true partnership and that she trusted him, even if no one else did. Standing at his back, she looked around at the courtiers, much as Guy had done, her expression defiant and imperious. William well recognised the language of power, and that this woman possessed it. She was no cipher, and he suspected that Guy was the one who must do her bidding, not the other way around.

A sudden commotion at the hall door heralded the arrival of a messenger who was brought directly to the King. He stank of hot horse and his garments were smothered in dust.

145

'Sire!' The man fell to his knees. 'Saladin has come with his host and laid siege to Kerak. The lord Reynald bids you come to his aid as swiftly as you may.' He presented Baldwin with a sealed letter.

A ripple of consternation spread through the room as the news carried outwards from the embrasure.

Baldwin gestured for the messenger to stand up. 'When did you set out?'

'A day and a half since, sire. I have changed horses and not stopped to sleep.'

'Go and refresh yourself and be ready to ride again as soon as you have rested.'

Dismissing the messenger, Baldwin stood up and used the higher level of the embrasure as a platform from which to address the stunned court. 'Saladin has dared to launch an attack on Kerak in the middle of the nuptial celebrations of my dear sister Isabella to the lord of Toron!' His voice rang out firm and strong despite his ailing body. 'If he prevails, he will capture both a vital fortress and many important members of our court. We must go to Kerak's aid as soon as we can muster, and we must strike hard. Light the beacons; tell them we are coming.'

Amid a babble of approbation and concern, Baldwin sent men running to give the order.

'I need a list of every fighting man who has the wherewithal to ride to Kerak,' he continued. 'Let the injured or sick give up their armour and horses to sound men who can take their place and let it be done without delay.'

The news about Kerak was alarming, but William's anticipation surged at an opportunity to prove himself.

'Who is to lead the army, sire?' demanded Badouin of Ramlah, stepping forward from their group, challenge ringing in his voice.

'I think that is already decided, my lord,' Guy de Lusignan spoke up before Baldwin could answer. 'As the King's acknowledged regent, it is my prerogative.'

'But the very reason so many of us are gathered at court now is to discuss your competency as regent and your ability as a battle leader,' Badouin retorted, his voice oozing contempt. 'It is not decided at all, my lord. How many here will follow you into an encounter with Saladin?'

Guy jutted his jaw. 'I think you will find that it is treason, my lord, to refuse.'

Baldwin raised his hand for silence as a groundswell of noise followed Guy's remark, mingling support and rejection in one tangle. 'You asked who is to lead the army, my lord of Ramlah. Then I shall tell you. I shall lead the army personally and I shall see succour brought to those in Kerak. And if you choose to give me the same answer you have just bestowed on my brother by marriage, I shall indeed consider you guilty of treason. We must all be one in this if we are not to see disaster come down upon us. Do I make myself clear?'

Bohemond muttered something under his breath that sounded like 'Dear Christ'.

Badouin did not flinch. 'Sire, I swear I will follow you behind the True Cross. This is our chance to deal with Saladin once and for all if we can take him by surprise and destroy him. We can wipe out the depredation of our enemy for a generation – but only if we are led by someone we trust to accomplish the deed. We all know you have defeated Saladin before.' He dropped to his knees and bowed his head, and was swiftly followed by every man in the chamber.

Baldwin stood tall before the swathe of kneeling men. 'God has granted me this opportunity to take Saladin, and I am glad. For now, let all other business be deferred. Once we have secured Kerak, then we shall deal with all matters pertaining. It would be foolish to further embroil ourselves in argument when we must deal with the enemy at our gates. The Count of Jaffa shall accompany me and assist me in any way I deem fit. That is my command. And let my nephew Baldwin, son of my sister, be anointed and crowned heir to the throne of Jerusalem before we depart. This is a dangerous undertaking, and I wish the succession to be clearly signalled. The debate concerning who shall act as regent for my nephew in times to come shall continue once we have relieved Kerak and with the full court assembled in Jerusalem.'

'Well,' said Bohemond as the gathering broke up and men started to leave to begin mobilising their soldiers and vassals, 'the lion has roared, but in whose favour? I did not think he still had it in him.'

'You underestimate him,' Raymond said.

Bohemond lifted his brows. 'Do I?'

William said quietly, 'Perhaps he hopes not to return.'

Raymond gave him a sharp look. 'Your meaning, messire?'

'Sire, the King is bearing his affliction with fortitude and dignity, but his time is borrowed. I have heard the tale of how once, when he was less incapacitated, he rode against Saladin and won a great victory that scattered his forces. Perhaps he hopes to do so again. If he succeeds he will buy time for the kingdom, and if he dies in the attempt, then it will be glorious. That is why he wants the succession settled.'

Raymond gave him a weighty look. 'I think you may be right, messire, but God preserve our King's life for a little longer yet.'

'Amen to that,' said Bohemond, and turned to William. 'I would welcome you and your men to ride under my banner to Kerak.'

William inclined his head. 'Sire, that is generous of you, but I should offer the King my services first and he should decide before I go elsewhere.'

Bohemond looked amused and also a little irritated. 'Then you must do as your conscience dictates, but if you do, remember you will be riding in the company of the Count of Jaffa, and I am not sure it is a good bargain for what you will receive in return, but as you will. My door is open and I am always willing to lend a listening ear.'

'Thank you, sire.' William understood perfectly what was being laid out before him and was thoroughly prepared to keep that door from closing.

Bohemond went off to make his arrangements and William approached Baldwin as the King prepared to leave the hall with Guy and Sybilla at his side.

'Sire,' William said, bending one knee. 'I offer to put myself and my men at your full disposal.'

'Your offer is gratefully accepted,' Baldwin replied brusquely. 'I need every fighting man we have, and now is your opportunity to display your mettle.' His ruined gaze was fierce and he had a gleam about him, as if a guttering stub had been replaced by a fresh new candle. Perhaps the last one in the cupboard, but it burned with the clear, strong light of the King's will.

'Sire.' William bowed again and stood back. Guy gave him a sour look but held his peace.

The King's attendants helped him into his cushioned litter and bore him away. Just before the litter curtain swished across, William saw Baldwin slump against the cushions, his head thrown back in utter exhaustion, and he realised how sick the King really was.

Guy turned to follow the litter with Sybilla, and shot a warning glance at William. 'The company you keep is noted,' he said.

'Then I am glad it is illustrious,' William replied calmly. He stood for a moment to watch the King and his attendants leave, then departed to his own lodging.

17

Manor of Caversham, April 1219

William became aware of a faint scent curling on the edge of his awareness, like the residue of incense smoke that had already risen in prayer, but as he strove to draw the fragrance deeper, it vanished. It had been more than thirty years since that perfume had haunted him, although it would never leave his memory and had played its part in defining who he became.

A movement at his side caused him to look up, half expecting to see a swirl of flame-gold silk and heavy dark braids shining through a veil as fine as mist. Instead, his gaze lit on two of his daughters, Eve and Mahelt, who were sitting with their sewing as they kept vigil.

'Papa, are you comfortable?' Mahelt asked. She was his eldest daughter, mother of his four grandchildren, forthright, honest, strong.

'Yes,' he said, although it was not true. He fiddled with a plain, scratched gold ring on the little finger of his right hand. 'Where is your mother?'

'At prayer,' Eve said. 'Shall I fetch her?'

William shook his head. 'Do not disturb her. She will come to me in her own time, and I am glad of your company.'

'You were talking in your sleep earlier, Papa.' Eve rose to smooth the coverlet and adjust his pillows. She smelled sweet, of summer meadows, totally unlike the perfume of a moment since. Mahelt helped him to drink from the cup at his bedside and he tasted the bitterness of whatever his physician was using to dull the pain.

'Was I? What did I say?'

'You said something about Lot's wife and a pillar of salt.'

'Ah . . .' He was relieved that it was nothing of consequence. He had always been so careful. 'Mahelt, bring me that box.' He indicated a small decorated coffer standing on a shelf.

She lifted it down and gave it to him, her dark eyes filled with curiosity. With shaking hands, he opened it and rummaged among the contents, moving aside various objects – small pieces of harness, a couple of tent pegs, a pair of dice, a crude nail wrapped in a piece of cloth – until his fingers lighted on a small red silk bag. Tugging open the drawstrings, he tipped a pile of milky white beads onto the coverlet. 'These are strewn all over the shoreline of the Sea of Salt,' he said. 'Some folk will tell you they are the jewels that Lot's wife was wearing around her neck when she was turned into a pillar of salt. Go on, taste one.'

Mahelt put one of the stones to her lips, gave a small lick, and then screwed up her face. 'Papa!' she admonished, and swiftly took a drink from his cup.

William chuckled. 'Yes, it is not palatable, but it is indeed a marvel of God's creation. Whatever you set on the sea refused to sink, although no ship could sail upon it for the water warped and corroded the planks.'

'What were you doing there, Papa?' Eve asked. 'You have never told us these things before.'

William gave his daughters a tired smile. 'No. It was a difficult time for me and I learned some hard lessons. What was I doing? I was on my way to relieve a castle, never knowing what awaited me there.' He shook his head and gazed toward the open window. 'It is something I need to remember, but not something you need to know. But stay, if you will. Your presence sustains me.'

18

The Shores of the Dead Sea, Early December 1183

At dawn, William walked with Ancel along the shores of the Dead Sea, the water reflecting hues of pink and rose-amber from the sky. The air was clear and dry and beyond the salt-scaled shoreline the earth was a dusty baked gold. It was bearably cool at the moment but the heat would burn up as the sun gained height in the sky. For all that it was early December, the temperature was as warm as France in the middle of the tourney season.

Ancel crouched by the shore, dipped his fingers and then tasted the water before choking and filling his mouth with saliva to spit. 'They say this place is one of the entrances to hell and that is why nothing will live in it or on it!'

William grinned. 'But surely priests tell us that the entrance to hell is lush and beautiful and paved with all manner of enticements?'

Ancel spat again, wiped his mouth, and made a face that said he was unconvinced. 'I can well believe this is the place where Lot's wife was turned into a pillar of salt.'

William stooped, picked up some of the smooth white stones edging the shore and put them in his pouch for a keepsake. Then he straightened and shaded his eyes to the sunrise, knowing this might be his last day on earth.

Ancel rose beside him and the deep rosy light fingered his cheek and burnished his hair. 'I hope you are right about the mouth of hell,' he said ruefully. 'I don't want to find myself back here if we die today.'

'Neither do I, but we have done our penance at the Sepulchre and received absolution, and that is all we can do.' A half day's ride would bring them to the walls of Kerak. If Saladin chose not to retreat, then they would be going into pitched battle against the full might of the Saracen army. Even with the protection of the True Cross, it was a daunting prospect.

Ancel said flippantly, 'Kerak will be full of jesters and minstrels present for the wedding. At least if we win through we shall be royally entertained.'

Hearing the bravado in his brother's voice, William gave him a rough hug. 'Whatever happens, we're together.'

Ancel returned the embrace, giving William a hard squeeze, but then self-consciously stepped back.

On returning to the camp to make their preparations, William was summoned to the King's tent to receive the order of march. Girding on his sword, he made his way to Baldwin's great blue and gold canvas pavilion, the royal banner fluttering from the top in the breeze. The flaps were hooked back to admit the army's lords and officers and a crowd had already gathered. William eased his way inside and found a space at the side near the entrance, trying not to tread on toes.

Baldwin sat on a raised wooden platform. He wore a knee-length quilted silk tunic and soft grey hose, for he was unable to bear the weight of a mail shirt. A thinly padded bonnet covered his head with a light coif worn over it. Raymond of Tripoli and Guy de Lusignan stood either side of him. The former, his hands clasped behind his back, was looking out over the knights with a composed expression. Guy was tight-lipped, his fists clenched around his belt.

Baldwin drew himself upright and raised his voice. 'Today we march to the relief of Kerak, and it may be that we shall meet the hosts of Saladin in battle should he choose to stay and fight. If that happens then I trust in the Lord God and His son Jesus Christ to be with us and to strengthen our swords and our resolve.

I shall be with you throughout, at the standard of the True Cross, and whatever happens on this day, I shall see it through to the end.

'My condition is such that although my will and spirit are strong, my body will not encompass all that must be done. I know there are differences of opinion among you and deep divisions, but now is not the time to air them. We therefore appoint the Count of Tripoli to act as overall commander of my army. He is known to all of you and is a steady hand with much experience. That is my decision. The Count of Jaffa shall attend on me and remain at my side to offer his personal support and succour.'

William heard the collective sigh of relief surge through the tent. Baldwin could not lead the troops in a fight however brave his words – he was incapable of holding a sword – but his barons would only follow Guy de Lusignan into battle under heavy duress. This way at least the rift was patched over until they had dealt with relieving Kerak.

Raymond of Tripoli stepped forward at Baldwin's invitation to give a rousing speech, followed by more prosaic instructions about deployment before dismissing everyone to their positions with a final instruction to be ready to ride on the moment. Guy sent a vicious look around the tent as it began to empty, but was forced by Baldwin's orders to remain by his side.

'Well, thank God for that,' muttered Bohemond to William as they left the tent. 'The lord of Tripoli is a fine man to lead the army and we know where we stand.' He sent William a shrewd look. 'The King is courageous but he cannot take an active part if there is fighting. It is his will that unites us and brings us here, but that is the most that can be said.'

'And the Count of Jaffa will protect him with his life?'

Bohemond snorted. 'The Count of Jaffa will do whatsoever the Count of Jaffa wishes – and that will be to protect his own life above all others. Saladin fears our King a great deal more

154

than he does the man who would follow him onto the throne of Jerusalem. He also has cause to respect the lord of Tripoli, but I doubt he has ever had a qualm about the name of Lusignan.'

William had his own qualms about the name of Lusignan. Guy could fight – indeed, he was vicious in a fray – but was too easily distracted by the heat of the moment. He was no commander; he did not have the gift in the thick of battle, and when it came to making plans he was a follower who would jump on a cart already in motion, but without knowing where it would end up. Many were swayed by his fair good looks and his arrogant air of entitlement. 'As you say, all will be well with the King to lead the True Cross and my lord of Tripoli to command the army.'

'You are a man after my own heart,' Bohemond said. 'I admire a bridled tongue.' He slapped William's arm. 'Good fortune. If all goes well, we shall speak again inside Kerak.'

Ancel reached for his water skin and pulled out the stopper to take a few swallows before passing it to William. The sun was at its zenith and had begun to beat down on mail shirts and helmets. Ever since setting out from their camp beside the Sea of Salt they had seen Saracen scouts in the distance shadowing their movements, close enough to taunt their approach but far enough away not to be caught. They would be reporting to Saladin that the King of Jerusalem had come in person to Kerak's rescue, bearing the True Cross, containing amid its glittering fabric a splinter of wood from the tree on which Jesus had hung and died.

William drank the warm water, tasting of leather, and returned the skin to Ancel. His belly churned with anticipation; he was ready for battle, ready to do his duty whatever the cost. Steady and alert. He and his men were riding on the left flank, on the outer edge of the knights protecting the King's palanquin. Baldwin was being borne on an open litter, the white silk curtains drawn

155

back to reveal him in his cloth armour. His face was covered by a gauze veil, but his figure, borne on high, was, like the True Cross, a marker and focal point for the men.

Guy de Lusignan rode close to the palanquin upon his white stallion, harness jingling with enamelled pendants. The links of his coif were gilded, so that although his blond hair was covered, he was still the shining golden prince. Riding at the King's other side, Raymond of Tripoli was sombrely garbed in a dark surcoat and seated upon a solid brown stallion, as though deliberately shunning the trappings Guy so flamboyantly embraced.

Dust rose in a gritty mist around the horses' hooves so that the army moved in its own cloud, while beyond them the air was clear and hard. High in the blue several large birds described lazy circles over the advancing men.

'Do you think they know something we do not?' Ancel asked, shading his eyes.

William squinted against the sun. 'Perhaps Saladin is asking the same question. Carrion birds always follow armies. Even without battle there are pickings to be had.' He patted his new stallion's neck to continue the bonding and reassurance. He had negotiated with the Templars for warhorses for him and his men and Onri had ensured that they had been given the best that could be found from among the order's remounts. His own, Flambur, was a golden dun with darker rings marbling his rump and shoulders. Ancel rode an inquisitive and greedy dappled grey that had already managed to dip its nose into the oat sack when no one was looking. Ancel had threatened to rename it 'Greedy-guts', the nickname of William's youth, but the horse was called Byrnie because the strongly marked dapples on his coat resembled a mail shirt.

Moments later two scouts came galloping in and reported urgently to the King. William was too far away to hear what was said, but the command went out to increase the pace from steady walk to trot.

A messenger joined him as they rode. 'Saladin is withdrawing from Kerak, but we may yet bite his baggage train in the backside if we make haste!' He spurred on, carrying the news to the next group, and the next.

William checked his weapons and his men, but was confident that every man knew his part. They had fought and trained and journeyed together for so long that they worked as one without conscious thought.

Through the dusty haze of their increased speed, Kerak castle reared before them, an imposing fortress of golden rock standing on the spur of a high plateau surrounded by a deep ditch with sloping sides rising up from the base of the rock. Scrubby bushes covered the unworked areas of natural stone. The defences showed signs of the battering they had received from the Saracen stone throwers, but banners waved defiantly from the battlements.

Ahead, the pace quickened to a canter and William heard shouts and the clash of weapons as they hit the tail end of Saladin's baggage train. A fight obstructed the ground in front of him and he had to swerve to avoid three knights who had brought down a Saracen horse archer. Small whirlpools of sporadic combat churned the dust. Loose horses milled around, among them a scrawny donkey heavily laden with two baggage sacks. Ancel grabbed the rope bridle. Despite its bony, flea-bitten condition, the creature flattened its ears and lashed out with its small, hard hooves, braying fit to deafen anyone in its vicinity, but Ancel held on tightly. The first rule of battle after survival, as every knight knew, was taking ransoms and acquiring plunder.

The siege machines that had been pounding Kerak's walls had been set on fire as Saladin's soldiers fled, and the heat and smoke flared out from their carcasses in burning wings of flame. Through the smoke and dust, William glimpsed the cloud of Saladin's rapidly retreating force. Arrows sang overhead and plummeted on the relief army like diving birds, but they were random and loosed as a distraction to slow the pursuit. One struck the ground close to William, and in front of him a horse was hit in the rump by an almost-spent shaft that sent it bucking and kicking and flinging its rider to the ground. William drew his shield in close to his body. Tents and debris from the Saracen baggage strewed the route – some of it burning, some still intact, most of it worthless. Saladin might be in full retreat, but it was in good order with his wealth and his best troops unscathed.

Swift orders were issued not to pursue the enemy but to secure the castle and relieve its occupants.

As a ragged cheer spread through the relieving army and gathered strength, William reined in Flambur and leaned forward to pat the stallion's damp shoulder. He had been prepared to fight and die, but was not sorry to see the Saracen army retreating before the banner of the True Cross. Their goal had been accomplished without loss, even if it was a pity that Saladin had had the foresight and time to move his most valuable assets forward through the ranks. Only the detritus of the baggage train remained to be picked over, and no one was going to get fat on that.

The ramparts of Kerak were lined with cheering people waving banners and cloths. William suddenly grinned and waved back, feeling like the champion at a tourney. Behind him the donkey brayed and he looked round with amusement. 'At least one of us has acquired some booty, although I don't think there is any need for you to share it out among the rest of the men.'

Ancel saluted him with a rude gesture.

The army paraded into Kerak in full military order, horses abreast, banners flying, the True Cross brandished aloft before King Baldwin's litter, and the midday sun flashing starbursts on armour and weapons.

William took note of the massive defences as they entered the castle. Such places were designed to resist assault for months if not years on end. He studied the damage to the stonework from Saladin's siege machines. The pock-marks and blurring, the chips and shards of broken stone. Yet the underlying structure remained intact and the inner defences were mostly untouched.

The first duty was to see to the horses, ensure they were watered and given adequate stabling, and to make sure the tack was stowed safely. Ancel investigated his donkey's baggage and was delighted to discover a red silk turban set with a huge sapphire pin, and a fabulous golden damask robe embroidered all over with pearls and gold beads. A pair of gilded leather slippers with turned-up toes completed the ensemble and fitted Ancel perfectly. The other sack contained a bag of charcoal, two battered metal cooking pots, and several dice in a lidded horn cup. Amid much joshing, they decided that Ancel had captured either a thief or a trickster's ill-gotten gains.

'You said I didn't have to share the spoils,' Ancel declared loftily, 'but you are welcome to the cooking pots and the charcoal.'

William cuffed Ancel across the top of his head. 'Generous to a fault,' he retorted with a grin. 'I hope to be equally generous when next I come into a fortune!'

That night a great feast was held with music and entertainments provided by the troubadours, acrobats, jugglers and sword dancers who were present at Kerak to entertain the guests at the marriage festivities of Baldwin's half-sister Isabelle and Humphrey the young lord of Toron. The nuptials were celebrated all over again with a thanksgiving for the timely relief that had arrived from Jerusalem.

William moved among the crowds in the hall, speaking to men, socialising, making useful connections, although his circle did not bring him anywhere near the high table where King Baldwin presided over the feast, seated on a great chair set beneath a blue silk canopy. William could see that the event was an endurance test for the young King who was visibly flagging, his posture slumped and his gestures slow. His half-sister the bride sat at his side, a quiet, fair-haired girl only just entering womanhood with slight breasts and a narrow waist. Her eyes were modestly down-cast and she said little. The bridegroom was a handsome youth but also subdued, and overshadowed by the grown men in the gathering with their beards and stubble and hard eyes, all watching each other and watching Baldwin.

Outside, the evening in the desert was cold and star-studded, but within, the press of so many people and the heat from the lamps and candles made for a pungent atmosphere. Seeking fresher air, William climbed to the gallery that ran around the top of the hall and looked down through the lamplight on a contortionist performing before the high table. The man's torso gleamed with blue paint and his golden loin cloth shimmered as he twisted his body into all manner of outlandish positions. William was reminded of the grotesques that populated the external walls of churches, warning everyone how close they were to sin, even in a holy place. Wondrous and disturbing.

He turned away to an embrasure to look out of the window instead. A full moon shone over the defences of a landscape scarred with the debris of the rapid Saracen retreat – the marks of their campfires, the smoking timbers of a destroyed siege machine. A jackal trotted over the terrain, sniffing, investigating, and paused to eat something it found on the edge of some heaped ashes.

William mulled over what had happened today and pondered strategies, turning over different scenarios in his mind – how he would have dealt with the matter of besieging this place if he had been Saladin, and how he would have gone about defending it too. Those trapped within Kerak had tried to set up a siege machine on the walls to respond to the Saracens but so fierce had been the bombardment that they had been forced to abandon their efforts. Many soldiers bore cuts and abrasions from flying chips of stone and numerous civilians had been slaughtered or seized for slaves during the retreat from the outer defences.

'Taking a respite?' Bohemond asked, wandering up to join him.

William turned. 'I was thinking, sire – ordering my mind.'

Bohemond's gaze was bright with curiosity. 'What is there to think about?'

William shrugged. 'What I would have done in the circumstances. It is always interesting to note each commander's actions and how he might have adjusted his strategy. If Saladin had filled in the moat before setting up the siege machines, his attack would have posed a greater threat.'

'Indeed so, and he will have learned from this – we must be ever-vigilant,' Bohemond touched William's arm. 'You have not been introduced to the bride and groom yet, have you? Or the Patriarch?'

'No, sire.'

'Then come, I shall take you. It will be instructive I think.'

William followed Bohemond with alacrity even though it meant returning to the crowded hall. His position in Outremer was ambiguous and fragile. In terms of status he could not mix with the high nobility unless supported by a patron such as Bohemond to vouch for him and make the introductions. It had taken fifteen years of hard work to develop his position at the Angevin court. Here he was a newcomer of unproven mettle, unable to move easily between the pools of influence to tap into the river. He knew Bohemond must want something from him in return and suspected it would be in the way of keeping his ears open and reporting what he heard, for that was a common way to advancement for newcomers. But Bohemond was only one of many playing the same game.

Reclining on his cushioned chair, Baldwin, who was eating nothing, saying little, but managing to preside, gave a languid wave of assent to Bohemond's request to present William to the other guests seated at the table picking at the subtleties of candied lemon peel and sugared roses.

Bohemond introduced William to the bride and groom. Baldwin's pale, fair-haired little sister was only eleven years old, and her response was the quiet murmur of a well-trained child. The bridegroom, a youth of seventeen, was also polite, but no more forthcoming. Here was no dynamic young warrior. At his stepson's side, Reynald of Châtillon clearly viewed William as just another chancer-come-pilgrim from Europe. However, the groom's mother, Stephanie of Milly, was more inclined to be gracious.

'What do you think of Outremer, messire?' she enquired with a polite smile. 'You have certainly been thrown into the thick of the challenges we face.'

William bowed. 'Madam, that is true, but in my own land I have fought many campaigns for the King of England and his son. Had it come to a full battle, I would have hoped to acquit myself well. I am humble to be in the land where Jesus performed His miracles and suffered on the cross to redeem us, and I shall strive to be worthy.'

She dipped her head and seemed satisfied by his reply. Her husband said nothing, but his hard look was tempered by speculation.

Bohemond then presented William to Heraclius, Patriarch of Jerusalem. He was dressed in robes of white silk that gleamed like the inside of a pearl shell scattered with mica. The skull cap set upon his iron-grey hair was made of the same glittering cloth, encircled by a band of rock crystals and pearls. Bohemond bowed deeply. 'Your Eminence, this is William the Marshal from England who has ridden with us this day. He has spent many years in service to the royal household of England.'

Heraclius extended his right hand so that William could kiss his amethyst ring of office. Then he motioned with his foot, and William realised what was expected of him. Second only to the Pope as the leader of Latin Christendom, Heraclius was ensuring that all knew it, especially the newcomers. Kneeling, William obliged and kissed the white and gold silk slipper.

'Indeed?' Heraclius gestured for William to rise now that his subservience had been established. 'I am pleased that the Prince of Antioch has presented you to me. Perhaps on another occasion we may talk about England.' His tone was smooth and urbane with platitude but already his attention was flicking to someone behind him who was waiting to have a word.

'My lord,' William said, feeling that matters were not progressing especially well. He had been acknowledged and passed over as just another formality.

Sitting at the Patriarch's side was a stunningly beautiful woman, richly attired in flame-red silk embellished with embroidery. Two plaits, as thick as ropes and as black as twisted jet, were looped under a veil of transparent white gauze edged with gold droplets. Her hands were smooth, the nails perfectly buffed, her fingers adorned with numerous rings. She sent him an enquiring glance from sable-dark eyes, subtly enhanced with cosmetics.

Bohemond hesitated, almost reluctant to make the introduction, but William waited because he was intrigued.

Bohemond cleared his throat. 'Madam de Riveri, may I present to you William Marshal, who is here on pilgrimage from England and who has helped bring the relief to Kerak.' He looked swiftly at William. 'Madam de Riveri is a valued member of the lord Patriarch's household.'

William absorbed the information with interest. So this was the Patriarch's concubine, and as important as the rumours suggested to judge by the richness of her clothing and her place at the high table.

'We are all in your debt, messire, for your timely arrival.' Her voice was musical with the hint of a Venetian accent.

William knelt to her, and of an impulse and with a tinge of mischief he kissed her shoes too. 'As I have greeted my lord Patriarch, so I greet his lady.'

She bestowed him an inscrutable look but allowed her foot to remain in his hand for a moment before withdrawing it. 'It is noted. Perhaps in the future you may be of assistance to His eminence, but for now I am sure you have concerns elsewhere.'

William rose to his feet and bowed again. Her composure was such that he could not tell if she was entertained or annoyed. Heraclius, who had been talking to others, fixed his gaze on William and the tightening of his lips told William not to presume further, but to bow once more and withdraw.

'The Patriarch looks very kindly indeed on the lady Paschia,' Bohemond said. 'Our beloved vicar is a worldly prelate, although at least he understands from personal experience the temptations to which all men are subject.'

William glanced over his shoulder and caught the woman's gaze on him in speculation, a slight curl of amusement on her red lips. Heraclius's beautiful concubine reminded him a little of Queen Alienor, only this version of Alienor was much younger and shone like a dark jewel.

Bohemond stroked his whiskers. 'She keeps company with the King's sister, the Countess of Jaffa. They are friends and allies, and Madam de Riveri and her network of relatives know everything that happens at court. That is part of her value to the Patriarch, but not the whole. It is more than business for him, but who can say with her? You should be careful,' he warned. 'The Patriarch is her patron and her family are protective of their asset. You would not wish to tangle with any of them.' Bohemond touched his arm and left to join Raymond of Tripoli.

Intrigued, William looked toward Paschia de Riveri again. She was whispering in Heraclius's ear. The Patriarch squeezed her hand affectionately and kissed her cheek. She summoned a young musician to sit at their feet and, with a warm smile and a light touch on his fair curls, commanded him to play for them. A woman of whom to be wary, but one whose patronage could prove useful.

Needing a moment to ponder, William went to empty his bladder and find his men. The first task accomplished, he was returning from the latrine when he came upon Guy de Lusignan deep in conversation with two of his own knights. Since he had to pass the men, William had to make his obeisance, no matter that it went against the grain. Guy might be under attack from factions at court and out of favour, but a wounded lion was still a lion and all the more dangerous because of it, especially with a fierce lioness to protect him.

'If you are seeking that brother of yours, he is playing dice with the common soldiers where he belongs. He knows his place as some do not,' Guy said with a sneer.

'Thank you, sire,' William replied blandly.

'It is difficult to know who to trust, isn't it? Which master's kennel you should crawl into next?'

William shrugged. 'I know where I should not go at least. Some things are clear.'

Guy bared his teeth in a humourless smile. 'Nothing is ever clear in Outremer. Like me you are an outsider and always will be. They will close their ranks against you if it suits their purpose. You might have had a high place in the Young King's retinue, but here you are just another fighting man. You have no one to watch your back, Marshal, and the nights are dark, and the knives long . . . that is not a threat, but it is a warning. Mind where you choose your affinity.' Guy moved on, and his knights followed him, pushing past William with enough force to knock him off balance.

William straightened and put his shoulders back. Guy was lashing out from his own insecurities for he had his own good reason to fear the long knives in the dark. William did not believe he was in immediate danger. Men might think him a jumped-up newcomer who had yet to prove his worth, but they had no desire to murder him.

William went in search of Ancel and did indeed find him playing dice in a room beyond the main hall. A pile of spilled coins lay at his elbow and he looked every inch the aristocratic lord in the jewelled silk tunic from the baggage panniers.

Looking up, he flashed William a playful if sour smile. 'I expected you to have your feet under the King's table by now.'

William gave his brother a playful cuff. 'And I thought you might have lost the tunic off your back.'

'Luck is with me tonight, even if not with you,' Ancel retorted.

'Who says it is not with me? I have finished my business that is all. I have several opportunities in hand for when we return to Jerusalem.'

Ancel took his turn with the dice, rolling a five and a four. 'Are you staying to play?'

William declined, but watched for a while and drank another cup of wine.

'Did you find out when we would be leaving?' Ancel asked between throws.

'No, but it will be soon – the supplies will dwindle too swiftly if we stay. The court will return to Jerusalem as soon as the King is rested and well enough to travel. There is a council tomorrow to deal with immediate matters, so perhaps the day after that.'

His wine finished, William left Ancel to his gaming and climbed to the battlements and once again was almost overwhelmed by Kerak's immensity. Compared to this, the keeps of England and Normandy were children's toys.

The night was still and cold with a thick dusting of stars over the arid terrain. As William paced the wall walk, thinking on the evening's events and remembering the enigmatic gaze of the Patriarch's concubine, he heard voices and instinctively stopped. A lantern held by a servant cast shadowed light over the figure of the King who was sitting in his litter chair facing an open crenel gap and gazing out into the desert with his almost sight-less eyes. The Patriarch was bending over him in urgent discussion.

'Sire, I beg you to reconsider.'

'No.' Baldwin's voice was hard. 'You can see how it is. The barons refuse to follow Guy and he undermines my rule at every turn. I am dying by inches, but by all that is holy I am not dead yet and I shall not be pushed aside like a pile of detritus. My mind is still sound and my will is as stalwart as these towers. This shall be dealt with once and for all and I expect your full cooperation. Do I make myself clear, my lord Patriarch?'

'Sire, I do not believe that is the Count of Jaffa's intent – he only wishes to ease your burden—'

'I did not ask what you believed,' Baldwin snapped. 'I said I expected your full cooperation and I asked if I made myself clear.'

'Sire,' the Patriarch replied, acknowledging while not giving an affirmative reply.

'Ah, leave me.' Baldwin flicked his hand and Heraclius departed, but along the wall walk on the side away from William, thus remaining unaware of his presence.

William considered retreating himself, but knew he might be seen, and caught as an eavesdropper, so instead he moved forward into the light.

Baldwin turned sharply toward the sound of his footfall.

'Sire, it is William Marshal.' William halted as Baldwin's attendants stepped forward to protect their master, swords drawn.

Baldwin gestured for them to sheathe their weapons. 'And what might you be doing here, messire?'

William cleared his throat. 'I was examining the defences, sire, and wondering how such scale could be adapted to the fortresses at home.' He gave a self-deprecating shrug. 'Also, I was preparing to retire and I have a habit of making sure all is secure.'

'But it brought you in my direction,' Baldwin said pointedly, 'and I suppose that your hearing is sharper than my eyesight.'

'Sire, my discretion is my honour.'

'Perhaps,' Baldwin said cynically. 'In my experience discretion and honour are rarities when men are offered bribes and inducement to listen and report. The Prince of Antioch seems particularly taken with you. My sight may be poor, but my vision is attuned nevertheless.'

'I served the Prince's cousin Queen Alienor,' William replied evenly. 'His interest in me is as a servant of the Angevin court, not this one, and as a trained soldier.'

'You also served my cousin the King of England.'

'Indeed, sire, and he is a great ruler.' Whatever else might be said of Henry, his greatness was not in doubt, nor his devious political ability.

'So we hear.' A light wind flapped the veil over Baldwin's ravaged features, making William think of a man breathing beneath his own shroud. Out in the darkness a jackal screamed. 'This country bleeds men, Marshal,' he said bitterly. 'They come here, they beget daughters and they die . . . or else they become lepers.' He turned his head toward William. 'You knew Guy de Lusignan in Poitou, but you have been most circumspect in your commentary on him.'

'Sire, it was a long time ago and in a different part of our lives.'

'But he was not your ally?'

'No, sire. We had different goals and different lords.' In a twisted way he owed his life to Guy, because after the Lusignans captured him, Guy had been sufficiently interested to keep him alive in order to test and taunt him. Perhaps Guy had even sought to preserve his life out of a perverse sense of guilt since he had been the one responsible for murdering his uncle.

'What was your opinion of him?'

William chose his words carefully, aware that Baldwin's servants were in earshot. 'He was a skilled fighter, but impetuous. He seldom considered the consequences. If he was fighting in a melee he would go for his man and not notice what was coming up behind him. He relied on others to watch the horizons, but he was always a strong and dangerous adversary in a hand-to-hand fight.'

'You say well and with tact,' Baldwin replied. He turned his gaze back to the night. 'Do you think King Henry would come and rule Jerusalem in my stead?'

William's first instinct was to say no, but he bit his tongue.

Henry's grandsire had left his lands in order to rule the Kingdom of Jerusalem, and he was also Baldwin's grandsire. Knowing Henry's personality, William doubted he would do so, but Henry could be unpredictable and he had sworn to take the cross as part of his atonement for the circumstances surrounding the murder of Thomas Becket. He had a treasure chest of thirty thousand marks of silver stored as aid for Outremer, as yet unspent, that could be used to facilitate his kingship. But would he be willing to give up the power he currently possessed in order to travel to a hostile place and begin again, even if that place was the land of Christ's birth? 'I do not know, sire,' William replied. 'It would depend on many factors.'

Baldwin fell silent again. After a while he said softly, 'The only pity is that Saladin retreated when we came to Kerak. I defeated him once when I was very young and still had the use of my limbs.' His voice strengthened with the remembered glory. 'He escaped, but we tore his army to pieces.'

'Yes, sire. We heard the stories of your prowess in Normandy and England.'

Baldwin waved his bandaged hand, dismissing the remark. 'I hoped back then that there might still be a miracle, but I know now it is not to be. My days are numbered. I have lived a full lifetime in ten years – there will not be another ten. What of Jerusalem when I am gone? All that Saladin need do is bide his time because mine is so short. Tell me, messire, as someone newly arrived in Outremer and without a faction – what would you do in my place?'

William suspected that Baldwin already knew the answer. 'I would look at the strengths and weaknesses in my court and ask who best served me and the kingdom and how could I position them to advantage. Men respect your rule because you command their loyalty.'

Baldwin made a rueful sound. 'But I cannot command that loyalty from beyond the grave, and what of Jerusalem then?'

'It would not be your remit, sire. You must make the best provision that you can and nurture it.'

The leprosy had destroyed the nuances of facial expression but William received a sense of bleak resignation, though steely too.

'You give me good counsel,' Baldwin said at length, 'but now you may go. Be circumspect in what you say to other men.'

William bowed. 'You have my word on it, sire.'

'And I trust to it, and to your honour.'

'Sire.' William departed, leaving Baldwin to his thoughts and his solitude. His chest was tight with angry sorrow at the unjustness that a young man of such ability and calibre was doomed to an early grave by this terrible affliction. He had watched Harry die in a matter of days, all that golden, flawed promise extinguished in stench and agony. Now he was set to keep vigil and bear witness as another young king fought a battle he could not win.

In the first light of dawn, William and Ancel walked together to the horse lines to check their mounts. Eustace was already there, busy at work. Byrnie had adopted the donkey as his bosom companion and the two stood side by side, legs touching. The donkey was eating as much as the horse, and faster.

'You'll need all your winnings from last night's dice to feed that thing,' William said, slightly horrified. 'Just look at it!'

Ancel grinned. 'It's like you,' he retorted. 'Your nickname was Greedy-guts when you were a squire. Don't begrudge him his food. He's lucky.'

William rolled his eyes.

Ancel pointed to the belt he was wearing – a confection of braided red and gold silk with a silver finial. 'I won this too, from a musician who stopped by to game. I could have taken him for more, but I asked him for a song instead. He belongs to the Patriarch's household, so I thought he would be useful to cultivate.'

'Yes, I saw him playing,' William said.

'He's called Ptolemy. He said he knew some good taverns in Jerusalem where we could go.' Ancel looked sidelong at William. 'He wanted to know all about us.'

'What did you tell him?'

'A great deal and very little.' Ancel wrinkled his nose. 'You think I am foolish, but I know when to keep my mouth shut. Musicians aren't to be trusted. They will milk you for information and then pass it on to the highest bidder – although I don't know why the Patriarch's gittern player should be so interested in us.'

'Because we are newcomers who know the English court. We have knowledge that may be useful and sometimes that knowledge has a different slant when garnered from friendship and dicing. Talk of the tavern, rather than of the counsel room.' William recalled how the young musician had sat at the lady Paschia's feet and the way she had smiled at him. Perhaps the information gathering had been on her behalf, and if so, just what did she want to know, and why?

'He thought I might be the leader of our party despite your introduction to royalty, since I was the better dressed,' Ancel said with a grin. 'I did not disabuse him.'

William gave an amused grunt and glanced up as he noticed movement among the horse lines. At other pickets, grooms and servants were saddling up and men were emerging from the keep, yawning and stretching, carrying their baggage rolls. A figure hurried from the buildings, tying his cap under his chin as he advanced toward the palfrey his squire was holding.

'Looks as though Guy de Lusignan is leaving,' Ancel said.

'Probably his best course of action.' William patted Flambur's glossy rump. 'The King is going to remove him from the regency today.'

Ancel shot William a keen look. 'Did you learn that at the courtly table last night?'

'No. The King said so.' William told Ancel about the meeting on the battlements. 'Guy cannot fight the numbers arrayed against him here. He has allies, but none who will stand up for him against the King.'

'So how does he know he is going to be deposed?'

William shrugged. 'At a guess, the Patriarch told him. As you say, spies are everywhere, including that musician.'

'So, the Patriarch does not support the King?'

'I do not know him well enough to say.'

The brothers watched the muster continue. By the time the sun was above the horizon, the Lusignan troops were marching out of the gate and it was clear that there were two parties – the slower foot soldiers and the faster mounted men who departed at a rapid trot.

'Do you think de Lusignan will rebel?' Ancel demanded, wide-eyed. 'What if he tries to take Jerusalem?'

William shook his head. 'He is not strong enough. The Patriarch has saved him a face-to-face moment and postponed the reckoning, that is all.'

'But he is leaving very early and in a great hurry,' Ancel said. 'Something is afoot.'

Everyone was gathered in the great hall for the King's audience. As Baldwin was carried into the hall by his attendants, William could see how sick he was, shivering and coughing. The night air on the battlements had settled on his chest, but he was forcing his will through his malaise. Raymond of Tripoli stooped to murmur in his ear and Baldwin gestured brusquely with one bandaged hand. The other senior barons came to stand at his back: the Prince of Antioch; Baldwin's uncle, Joscelin of Edessa; and the Ibelin brothers, Badouin and Balian.

Onri and Augustine joined William, Ancel and the other knights to one side of the dais.

'No sign of the Count of Jaffa,' Augustine said.

'Ancel and I saw him leaving at dawn,' William replied. 'Riding westward in haste.'

'Small wonder the King and his advisers look so out of sorts,' Onri said. 'Their bird has flown, and they would have done better to keep him confined.'

The Patriarch arrived in a flurry of silk robes, bowed to Baldwin and sat in the vacant chair facing him. The ushers called for silence and the low hum of conversation ceased.

Baldwin pushed himself upright on his cushions and thrust his head toward the Patriarch. 'I heard that the Count of Jaffa left Kerak at first light,' he said frostily. 'What do you know of this business?'

'Nothing, sire,' Heraclius replied smoothly, adjusting his robes to accommodate his chair. A practised gesture of his right hand displayed his ring of office to full effect. 'The Count of Jaffa departed of his own accord – I have only just heard about it myself.'

'That is a specious reply, my lord. If you have only just heard it is because you instructed your servants not to tell you, but I think you knew very well what he would do. Well, no matter. We shall speak with him soon enough. You know why I have called this meeting.'

'Indeed, sire, and I am deeply concerned and saddened.' Heraclius flicked a glance at the men standing behind Baldwin. 'I urge you to reconsider what you intend to do. Surely this matter can be resolved by less drastic means? Is there no way forward whereby you can work with the Count of Jaffa to heal this rift between you?'

'Apparently not when he rides out rather than face me in council,' Baldwin said to nods of approbation from the nobles behind him.

'Guy de Lusignan seeks to usurp your power, sire,' said Badouin of Ramlah. 'He turned the head of your sister. They only married because he seduced her out of her common sense at a time when she was a vulnerable widow.'

Baldwin raised his bandaged right hand in a silencing gesture.

'Have a care what you say about my sister,' he warned. 'She is of the royal house and my closest kin. I agree that the marriage was made inadvisably and I am to blame in part for yielding to pressure and allowing it to happen. I believed I would have a staunch ally and useful deputy in Guy de Lusignan, but he has proven himself arrogant and lacking the judgement I expect in a man designated to govern men and lead armies. Therefore, my lord Patriarch, I desire you to dissolve the marriage of my sister and this man. You shall summon them to appear before you in your court as soon as we return to Jerusalem.'

A collective intake of breath rippled round the chamber, for Baldwin's command escalated the matter from a disagreement to a major division.

Heraclius had recoiled at the suggestion but now he leaned forward again. 'Sire, I beseech you to reconsider what damage this will do. At least wait until we return to Jerusalem.'

Baldwin drew himself up. 'For a last time, my lord Patriarch, I tell you that my mind is fixed on this matter. The Count of Jaffa and my sister shall not stay wed. On our return to Jerusalem we shall indeed hold further council, but I expect you to set a date for your court to annul the marriage.'

Heraclius took the news in tight-lipped silence but eventually bowed his head. 'As you wish, sire.'

'Good, it is settled.'

Baldwin made a peremptory gesture to his attendants who bore him from the chamber, followed by his barons. Heraclius left too, stalking off in a different direction, his expression blank, but the underlying anger and frustration clear to all.

'The Patriarch certainly favours de Lusignan,' William said.

'It is more that he favours the Princess Sybilla,' Onri replied, 'and she is devoted to her husband. The Patriarch wants everyone to unite behind Sybilla as ruler with de Lusignan to carry out her bidding, but unfortunately de Lusignan is unpredictable and those who could temper and restrain him are disinclined to be his allies.' Onri pursed his lips. 'The Patriarch is a slippery fish. He will prevaricate with his date and in the meantime try to soften the King into conciliating.'

'Can the marriage be dissolved?' William asked.

'Heraclius will find all kinds of legal difficulties to push his argument,' Onri replied. 'I am not aware of any consanguineous link between the two that could be exploited. I supposed the King might claim the marriage was forced and that his sister was betrothed to Hugh of Burgundy at the time.'

'Was she?'

'It was being mooted but had not gone beyond a notion. But forged documents are no rarity in these parts and who knows if "proof" will suddenly appear.'

William folded his arms. 'If the marriage is dissolved, who then will govern?'

Onri shrugged. 'Who can say? The King's days are numbered but only God knows his remaining span. Envoys will go to England and France and offer the throne of Jerusalem to the princes there, but no expedition will set out until late spring at the earliest. And who knows if such a prince will come. For now, all we can do is bide our time and pray.'

Baldwin remained at Kerak for two more days, attending to business and gathering strength for the return to Jerusalem. William used the time to train his men and horses, for skills had to be kept sharp, and since everyone of influence was gathered here, it was an opportunity to display their military talents to interested parties. Since a wedding had recently been celebrated and Saladin thwarted, the session soon turned into an impromptu tourney to celebrate the earlier curtailed festivities.

William and his men had tourneyed and fought together for so many years that even without recent training they were a tight unit and proudly displayed the lance, sword and horse work that had made them famous across the tourney fields of France and

Flanders, Normandy and Hainault. Knights from other retinues armed up and took to the dusty ground outside the castle walls, and there were some determined exchanges between the teams, even if the mood was amicable. As William seized the bridle of an opponent and rendered him hors de combat, he experienced a sunburst of joy and exultation. For a moment he was a young knight again, thundering across a grassy field on Blancart, his first destrier, with the world at his feet. The image superimposed itself on the arid practice ground and the dust smoke burning around Flambur's hooves as he manoeuvred in his natural environment, displaying the valour and burnish of his troop to an audience of discerning potential clients. Bringing the opposing knight, a man of Ibelin, to yield, William could clearly sense Harry's presence at his shoulder, a laughing, golden-haired phantom, urging him on.

Taking respite to drink watered wine and eat some bread while waiting for his second horse to be saddled, William developed a distinct feeling that he was being watched, but a sweeping search of the gathered audience yielded no result.

'We've taken four knights for ransom already, sire!' Eustace's face was alight with enthusiasm.

William grinned at the squire. 'And more lining up for the privilege. If we can take another four between us, it will keep us solvent beyond Christmas.'

Ancel joined them, red and sweating. 'The one on the roan stallion,' he panted, 'in the blue surcoat. That's a horse worth having. Turns on a penny, and look at the rump on him – there's speed.'

William followed Ancel's gaze to a knight who had recently joined the field with his retinue. The sheen of the stallion's coat was almost metallic and its movements as fluid as water. The knight was accomplished and swift, like his horse. It would be no easy matter to take him, but if he could be overcome, then the reward would be to great advantage.

William donned his helm and mounted Flambur. Gathering the reins, he glanced at the crowd through the helm's eye slits and this time, because his own gaze was concealed, he trapped his watcher. The Patriarch's concubine, Paschia de Riveri, was studying him intently. Taking one hand off the reins, he flourished a salute. She immediately lifted her chin, and turned to speak to the lady at her side as if he was of no consequence.

William grinned inside the helmet and took up his lance. Ancel joined him on Byrnie and together they mustered their team and returned to the field.

The knight on the silver roan was immediately eager to challenge William and made his horse caracole and paw the air. William signalled his answer and pricked Flambur with the spur and launched him toward his opponent. The roan sprang from its hocks in a dazzling burst of speed and William swiftly adjusted his position and shield angle.

His opponent's lance struck his shield and splintered, and if William had been less skilled or experienced he would have been hurled from the saddle. His own lance had shattered too so he cast it aside and caught the fresh one Eustace tossed to him. Again the knights charged together and broke their lances, dust billowing.

William's adversary reached for William's bridle to try and drag him from the field. Two more knights galloped up to help, intent on bringing down this newcomer from England, and William drew his sword and pressed with his knees, commanding Flambur to rear and kick and break the hold. As the stallion pawed the air, the knight lost his grip and William pivoted, won free and spun away to cut behind one of the other knights, seize his bridle and in turn take him captive.

The knight on the roan pursued William, who immediately transferred his prisoner to Ancel, turned again, reversing the pursuit, and entered the killing space behind his adversary. Bringing his sword down on the warrior's helm, he dealt a vigorous blow, making the forceful point that if this had been a true battle the knight would have died. Urging Flambur alongside the roan, it was now his turn to grab the bridle and attempt to drag his prize to the side of the field and secure his win. The horses pushed and barged each other, shoulder to shoulder, and the knight struggled to escape William's grip, but was caught fast as Geoffrey FitzRobert arrived on the other side and hemmed him in.

William and his team brought their 'prisoners' to the refuges at the side of the field, there to take pledges of ransom. William's opponent proved to be a knight attached to the Patriarch's household, one Thomas of Auvergne. While not overjoyed at being taken for ransom, he accepted his defeat manfully, preferring to pledge money for his horse rather than hand him over to William. He was also eager to return to the field to win some of that pledge back from others less talented. William was courteous and affable and let him off lightly. It was always useful to grease the wheels of courtesy with fellow warriors.

'You could have taken him for a lot more,' Ancel said as they watched their man spur back into the fray. 'His horse alone would have fetched a hundred marks at home.'

'But better an ally than an enemy,' William replied, and glanced toward the audience. The lady Paschia had risen to leave but at the last moment she glanced at him over her shoulder and half smiled, before turning away.

The next morning Baldwin set out for Jerusalem, leaving a detail of labourers and serjeants to repair the walls and bolster the garrison. Saracen scouts tailed the column and lightly harassed the baggage train like bothersome flies, but were periodically chased off by parties of knights. The lighter-armed Turkish warriors had no intention of coming within range of the muscular power of knights on warhorses, and the knights in their turn did not wish to become victims of the highly skilled Turkish horse archers. It was a game of tease and taunt. William took his turn among them and galloped out a couple of times with his troop, returning with two arrows buried in his red lion shield.

On approaching Jerusalem, Baldwin had himself transferred from his litter onto a docile white palfrey so that he could enter the city as a victorious sovereign and leader. William had been helping to keep the path clear as they neared the city. Riding close to Baldwin, who was flagging, he could tell that the King was in great discomfort. Briefly he thought of Harry – all that life and energy wasted in battling his father for the right to rule more than just a tourney field, and now this other young king, burdened with overwhelming responsibility and clinging to the edge as it crumbled away.

'Sire, if I may assist you to your litter,' William said as they arrived at the royal enclave close by the city gate. He dismounted, threw his reins to Eustace and went to help the King. A miasmic odour of sweat and rot emanated from Baldwin's body, but William ignored it, concentrating on performing the task with dignity and honour.

'Attend me,' Baldwin commanded, and his bearers lifted his litter and bore him into the palace where more servants waited to see to his needs. 'Take me to the Countess of Jaffa's chamber,' he instructed. 'I have business there.'

Exchanging looks but not speaking, the bearers carried Baldwin along a corridor and up a short flight of steps to an arched doorway that led into a room of tumbled and strewn disarray.

Standing behind Baldwin, William gazed at empty coffers, rumpled bedclothes and an overturned stool. The braziers that should have warmed the room and imparted a delicate scent of incense were silted with ashes. A mouse sat in the middle of a crumb-strewn platter nibbling a morsel of stale bread. Startled, it whisked down an abandoned silk scarf trailing over the edge of a coffer and vanished under a cupboard.

Baldwin clambered out of the litter and struggled to his feet.

'Where is my sister?' he demanded. 'Why is she not here to greet me? Someone find her and bring her to me – and my nephew.'

'She is not here, my son,' Baldwin's mother announced from the door. 'Thank God you have returned and that you are safe.'

William turned to regard Agnes of Courtenay. If she had been slim before, now she was almost skeletal, her skin yellow-tinged. William had been at court long enough by now to have heard the many tales of the power she had once wielded. Of her beauty, her driving ambition and her supposed affairs, including one with the Patriarch. But the lady who stood here now was an old woman, struggling with serious illness.

'What do you mean she is not here?' Baldwin snapped. 'Where is she? And where is Guy?'

'I mean precisely what I say,' Agnes replied curtly. 'Guy arrived in haste, and said they must leave immediately. I tried to stop them, but they refused to listen. I was worried that there had been a disaster at Kerak, because Guy was wearing his armour, covered in dust and would tell me nothing.'

Baldwin made an exasperated sound. 'We reached Kerak in time and sent Saladin on his way with his tail between his legs. I have dismissed Guy from the regency and I need my sister here in Jerusalem.'

Agnes shook her head. 'It is too late, my son; they will be halfway to Ascalon by now and they have taken the children.'

Baldwin went very still. 'You should have stopped them.'

'How was I supposed to do that?' Agnes retorted. 'Sybilla is their mother and Guy was still acting regent when you left for Kerak. I had no reason to prevent them.' She clasped her hands beneath her breasts and drew a sharp breath.

Seeing how livid her complexion was, William offered her his arm and assisted her to sit down upon the bed, where she leaned over, breathing shallowly.

Baldwin limped several paces across the room and turned around. 'I am sorry to hear that, Mama. You should go and rest,' he said brusquely. 'I have ordered the Patriarch to summon Guy and Sybilla to his court in order that their marriage be dissolved. If they do not appear, I am within my right to bring an army to Ascalon and demand a reply. And I shall take my nephew back into my personal custody.'

Agnes looked up, her face contorted with pain. 'Is that what you truly intend? To annul the marriage?'

'Yes, it is, Mama. Guy is not fit to rule. Sybilla must have a new husband and in the meantime we shall find someone else to act as my regent.'

Agnes leaned over again. 'Your sister will never agree to such a thing.'

'Then she shall be made to do so,' Baldwin said grimly. 'I intend to have this marriage dissolved before it breaks my kingdom apart. I should never have agreed to it in the first place, but I was persuaded against my better judgement.'

'You say that now, but at the time you believed it would solve your difficulties – you were even pleased that your sister had found a consort to her liking,' Agnes said wearily. 'Be very careful, my son. Sybilla is your sister and the mother of your heir.'

'I do not need that reminder, Mama,' Baldwin snapped.

'I think perhaps you do.' She gave a tired sigh. 'I shall order the room to be tidied now, but I wanted you to see it and know the value your sister sets upon her union with Guy. It will be no easy task to put their marriage asunder.'

William noted a hardness in Agnes's expression beyond the exhaustion. Challenge perhaps, and anger. A trapped animal seeing the inevitable but still determined to bite even as the killing blow descended. Her son was a leper on the inexorable road to death and her daughter was wed to a man who was unfit to succeed.

Baldwin drew himself up. 'Then it is the same as every other task I have faced, but it will not stop me from striving.'

19

Manor of Caversham, April 1219

William knelt in prayer with his men and a multitude of others including King Baldwin in the church of the Nativity in Bethlehem, his emotions a juxtaposition of deep unworthiness and exaltation as the Patriarch celebrated the birth of Jesus Christ, born of the Virgin Mary, the conduit between the pure Almighty and sinful man. God made flesh and the redeemer of all by His birth and His suffering. Such was the miracle, and his heart welled with emotion that he was here now in that very place celebrating.

Eyes closed, breathing in the scent of incense, he heard a woman speaking his name, her tone low and gentle but insistent. His vision filled with an image of the great star shining above the stable of Christ's birth and he could feel himself being absorbed into that light.

He was suddenly inside another church, in Normandy this time, and a choir was singing. Light streamed in through high arched windows and Isabelle was there, prostrated before the altar in a pale silk gown. A nurse held a small baby in her arms, wrapped in swaddling and draped in a blue blanket. 'My son,' he thought, and love filled his body with luminous joy. The voice came again, comforting, gentle, but insistent, and he felt a hand take his in a warm clasp.

'William?'

He opened his eyes, and this time he was in his chamber at Caversham and his bed was bathed in morning light. Isabelle was leaning over him, with a smile on her lips but concern in her eyes which were shadowed and tired. 'You were restless, my love.' She lightly touched his face. 'Tears?'

William swallowed. 'I was dreaming,' he said, 'and I was remembering.'

'What were you remembering to make you weep?' She fluffed up his pillows and helped him to drink a cup of spring water laced with honey.

'The Nativity in Jerusalem, the first year I was there, and what a great and holy thing it was. And then I remembered the day of your churching after you had borne Will, and how I was so proud that I almost burst. I was so thankful to God that He had granted me bounty beyond all that I deserved.' He squeezed her hand. 'If there are tears on my face, they are of remembered joy, and in remembering they give me joy again, even now.'

Isabelle bit her lip and her chin dimpled.

'I would not have you weep for sorrow,' he said gently.

Her face started to crumple. 'Then do not die.' She stood up and moved away, wiping her eyes on the heel of her hand and sniffing. But then she drew a deep breath, composed herself and, picking up her weaving frame, brought it to the bedside.

'That is not within my power, but God's,' he said softly. 'We must all take that road. I never thought to be worthy of so much wealth and grace and I am grateful for all that I have been granted.'

She began to check the tension on the strands and he gazed at the pattern, which was worked in restful shades of blue, green and soft gold that reminded him of the seashore near Pembroke under a kind morning sun. Her fingers wove like fish through fronds, sure and quick, even though he knew she was upset and trying not to show him. Always practical, always strong. His Isabelle. His angel and saving grace.

'I never had any love for Guy de Lusignan,' he said, 'but for all his folly, arrogance and stupidity he loved his wife, and that at least was something steadfast in the man.'

She sent him a questioning look, her eyes shimmering with tears, but still that summer-ocean blue that had captivated him thirty years ago.

He had always drawn a veil across his time in Outremer, save for a few diverting tales about a favourite horse, or the food he had eaten, or the clothes the ladies wore. He had been so careful, but now that veil was gossamer-thin.

'At the outset I saw him as a man using his wife as a pawn to aggrandise himself, that she was just a rung on his climb up Fortune's ladder, but I came to realise that he truly loved her, and she him. They had a marriage like ours – through thick and thin, even when times were threadbare indeed. His power came from her. Without her he was nothing, and they allowed no one to come between them – not kings, or prelates, or the knife of politics.' Only death, he thought. Their steadfast need for each other had brought down the Kingdom of Jerusalem to ruination and destroyed so many lives. In that way, he and Isabelle were very different.

20

Jerusalem, Late January 1183

William watched the groom walk the horse around the stable yard and assessed its conformation and temperament with an expert eye. The palfrey was tall and strong with an elastic step and well-sprung hocks. The predominant colour was white with shadow-rings of dapple on rump and forequarters and the muscles rippled under the tight, firm hide as it followed the groom, its manner docile but its ears pricked.

'You will find no better horse in the Kingdom of Jerusalem,' the trader said. He was a shrewd, hard-eyed Norman settler from Jericho.

William nodded to show he had heard, but gave nothing away. Bohemond of Antioch stood beside the trader, his chin cupped in his hand. He had asked for William's opinion on the stallion since William's reputation for expertise in that area had gone before him.

William gestured for the groom to stop so that he could conduct a thorough examination of the horse, picking up its hooves, checking the articulation of the hips, the movement of the shoulders, the size of the rump. He lifted the silver waterfall tail to check beneath. Then round to the head to examine the teeth. The stallion stamped a little, but calmed when William spoke gently and soothed it with his hands. He mounted up and trotted around the yard. The horse responded to the lightest touch on the bridle, his ears continuing to flicker, revealing that he was attuned to the rider without being afraid.

William dismounted and returned the reins to the groom.

Bohemond nodded to the seller. 'I will send word within a day to let you know.'

'Sire.' The man bowed and retained his aplomb. 'I have had other enquiries, but I shall hold him for you until tomorrow.'

'What did you think?' Bohemond asked William as they walked back toward the royal palace.

'A fine animal,' William replied. 'Intelligent, well proportioned and of a biddable disposition while still being spirited. And a good size. Any man who rides him will be taller than those around him in a crowd.'

'I thought so too,' Bohemond said. 'So, tell me, Marshal, why is the price so good? I would expect to pay a third as much again for a horse of this quality. That is why I asked you to look at him – I will not be duped.'

'I heard a rumour that might explain the reason for the price,' William said.

'Indeed?'

'My brother was told that the horse was intended as a gift to the Count of Jaffa from his wife, but the Count and his lady have been in Ascalon for six weeks now and your trader cannot keep the animal indefinitely.' Six weeks in which the King had summoned Guy and Sybilla back to Jerusalem on numerous occasions to answer in the Patriarch's court and been met first by the claim that Guy was too sick to attend, then by silence. Soon King Baldwin was setting out to Ascalon to confront the couple in person and demand their obedience.

'I see.' Bohemond looked amused.

'Perhaps too,' William added, 'you are known as a man swift to settle his debts and it is better to have the payment now rather than feeding and stabling the horse for another month and not receiving the due fee for even longer.'

Bohemond's eyes lit with a sardonic gleam. 'It is good to know I am trusted to pay my debts while others are not. I shall send word tomorrow and buy him. It will give me great pleasure to ride him in certain parades.'

William responded with a dry smile, knowing that the Prince of Antioch would deliberately ride the stallion in Guy's presence whenever the opportunity arose.

Bohemond paid William a generous fee for his help and to further show his appreciation took him to eat at an exotic establishment not far from the palace. As he entered the brazier-warmed room and had his cloak taken by a smiling, dark-eyed woman, William thought wryly that Onri would have had him down on his knees in a trice doing penance.

Colourful rugs covered the floor and large cushions were arranged around the room upon which guests could recline. Platters of small spicy delicacies and sweetmeats flavoured with rosewater were set out on low tables, and incense burned in shallow silver bowls, spiralling thin white smoke toward the vaulted ceiling.

Two women were dancing to the pat-pat of a drum, bodies weaving with supple suggestion. Silver bells tinkled on their ankles and wrists and multiple flimsy layers of silk garments enveloped them like coloured flames as they moved. William was accustomed to the prostitutes who frequented the Angevin court and the tourney circuits; but these women were more exotic and striking. They probably cost a lot more too.

'Choose whichever one you want,' Bohemond said affably. 'I will pay. The dark one is a Bedouin and knows all the arts of the Perfumed Garden, and the fair-haired one comes from the lands of the Rus – both are good. Or the one over there with the red ribbons.'

'Thank you, sire,' William said, thinking that a night of indulgence was perhaps unwise because he had to prepare for the morrow's ride to Ascalon. But there was no harm in looking, and folly might still get the better of him.

The door opened as the Patriarch's musician Ptolemy arrived

with a cluster of friends, Ancel among them. They had already been drinking elsewhere to judge by the flushed faces and glittering eyes. Ancel detached himself to come and greet William, stumbling a little upon the cushions. Righting himself, his complexion scarlet, he apologised profusely. 'Do not worry, Gwim, I will not interrupt you.' He bowed clumsily to Bohemond.

'I am not worried,' William replied. 'Just have a care with your own company, and watch your drink.'

Ancel made an ironic salute and stumbled off to rejoin his companions. The patriarch's musician had ostentatiously dropped a hefty pouch of coins on the low table around which his group had gathered. Wine was commanded and the dice came out. William noted with relief that Ancel sobered up very quickly indeed.

'Your brother has become friendly with the Patriarch's musician,' Bohemond said, a note of censure in his voice.

William shrugged. 'Ancel can take care of himself. It is useful to have contacts at court. Ptolemy fishes for information from Ancel, and Ancel baits his own line.'

'Ah.' Bohemond stroked his beard. 'And just what does each hope to gain from the other?'

'For Ancel it is the lure of the dice and places such as this, and he delights in music. It gives him a taste of what he had when we followed the tourneys. The musician, I do not know. I would say that like all of his kind he can slip like a fish through all streams of society. His music gives him access to bowers and bedchambers, and information is a valuable coin.'

Bohemond nodded and looked thoughtful.

'He will glean nothing worthwhile from my brother though. Ancel has perfected the art of saying a great deal without saying anything at all.'

'Rather like yourself then.'

William chuckled and raised his cup. 'Perhaps, but in a different kind of way.'

Bohemond studied the musician. 'He is much favoured at court and a protégé of the Patriarchess – as you may have noticed.'

William gave Bohemond a sharp look. The latter's voice held no particular nuance, although its very neutrality was an indicator. 'Yes,' he said.

'Of course, he is the Patriarch's musician too.' Bohemond leaned back against the silk cushions. 'Madam de Riveri's relatives and favourites receive Heraclius's patronage and serve in his court – and they are a nest of scorpions. Whether you are stung or not will depend on whether you are perceived as friend or foe. I prefer to keep my distance.'

'Is the musician a relative?'

Bohemond shook his head. 'No, but he is from a family who have dealings with hers and is part of her network.'

Ptolemy beckoned to the woman with the red ribbons and a moment later they disappeared behind a heavy curtain. Anccl remained at the dice table but smiled over at William as if expecting him to follow suit with one of the other ladies. William returned the smile but stayed where he was. He had been in two minds, but now had no intention of following the musician through those curtains and having his deeds reported upon to the Patriarch and Madam de Riveri.

A short while later Ptolemy returned, adjusting his crotch. When a companion made a quip about what he had been doing, he laughed, and cupped himself through his braies. 'No woman can resist my charms, be she lady or whore – there's no difference between any of them when you lay them on their backs, believe me.'

'What about the money?'

'Hah, one pays for the other?' The musician flashed a grin. 'They both beg for it nonetheless.'

William and Bohemond exchanged glances.

Three more men arrived, and on seeing Bohemond they immediately made their salutations. The older man was in his forties, his black hair beginning to silver at his temples, and his eyes hard as obsidian. They fixed on Ptolemy as soon as they walked in. His companion was a broad-shouldered knight of about William's age, olive-skinned with a knife scar marking his left cheek beneath his eye, and hawkish features. The third was a slender dark-haired squire.

'Your brother should be wary of those men if he keeps the musician's company,' Bohemond said quietly. 'I was speaking of scorpions, and here are three. The one on the left is Zaccariah of Nablus, the Patriarch's gatekeeper and uncle to Madame la Patriarchess. The other is Mahzun of Tyre, a mercenary whose services they purchase from time to time. The youth is one of Zaccariah's squires and kin of some sort.'

William lifted his brows.

'If they look at you, do not look back unless you expressly wish to garner their attention or put business their way. They serve a purpose in that they keep the other vermin under control, but they are dangerous men.'

William drank his wine and observed circumspectly. Zaccariah was watching Ptolemy with narrow intensity and the young musician was on edge, flicking wary glances, perhaps even a little fearful in contrast to his earlier bold stance.

The newcomers crossed the room to join the dice game and Zaccariah tossed a pouch of coins on the table as his credentials to play.

'And their intent at the moment?'

Bohemund shrugged. 'Zaccariah is always hunting. The lady's gittern player is one of his information gatherers.'

The company settled down to their game and Ptolemy lost several throws. Seeing his pile diminish, he rose to leave, but Mahzun of Tyre put his hand on his sleeve and flashed a dangerous smile. 'Come now, no cause to run home just yet. Your luck might turn.'

Reluctantly the musician settled back down, his throat bobbing as he swallowed. Ancel cast William a mute entreaty for help. William gave a slight nod in reply but made no immediate move, although he spoke to Bohemond in a quiet murmur. He allowed the group to play another couple of rounds during which Ancel and the musician both lost again, and then, having thanked Bohemond for his hospitality, he rose to his feet and sauntered across to the table. 'Time to retire.' He squeezed Ancel's shoulder. 'We have a long journey in the morning and preparations to make.' He bowed courteously to Zaccariah of Nablus and Mahzun of Tyre.

Ancel nudged Ptolemy. 'Do you want to accompany us? You will be riding tomorrow also?'

Ptolemy shot him a grateful look and began scraping together his few remaining coins. 'Yes,' he said, 'thank you.' His friends were also disinclined to stay.

As Ptolemy turned to leave, Zaccariah grabbed his arm. 'Remember who employs you and the songs you are paid to sing,' he growled. 'It would be a pity if you were to lose your fine voice or your wherewithal to play.'

Ptolemy wrenched himself free, but more because Zaccariah had relaxed his grip than from any strength of his own.

'Their dice were loaded,' Ancel muttered in an aggrieved voice once they were out of the door and heading toward the palace.

'Their dice are always loaded,' Ptolemy replied sourly.

'Zaccariah of Nablus seemed to have a particular bone to pick with you, yet you dwell in the same household?' William said.

'Our services are very different,' Ptolemy replied, giving William a sidelong look. 'He thinks I am a threat because I know things.'

'But surely hinting to others that you "know" things immediately makes you a risk.'

'I have protection,' he replied defensively, but dropped his gaze.

William raised his brows but said no more as they came to the postern of the Patriarch's palace and Ptolemy bade them good night with cheerful bravado before going inside with his friends.

'What do you think he knows?' Ancel asked as they made their way to their own lodgings.

'Perhaps safer not to know. Has he said anything to you?'

'No, he just keeps hinting about the things he could tell. But he's a musician. It is the nature of his employment to go from place to place passing messages and keeping his ears open. The wonder would be in his trade if he did not.'

'He is still your friend though?'

Ancel shrugged. 'He is my friend because he wants to know about our life at court in England. He likes too that I am a newcomer. He can brag and tell the stories that everyone else already knows. And why not? I like his music and he entertains me as much as I do him. But he is fickle and will do whatever he must to further his ambition.'

'He should have a care, because clearly others will try to stop him if he threatens their interests.' William shook Ancel's shoulder. 'Just do not get caught up in it.'

'I am not a fool.' Ancel shrugged him off, looking aggrieved.

'No,' William said, 'but it still behoves me to look out for you.'

Ancel rolled his eyes. 'Worry about yourself, not me,' he said, and thumped William's arm.

King Baldwin came to Ascalon on a cold early February morning with sharp rain lancing through a bitter wind to sting William's face. It was almost like being back in England. A little warmer for the time of year perhaps, but the tales told of Outremer at home were always of desiccating heat, never inclement weather like this.

Ascalon lay on the coast, two days' ride from Jerusalem, strategically guarding the approach to Egypt. Won from the Saracens more than thirty years earlier, the city was a major port controlled by the Count of Jaffa.

Today Ascalon's gates were barred against all comers and guards stood on the city walls, spears to attention. The sky behind the banners on the roofline was a dark, roiling grey. To a fanfare of trumpets, Baldwin's heralds spurred forward to the massive gates to formally announce the King's arrival and demand admittance. Their answer was a taut silence from the walls, the only sound the roar of the wind and the jingle of harness from the troops assembled outside.

Baldwin had ridden the last few miles on his white palfrey with an adapted padded saddle. Now he signalled William to help him down – it had become his preference to have William perform this service for him. Setting his feet on the ground, he steadied himself. The veil covering his face tugged this way and that in the brisk wind, lifting now and again to show his ravaged features. Patriarch Heraclius dismounted from his big chestnut and joined them, his expression set and grim.

'See, my lord Patriarch?' Baldwin said with angry contempt. 'I am refused entry into a city where I have final jurisdiction. This is how my brother-in-law serves me. Come, let us have an end to this. We at least shall observe the formalities.'

Heraclius took Baldwin's arm and guided him the short distance to the city gates. Baldwin was hampered by the wind flurrying against his robes, but although he was barely able to walk, he was determined. He clutched an ebony rod in his better hand, and upon reaching the gates he lifted it and beat three times on the wood as hard as he could, raising his voice and pushing all of his strength into a great shout so that it was not the cry of a sick leper, but the command of a sovereign lord in full fury. 'Guy de Lusignan, I command you to open the gates to your King!'

Silence, and a growing tension within that silence.

Again Baldwin raised his voice. 'Guy de Lusignan, I command you to open the gates to your King and answer the summons of the Patriarch!'

Still no answer came from the people lining the city walls.

William had no doubt that Guy and Sybilla were among them, watching, but choosing not to show themselves. A fresh gust of wind almost knocked Baldwin off his feet. He gripped Heraclius, mustered his reserves and commanded the Patriarch to knock full force with his own staff. Heraclius hesitated, clearly reluctant, but at last did as he was bidden. For a third time Baldwin shouted his demand, and for a third time was answered by silence.

'There, my lord Patriarch,' Baldwin said with bitter triumph. 'You see how I am served? My sister and her husband show me only defiance and perfidy. They refuse to open their gates and answer to their King. If I can come to them sorely afflicted as I am, then my brother by marriage would have to be on his deathbed not to face me. The only sickness he has is that of treason.'

'Sire, calm yourself,' Heraclius entreated. 'You will do yourself harm. This matter can be settled by diplomatic means, I promise you.'

'So you keep saying, my lord Patriarch,' Baldwin snapped. 'But I do not see how since it is clear we are not going to be admitted and no one has seen fit to answer my demand. Know this: Guy de Lusignan and my sister shall not defy me with impunity.'

The galley climbed the wave and then dipped into a trough, spray bursting against her prow and lacing her flanks. White caps frilled the crests and the wind was blowing hard from sea to shore. William's stomach echoed the motion of the ship and he swallowed nausea. He had been well enough at the outset of the journey as King Baldwin embarked from the port of Jaffa, heading for Acre a hundred miles up the coast, but as the voyage progressed, William had begun to feel the all-too-familiar wallow in his gut. Ancel, cheerfully unaffected, was talking to the crew and enjoying himself. Now and again he cast an almost smug glance William's way, because he was unaffected, and so much better at this than his brother.

194

They had spent several days in Jaffa which, unlike Ascalon, had immediately opened its gates to them. Baldwin had removed the city from Guy's control and appointed a governor, ignoring Heraclius's peace-making remark that Guy and Sybilla must have sent instructions to open the gates to Baldwin and the only reason Ascalon had remained closed was that the couple feared being seized and forced to comply with the annulment. Now Baldwin was moving up the coast to Acre and calling a council to decide what was to be done. Guy and Sybilla were required to attend but no one expected them to appear.

Other members of the court were travelling on the same ship as William, including several women, among them the Patriarch's concubine Paschia de Riveri. She stood not far from William, gripping the ship's side and staring at the horizon. Every now and again she swallowed and her shoulders quivered. Recognising the symptoms all too well, he made his way over to join her, thinking to distract himself from his own discomfort. He was mindful of what Bohemond had told him, but there was no harm if he was respectful.

'It is brisk weather, my lady,' he said.

'Indeed, messire, but it makes the journey swifter.'

The galley struck another wave, spray bursting against the side of the ship, spattering the voyagers, and then they were plunging again. She staggered and clung to his arm for support.

'Are the seas rough where you come from, messire?' she asked as the surge subsided.

'Yes, madam, especially in winter. The King often crosses from one shore to another. The journey is less than half a day if the wind is in the right direction, but the seas can be treacherous and stormy.'

She watched the galley bearing Baldwin and Heraclius that was ploughing the waves ahead of them. 'You must have crossed it many times in service to your King and Queen.' Her dark eyes appraised him.

'Indeed, yes, my lady, although I confess it has never been my favourite form of travel.'

He had to suppress a retch as the galley threshed through another strong wave. She gripped his wrist harder, and did not know who was supporting who. Her hands were fine-boned and small, but they were strong. He could imagine them gripping reins or cutting cloth with clean precision. Numerous gold rings adorned her fingers, including one that glistened with a ruby the size of a quail's egg.

'My mother saw your Queen before I was born – a fleeting glimpse only as she rode through the streets of Jerusalem, but enough to leave a lasting impression. My mother said she was golden-haired and very beautiful.'

William gave her a strained smile. 'She still is.'

'And her husband's prisoner now, if what we hear is true?'

William hesitated, wondering what to say, remembering Bohemond's warnings about becoming trapped in a net; and yet her interest seemed sincere and of the moment rather than possessing an agenda, and he had approached her after all. 'Yes, it is true, and I am sorry for it, because I have served both with loyalty. Their eldest son was my lord, and the reason I came to Jerusalem – to pray for his soul and my own, and do penance for my sins before God and His Holy Mother.'

'Yes.' She gave a sympathetic nod. 'I am sorry that you have lost your lord, but glad that you have been able to find spiritual solace.' Her smile appeared again. 'Is the King of England a good traveller? Does he suffer on the ocean?'

William shook his head. 'No, my lady. He is one of the most enduring travellers I know. He will eat burned bread, drink sour wine and sleep rolled in his cloak at the side of the road if he must. He will also journey from dawn to dusk without respite. His court can barely keep up with his pace and his vigour.'

'So, King Henry is strong and tireless,' she said. 'And a man accustomed to governing and bringing people to do his will.'

'That is a fair assessment, my lady.'

'And might he too come to Jerusalem do you think? The Patriarch has hopes.'

Her voice was warm and interested as she continued her political probing. William steadied his feet as another wave rolled under the keel, bumping them together, hip to hip.

'Perhaps, my lady,' he said diplomatically, and then compressed his lips.

Her maid arrived with a steaming lidded cup of tisane that she had brewed over a small covered pot of coals. 'Might you be able to drink this, madam?' she asked.

Another heavy wave smacked the ship and spray boomed over the strakes. William's stomach gave up the fight and he had to dive for the side and hang there, vomiting and retching, all efforts at chivalry abandoned to his heaving belly. Finally, empty and sore, feeling utterly wretched, he collapsed against the straking.

The maid, Zoraya, gently touched his shoulder and handed him the tisane. Much of it had spilled as the wave struck, but about a third remained. 'My lady says you are to have this for you are in more need than she is,' she said.

William weakly thanked her, took the cup and, closing his eyes, forced himself to take a swallow. The bitter herbal taste cleaned his mouth but didn't make him feel any better.

The Patriarchess had retreated to the other side of the galley. Her gittern player Ptolemy huddled miserably at her side, arms folded, clearly another victim of mal de mer.

William abandoned the tisane, huddled in his cloak and tried to sleep.

King Baldwin lay on the couch in his bedchamber in his great fortress at Acre and stared out of his open window toward the deep blue sea, frilled with white caps but devoid now of the turbulence that had driven them up the coast from Jaffa faster than a galloping horse. William, having recovered from his sea-sickness, was attending upon him with the rest of the court, all gathered for the day's meeting. He wondered how much Baldwin could see of the deep blue water, busy with merchant ships and fishing boats. The port of Acre was greater than London or Rouen. Indeed, its annual income outstripped the entire revenues of England.

The court was about to discuss the mission to ask the princes of Europe to aid the beleaguered Kingdom of Jerusalem, but everyone was still awaiting the arrival of the Patriarch who had been designated to lead the undertaking. William had overheard mocking comments that he was probably still abed with his concubine, and that she was giving him advice about what to do. The humour was sour and exasperated, because until Heraclius arrived the discussion could not start.

Baldwin sent one of the household knights to fetch the Patriarch. 'Do not return without him,' he commanded. 'Whatever excuses he offers.'

A short while later the man returned, Heraclius stalking in behind him, his crosier clutched in one hand and a handful of parchment notes in the other.

'Ah,' said Baldwin, 'finally. Now perhaps we can discuss the matter of this mission to the Kings of France and England.'

'Indeed, sire,' Heraclius replied, 'but first we must deal with another matter.'

'And what matter would that be, my lord Patriarch?' Baldwin asked frostily.

Heraclius cleared his throat. 'That of your sister Sybilla's marriage to the Count of Jaffa. I beg you not to pursue your intention of putting asunder their union and to reconsider. If you were to show generosity, I know it would be reciprocated.'

'I doubt that,' Baldwin snorted. 'Have I not shown them utmost generosity already, and look at where we stand now! I agreed to the match in the first place because I was tender-hearted and disposed to heed the pleas of my sister and my mother. I gave

Guy de Lusignan riches, status, and every opportunity to prove himself, and he has thrown it back in my face and been a sad disappointment. He is a poor leader of men and an unsatisfactory commander. He has begotten two girls on my sister thus far, and that is not the mark of a man. Where are the sons? When I asked him to exchange Tyre for Jerusalem for the good of my health he refused. My barons have no confidence in him and now he refuses to answer my summons and bars me from Ascalon. Yet you still believe I should show him clemency?'

Heraclius had flushed beneath the onslaught. 'Sire, I know you feel he has a cause to answer but—'

'Feel!' Baldwin struck his chest. 'You know nothing of what I feel, my lord, and I am within my full right!'

'But do you not see this path is taking us nowhere?' Heraclius implored. 'This is dividing the kingdom when we have enemies on all sides. We cannot afford to turn our swords inwards and fight each other. Let us keep the Count of Jaffa for the time being and assess the matter later. If we continue now, there will be bloodshed. Saladin will see that we are divided and will strike at us anew. We should resolve this matter by diplomatic means.' His eyes were moist with tears. 'I can say no more.'

'You were not asked to say any more,' Baldwin snapped. 'You and your priests are unworldly fools. This matter needs dealing with by someone who will not bow down to the pressure of women. You think I do not know that my sister is behind this? I tell you, my lord Patriarch, you accede to my plan, or you are nothing.'

'In the name of all that is holy, I cannot.' Heraclius shook his head. 'Even if I wished it, I have no power to do such a thing. Whom God has joined together no man can pull asunder. Your heart is hardened against this man, but there has to be a way to restore peace and integrity to the kingdom.'

'Peace and integrity!' Baldwin was incandescent. 'You would see him walk all over you and stamp on your head and not say a word. This is not the way forward. Let Guy come and answer to me and then we shall see.'

'There is nothing more I can do, sire,' Heraclius said with weary resignation, 'and I take no side. Surely if we all rally together it has to be better than this strife.'

Baldwin turned to the Grand Masters of the Templars and Hospitallers who had been standing to one side listening in taut silence. 'And you, my lords, do you agree with this?'

Arnold de Torroja stepped forward, his jaw thrust out and his eyes hard. 'Sire, I do. I petition you to beware the consequences of your actions.'

Baldwin stiffened in astonishment and drew himself up.

De Torroja continued, 'Should it come to your passing, sire, which is the reason for all this discussion and preparation, you will leave the seeds of a divisive war with us, one I know you do not wish for your subjects. We implore you on God's behalf to make peace with your brother by marriage. We abhor this conflict of brother against brother and we implore you to do good by us . . . sire.' De Torroja bowed and stepped aside to stand beside Heraclius.

'And you, my lord.' Baldwin turned to the Hospitaller Master Roger de Moulins. 'Is this your opinion too?' His tone was quiet now – ice on steel.

De Moulins was a younger man than his elderly Templar counterpart. Handsome and more softly spoken, but with charisma and authority. 'Sire,' he said, 'we are one with you in our passion to serve Christ and to cherish the Kingdom of Jerusalem. If Guy de Lusignan stands against you, then we must reconcile him. He is your sister's husband and the father of your nieces. Would you rend all that asunder?'

Baldwin was silent for a long time, his earlier anger now solid and dark. Eventually he shook his head. 'I cannot answer your petition at this time,' he said flatly. 'It is not within me to do so.'

Heraclius stood firm. 'Clearly, sire, we cannot discuss the matter of our mission to France and England until we have an accord. We dare not leave the kingdom in this unsettled state.'

The three Church leaders made their obeisance and walked out of the meeting. Silence fell on their heels for Baldwin had no authority to order them back by force. It was clear to William that Baldwin would have to drop his demand for the annulment if he was to have the support of the Church. William understood the point that Heraclius and his associates were making. The kingdom had a king who was almost blind and had virtually lost the use of his limbs, a king who was dying lesion by painful lesion, and whose anointed successor was a child. Sybilla, that child's mother, would have to be considered for rule. She had a physically robust and strong man at her side to help her carry out the role of regent. The difficulty was that he had neither baronial support nor aptitude, but William suspected that the military orders, the Church and his wife hoped to control him and use him as their figurehead.

The following day Baldwin had himself borne from Acre to visit Heraclius in his tent outside the walls, and William formed part of his entourage. Overnight the King had shed his rage and the man who climbed into the litter possessed an air of compressed, grim determination.

Heraclius greeted Baldwin courteously as if yesterday's altercation had never taken place, and sent for the Templar and Hospitaller Masters. Attendants presented Baldwin with a goblet of sugared lemon juice and water and brought extra cushions to support his body. A red silk curtain divided the Patriarch's tent front from back and William saw it twitch gently and sensed a listener's movement behind its folds.

'So,' Baldwin said, when everyone had gathered, 'what is to be done? Whatever our differences, you must see that I cannot have defiance in my realm. You say that a war between ourselves would weaken us and bring Saladin down upon us, and I agree.

He constantly tests our boundaries and it troubles me greatly for I know I have little time left in this world and I wish everything to be settled and stable before I leave it.' He leaned forward in his customary hunched pose. 'Tell me honestly, my lords: what am I to do? Can any of you truly say that Guy de Lusignan is the best man to lead this kingdom?'

Heraclius cleared his throat. 'No one is denying it is a difficult position, sire, but the kingdom is being damaged by this dispute and we must reach a solution.'

'Indeed,' Baldwin said with cynicism. 'So then, my lord Patriarch, what do you suggest I do other than unwed my sister from her husband? Bearing in mind that most of my lords will not follow him.'

Heraclius steepled his hands under his chin. 'You have declared your nephew as your heir, but he is a child, and should you become unable to rule, he cannot take your place. Someone has to govern in his stead. I do not deny that Guy de Lusignan has made errors of judgement, but we are all fallible. The other lords have condemned him out of hand as unfit to rule, but perhaps they are too swift in their judgement and jealousy.'

Baldwin made an irritated sound but did not retort.

'The Countess Sybilla is strong and competent to make non-military judgements and she could certainly guide her son – and help you if you would allow it.'

'But not Guy,' Baldwin said, and his voice was full of raw pain. 'I give orders and he countermands them. If we are both in a room, then everyone avoids looking at me because of my condition. Instead they look at him and I might already be dead. I am told that he does this, or that, and he revokes my will. That man is no king.'

Now they came to the crux of the matter, William thought. Baldwin's resentment at being pushed aside by de Lusignan. The walking corpse in the presence of the golden god.

Heraclius pursed his lips. 'As I said, I do not think he has been

202

given the full benefit of the doubt, but I accept your stance on that. What I cannot do is break the marriage. There is no consanguinity involved. The Count of Jaffa and your sister are devoted to each other and may yet produce sons. Their affection for each other is the main reason they have fled to Ascalon. The Count of Jaffa has accepted the anointing of his stepson and demotion from the regency since you say you are capable of ruling again, but he will not countenance the annulment of his marriage and your sister stands by him in this.'

Baldwin arched his brows. 'You are very well informed, my lord Patriarch. Do I take it that your lady's doves have been busy in flight between Ascalon and Acre?'

Heraclius faced out the enquiry with a bland expression. 'No busier than anyone else's, sire. I take no sides in this. I can only state the position of the Church which is that the marriage cannot be annulled because there are no grounds for separation and the parties themselves believe their bond is indissoluble.'

'And that is precisely why I have come to you this morning,' Baldwin said. 'We must solve this problem. We need someone to govern and to make good judgements.'

Heraclius gave a cautious nod. 'Certainly, sire; we are all in accord about that.'

'Good. What I propose is that you, my lord Patriarch, and your colleagues of the Temple and the Hospital travel to the princes of Europe as we have discussed and request their succour and aid, with especial recourse to the Kings of France and England. You will invite each of them to take up the rule of the Kingdom of Jerusalem until my nephew comes of age. I would in particular be interested in approaching Henry of England since he is my cousin. He has many sons to follow in his stead, and he also has money set aside for the protection of the kingdom that he could use to good effect. How much has the King of England deposited in the treasury thus far, Grand Master Torroja?'

The Templar rubbed his chin. 'Thirty thousand marks of silver thus far, sire, and two thousand added each year under the terms of his atonement following the death of the Archbishop of Canterbury.'

'So, he would come to us richly endowed. That, my lords, is what the kingdom requires, and I entrust this mission to you.'

'And in our absence, what of de Lusignan?' de Torroja asked, to the point.

'I suggest a compromise,' Baldwin said. 'The question of the dissolution of the marriage shall be held in abeyance while you are gone. I will think on what you have said and I promise to make no further move on the matter until you return with your answer. Should I die in your absence, I want it clearly understood that Guy de Lusignan shall not be named as regent for my nephew. Someone else shall take on that role while we wait. Do we have an accord?'

Heraclius and the other men looked at each other and an unspoken exchange passed between them, signalled by slight nods.

'Very well, sire,' Heraclius said. 'We agree to go and seek aid from those princes and request that one of them come to take up the rule of the Kingdom of Jerusalem. And you will agree not to pursue the annulment of the marriage until our return.'

'Then it is settled,' Baldwin said with palpable relief. 'We shall return to Jerusalem and prepare for this mission. The Count of Jaffa may remain in Ascalon. Since he has expressed no desire to come to court, I shall not invite him again, although my sister is always welcome and may come to me under safe conduct and without fear. Her son shall dwell with me. I shall write to her myself – although I am sure she will receive the news sooner than any messenger I can send.'

Heraclius said nothing, merely inclined his head, and continued to look bland and mild.

William glanced toward the red curtain. The drapes were completely still, but that made him all the more aware of the listening presence on the other side.

21

Manor of Caversham, April 1219

On Easter morning, soon after dawn, William was once more borne into his chapel at Caversham, his padded litter carried by his eldest son and three knights. William's shoulders and spine were well supported by firm pillows, and the blankets and furs tucked around his wasted body kept him warm. Isabelle walked at his side with quiet dignity. When he looked at her she smiled, but he could see the strain in her face and the bruised shadows under her eyes.

He had insisted he would celebrate Easter in the chapel he had endowed to the Virgin Mary, with his family around him, rather than have the priest brought to his bedchamber. It was a time of renewal and replenishment; of Christ's rising from the tomb and the redemption of mankind. It had always been a meaningful celebration to him and it was for the final time in this life.

Today the open shutters allowed the spring light to flood into the chapel and shine upon the jewelled crown of the Virgin statue in her niche before the altar. The Easter triptych which had been fastened with gold clasps during the months of Lent was now open, its three images of the crucifixion, resurrection and Christ in majesty blazing out in triumphant colour.

The Holy Lance, said to be the very spear that had pierced Christ's side and brought back from the Holy Land by Robert of Caen, son of the Conqueror, was presented before the altar with deep reverence. Members of the congregation went forward to kneel and kiss the iron blade. The relic was brought to William too, and he stretched out a trembling hand to touch the cold ancient metal while cries of 'Alleluia!' rang around the church and candles were lit, burning light into every corner. There was a nail too, which he had brought from Jerusalem, said to be from Christ's very cross, and in a way perhaps it was. They had been skilled men in the Patriarch's workshop after all and the mould was ancient.

'I am glad to see you here, my lord,' said one of his chaplains, Edward Abbot of Notely, who was presiding over the service.

'Did you think I would not come, Edward?' William said with a weak smile. 'I would not miss this opportunity.'

The Abbot gently pressed his shoulder. 'No,' he said. 'In truth I knew you would be here if you were able.' He bowed and turned back to continue with the ceremony.

William listened to the voices carrying toward the arched rafters of the chapel, heard the singing of the choir, sweet and pure, and saw everything through a blur of golden light shot through with darkness.

22

Jerusalem, Easter 1184

The church of the Holy Sepulchre waited in darkness. William could hear people breathing and shuffling around him. The murmur of prayers, the intense moment of waiting for the breath of God to kindle the lamp in the tomb of Christ and restore light to the world. Like everyone gathered in the round outside the edicule he clutched a candle, ready for the moment, filled with belief, but at the same time, deep under the surface, assailed by a treacherous darkness of doubt. What if the flame did not kindle? What if the weight of their sins was too great and God chose to show his displeasure by denying the light?

He pondered about the lies men told to comfort themselves, and a cynical part of him wondered just what the Patriarch was doing alone within the edicule without witnesses. What conferred on him, a worldly prelate who dressed in jewelled silks and kept a lovely young mistress, the privilege of receiving the Holy Flame, symbol of Christ's resurrection? He strove to quash that thought and murmured his prayers like everyone else. Even if the fire was caused by human intervention, it did not negate the miracle of Christ's death and resurrection.

Baldwin's litter had been borne as close to the edicule as possible, and since his leprous fingers were unable to grasp the candle, his little nephew, heir to the throne, held it instead in his small, perfect grasp, his gaze clear and steady and his infant features petal-smooth. His mother stood at his side: she had come to Jerusalem for Easter under safe conduct to make peace with the King, but would soon return to Ascalon and her husband.

The waiting time lengthened and the prayers developed an edge as tension escalated in the packed rotunda. Somewhere a child wailed and was shushed by its parent.

Suddenly, a sound like rushing wings came from within the edicule, then a soft cry of triumphant elation and Heraclius emerged, ducking under the arch and then standing straight in his glittering patriarchal robes, light shining around him. He held a burning candle in each hand and the flames shone a strange ethereal blue that sent a gasp around the rotunda. Priests hastened to light bundles of tapers from the Patriarch's candles while Heraclius himself stepped forward to kindle young Baldwin's taper.

In widening circles the rotunda filled with a blaze of heat and light as the fire was sent from person to person, no longer ethereal blue but customary gold, and wisping with smoke that draped the air with the smell of burning wax. William took the flame from Onri and passed it on to Eustace and Ancel, who in turn passed theirs to the rest of the men, and as the wicks flared the cry went up that Christ was risen and mankind saved. Amid chanting, praise and joy, the light was borne in procession out into the streets of Jerusalem and shared among its relieved and joyful citizens. William's heart brimmed with bliss and humility and a tender, almost painful feeling that he was unworthy and should strive to be a better man. All at once his cheeks were wet as a sob shuddered through him.

Ancel touched his shoulder in concern. 'Gwim?'

He shook his head. 'I was thinking of Harry and how we are witnesses for him. He should have been here to see this and kindle his own flame, but we are here in his stead. This light is for all of us, but it is for him especially.'

'And now it is complete,' Ancel said, and crossed himself. 'Amen.' His eyes were clear and open and William realised that for his brother their arrival in Jerusalem had been an end to their trials, all debts paid and matters set to rights.

'I doubt it will ever be complete – for me anyway,' William said. He wiped his eyes, stinging from tears and smoke, and drew a deep, steadying breath. He was conscious of the great privilege he had been granted. So few in the world were given the grace of witnessing this miracle.

Ancel opened his mouth to speak but he and William were suddenly parted by a group of people forcing a way to the door. William recognised the men from the Patriarch's domestic household – Zaccariah of Nablus and the mercenary Mahzun of Tyre with several henchmen. Following in the path they had cleared, clad in a gown of dark ruby silk, walked Paschia de Riveri. A blue cloak was fastened across her breast with gold chains and her hair was concealed under a headdress winking with small sapphires. Her gem-embroidered shoes peeped out from under her robes with each step she took. She saw William and gestured him to walk beside her and he had perforce to oblige, even though he was still off balance and swallowing emotion.

'I trust you have fully recovered from your encounter with the rough sea, messire Marshal?' she enquired with a gleam in her eyes. An exotic perfume of rose and musk wafted around her.

'Yes, madam,' William said wryly. 'And you also?'

'I am well, thank you for asking, and I am pleased to hear of your own good health since I have been thinking much on the matter of how you might be of help to the Patriarch.'

William bowed. 'If I can be of service I shall be glad to assist. What may we do for you, madam?'

Her expression lit with a smile. 'The Patriarch is hosting an event at the palace with readings and music the day after tomorrow,' she said. 'If you wish to come I am sure there are matters you could both profitably discuss.' She emphasised the second to last word and, setting her hand on his wrist, leaned toward him briefly. Her breath smelled sweetly of liquorice and cardamom. 'You may not think that such a gathering would suit a military man, but you would be very wrong.'

William was wary but intrigued. 'It will be my honour, madam. I used to value such gatherings when I served the Young King.'

When we were at Kerak, I watched you and your men performing on the tourney ground. I admired your skill – you were outstanding. In Outremer we have many fine knights, but you are their match. I am not easily impressed by the flash of armour and ready courtesy. Many have tried that road to gain my favour but I am wise to their guile – and their inevitable shortcomings.'

'I hope I am not one of them, madam.'

'So do I.' Her glance was frankly appraising. 'My point is that I recognise talent and I am willing to reward it. Bring your men too. I am sure they will enjoy the entertainment and it is good to have fresh blood among us.'

William was fully alert now for she was blatantly weaving her political strands around him and drawing him into her net; but she was an alluring, powerful woman and his interest was piqued. 'I am at your service, madam.'

'Indeed.' She released his wrist and a mischievous sparkle lit her gaze. 'I am counting on you to have a steady stomach this time – and not to worship at my feet unless I bid you.'

He grinned and swept her a bow. 'Madam, I can fulfil both of those requirements.'

'I am pleased to hear it.' She turned away with her ladies, showing the flick of an embroidered undergown and a peep of dainty embroidered slipper as she did so. Greeting another lord, she laid her hand on his arm in exactly the same wise, leaned toward him, and began asking after his family.

Ancel rejoined William with a question in his eyes.

'You are going to need your silk gown from Kerak again,' William said. 'We are all required to present ourselves at the

Patriarch's palace in two days' time for an informal event. There will be food and entertainment.'

Ancel raised his brows. 'Do we have to sing for our supper? I assume we've been invited as the entertainment.'

William's eyes were drawn again to the lady Paschia who was now engaged with someone else, laughing softly at something the man had just said. Indeed it was difficult to look away. She strongly reminded him of Queen Alienor in the way she was witty, intelligent, interested in her subject for the duration of the conversation and then moving on. She was a great asset to Heraclius even if her position was ambiguous and frowned upon by many. 'I suspect that since the Patriarch and the Grand Masters of the Temple and Hospital have agreed to lead a mission to France and England, they will want to know everything they can about those courts.'

'Are you going to tell them?'

'Not everything, obviously.'

'Do you think Henry will come?' Ancel asked. 'Or one of his sons?'

William shrugged. 'Henry is a law unto himself. I would say not, but he is so contrary that he might do it to shock everyone.'

Ancel nudged William with his elbow. 'If Henry does decide to come then our fortune is made. He's bound to make you his Marshal. He might even get rid of de Lusignan. We could marry heiresses and become great lords.'

William shot Ancel a look of tolerant affection and shook his head. 'I would not light the fire under the pot just yet.'

'Do you remember when we were boys and we would sit in the barn and dream of having such things even though we were younger sons and knew it was unlikely to be our lot?'

William chuckled. 'I recall you stealing a jug of the best wine from the barrel in the undercroft and we knew we'd be thrashed if we were caught.'

'But we weren't caught, were we? And now look at us. Truly, what is there to lose since we started off with so little?'

William conceded Ancel the point, although it could be argued that they had gone from stealing wine to robbing shrines, with many murky places in between. But there was always the dream to strive for.

'Besides,' said Ancel, 'if they believe the King of France or Henry or one of his sons is going to rule in Jerusalem, we shall reap the benefit of their patronage for a little while at least. They will want to favour us in return for all the favours we may potentially do for them.'

William laughed sourly. 'Now you truly are thinking like a courtier, brother.'

The Patriarch's palace stood cheek by jowl with the church of the Holy Sepulchre and was a magnificent edifice with decorated arches and columns, and domed roofs. Most of the High Court of Jerusalem was attending the Patriarch's gathering, although King Baldwin was absent. Recent events and the long Easter celebrations had taken their toll and he was resting in his own palace, being treated by his physicians.

Food had been set out along trestle tables where guests could help themselves, although the ranks were separated and the higher end of the hall was reserved for the most exalted attendees.

William wore a green silk tunic and a cloak of soft dark-red wool purchased in the cloth market. He had visited a bath house that afternoon and had been scrubbed and pummelled until his skin glowed. His hair had been trimmed and his beard closely shaven so that it hugged his firm jawline. Colourfully attired and perfumed, he blended with the rest of the court, no longer standing out as a raw newcomer.

A roast pig doused in sandalwood sauce was the centrepiece of the banqueting board.

'It looks like Ancel's face when he takes off his helmet after a tourney,' Eustace declared. 'You wouldn't catch me with a face as red as that!'

'Oh I don't know, it would depend on the circumstances, wouldn't it?' Ancel, resplendent in his tunic from Kerak, good-naturedly thumped Eustace's arm as he retorted.

Amid the joshing, William looked round, absorbing details. The Patriarch sat at the head of the hall with his high-ranking guests – mostly the barons who had opposed Guy de Lusignan. Their wives were present too, and Sybilla, the King's sister. Madam de Riveri sat at her side, gowned in her blood-red silk, and the two women were smiling and talking together in the relaxed manner of friends.

An attendant mounted the dais steps and stooped to speak to the Patriarchess. She thanked him and her eyes sought and met William's. Murmuring to Sybilla, and lightly touching Heraclius's arm, she left her place and crossed the room.

'I am glad you have come.' She offered William her hand. 'The Patriarch will be most keen to meet you again.' She sent her dark gaze around his men. 'And these are your companions? What fine knights. I was impressed, messires, with your perfor-mance at Kerak.'

William performed brief introductions and she had a gracious word and a smile for each one. 'Your brother?' She looked almost surprised when William presented Ancel.

'I am the handsome one, my lady.' Ancel flashed a grin.

She arched her eyebrows in amusement. 'There is a certain resemblance between you. Indeed, I saw you at the tourney. I hope the ground was not too hard, messire.'

Ancel flushed but his smile remained. 'No, my lady, I bounce well. It is one of my particular skills.'

She laughed softly. 'And a very useful one to have I am sure.' She took William's arm, laying claim to him. 'Come, messire, I will introduce you to the Patriarch. It has been good to meet you, gentlemen.' She swept a look around William's men, dismissing them with courtesy but firm intent.

'I told my lord that you might not seem to be anything out

213

of the ordinary, but that you had great potential and might be of use to him.' Her brief glance as she led William to the dais was mischievous.

'I am glad you think so – the second part certainly,' he answered in kind. He was on his mettle for this was an important moment and it was vital he judged it well.

'Oh, the first part always makes the second more interesting I find.' Her voice was as smooth as dark silk. 'Like unwrapping a gift.'

Her words sent a frisson through him, and he was intensely aware of her light grip on his sleeve, and her scent, an intoxicating blend of incense and roses.

They reached the high table and she curtseyed to the Patriarch, while William bowed.

'Sire,' she said, 'this is the young man I mentioned to you. He has served the King of England and is familiar with the French court.'

Heraclius folded back the sleeve of his gilded overgown and exchanged an indulgent look with his mistress, before fixing William with a sterner one. 'We have been introduced before.'

'Yes, my lord, at Kerak.' William bowed again.

Heraclius's expression grew shrewd and calculating. 'I have seen you often in the King's entourage, and you appear to have found employment with others including the Prince of Antioch.'

'Sire, I have helped when I have been requested, but I am my own man.'

'That may be so,' Heraclius replied, his tone interested but sceptical. 'Madam de Riveri thinks well of you and believes you may be useful, but I would know more about you before I make that decision.' Leaning back, he stroked his chin. 'What were your duties when you served the King of England?'

'My lord, I served his son until he died. I was his tutor in arms and master of his military household,' William replied gravely.

'Was not the young man at war with his father?'

'Indeed, sire, and it was a tragedy to witness the strife between them, but I had pledged my oath to the Young King and I served him loyally. King Henry wished me Godspeed on my mission to lay his son's cloak at Christ's tomb and he has promised me a position in his household on my return. I am familiar with his court and my older brother is his master marshal, as was our father before him.'

Heraclius proceeded to question William in detail, and now he was incisive and demanding, wanting to know exactly what his duties had been, how many men answered to him, who he knew, how close he truly had been to King Henry and his sons. Ancel had spoken to William of singing for their supper, and now William had to do just that, but seriously and without any of a minstrel's boastful glitter. Heraclius wanted facts and detail, clear and hard without evasion.

William was conscious of Paschia de Riveri watching the exchange like a cat at a mouse hole, missing nothing, a half-smile curling her lips. He knew how the game of patronage played out at court and he included her in the discussion by meeting her gaze and bowing his head, acknowledging that it was her influence that had brought him here. He afforded Sybilla Countess of Jaffa the same courtesy. The women of the court were the keepers of its undercurrents and tides, and the most powerful knew how to move men along and through such waters. He was aware of them feeding on the information as if it was rich suste-nance, and from the glint of satisfaction in Madam de Riveri's eyes he understood she was pleased by his responses. As if she had brought a gift to her lord and was proudly satisfied at having her judgement borne out.

Gradually the Patriarch's guard relaxed. He smoothed his silk gown over his knees and said, 'I believe you may indeed be of use to me and my colleagues in planning our mission. I am hosting a meeting tomorrow after Compline and I would like you to attend and give us the further benefit of your expertise.'

215

William experienced a warm feeling of achievement at the Patriarch's offer. 'It will be my honour, my lord.' Dismissed, he bowed and then backed from Heraclius's presence. The Patriarchess murmured to her lover and kissed his cheek while he fondly patted her arm. She lowered her lids and looked demure before flicking a glance at William and smiling. He was uncertain whether it was for him or merely a sign of her pleasure that matters had gone as she wished.

'Messire Marshal.' Heraclius advanced to greet William and usher him into his chamber, his manner more informal and welcoming than it had been in public the previous evening. A concentration of lamp and candle light fell upon a table around which a dozen men sat on benches like disciples at the Last Supper. William noted the presence of the Templar Grand Master Arnold de Torroja, and beside him his seneschal Gerard de Ridefort. The Hospitaller Grand Master Roger de Moulins was here too, his posture alert, but more relaxed than his Templar associates, and he too had a companion Hospitaller with him. Also at the table were the secular lords Raymond of Tripoli, Bohemond of Antioch, and the brothers Badouin of Ramlah and Balian of Ibelin, and a scattering of clergy. A mixture of factions, but all prepared to come together tonight.

Heraclius presented William to the men and then directed him to a place on the bench at his right-hand side, where a servant furnished him with a cup of wine.

'My lords,' Heraclius announced, once everyone was settled. 'We are here to do God's work today, whether we be lay people or clergy. This man knows the courts of England and France well and has served the King of England and his household. I trust him to tell you from his own heart what he knows of these matters and let you all be the judge of his veracity.'

William cleared his throat, aware of their keen scrutiny and knowing he must measure his words for they in turn would be measured. 'I hardly know what to say to you, my lords, but I will do my best to give you useful knowledge. There is great trouble at the courts where you seek support, but all are firmly united in the wish to preserve the Kingdom of Jerusalem. As you know there is a deep bond between my lord Henry's court and this one.'

He received nods of agreement around the board.

'It is true that my lord King Henry and Queen Alienor have been embroiled in many disagreements recently but they were united in their wish for me to present the cloak of their son at the tomb of Christ, whom I commend to the eternal master of us all. However, I ask you to consider the part of a man with four grown sons, all jousting for position at his own table, and the father being jostled upon that table. It is a precarious position at times but one he is more than able to sustain through his own tenacity and power.' He paused to add water to his cup, for the wine was strong and he did not want his tongue to run away with him.

'His court is served by diligent men. Each matter is dealt with in its turn and there are trusted servants and officials ready to see that orders are carried out. The court is held together by an able king whom people agree to serve, fearing otherwise, if they did not serve truly. Even his own sons he rules with a rod of iron and brooks no instance of contradiction or insurrection, and so he keeps a tight rein on everything.'

Heraclius pursed his lips. 'Would you say that Henry was willing to give his sword to Jerusalem?'

'I do not know the answer to that, sire,' William replied diplomatically. 'Jerusalem is truly a place that enriches the soul, but what of the heart? My lord King has fought long and hard for his domains.' He saw the gathered men exchange concerned glances. Their dilemma was how to persuade Henry to release the reins he currently held in order to grasp those of Jerusalem.

'Indeed, that is interesting,' Heraclius said. 'How then may we encourage him? Will he not come now and follow his son's trail to the Sepulchre?'

An image of the Young King's cloak upon the tomb crossed William's mind and struck like a hammer to his heart. 'That I cannot tell you, my lords. He is a courageous man, but he has his own wars to fight. Whether he will take on the wars of Jerusalem, I know not. I can assure you he is a great ally to have and decisive, but it all depends on the opportune moment.'

The flagon was passed around while the group digested William's words.

Heraclius said, 'We know that the King of England is very generous in his monetary wishes for the kingdom too.'

William inclined his head and murmured a platitude. Talking about Henry's silver was delicate ground. 'King Henry cares for appearance and material wealth only as it suits his purpose as a monarch. This wine, for example. Never have I tasted better, but it would be wasted on my sovereign lord were you to present him with a tun of it. The wine of the English court is like vinegar and one must often filter it through one's teeth while trying not to shudder.' He was amused to see the grimaces exchanged among the gathered men. 'I do not seek to disparage my King, only to tell you what to expect. He also does not care for elaborate banquets or rich food. In truth, he barely notices what he eats. Food to him is no more than sustenance. He is unable to remain still for longer than a moment. If he talks to you, be prepared to have him pace the room and constantly fidget. But do not make the mistake of believing he is not listening. He has keen ears and even sharper intelligence, and he will give you no mercy in conversation. He is a man like any man, but he is also a great king, even if he shuns many trappings of that kingship. Do not be misled by his appearance. He is decisive and forceful, and he can see through deception at a glance. You must be direct with him, yet at the same time you must be subtle.'

218

Heraclius stroked his chin. 'What would be the best advice to bring him to a positive decision to come to Jerusalem?'

William considered the question. 'I would say do not try to press an answer from him, for you are unlikely to receive one if he thinks you are pushing him in a particular direction. You would be wise to make allowances and bide your time.'

Further questions followed – about Henry's advisers, about his sons, and about Philippe of France, who was also sworn to make pilgrimage to the Holy Land.

'Would you agree that the King of France is a fine man?' Heraclius asked.

William managed to keep a straight face. There were different interpretations one could put on that term. 'He is an adept politician, my lord. He treats his foes and allies alike and in this way always keeps himself at the centre of events.'

'How would he behave if King Henry were to come to Jerusalem?'

'My lord, I think his purpose would be to help himself, rather than assisting in the venture,' William replied, 'although he would make it seem that he was offering every help.'

'Perhaps if the King of England and the King of France were to be brought together in diplomacy,' said Roger de Moulins. 'If they were to make a joint venture rather than just one or the other.'

William suspected that pigs would fly before such cooperation happened. 'That again I cannot say, sire. All I can tell you is what I know from my experience at both courts.'

William's part in the meeting finished soon after that and Heraclius saw him to the door personally rather than dismissing him with a servant. 'I am in your debt,' he said. 'And I thank you for your advice, as do my companions. We shall need to talk to you again because we have so much to prepare before the summer.' He removed a gold ring from his little finger, and presented it to William. 'Show this at my door and you shall be passed through.'

'I shall await your summons, sire.'

Heraclius gave him a meaningful smile. 'Do not worry, it shall be to your advantage,' he said, and returned to his guests.

William looked down at the ring in his hand and wondered at the twists and turns of fate that had brought him here from the soft green pastures of home. What was he to do with this, for it was clearly another offer of reward and patronage. Accept and attach himself and his men to the favour and protection of the head of the Church in Outremer? But at what price? What else did Heraclius want from him?

As William turned to leave, Paschia de Riveri emerged from another doorway clutching a fluffy tabby cat in her arms, and he had to side-step swiftly to avoid a collision.

'Messire Marshal!' she declared with surprised delight. 'Of course, I had forgotten, you are here to talk with the Patriarch.' The cat leaped from her embrace and stalked off down the corridor, its tail waving like a bushy banner. 'I trust the meeting went well?' Her thick black hair hung in loose ringlets tonight, her only head-covering a slim band of gold silk beaded with sapphires.

William suspected that she had not forgotten at all – that this meeting was more than happenstance. 'Favourably well I think, madam, but you will have to ask the Patriarch for a fuller accounting.'

'Indeed, I intend to.' Her look sparkled with flirtation. 'I hope your assistance will reap suitable reward.'

'Thank you, madam. If I can render any service to your household, I shall do so gladly.'

'Be assured I shall take you up on that offer – should the need arise.'

The cat returned and twined around their legs, rubbing and purring. She stooped and picked it up, and it butted its head beneath her chin, its paws kneading.

'Madam.' William bowed and took his leave, his step light with the knowledge of a task well accomplished. He had given a good account of himself to the Patriarch and the others; his information had been judged a thing of value, and that meant more doors opening to him and his men.

The lady Paschia intrigued him too; she reminded him so much of Queen Alienor, or Alienor as she must have been when she was a vibrant young woman at the French court, engaged in the game of playful flirtation. The thought gave him a frisson; a pleasurable sense of challenge and danger. Looking back over his shoulder he saw that she was still standing where he had left her, watching him, the cat in her arms, her cheek pressed against its fur.

William was summoned to several more meetings between Heraclius and his associates concerning the expedition to France and England. Some were conducted at the Patriarch's palace and some in the King's chamber with Baldwin presiding. Between such gatherings, William and his entourage were kept busy with various employments, particularly advising the nobles and clerics of the court on the purchase of horses, saddlery and harness – one of the senior duties involved in the Marshal's role in Outremer. William was also employed to source horses and tack for specific commissions after word of Bohemond's purchase went around the court.

William and his men gave instruction in weapons and tourney training to young knights and squires, and provided armed escort on the pilgrim route between Jerusalem and the River Jordan, where the road was particularly susceptible to attacks from bandits and thieves. At times they were pilgrims themselves, visiting and worshipping at the numerous holy places surrounding Jerusalem – Nazareth, Bethlehem, Bethany. They visited the River Jordan and were cleansed and baptised anew, and they rode up to the shores of the Sea of Galilee where Christ had walked upon the waters and called his disciples to him.

With Heraclius and the leaders of the military orders preparing their mission to the courts of Europe, their knowledge was much in demand. Should Henry or Philippe of France agree to come to Outremer, then William and his men would be positioned to play a vital role in the royal entourage and thus, as Ancel had predicted, they were feted and cultivated by the Jerusalem court. William suspected that the outcome would not be as the envoys desired, but until they had their answer the rewards to William and his men were generous.

Returning one day from a visit to a horse trader, William met Augustine who had been about his own business for the Templars and was also returning to the city. He admired the four horses William had bought. 'I hear you are acquiring quite a reputation,' he said.

William grinned. 'An honourable one I hope.'

'Yes indeed, and not just about horse flesh – although you are also the subject of much speculation. Many are saying you are King Henry's harbinger.'

'If I am, it is news to me,' William said ruefully. 'For the moment I am but a horse master.'

'And word from the horse's mouth is always the one to bet on – is that not what they say also?'

'I thought the saying was about gift horses,' William retorted, making Augustine laugh.

'I suppose it depends on what you seek . . . My own news is that I am to travel with the Patriarch and the Grand Masters on their mission.'

'You will be a valuable asset. We could not have managed without you on our own journey.'

'Oh, you could have,' Augustine said with a dismissive wave. 'We were all a part of a greater whole.' Nonetheless he looked pleased. 'Our journey is the reason I am well seasoned now.' He gave William a keen look. 'Do you believe the Patriarch will succeed?'

Everyone asked William that question and his answer was always circumspect. 'The Patriarch is a man of the world, and a fine orator – I hope that will be enough to persuade either King Henry or Philippe of France.'

'King Baldwin is very sick,' Augustine said, his expression sombre. 'We all know his days are numbered and that we need aid – we cannot stand alone.'

'Yes, I know,' William said quietly. 'We can only pray.'

Having stabled their horses and attended to the four new ones, William and his men repaired to their lodging. Ancel hesitated as a sturdy woman came walking toward them, a covered basket over her arm. Seeing Ancel, her homely face creased into a beaming smile.

Ancel flushed. 'I will see you in a while,' he muttered to William, and broke away to speak to her.

William observed their greeting – the pleasure on both their faces, the light touch of hands. 'Should I know about this?' he asked Eustace.

The squire shrugged. 'We buy food from her sometimes – bread and cheese, and pies.' His eyes lit up as he mentioned the latter. 'Lots of pies.'

William vaguely remembered seeing her. He had had so much on his mind recently that a woman selling food in passing to his men was of little consequence.

Ancel gestured to William to continue on his way, from which William deduced that it had gone further than just a matter of tasty pies. Thoughtful, diverted, suddenly seeing Ancel in a new light, he walked on. A glance over his shoulder revealed that his brother was now carrying the woman's basket and that she had linked her arm through his.

William sent his men on to their lodging while he paid a visit to the patriarchal palace to report his return and that he had found four horses, two of which might suit Heraclius's stable.

Expecting to leave a message with one of the Patriarch's servants, he found Heraclius himself cloaked and spurred, standing in the courtyard having just dismounted from his bay stallion. As William approached, Heraclius threw his soft hat on the ground, his face flushed with anger as he shouted at his groom, uncharacteristically out of temper.

'How has this happened?' he demanded. 'Do you know how much time this will cost me? Where am I to find another horse?'

'Your eminence, may I help you?' William asked, bowing.

Heraclius glowered. 'I doubt it,' he snapped. 'My palfrey has the colic and now my remount is lame. I have important business in Bethany. How am I supposed to go there when the only other beast of worth in the stable is my lady's palfrey and in foal? By all that is holy, I do not believe this! My grooms are idiots!'

Having served King Henry, William was accustomed to dealing with outbursts of enraged exasperation when confronted with mundane problems that foiled imperious intent. 'Shall I take a look, sire?'

'As you wish.' Heraclius gestured irritably and swept his hand through his hair. 'Front nearside. I cannot believe this!'

'Hold him steady,' William ordered the stable boy. Soothing the horse with gentle words, he ran his hand down the affected leg from shoulder to hoof, noting that there was no heat or signs of tenderness. The bay's ears flickered, but it displayed no serious signs of pain. William coaxed the stallion into lifting his hoof and looked at the underside. With a calm, steady movement he unsheathed a small knife from his belt and, gripping the bay's leg firmly, cleaned out the inside of the hoof, dislodging a small but sharp chip of stone from the frog. 'Here is your culprit.' He set the hoof down and showed the fragment to Heraclius; then patted the bay's neck and directed the lad to walk him round the yard. The horse moved gingerly at first but picked up smoothness and pace with each long stride.

'He might be a little tender on that hoof so do not press him, but he should take you to Bethany. You might want to encourage your stable hands to be more diligent.'

Heraclius's colour remained high, but his expression had turned to one of relief. 'Oh, I intend to. I will not have this kind of sloppy care of my horses. You have saved me much aggravation messire Marshal. It is always difficult finding a comfortable and trustworthy mount.'

'I have just returned with four good horses from a trader near Tiberius,' William said. 'You might wish to look at them for your own stable.'

'I would indeed be interested,' Heraclius said. 'Bring them to me the day after tomorrow.' He turned to the bay but paused as his mistress and her maid emerged from a doorway. The lady Paschia was wearing a very fetching headdress decorated with peacock feathers.

She greeted Heraclius with a touch on his sleeve and a smile. 'I am going to the market,' she said. 'I thought you would have left by now.' She acknowledged William with a dip of her head and a swift glance from her dark eyes.

'Messire Marshal has just cured Charol of lameness,' Heraclius said, 'otherwise I would be going nowhere.'

'It was but a stone fragment that needed cleaning out of the hoof,' William said. 'From the way he is striding out I do not think much damage has been done beyond slight bruising.'

'But you knew what to do and how to go about it in a way that did not upset the horse, and I am most grateful.' Heraclius looked shrewdly at William. 'It occurs to me that I have sufficient room to lodge you and your men. You will be more readily available to my summons while I make ready to leave. I can provide a roof over your heads and food in your bellies and in return make you responsible for my stables and horses – as befitting the role of a marshal.'

William hesitated, uncertain how to respond. There were so many factions vying for dominance and he did not want to be seen favouring one side over another lest he become caught up in the rivalry. Yet the offer was tempting. Bohemond had returned to Antioch and that particular patronage had ceased. Heraclius's household was well organised and comfortable whereas their lodgings were a trifle cramped. It would be pleasant and logical to dwell here while awaiting King Henry's decision. There was room to stable his own horses and it was no small consideration to have food and shelter provided. 'That is most generous, sire.'

The lady Paschia gave Heraclius a melting look and stroked his hand. 'You must accept, messire Marshal,' she said, turning a dazzling smile upon William, making his stomach jolt. The peacock feathers waved jauntily in her headdress.

He bowed. 'Madam, I shall give the matter full consideration.'

'I am glad to hear it.' She kissed Heraclius on the cheek and continued on her way. Heraclius briefly followed the sway of her hips before he dragged his attention back to William, who had swiftly dropped his own gaze.

'You do not have to agree here and now,' Heraclius said, reaching for the bay's bridle. 'Come and see me when I return and we shall discuss terms . . . although you will save yourself trouble if you agree sooner rather than later. My lady always gets her way.' With a wry smile he mounted his restored horse and trotted from the yard, leaving William to his interesting dilemma.

It was late when Ancel returned to the lodging with heavy eyes and the expression of a man well fed and well pleasured. The others, who were playing dice, greeted him with cheerful whoops of welcome and accosted him with bawdy remarks and gestures. Ancel flushed bright red and stooped to make a fuss of Pilgrim who had dashed up to him, tail wagging so frantically that his back end almost collided with his nose.

William was sitting at another table adapting a bridle for a baron's troublesome horse. He gestured to the scanty remains of a couple of roast hens and a dish of spiced lentils. 'We left you some, but I doubt you're hungry.'

Ancel sat down on the bench beside William and continued to fuss the dog. 'No,' he said, but helped himself to a half-cup of wine. 'You are all just jealous,' he toasted the others, and received another barrage of good-natured banter.

William looked at his brother and experienced a rush of affection and protective amusement. Curiosity too, but he reined it in and waited.

'It's like being at home when I'm with Asmaria,' Ancel said quietly once the others had settled back into their game. 'It's safe and it's comfortable.'

'And this is not safe or comfortable?' So that was her name – Asmaria.

'Well yes, I do not mean it in that way.' Ancel screwed up his face. 'We are brothers in arms and together, but it is not the same as sitting at a hearth watching a woman stir a cooking pot, or knead bread while she sings to her children, and the man looks on with his feet stretched to the fire, knowing he has to provide for them, but they also are providing for him.'

'I do not suppose it is,' William said. There had been little time for such moments of idyllic domesticity in their childhood, although the occasions when it had happened made the memory all the more precious and he could understand Ancel wanting to taste that sweetness. Strange to come all the way to Jerusalem to find such comfort. 'So the lady has children?'

'A boy and a girl,' Ancel said. 'Her husband was a cook but he died a year and a half ago. Now she sells food to pilgrims and launders and mends.'

'And provides other services too?' William set the harness aside and refreshed his brother's cup.

Ancel shook his head. 'No, that is not her trade.'

'But you paid her?'

Ancel flushed. 'She did not ask for money, it was not like that.

227

Yes, I gave her money to lighten her burden and buy something for the children – but it was not payment. It was provision and caring.' He jerked his head toward the others, indignation sparking in his eyes. 'They do not understand that. All they think of is money paid to a whore for spreading her legs.' He lowered his voice a further notch and said vehemently, 'Asmaria is no whore and I will not have her named thus.'

William heard the sincerity in Ancel's tone, and the steel. Since arriving in Jerusalem his youngest brother had changed, becoming more of his own man, and if this woman gave him comfort and stability, he would not stand in his way. 'She shall not be named thus in this household, you have my promise on that.' He poured wine into his own cup and changed the subject. 'While you were away about your business, I had a proposal.' He told Ancel about Heraclius's offer. 'I have said I shall think on it.'

A frown crossed Ancel's face. 'Does that mean we shall have to kneel to him and swear allegiance?'

William shook his head. 'It will be open to discussion how far our service goes, but I think it no bad thing while we await the outcome of his mission. When he returns we can decide whether to remain or leave.'

Ancel pursed his lips, considering. 'So, we would have lodging in the Patriarch's palace and use of his stables and eat at his expense?'

'In essence, yes.'

'Then I think it a good thing too,' Ancel said, 'as long as I can come and go as I please outside my duties.'

'Of course.' William gave his brother a knowing look. 'This is the Patriarch's favour in return for our information and the keeping of his yard. He has us close to hand for his own convenience. That is all.'

Ten days later William and his men moved into the Patriarch's palace. Heraclius was absent again about other business, but they were shown to their quarters by one of his stewards. William's knights were provided with sleeping space in the guardroom and William was given a small wall chamber above the Patriarch's hall on the side nearest to the stables. There was space only for a bed and a stool, but it had a narrow window and a niche for a lamp, and since it was within the palace itself was a mark of high favour. In negotiating the terms of their occupancy Heraclius had not asked William to swear allegiance to him, but in return for food and lodging expected him to be available when summoned, and to care well for his horses, acquiring new stock as necessary.

William was summoned to attend several more meetings to discuss the machinations of King Henry's court until he wondered what else he could possibly tell them. One day Heraclius requested his presence in his private chamber. The room was separate to the one where he usually conducted his business, and was more intimate, with cushions and low tables. Rich hangings draped the walls and small bowls of burning incense sent fragrant smoke wafting in layers like the finest muslin. Servants came, soft-footed, and poured wine, and the lady Paschia set a platter of rose-flavoured sweetmeats before the men, and then with a swift smile retired to the far end of the room with her maid.

Once they were settled, Heraclius said, 'I have asked you many things about your King, and you have answered me fully and courteously, but now I must ask you about the silver he has promised to aid our cause, but that yet remains beyond our reach with the Templars.'

William had known they would come to this. As well as requiring a ruler and material aid such as horses and equipment, the Kingdom of Jerusalem was hungry for money. He understood that Heraclius wanted reassurances but William had no intention of committing himself on issues beyond his remit. 'It is a matter for King Henry himself,' he replied. 'I cannot say.'

Heraclius gave him a sharp look. 'But you must know something about it if you have been at close quarters with him. He made a solemn promise to God that he would pay recompense to atone for the death of his archbishop, and he has done this, but has yet to release any funds. Surely a man of his standing would not go back on his word but I would know his mind on this.'

Many opined that the Patriarch was bland and pleasure-loving; having come to know him better, William thought him smooth and urbane – a man with a taste for luxury and fine things, but it was like thick padding over a pillar of the utmost granite. Heraclius was no fool.

As he hesitated, Heraclius continued: 'I am led to wonder what will happen to the money if he chooses not to come.'

'My lord, I do not know.'

Heraclius took a sweetmeat and held it delicately between forefinger and thumb. 'You were eager enough to give us personal information that showed how close to the King you were, and now you have no inkling about the matter of his finances, which is surely a highly public one. What are we to believe? How far are you to be trusted? That is what I ask myself.'

It was plain that Heraclius intended to push hard.

'Sire, I can vouch for the fact that King Henry will keep his promise, but I cannot speak for him on when and how. That is for you to discuss with him in England.' William spoke politely but firmly, holding his ground.

'And how may we obtain this money from him?' Heraclius asked. 'Are we to remain empty-handed? We have many needs at the present time. We must protect our cities and defend them against Saladin.'

William took a drink of wine and allowed the moment to draw out while he decided on his answer. Heraclius was clearly seeking information to open the coffer lids, some chink in Henry's armour that he could exploit. 'I have seen many buildings rising to the glory of God in Jerusalem and elsewhere, and many magnificent castles too. Indeed the money would pay for another weight of mortar to cement the kingdom, but you press me into ground that is not my own. I cannot speak for my King on this matter and he has given me no brief to do so. You must ask him yourself, as I have said, when you visit him with the Grand Masters. You may tell him you have spoken to me, and that I have said that I have neither the authority nor the information to tell you more.'

Heraclius narrowed his eyes, but not in hostility. Exasperation perhaps, but also in acknowledgement of a worthy opponent, and one with loyalty and judgement. 'Well then,' he said a little ruefully, 'it seems that you have told me as much as you are able, and it would be fruitless for both of us to push the matter further. I shall speak to your King – and I shall commend you to him as a man of strength and loyalty.'

'Thank you, sire,' William replied, relieved that Heraclius had taken the matter in good part. He rose to leave soon after that and Heraclius saw him out.

'We shall still speak again,' Heraclius said, 'but we know where we stand. I recognise your faithfulness to your King, and I applaud you for it.'

William bowed and departed. Glancing over his shoulder he saw that the lady Paschia had joined Heraclius and he was leaning down to listen to her as she spoke softly in his ear. Her eyes met William's across the room and held his for a long moment before she looked away.

The following day William was invited to a gathering at the court as the nobility of Jerusalem took shelter from the burgeoning late spring heat within the cool walls of the palace and he found himself sitting with a group of ladies who were desirous of knowing all about the fashions at court in England, what tales were being told and what songs being sung. William obliged them, enjoying himself. It had been a long time since he had had an opportunity to relax in the company of women and the conversation was a pleasurable respite from the serious military and political discussions of late.

The lady Paschia was present among the women, and had directed the subject by asking him about his life at court, its etiquette and manners, and especially wanted to know about Queen Alienor.

'She is a great and gracious lady,' William replied. 'I served her when I was a young hearth knight – and I still do.'

'But we hear that she is estranged from the King of England.'

'That is so, madam,' William said guardedly.

'And are you not torn yourself? Surely it must be difficult to serve your Queen and yet remain loyal to your King?'

'Their estrangement is a source of grief to me, I freely admit. I served their son, and he rebelled against his sire, but I pray that all will come to unity in future.' He kept his tone neutral and diplomatic.

'Prayer is always of benefit, but I have found that sometimes prayer needs all the assistance that men and women can provide,' she said, to the point. 'Do you believe they will reconcile?'

'The King has been a little gentler to the Queen since my young lord's death,' he replied, 'but if it will continue, I do not know.'

Her look told him she thought he was holding back but her smile was tolerantly amused. 'So where does your loyalty truly lie, messire? With the King, or with the Queen?'

William inclined his head to her. 'With my honour, my lady.'

She laughed softly and crossed one leg over the other in a rustle of blood-red silk, exposing the tip of a gold-embroidered shoe which she pointed in his direction. 'A diplomatic if evasive answer, messire.'

William returned her smile and bowed his head. 'Not at all, madam. I answered you with the honest truth.'

She arched her brows. 'That is a refreshing change in court circles, although I must judge for myself how honest your truth is.'

'Indeed, madam, but I esteem you a shrewd judge of character.'

Her lips twitched and she gently swung her foot, allowing a glimpse of a slender ankle clad in pale silk hose.

Ptolemy, her musician, sat down at her side and began playing a beguiling tune on his gittern while at the same time casting languishing glances in her direction that she ignored by turning her head away and frowning. The line of her neck was gracefully enhanced by her earring from which dangled three pearl droplets on fine gold wires.

William recognised the moves. Young men of the court played the game of longing after unattainable women and directing their creative talents to winning a corner of a heart while constantly being shunned. Ptolemy was a past master of the art, although today his lady was clearly disposed to be indifferent to his persuasion and turning her attention elsewhere. William was well aware of the dangers as well as the delights of the game. Queen Alienor had played it with him to a degree, but always within the boundaries. But here in Outremer, the holiest place on earth, those boundaries were more fluid than at home, and the temptations more intense.

'Perhaps you would tell us a little about your tournament days in France,' Madam de Riveri said, keeping her head turned away from her musician and leaning toward William. 'You must have won many prizes.'

'A few,' he said warily.

'One of your men was saying that you have taken the ransoms of five hundred knights all told. That is a great amount.'

'It may be that many, my lady, but I cannot say for certain, and I would not boast of such a thing since deeds always speak louder than words.' He would have to warn his men to be careful in their conversation because all was clearly being noted.

'Indeed they do,' she agreed, her smile sparking with challenge.

He hastily told the women a self-deprecating story about losing a man he had captured for ransom when the knight had leaped from his saddle and shinned up a passing house gutter.

His tale was interrupted by a sudden flurry at the end of the room as more people arrived, and William was surprised and a little dismayed to see Guy de Lusignan escorting his wife, the Countess of Jaffa. Obviously he had now deemed it sufficiently safe to emerge from Ascalon and rejoin the court. Immediately the social circle broke up and people hastened to greet the newcomers. Heraclius was effusive, guiding them to a settle.

William had no choice but to make his obeisance to Guy, who accepted his bow graciously.

'I hear you are working for the Patriarch now,' he remarked.

'I have some duties for him concerned with his forthcoming journey, sire,' William replied diffidently.

Guy nodded. 'Well, I suppose it is useful to have you to hand.' He spoke as though addressing a servant, but his smile was magnanimous. He turned to greet someone else and William was able to distance himself.

He would have left then, but he was accosted by a baron who wanted to talk about horses, and that led to further conversation about harness by which time a formal meal had been set out and William had to stay and dine and socialise. He was nowhere near Guy at the board, but it was still too close for comfort, and he was aware of the lord of Jaffa glancing at him every now and again with a speculative eye. He noticed that Guy often touched his wife's hand, and their shoulders brushed as they conversed. The lady Paschia attended on Sybilla and the women clearly enjoyed each other's company. From the swift whispers and smiles, he judged that they were sharing confidences, and suspected at one point that he was the subject of their discussion for Sybilla's gaze ranged over him in speculation as Paschia spoke in her ear.

Ptolemy was called upon to play his gittern and sing for the company, which he did both in French and Lengua Romana of Aquitaine, his voice soaring and liquid. For his final piece he performed the tale of a spurned lover mourning his lady's coldness toward him because she would no longer grant him her favours. He sang with a wobble in his voice, his eyes fixed tearfully on his mistress. As the song ended, Ptolemy bowed over his instrument for a moment, then rose and saluted his audience.

Giving him a brittle smile, the lady Paschia presented him with a mirror in a small ivory case. 'So you may reflect on your life, Ptolemy. Those were beautiful songs, and now you have my leave to go.'

He hesitated, and then made an exaggerated flourish before departing with set lips and tears on his cheeks. William thought the reaction a little untoward. Glancing at Madam de Riveri, he saw that her own lips were pressed together with irritation; but when Heraclius spoke to her she was immediately smiling and attentive.

William was eventually able to make his obeisance and, with relief, leave the gathering. Walking toward his own chamber, he became aware of two men standing against a pillar in the near darkness by the stairs, talking in subdued voices.

'It has gone far enough,' one said. 'It is not the first time this has happened with her, and I doubt it will be the last, but it must be managed. He is becoming too much of a liability.'

'I shall see to it,' the other said. 'Leave it with me. I know a reliable man.'

'The usual fee.'

They looked up as William walked toward them and he recognised the lady Paschia's uncle Zaccariah of Nablus and the mercenary soldier Mahzun of Tyre. He nodded briefly as he passed and experienced an involuntary tingle between his shoulder blades. He resisted the urge to look back, but harboured an image of them circling him like wolves contemplating a lone deer. He knew such men well. King Henry employed them as doorkeepers and messengers, often with dubious remits on the outskirts of their duties. What he had just heard did not bode well for someone at court, although he could do nothing, and if he became embroiled he would endanger himself and his men. He only had to glance at the fading scars on his wrist to know it was not worth it.

William and his knights spent the next three days escorting parties to the banks of the River Jordan. Onri was commanding the detail, leading the pilgrims through what was dangerous terrain unless one had armed protectors.

At Jericho a rest camp with abundant date palms and sweet water awaited the weary travellers, with space to pitch their tents for the night. Beyond lay the verdant River Jordan itself and the very place where John the Baptist had baptised Jesus. Here the pilgrims attended ceremonies, prayed, were christened anew in the waters of the river, and filled their flasks to bring the precious waters home. William had been on the detail several times now and the duty had become almost mundane. No brigands were going to attack a pilgrim party guarded by a dozen knights on warhorses. The assaults happened when folk chose to travel alone without armed escort.

'They are like sheep,' Onri said, 'and we are both shepherd and sheep-dog, but it is also our duty to serve them. You would think they would realise what happens to strays, but there are always the foolish ones who strike out on their own and pay the price.'

The late spring heat was increasing daily and the men wore surcoats over their mail to protect them from the sun's strength, and carried full flasks which they replenished at Jericho. Since fully fledged Templars were not permitted to speak to women, and there were women among the party, it fell to William and his men to give instructions and interact with the pilgrims, a duty that William rather enjoyed. Many people had come via ship and so had fairly recent news of home where for the moment all appeared to be quiet, which made William wonder if perhaps Henry would indeed decide to visit Outremer.

They returned to Jerusalem in the late afternoon of the third day. The sun was uncomfortably hot and the pilgrims with their blistered feet, dusty clothes and red, sore skin were relieved to stagger back into the city, waving their palm branches and raising hoarse voices in hosanna to God.

'Most of them will seek out the nearest tavern to quench their thirsts,' Onri said wryly, 'but still we serve them as knights of Christ, and when their heads have cleared in the morning a few will come to church and do penance.' He turned his horse toward the Temple Mount. 'I must go and report to my commander, and in truth I shall be glad to be rid of this armour.' He gave William a dubious look, albeit edged by a smile. 'And I suppose you are returning to your den of iniquity?'

William laughed at his gentle barb. 'The Patriarch would be dismayed to hear you describe his palace thus.'

'I am sure he would, but perhaps not surprised.' Onri saluted laconically and rode on, the pied Templar banner waving on its stave.

William returned to the palace and saw the horses settled before going to scrub away the heat and dust of the road in the Patriarch's bath house. Cooled and refreshed, his hair damp and sleeked back, he was making his way toward his chamber when the lady Paschia came running around the corner, sobbing, half stumbling on the hem of her gown.

'My lady.' He caught her sleeve to steady her. 'Is there something wrong? Can I help?'

'It is too late for that, much too late!' Her tears had made running dark smudges of her eye cosmetics.

William was bemused. Removing a stone from the hoof of the Patriarch's horse was one thing; comforting his weeping concubine was quite another, and there was no etiquette for such a situation. 'Madam, come, I will escort you to your ladies and they will help you.'

She shook her head vigorously and an expression that was almost panic contorted her face. 'No! I have just come from there

'– I do not want them. I need to breathe clean air. Take me to the garden if you will and let me sit a while.'

Concerned, but alert and on edge, William brought her to the Patriarch's garden – a walled-off area on the east side of the palace shaded by fig trees, with flagged paths leading to a three-tiered fountain at its centre. He helped her to sit on a stone bench facing the silvery loops of water where she knotted her hands in her lap and bent her head, her whole body trembling.

'Shall I bring you a drink?' He started to move away.

Her head jerked up. 'Oh, don't go! Please! Just stay with me for a moment.'

Tentatively William sat on the edge of the bench and glanced round. No one else was in sight, not even a gardener.

Three doves landed near the fountain and began pecking around for kernels of grain that someone had cast down earlier. A warm breeze rustled the leaves on the fig trees. Somewhere a workman was chiselling stone and the metallic clink of his hammer rang out, marking beats of time.

'May I ask what has upset you?'

She shook her head and dabbed her face on the sleeve of her gown, leaving dark smears. And then she drew a shuddering breath. 'It is my musician, Ptolemy,' she said. 'He is dead.'

William stared at her in shock. 'That is terrible news, my lady. What happened to him?'

'I do not know.' She swallowed. 'The Patriarch just said he had been found dead in his chamber. I think he wanted to spare me the details. In truth I do not wish to know, although I think he believes he killed himself, and that is a mortal sin.' Tears rolled down her face. 'I am sorry. You must think me a poor, weak creature.'

'No, madam, indeed not. You are understandably distraught.' In his other encounters with her she had always been composed and in control of her environment; a woman of shrewd political acumen and a gracious hostess. Now, beneath the painted face of a courtesan, he saw a vulnerable young woman playing the best game she could to survive and it moved something inside him.

'I knew him from when he was born,' she said, her voice catching. 'I was like a big sister to him when we were little. I looked after him sometimes for his mother – and then when he came to court seeking a position, I helped him because I could, and why should I not?' She jutted her chin. 'I know what it is to hunger. He wanted to rise high, and he was hand-some and talented. I wanted everyone to know how skilled he was.' She bit her lip. 'He was a beautiful, thoughtless boy and it should never have come to this. I blame myself.' Suddenly she pressed against William's shoulder and sobbed heartbrokenly into his sleeve.

William was decidedly uncomfortable, wondering what would happen if someone came in search of the Patriarch's lady and misconstrued the scene. The exotic scent of her, the feel of her in his arms, kindled both his protective instincts and more shameful ones, which he tried to ignore because they were not right in the face of her grief and distress. 'Madam, it is not your fault,' he said in a constricted voice.

'It is,' she wept. 'You do not understand. How could you? I could not explain even if I wished, nor would it be wise, for this place is filled with darkness – and he was an innocent fool!' Shuddering, she withdrew and looked up at him with her eyes full of desolation, her lips slightly parted as if inviting a kiss.

'My lady, I cannot stay any longer, I must go.' Gently disen-gaging, he rose to his feet. 'You are distraught and you should not be alone, but better with your ladies or the Patriarch. I shall send someone to you.'

'Don't go.' She held out her hand. 'Please.'

'My lady, I am sorry for your loss but I cannot stay.' Her grief was like a fierce tide washing away the cliff, revealing the unstable, underlying strata and exposing his own susceptibility.

He bowed deeply to her and walked away, his mind turning swiftly and his heart pounding. Ever since squirehood he had engaged in flirtation and witty by-play with the ladies of the court and he excelled at it, but he knew the hazards. He had once been falsely accused by rivals of having an affair with Harry's young wife and although exonerated, the incident had scarred his reputation. The court of Jerusalem was more intense than the Angevin one and the dangers on all sides were far greater.

Reaching the palace, he went in search of her women but encountered Heraclius first, who was hurrying along the walkway, a grim set to his mouth.

'Your Eminence, Madam de Riveri is sitting in the gardens by the fountain in much distress,' he said. 'I am searching for her ladies to succour her.'

Heraclius pressed William's arm. 'Thank you. I will go to her myself.'

'I am sorry – she told me the news about Ptolemy.'

'Indeed, it is a terrible business,' Heraclius said sorrowfully. 'I know he was troubled, but I had no idea that he would hang himself.'

William raised his brows. 'Is that what he did?'

Heraclius grimaced. 'He smashed his instrument to pieces on his chamber floor and then he hanged himself from the lamp hook above his bed. God have mercy on his soul.'

William crossed himself. 'I would not have thought that of him either.'

Heraclius shook his head. 'If only he had come to me. But who knows the darkness that possesses men's souls at such times?' He raised his hand in warning to William. 'My lady must not know that this was his end. She has personally promoted his cause at my court and she has known him since girlhood. It would distress her beyond the grief she suffers now to know the true manner of his death. Let her know only that he was found dead in his chamber and let no one speak of how it happened. Men are carried off in this land by sudden fevers so often that it will suffice as good reason.'

William nodded brusquely. 'You have my word, sire.'

'Good. I know I can count on you.' Heraclius pressed William's shoulder and looked relieved. 'I shall find Madam de Riveri a new musician as soon as I may, although I fear it will be difficult to replace Ptolemy.'

Heraclius hastened toward the garden and William returned to his men in a distracted mood.

Ancel, newly returned from a visit to Asmaria, looked up from sharpening his sword. 'Have you heard about Ptolemy?'

William poured himself a cup of wine and drank it down. 'The Patriarch has just told me.' He made no mention of the moment in the garden, but went to sit on a stool and leaned his back against the wall with a sigh.

'I saw him the day before we rode out on patrol and he was well enough then,' Ancel said. 'He played too recklessly at dice and almost lost his shirt, and he drank too much, but that was usual for him and there was no indication he would do this – that is if he did hang himself of course.'

William eyed him sharply, for Ancel's words were precisely what he had been trying not to think. 'You have reason to believe he did not?'

Ancel sheathed the sword. 'Only that troubadours often carry information and he was always hinting at things he knew – what he could tell us all if he chose. Perhaps someone decided to silence him.'

William rubbed the back of his neck. He thought about what the lady Paschia had said – that she could not tell him, that he would not understand.

'Do you remember when we were with him in that hostel not long after we had arrived, and there was some business between him and the Patriarch's men?' Ancel asked.

241

'Yes,' William said. 'And before we went to the Jordan, I over-heard Zaccariah of Nablus discussing business with Mahzun of Tyre that involved silencing someone. It might have been Ptolemy.' He shook his head, grimacing. 'I cannot believe Heraclius would be involved. He seemed genuinely shocked when he told me, although he also strikes me as a man who sees only what he wants to see.' Perhaps that was the best way to be. If a man went digging, he was bound to find corpses. He suspected that Ptolemy's threats to tell what he knew had been his undoing. How that undoing had come about, and who had given the order, was another reason to tread very carefully in this land.

23

Manor of Caversham, April 1219

Someone was playing an instrument in his chamber, a gittern like the one that Ptolemy had owned, but the notes fell more gently, like soft rain rather than Middle Eastern sun, and the voice was different with a higher pitch, clean and light. The person was singing a hymn in praise of the Virgin and the notes went straight from William's ears to his heart and filled him with a sweet, poignant longing.

Poor Ptolemy. The words formed on his lips but he did not use his voice because he did not want the musician to stop playing. Heraclius had given Ptolemy a Christian burial and the truth about his demise, whatever it was, had been kept silent and hidden away in the places where all such secrets were concealed. Prayers had been said for the young musician at the Sepulchre, and candles lit. So many darknesses in the palaces of light. So many heavy secrets taken to the grave.

William drifted on a sea of exquisite sound. A new musician had taken Ptolemy's place – another young lad, fair-haired and freckled, but with a very different air about him, and it was plain from the outset that he was never going to win the lady's favour and patronage. That brightness had been quenched.

24

Royal Palace of the King of Jerusalem, May 1184

'So,' said King Baldwin, 'I understand you have moved your quarters to the Patriarch's palace and are acting as marshal in charge of his stables.' His voice was hoarse and a trifle slurred, a result of his advancing leprosy. He was sitting on his cushioned chair, his customary light veil draped over his face. Long tables had been set out in the hall with food for all and people were mingling and talking, mostly about the forthcoming expedition to England and France. William had been summoned to give his own progress report to the King.

'Yes, sire.'

Baldwin signalled, and a servant assisted him to drink from a cup of watered wine. 'But you have not sworn your allegiance to him?' The question was sharp.

'No, sire,' William replied. 'He has not asked it, but he deems it more convenient for discussions if I am under his roof.'

'And you agreed?'

'Yes, sire. My allegiance is to my lord King Henry, but I said I would do all I could to assist the Patriarch in preparing his deputation.'

Baldwin nodded. 'We all pray that it comes to a good outcome.'

'Indeed, sire.'

William hoped Baldwin would not ask him if he believed it would, although a certain nuance in the ailing King's voice told him that he was holding to his course while being grimly aware of the rocks beneath. One of those rocks was present now in the form of Guy de Lusignan. Since the matter of annulling his marriage to the Princess Sybilla had been deferred until at least the return of the envoys, he had gradually returned to court, and an uneasy truce lay between the men. They were civil to each other, with wary caution on both sides, and Baldwin had made it clear that while he would tolerate Guy if he must, he was to have no say in the rule of the kingdom. Even so, Guy was making his presence felt, exerting his charm, wearing magnificent tactile fabrics, showing how whole and manly he was, and being especially solicitous of Sybilla and his little stepson.

'You strike me as someone who is not easily influenced or duped,' Baldwin said.

'I hope I am not, sire,' William replied, avoiding the thought of what had happened in Constantinople.

'I do not see well, and you know the limitations of my limbs. I cover my face to disguise my ravaged appearance. My body is weary and this disease devours a little more of me day by day.' He thumped his breast with his bandaged hand. 'But inside, in here, I am strong. In here I am steel. But do they know it?' He extended a knuckled stump outwards to his courtiers. 'Or would they rather follow that which is fair, but in the end has nothing to sustain them? You are still on the outskirts, tell me what you think.'

William cleared his throat. 'Sire, there are those who will always be drawn in by appearances and golden words, but many are not so easily swayed. You must use your own judgement and not be distracted from your path by how others choose to walk theirs.'

'I am not dead yet,' Baldwin said softly, 'and he shall acknowledge that.'

He spoke more to himself than William, who murmured assent and then bowed from the King's presence as Raymond of Tripoli arrived to speak with him.

Heading toward the banquet table, avoiding Guy but intent on finding something to eat, William paused at a touch on his arm and, turning, found himself face to face with the lady Paschia. He was immediately wary because of what had happened in the Patriarch's garden ten days ago. Since then he had only seen her from a distance because she had either kept to her own chambers or had been attending on the Countess Sybilla. And in truth he had been avoiding her too.

'Messire Marshal,' she said, 'you have been most elusive.'

'I have been about my duties, madam,' he replied, bowing. 'I did not know you had been seeking me.'

'I wanted to thank you for your care when I was shocked and grieving. I am in your debt, for there is much ambition and very little kindness at court these days.'

Once more William felt the frisson of crossing the line from safety onto perilous ground.' Her earrings were set with rubies tonight and they caught the candle light like red sparks.

'I was glad to be of service, madam, and very sorry to learn of the death of your musician.'

'Indeed, a terrible thing. I have had many masses said for his soul. It may have seemed nothing to you, but you were a great comfort. I am grateful, and I do not forget.'

William bowed and said nothing, and silence hung between them until she raised her chin and changed both the subject and her manner, putting on the smile of a courtly hostess donning a mask. 'So, tell me, messire,' she said brightly, 'what do you think of the court now you have had time to settle in and observe us about our business?'

'I think it surpasses many a court in England and France,' he replied tactfully.

'In what way?'

'In its sophistication, in the wealth and knowledge of those who frequent it. In its taste and fine manners and richness of apparel.'

She considered him shrewdly. 'And what advantage do other courts have above ours? There must be some.'

'Perhaps there is more plain speaking,' he said, 'or at least men come more swiftly to it. Sometimes less embellishment helps one to see more clearly. A magnificent sword scabbard does not always house the best sword for war.' He deliberately avoided looking at Guy de Lusignan. 'In many ways, the courts are similar. Each person plays to his or her advantage and makes allies of those who support that advantage.'

'And what do you see as your advantage, sire?'

They had reached the banqueting board and William offered her a platter of almond and sugar sweetmeats. 'That I am an outsider,' he said. 'That is not always a good thing, but it enables me to observe, as you have said. My skills with lance and sword and my knowledge of horsemanship are sought by many, so I have plenty of opportunities.' He nodded toward a man who was deep in conversation with Heraclius. 'That baron was at the stables earlier today. He desires two horses from the Patriarch because he says his own are growing long in the tooth and he cannot patrol his domain without better animals. So, I will find two such horses and my lord Heraclius will bestow them as gifts and I will advise on their value.'

'Indeed, then you do have many advantages, as you say.' She bit into an almond sweetmeat and nibbled it daintily. William ate one himself, followed by a small delicious tart stuffed with minced dates. She wanted to know his impressions of this man and that in the room, and he obliged her with short assessments. 'And the Count of Jaffa?' she asked. 'What is your opinion of him?'

William wondered if she was trying to catch him out, or genuinely seeking his opinion. Since she was a close companion of de Lusignan's wife and he had often seen her in Guy's company too, he needed to be careful. 'I think he is a man of prowess,' he said neutrally.

'And a worthy contender?'

'As many are, madam.'

'But they are not kin to the heirs of Jerusalem.'

'Indeed not.'

She gave him a thoughtful look. 'Many men become great by marriage in Outremer. Do you have a wife at home, messire Marshal?'

William shook his head. 'No, madam; I am unwed.'

'I thought so.' Her tone became lightly teasing. 'Well then, that might make for many an interesting conversation, do you not think?'

She was clearly speaking of rewarding him, perhaps with an arranged marriage to an heiress of rank, but William wondered at her motive, suspecting that she wanted to weld him to her own allegiance, which was to the Lusignan cause. He fixed her with a direct, firm gaze, devoid of the courtly game of flirtation. 'Mayhap not, for I will find my own bride when the time is right – and of my own intent.'

She smiled, but with an edge now. 'I can tell that you are a man of decision, and I like that, but you should think on the benefits that might come to you should you choose one path over another.'

William bowed. 'Indeed, I shall think on it, my lady, but please do not feel you have to pay my future any special attention – I can manage for myself.'

She raised her brows. 'I daresay you can, messire, but without my help how far do you think you would have come by now?' She laid her hand on his wrist so that her nails lightly dug into his skin. 'A word of timely warning: do not be hasty to dismiss friendship when it is offered, for a man isolated is a man easily picked off or ignored.' She released him and walked away to join the group of courtiers standing around Guy de Lusignan. Her patterned silk gown emphasised the sway of her hips. The red earrings twinkled. He realised that she was not a younger version of Queen Alienor at all but a beautiful, ambitious seductress, politically adept, intriguing and highly dangerous, not least because she had unbalanced his certainty in himself. She was right about how isolated he was.

When he took his leave, she neither looked at him nor bade him farewell, but he could feel the intensity of her focus like an invisible cord between them. He looked over his shoulder and she met his eyes with a single challenging glance before deliberately turning her back and continuing with her conversation.

A few days later Heraclius was in the stable yard, inspecting a new saddle William was making for him in preparation for the leaving parade eight weeks hence. Of sumptuous green leather, padded and carved, it was comfortable too. Heraclius expressed his pleasure at how swiftly and competently the work had been done, and prepared to go on his way, but then touched his forehead. 'I almost forgot. Madam de Riveri wishes to see you and I said I would tell you to call upon her.'

William's chest tightened. 'Certainly, sire,' he replied. 'Do you know why my lady wishes to see me – so that I may be prepared?' Ever since the meeting at the palace he had avoided her, although he had been acutely aware of her presence when eating in the hall with his men, or attending mass in the Sepulchre. If not with Heraclius, she was usually in the company of the Count and Countess of Jaffa.

Heraclius waved his hand. 'Her husband was a draper and her family retain connections with that trade. Mostly they deal in silk, but she desires me to bring some English cloth for her when I return.'

William was puzzled. 'Sire, I do not understand how I may be of service then. If my lady was asking me about swords or harness then I could help, but I know nothing of fabric.'

Heraclius looked amused. 'But you have been close to the court and you know the suppliers – the names of the men who provide the cloths. Whether you are able to help or not remains to be seen, but I counsel you never to deny a woman's will –

although I am sure you are wise enough to know that yourself. She expects you as soon as you may, so do not keep her waiting. Ah, Guy!' Heraclius turned as de Lusignan strolled up. 'I was just coming to see you.'

Guy smiled lazily. 'Yes, I was wondering where you had got to.' His sharp blue eyes flicked over William.

'Just finishing arrangements for my new saddle.' Heraclius gestured to the item. 'See how fine it is.'

'Indeed,' Guy said. 'Perhaps you could make one for me, Marshal?'

'Perhaps, sire,' William replied in a noncommittal tone, knowing that hell would freeze over first.

'Well, we shall see. Who knows what the future will bring.'

Guy and the Patriarch went on their way together and William slowly unclenched his fists.

Ancel left the horse he had been attending to, wiping his hands on a cloth. 'What did de Lusignan want?'

William grimaced. 'To harness us to his cause,' he said.

Ancel snorted. 'That will never happen.'

'No. I have to go and see Madam de Riveri.'

'She wants to harness us to his cause too?' Ancel asked with innocent eyes.

'I do not doubt it; however, she says she wants advice on where to obtain goods from England.' William gave Ancel a bear-cuff. 'I will see you later.'

Ancel grinned. 'You might; then again you might not.'

'Then give Asmaria my greetings,' William retorted with good humour.

Ancel departed to finish his task and William went to wash and don clean garments. He was tense with anticipation. He wanted to see Madam de Riveri and talk with her, and at the same time he wished he was a hundred miles away on a fast horse. The latter was certainly the safer place to be.

The lady Paschia had her own domicile adjoining the palace

250

precincts, accessed by a door painted deep red and bound by ornate black ironwork. It was opened before William could knock by a doorkeeper, but to let out the lady's uncle, Zaccariah of Nablus, who was clutching several scrolls under one arm while twisting to secure his money pouch at his belt. He acknowledged William with a brusque nod, and a narrow look that told William his presence here had been marked.

The doorkeeper escorted him across cool tiles to a chamber with a marble floor glistening like mother of pearl and partially covered by a large rug woven in shades of red and gold. The lady Paschia sat at a fretwork table before an arched window. White doves pecked at crumbs on the sill and hangings of diaphanous bleached linen wafted in the breeze. Her cat lay at her feet, indolently flicking its tail and blinking sleepy green eyes. Incense twisted into the air from a brazier burning small lumps of resin and mingled with the perfume from a crystal ewer filled with roses.

She was dictating to a scribe who had been busy all morning judging by the numerous wax tablets piled up at his side. An ebony-skinned page boy was pouring wine into a cup from a glass flagon.

'You sent for me, madam?' William said.

Taking her time, she rose to her feet and told the scribe to go and make fair copies of what was written on the tablets. In the privacy of her own chamber she wore the lightest of silk veils, fine as cobweb, exposing her heavy black braids which were twined with golden ribbons. She gave an offhand wave. 'I daresay the Patriarch told you that I wanted your help in making some purchases.'

William tightened his lips, knowing she had deliberately manufactured this encounter and was playing with him. He had better things to do and contemplated turning on his heel, but that was possibly more dangerous than remaining. 'The Patriarch did tell me, but I do not see that I can help you – with all due respect, madam.'

'Then with all due respect you are wrong, messire.'

She stooped to a row of wicker cages set under the window occupied by cooing pigeons and removed one. It nestled into her cupped palm and she stroked it gently, the motion sensual, drawing attention to her elegant fingers. With dexterity she tied a small message strip to its leg before casting the bird from the window into the wide blue sky where it took off with a clap of swift grey wings. Her action emphasised the lines of her body – the taut waist, the graceful sweep of her arm before she turned back into the room and directed her page to pour more wine.

'I wish to know the names of drapers and mercers who can be contacted so that Heraclius may obtain good English cloth to bring home for me.' Her tone neutral now, business-like. 'I could ask him, but it will be easier if he knows who to contact and can send someone to deal with it. You have been at court and as a marshal you know the sources that your King uses. The same for English embroidery. Your homeland is famed for such work and I desire fine examples to bring to Jerusalem.' Sitting down again, she gestured for William to take the chair the scribe had vacated.

He did so, and watched her make notes on a wax tablet with the unthinking ease of second nature. He was unsettled, for he had never learned to read and write. He had been tutored but to no avail. Even the beatings had not made the words any clearer to his mind.

He gave her a few names, including that of the King's tailor who bought in cloth supplies for the royal garments, and she wrote them down. She then rested her stylus and looked at him. 'I know you think this a trivial thing, and one for which you have little time, but it will be of great use to me and my family – and that in its turn will benefit you. I meant what I said the other day: I admire a man who knows his own mind and is strong in his resolution. They are qualities that anyone would want to add to their affinity.'

She pushed a small pouch of gold bezants over to him. 'This is for you, in gratitude.'

William's body stiffened with tension as he sensed danger. He made no move to take the coins.

'Please,' she said. 'Your information is useful – it is not as if you are selling your soul, is it? Heraclius would want you to have it. Indeed, he would expect me to pay you.'

William looked at the bag of coins. He did not want to be beholden to her, but he and his men needed to eat and were dependent on largesse. This would go a long way to keeping the wolf from the door. Had Heraclius given him the money he would have taken it as his due. In a way the coin did belong to Heraclius, for she depended on him for her wealth and power. And yet she had overpaid him for that information and it was like setting a collar around his neck as she would a pet dog.

'Thank you,' he said woodenly, and took the pouch, feeling distinctly uncomfortable. 'Will that be all, my lady? I have to go and instruct my men about tomorrow.'

She gave him a long, evaluating look. He imagined what it would be like to kiss her mouth. To put her to the test.

'Yes,' she said, her wave as dismissive as that which had beckoned him inside. 'But do not go far because I may need to speak to you again later.'

So, she had lengthened the leash and given a small tug on the choke chain. And she knew exactly what she was doing and believed that he was under her leverage. Well, perhaps she played that game with others, but she would not play it with him.

He rose to leave. 'As you wish, madam,' he said, and, without a flicker of emotion, bowed and formally departed. He closed the door after him with quiet deliberation and walked away slowly, irritated and on edge, his body saturated with a dull heaviness of sexual tension. He had never encountered anyone like her before. She made him unsure of his ground, and that was a challenge. He wanted to seek beneath her surface and find what lay there, as if he had glimpsed a siren's jewels underwater, shimmering and beguiling, just out of reach, luring him to his doom.

The pouch of coins banged at his hip and reminded him of the time he had robbed the shrine at Rocamadour and received his wages from the Young King, and it made him feel a little sick. The moment he returned to his chamber he unfastened it and thrust it into a wall niche, concealed by the icon of the Virgin Mary he had bought in Constantinople.

The preparations for the departure of the envoys continued. The baggage train needed to be arranged for the journey and no expense spared because Heraclius knew the value of pomp and display. William advised him that King Henry was not a man for such ceremony but Heraclius would not be dissuaded, because bejewelled garments and ceremony were his own natural preference.

'But your King will expect visiting dignitaries to make a fine presentation,' he objected when William tried to make his point one day in his chamber. 'I did not come to Outremer until I was in my fortieth year, and I was visiting Paris when I saw the envoys your King sent to Louis of France when he desired to make a match between his heir and Louis's daughter. Never unto this day have I witnessed a parade of such splendour. Cart after cart pulled by matching horses, brimming with the treasures of England, and every man in scarlet livery. There were even monkeys sitting on the horses – so do not tell me that your King does not appreciate the advantage of putting on a fine display!'

Despite the criticism, William smiled. 'Indeed, sire. My father was responsible for assembling both horses and monkeys and for keeping order of the entire menagerie until it crossed the Narrow Sea. I begged him to let me have a monkey, but he said that he had enough trouble in his household already without adding that sort of mayhem to his chamber.'

Heraclius grunted with amusement, but was not moved to alter his intention.

'King Henry was a very young man at that time and since then he has sobered and become more careful of his largesse,' William said. 'He values plain speaking above embellishment.'

Heraclius frowned, clearly unconvinced. 'I am the Patriarch of Jerusalem,' he said, 'and I must present myself in a manner fitting my position. I am sure the King of England will appreciate this.' He indicated several enormous keys gleaming on the table at his side. 'These are for the gates of Jerusalem, for the church of the Holy Sepulchre, and the Tower of David. Replicas of course, but they symbolise the great honour, responsibility and power that a king would take up in accepting them. I shall present them to him with my plea.'

'I think he will appreciate that gesture,' William said. Reaching inside his tunic, he removed a folded parchment map. 'Sire, this was given to me by the Templars when I set out from England. Perhaps it may be of use to you on your journey.'

Heraclius took it from him, opened it out and read it with interest, tracing the cities marked and the notes written by a scribe. 'This is very fine calligraphy,' he said, and called other members of his household over to view the length of parchment. His finger stopped on one of the cities and he raised his brows at William. 'Constantinople?'

William made a wry face. 'In hindsight, sire, our road would not have led us that way either.' He made a conscious effort not to look at his arm.

The door opened and the lady Paschia arrived with her women. Servants followed bearing food and drink. Her gown of flame-coloured silk shimmered as she walked, and her hair was twisted in individual ringlets that fell to her waist. She looked utterly ravishing. William made to leave and return to his duties with the horses, but Heraclius bade him take some wine first and called Paschia over to look at the map.

She gave William a smile and a sultry glance before leaning over Heraclius to study it. 'Indeed, it is fine penmanship.' She traced her forefinger slowly from city to city. 'I can see that it is well travelled.'

'Yes, madam. It . . . was given to me at the Temple Church in London and we used it for much of the way.' He inhaled an intoxicating scent of roses and musk from a swinging lock of her hair.

'I am sure that the Patriarch will be able to make great use of it. It is kind of you.'

'Indeed so,' Heraclius replied. 'I thank you with true gratitude.'

'I am glad to be of service,' William replied. 'By your leave, I must return to my duties.'

'By all means. I know you still have much to do . . . and do not worry. I shall not ask you for monkeys.'

William's lips twitched. 'I am glad to hear it, your eminence.' He made his obeisance and went to the door.

The lady Paschia insisted on seeing him out. 'Monkeys?' She arched her brow.

'We were discussing an occasion when King Henry sent envoys and monkeys to the King of France,' he replied neutrally. 'Doubtless the Patriarch will tell you.'

'Doubtless he will.' She gave him an amused, slightly exasperated look. 'We shall see you later perhaps.'

William made his bow serve as a reply and took his leave. Returning to his duties he was preoccupied. The way she had leaned over Heraclius and used her finger in that sensual way to trace over the map had sent a lightning bolt of arousal through him. She had known exactly what she was doing in the same way she had known when she looked at him with slumberous knowing. He was being hunted down and did not know whether to run, fight back, or surrender.

Since William had to attend on Heraclius most days, he continued to come into frequent contact with the lady Paschia, but he tried to ensure there were always others around at the same time and he dwelt in constant anticipation and dread of another personal summons from her – although none materialised.

When Paschia was with Heraclius she was devoted to him and solicitous of his well-being. She ensured that refreshment was always to hand and placed comfortable cushions at his back. She was quietly efficient in the background, but swift to come forward at need and play the gracious hostess. She threw herself whole-heartedly into the preparation for his mission and made it clear that her life's purpose was satisfying him and seeing to his welfare. She was affectionate, kissing his cheek, holding his hand, protecting him when he needed a quiet moment – playing her role to the hilt.

If people considered her actions inappropriate or condemned him for a worldly prelate, they said nothing in public even if eyebrows were raised behind closed doors. Everyone knew that the lady had powerful connections and that her influence was far-reaching, and depending on one's faction could either be a safety net or a pernicious web.

In public, Paschia would often slant William looks, reminding him of the power she wielded. In conversation, she was cour-teous and witty. Sometimes she would play chess with him and William greatly enjoyed these sessions even while he knew he was dancing with fire. It was a chance to test each other's mettle and probe for weaknesses, and at the same time in juxtaposition to build a rapport. The safety net and the web. Her play was keen and her ruthless business sense fully to the fore, although again, in paradox, she was mercurial and prepared to take enor-mous gambles if she thought they would pay off, and in doing so she continued to keep him off balance. They won and lost an equal number of games, but she would always leave the table at a point when she was victorious; and she would look at him and smile.

One day she showed him her pigeons, explaining how the messages were attached to their legs and how they were sent to specific lofts elsewhere in order to speed the carrying of information. Such a system could be adapted for use in King Henry's domains and William was keenly interested.

'But some must fall to hawks,' he said.

'Indeed, that is why we always send more than one – and sometimes decoys if we suspect we are going to be intercepted. The Patriarch has delegated the task to me because he knows I work well with the birds and can be trusted.'

William remembered the pigeons he had seen winging their way toward Ascalon from the King's camp at Caesarea back in January. The red curtain in the Patriarch's tent and the listening silence behind it. So many secrets and conspiracies.

A few days later Heraclius asked William to find Paschia a new mount. 'Her grey is heavily in foal,' he said, 'and my lady can no longer ride her. She will have duties while I am absent that will require her to ride out. I need a good horse of sound temperament and suitable disposition. I leave it in your hands to find the right beast, and do not stint on the cost.'

'Oh!' Paschia gasped as she stared at the palfrey William was holding in the stable yard. Her eyes alight, her expression that of a delighted child, she hurried to his side. 'What a beauty!' She looked round at Heraclius who was standing with his arms folded, a smile on his lips. 'Truly for me?'

Heraclius said indulgently. 'For who else would I have gone to such trouble? I sent William here to the Bedouin to find you a mount and he has done us proud.'

'Indeed, more than that!' She bestowed on William a smile as bright as the sun and his heart somersaulted within his chest. He had groomed Rakkas until his hide shone like a bronze mirror reflecting a dark pool. He had combed and braided his lighter mane and flame cascade of tail and harnessed him with a bridle and a ladies' saddle of embossed red leather that Heraclius had ordered several weeks ago.

She ran back to Heraclius and stood on tip-toe to kiss his cheek. 'Thank you, thank you! I want to try him – now!' She twirled, laughing like a child, her face radiant and joyous.

William had never seen her like this before, and it was a revelation that stunned him.

'And so you shall, my dear,' Heraclius said indulgently, 'but I have business to attend to. Messire Marshal will escort you and I shall speak with you later.'

William had other duties waiting too, but had no choice but to comply with the Patriarch's order. He let Paschia feed the gelding two plump brown dates and then led him to the mounting block and assisted her to the saddle, which she gained with ease, her hands confident on the reins. William sent Eustace to saddle Chazur and swiftly organised his knights to fetch their horses and provide a mounted escort. Several of Heraclius's own men joined them, including Paschia's uncle Zaccariah and the mercenary Mahzun of Tyre. William was deliberately courteous toward them, and they responded in a similar wise, but an atmosphere of bristling watchfulness verging on hostility prevailed, like dogs circling each other's territory.

Leaving the Patriarch's palace, the group rode toward St Stephen's Gate and the leper hospice on the western side of the city, intent on following a circuit of the walls. Paschia's new mount responded to her lightest touch of rein and heel, and was curious but little bothered by the crowds and the cries of the beggars and hucksters they encountered on their way out of the city.

'Make way!' bellowed Mahzun of Tyre in his huge voice. 'Make way for the Lady Heraclius!'

She smiled and threw handfuls of coins into the crowd from the generous pouch with which Heraclius had presented her, and she made gracious flourishes, like a queen. William was fascinated by her power – how much she had and yet how little because it was all dependent on the Patriarch. But he admired how well she used it.

'This is a beautiful horse,' she said to William as they rode out of the gates and turned eastward toward the Postern of the Magdalene. 'You truly do have a skill.'

'I learned almost from birth,' he replied, 'but the Bedouin have the finest mounts I have ever seen. Most are too lightly built to be destriers, but as palfreys and chasers they have no compare.'

'He is like his name. He dances.' She touched him lightly with her spur and the horse sprang into a bouncing trot. Then she reined him down again and looked at William. 'You know Heraclius pays the nomads for information.'

William returned her look blandly.

'I am not giving away any secrets,' she said with a glint of impatience. 'You must already have guessed as much.'

'Yes, my lady,' William said, wondering if he was being further tested for his prudence, and what the implications were.

'Mostly it comes to naught, but they travel far and wide and they trade with everyone. They take word to Saladin about our movements, but in the same wise they will feed Saladin's intent back to us, so it behoves us to keep them as our allies. Everyone has his use . . . and his price. The trick is to know what that price is.' She gave him a loaded look.

William maintained a neutral expression. 'That is true to an extent, but some prices are too high to be paid and there are some who would rather die than be bought.'

Paschia's uncle interrupted from behind, his tone grating and harsh. 'Then you persuade the first to lower his price, and you arrange for the second to have his wish. That is the way business is conducted in this land.'

William looked round to meet Zaccariah's cold, dark eyes and experienced a fresh surge of antipathy for the man. 'So I have observed, sire, and I would fill my own entourage with honourable men of the second persuasion and discard the rest.'

'You have high ideals, messire.' Paschia's gaze was speculative. 'But perhaps they have never been put to the test?'

'As far as I have been tested, I have striven to remain true,' he replied. 'And I maintain that is so for my men also.'

She nodded, as if accepting a challenge, and urged her new mount along the path until they came to dusty open ground not far from the Stable Postern on the Temple Mount.

A group of soldiers was training on the sun-burned field, practising charging in formation and executing skilled lance work. 'See, messire Marshal,' she said with humour and asperity, 'you and your knights are not the only accomplished warriors in the Kingdom of Jerusalem.'

'I am glad that is so, my lady, for where would the kingdom be without its skilled warriors?' Watching the men, he recognised one of the foremost fighters, confidently arrogant in the saddle, and compressed his lips, knowing that she had deliberately ridden this way in order to bring him to Guy de Lusignan and his household knights at their training.

'Where indeed?' She drew rein to watch, making no attempt to ride on. After a hard-fought skirmish, which de Lusignan won with panache and brutality, the knights paused to regroup and Guy removed his helm, turned his horse and trotted over to the observers.

His red face and sweat-streaked exertion made his eyes dazzle like chips of blue ice. Sweat hung like rain drops in his tangled hair. Once greetings had been exchanged, he admired Rakkas, although he did not dismount to look at him, and on hearing about William's part in his selection, he gave a supercilious smile. 'You always were a good horse trader, Marshal. Perhaps we could discuss your talents at some point. And I'm still waiting for that saddle.' Without waiting for an answer, he turned to Paschia, the angle of his shoulder dismissing William as a hireling of no consequence. 'I would invite your men to join us, but I can see they have escort duties, and we are finishing soon before the heat becomes too great. Another time, I would value their company and expertise.'

'By all means, sire,' she replied. 'Indeed, they would welcome such an opportunity to practise and learn from you.'

Guy spun his stallion, making it caracole, and then galloped back to his troop. Striving not to grind his teeth, William acknowledged that Guy knew how to make a good display. In looks, in outward trappings, he had always been a king, but it was a hollow construct.

'I hope you were impressed by what you saw.' Her voice held challenge as they made to ride on.

'It will keep the wolf from the door,' William replied, stiff-lipped and struggling with his courtesy.

She arched one eyebrow. 'You would do it better, messire?'

William made a back-and-forth motion with his hand, suggesting possibly.

'But even so you would need someone as an overall commander to follow, someone to give you order and direction.'

William looked down at his reins and said nothing, doing his best to be diplomatic, but it was not enough and she saw through him.

'Why would you not?' she demanded. 'Admit it. The Count of Jaffa is competent and he shows a good display.'

William wanted to say 'But what happens when he is tested?' but he bit his tongue and raised his head to her. 'I have nothing against him if you desire my opinion, but I would not follow in his train because he is not a man for whom I would give my life.'

Two frown lines appeared between her brows. 'You do set your mark very high – or perhaps lower than I had thought.'

'That is for you to decide, madam. I can only give you my honest opinion.'

They rode in silence for a while, but within a charged atmosphere, like two opponents who were not enemies, but each intent on mastery.

'Perhaps you would consider attending a meal tomorrow with

the Patriarch. The Count of Jaffa will be there and you can engage at closer quarters and gain a different insight.'

Her persistence was backing him into a corner.

'I do not think so, my lady,' he said firmly.

She sat up straighter, a glint in her eyes. 'Do you not indeed?'

He sighed, concluding that being straightforward would serve him better than this tortured diplomacy. 'Madam, I have been at close quarters with this man in the past and we were not allies then. I have no wish to be any nearer to him than I am now. I will never follow such a man and therefore courteous avoidance is my best choice.'

She stared at him, wide-eyed now and clearly taken aback. Heraclius had warned him that she was seldom denied anything she desired.

'He is not the man to lead Jerusalem,' William continued. 'You need someone stronger for the task. I would lay down my life for every one of my own knights, but I would not do so for the Count of Jaffa because I do not hold him in the same esteem.'

'You are mistaken,' she said, her eyes narrow with anger. 'He is the one man who could unite Jerusalem with the right kind of support. I hoped you might be one of those who would have the vision to give it.'

William stood his ground. 'Madam, Jerusalem is united behind King Baldwin, and very soon the Patriarch and the Grand Masters will leave for Spain and France and England to seek aid from the kings there. Let the Count of Jaffa support such men as well as he is able, and that will be my undertaking too – and as such we shall be allies, if not bosom companions.'

She tossed her head and looked away, and they rode the rest of the way in silence until they reached the palace and he helped her to dismount. Mahzun of Tyre departed to other business. Her uncle lingered, scowling, until she dismissed him with a peremptory wave. 'I will be but a moment,' she said. 'I want to see Rakkas settled.'

He raised one eyebrow, gave William a pointed look, and left.

She fussed the horse, feeding him more dates, kissing his muzzle. 'I have never met anyone like you,' she said after a moment. 'So principled, so stubborn, some might even say pig-headed – to your own detriment.' She scratched the whorled-star marking between the horse's eyes.

'What they say is up to them,' William replied. 'I can only follow my own truth.' He brought a rope halter to replace the gelding's ornate bridle.

'You could make your life here you know. You could be a great lord with a fief of your own and lands and status to your name. You could give wealth to your followers – to that brother of yours. We are short of fighting men of your calibre.'

'Madam, I am sworn to return to England and Normandy,' he said doggedly.

She gave a short laugh. 'For what? A life as a hearth knight? Here you would be vouchsafed a greater future, perhaps even a magnificent one.'

William shook his head. 'I do not understand why it should matter to you.'

'Do you not?'

He was caught in a full and candid stare that left nothing in doubt. Her hand grazed his as he started to remove the bridle and replace it with the halter.

'Perhaps you are blind as well as pig-headed.'

Pivoting on her dainty leather shoe, she stalked off in the direction her uncle had taken. William watched the sway of her body and fought the urge to go after her, spin her around and show her exactly what she was playing with. But then, lips compressed, he turned away to deal with the horse.

He knew that the sensible thing to do was to leave Heraclius's employ forthwith and swear himself to the Templars as a secular knight for the duration of his stay; perhaps even request that they send him to Acre or Caesarea. Yet, to walk away now would be like walking off a chess board in mid-game. Besides, her patronage would cease, and if she chose she could do him and his men untold damage in the same way that she had favoured him. Whichever way he moved, he was challenged.

Ancel returned from stabling his own horse, Pilgrim trotting at his heels. 'What's wrong, Gwim?' he asked, slapping him on the back.

William shook his head. 'Nothing.'

'Did Madame la Patriarchess like her new horse? She was smiling when I saw her a moment ago.'

Ancel's question was innocent, but for William it bore a double meaning. He had no intention of being saddled and controlled by her. 'Yes,' he said. 'She did.'

'Then what's wrong?'

'Nothing, I told you. I have no love for Guy de Lusignan, and riding out to watch him parade around like a king might not be my notion of time well spent.'

'I suppose not,' Ancel said with a shrug. He rumpled his hand through his hair. 'I am going to visit Asmaria. Come with me and have a drink.'

William started to refuse and then changed his mind. 'Why not?' he said.

Leaving the yard, he accompanied Ancel to the small house at the end of Malquisnet Street. Asmaria greeted Ancel warmly with a kiss on the cheek and curtseyed clumsily to William, her face red from her toil over the fire. However, she swiftly overcame her embarrassment and set about pouring the men wine and putting oil, bread and salt on the board for them. The children came forward and were introduced to William – a boy of six and a girl of four. The latter clambered confidently onto Ancel's lap and hugged him while her brother brought his new small bow and set of six arrows to show to Ancel.

The atmosphere of relaxed warmth enfolded William. Asmaria's dwelling was humble with one room and a ladder up to the roof, but it was swept and cared for with pride and just now it was more welcoming than any palace. The wine was plain but excellent, as were the bread and olives. He understood why Ancel preferred to spend his off-duty time here rather than in the Patriarch's guardroom. Here was comfort and acceptance; the sense that he could stretch his legs, unfasten his belt and belong. He was pleased for Ancel, and perhaps a little envious.

Having finished his wine, he took his leave, and bowed to Asmaria with the same respect he afforded the ladies of the court. 'Thank you for your hospitality, and thank you for looking after my brother.'

She beamed at him. 'No, sire,' she said. 'He looks after me.'

'We look after each other.' Ancel squeezed her hand.

Refreshed, William strolled back to the palace. The time he had just spent with Ancel and his woman was far superior to banqueting with the likes of Guy de Lusignan and nothing would ever change his mind on that score.

25

Manor of Caversham, April 1219

William woke to talons of pain stabbing his chest and belly and he clenched his teeth to endure the agony and not cry out. For his pride. So as not to burden and alarm those who cared for him.

'Hush.' The voice was a whisper, tender and soft. Gentle fingers smoothed his brow. 'Hush now. All will be well.' A soft kiss at his temple. 'I always loved you . . .'

He twisted on the edge of pure agony, and somewhere, deep within him, deep as the talons, caught on the hooked tips, he knew that love came in many guises, some of them cruel and terrible.

'Papa? Here, drink this.'

The rim of a cup touched his lips and he tasted the bitter poppy tincture that brought the vivid dreams and took away the talons even though he knew they were still embedded in him. He saw the sweep of long fair hair twined with red ribbons. 'Ysabel?' he whispered. He had almost expected the hair to be as black and thick as a starless night, not his daughter's soft wheat-gold.

'I should fetch the physician.' Her eyes were concerned as she withdrew the cup and set it on the bedside coffer.

William shook his head and took her hand. 'You do me more good than any physician. Stay a while and comfort me.'

She acquiesced, and as he forced a smile, he saw her do the same. She had her mother's beauty and like all of their offspring she was courageous and true.

She fussed with the bedclothes, smoothing and patting. 'The time was when you used to tuck me up in bed and protect me from all harm. I always knew I was safe and loved and that nothing could hurt me.'

'And now you are doing the same for me.'

'But you are in pain, Papa; I wish I could take it away.'

'You ease it with your comfort and presence. Come, no tears.' He lifted his knuckles and gently brushed her cheek. 'I would not have you weep.'

She sniffed and smiled again for him, and the light from the window shone on her fair twists of hair, making a nimbus around the crown of her head.

'There,' he said. 'Sunshine through rain.' The talons were relinquishing their grip as the poppy syrup took effect. His eyelids began to droop.

'Before you spoke my name, you said another.'

'Did I?'

She picked up her sewing. 'Who is Paschia?'

He forced open his heavy lids as the name caused a sluggish jolt through his body. 'It was long ago in Outremer. Many years ago. I thought I had made my peace, but strands still remain to be woven and cut off.' He gave her a weary smile. 'Now I have you, I have your mother, and your sisters and brothers. I never believed I would be so blessed and fulfilled. You hold my heart and it overflows. That is all you need to know.'

He closed his eyes and heard her gasp as she stifled a sob, but was unable to reach out to her because the drugged wine was taking him down and the soft voice was saying again that all she had ever wanted was love; that she had never intended what had happened . . .

26

Jerusalem, July 1184

On a hot morning in mid-July, the Patriarch and the Grand Masters of the Templars and Hospitallers departed on their great mission to the princes of France and England. The previous day Heraclius had performed the ritual procession around the outside of the city to mark the triumphant taking of Jerusalem by Christian armies more than eighty years since, and preached an eloquent sermon before a wooden cross marking the place where the troops had breached the city walls. Everyone in Jerusalem had taken part amid prayers and rejoicing. A great banquet had been held in the patriarchal palace, spilling out into gardens and courtyards in order to accommodate the numerous guests. William had been on duty, his marshal's experience being invaluable for organising so many people, including those who would have preferred not to keep each other's company.

Today, William rode among the soldiers of the Patriarch's household. Garbed in white robes glittering with silver and gold embroidery, escorted by the staff of the True Cross, Heraclius and the Grand Masters of the Templars and Hospitallers rode to the Gate of David to take their leave. As with yesterday's procession almost the entire city was present, including the King borne on his painted litter – although suffering, determined to play his full role.

Once more Heraclius addressed the crowd, taking into his hand from a silk cushion the keys of Jerusalem and the Sepulchre and holding them aloft. 'I bear these keys of our most sacred city and church to offer up to King Henry of England and to King Philippe of France and entreat them to come to our aid and succour!' he cried. 'I hope to return as soon as God wills with joyful tidings and all the succour and support our belea-guered land requires. I entreat you all to be of good cheer until our return and keep your hearts and courage stalwart. Support your King in every endeavour to keep the kingdom safe and serve God faithfully.'

Following more prayers and speeches, the cavalcade finally set out on its way with rippling banners and bright garments, glossy horses, and carts piled with gifts. It would take the proud array four days to reach Acre, and from there they would embark for Brindisi, and then to Rome for an audience with the Pope.

William and his knights returned to the city, now escorting the King who was deep in conversation with Raymond of Tripoli. In another litter the Countess of Jaffa rode with her son, the little king. And behind them came Guy de Lusignan, talking to the Templar Gerard de Ridefort who was to take over as acting head of the order while Grand Master Arnold de Torroja was absent on his mission. William had yet to make up his mind about de Ridefort. He was proud and autocratic, but seemed honourable enough. William had not had time to talk to Onri about him, but intended to on their next patrol.

The lady Paschia rode on Rakkas not far from the Count of Jaffa's entourage with her uncle Zaccariah and his dark-haired squire, Alessandro, acting as her chaperones. Her head was bowed and her attitude modest and discreet. She had bidden farewell to Heraclius in the palace earlier with fervent kisses and tearful entreaties that he return safely to her, and Heraclius had tipped her chin with his finger and promised he would do so if ever he could.

'Make sure that you do,' she had said, swallowing tearfully, 'because if you do not, I shall be lost.'

William had thought it a pretty show. Her words, although

they sounded bereft, were also the pragmatic truth. Without Heraclius's wealth and protection she would be thrown back on her own resources, and they would never amount to the privilege and power of her present position.

She had ridden in procession on the road for their leave-taking, but not at his side, and her garb had been rich but understated and plain. A good and modest wife bidding farewell to her dear lord. And the same on her return to the city – eyes lowered, her aspect almost that of a nun. William glanced at her several times, but she neither looked up nor acknowledged his presence.

William attended to stabling the horses. He helped Paschia to dismount and took Rakkas for her. She thanked him modestly and with folded hands and downcast eyes departed to her dwelling with Zoraya and her attendants. William saw to the palfrey himself rather than leave it to a groom. It always soothed him to perform such tasks. To disengage from human and political social battles for a while and just enjoy the sweet hay-scented breath and nudges of a contented, glossy horse.

Hearing a soft sound behind him, he turned to discover Paschia standing in the stable doorway. The clothes of the modest widow had been replaced by those of the courtesan. The red silk gown clung to her figure from breast to hip and then flared out around her feet. A large golden tassel decorated the end of her belt. Her hair was covered by a light veil but her braids hung below it, loosely plaited. The scent of spice and roses emanated from her skin. Around her neck, on a red silk cord, dangled a small but ornate door key. He had glimpsed her wearing the key before, but she was touching it now, and drawing his gaze to it deliberately.

'Madam?' He had to swallow for his own throat was as dry as dust.

'Leave the horse to the grooms,' she said. 'Come, I have something to show you. It is important,' she added when he hesitated.

He wondered what could be so important just a short while

271

from Heraclius's departure. Surely whatever it was could be dealt with by her uncle. He could almost taste the danger and suspected that if he took but one step, his fate would be sealed. 'Then I am at your service, madam,' he heard himself croak.

She gave him a sultry look and her gaze flicked over him from head to toe. 'Indeed, I hope you are.'

She led him down the steps and brought him to the Patriarch's domestic private chapel. Many of the fittings had departed with Heraclius on his mission, but a pair of candlesticks stood on the small altar along with a gilded cross set with pearls and garnets. The walls were painted with glorious frescoes detailing the life of Christ and the air was heavy with the scent of incense.

Going over to a heavy red and gold curtain hanging against one wall, Paschia hooked it to one side, revealing a small door scrolled in wrought iron. She took the key from around her neck and set it in the lock. 'Few people know this is here,' she said. 'And the only keys are mine.' She opened the door on to a narrow spiral staircase.

'Go on up,' she commanded.

William did so, his whole body alert with an awareness of danger. The treads were almost too shallow for his feet, and the light was like the world at dusk, although growing brighter as he climbed. Behind him, he heard Paschia locking the door.

At the top of the steps another wrought-iron door stood open to provide light for the stairs and led into a small domed chamber. A bed stood in the centre of the room, made up with an embroidered quilt and many colourful cushions. The sun shone rays of light through the high windows like the spokes of a wheel and above and below the walls gleamed with mosaic in vibrant colours. The room was only large enough for the bed, and a simple table on which stood a jug and a dish of swirled glass holding grapes. A plinth ran all the way around the edge of the room and there were cushions on it, small glass phials and ornaments.

Paschia stepped in behind him and quietly shut the door, then leaned her back against it. 'This is mine,' she said. 'To do with as I wish, and to have as my desire. It is my payment and my consolation for everything.'

Her breathing was swift, her eyes wide, dark pools. William knew with all his being that he should not be here, yet she was between him and the door, and there were tiny beads of sweat on her brow, and that tender pulse beating in her throat.

'My lady, I . . .'

She moved then, and pulled him to her by the front of his tunic. 'I want to have you in my life,' she said fiercely. 'Never have I desired anything so much as to lie with you on that bed and take you and discover who you really are in truth. I would know you underneath your clothes. I would know you as a woman knows a man. All the courtly words, all the flourishes and gestures – it all comes down to this, doesn't it? I know you want me as much as I want you. You fight it, but why should you when I offer it to you freely?'

'I cannot . . .' he said. 'Heraclius—'

'Is not here.' A note of bitterness crept into her voice. 'I am a concubine. Heraclius bought my services from my husband for ten bags of gold bezants and I had no choice but to go down on my knees and serve God's vicar with my mouth. When my husband died, Heraclius offered me that position permanently. Oh yes, he rewards me with jewels and kindness – anything I want in return for what I do. But all that I have depends on his goodwill. I gave him no oath; I am not his wife, even if they call me "Madame la Patriarchess". I see the looks in their eyes and I know what they think I am worth.'

'And what of that goodwill now?' William asked hoarsely. 'Are you not afraid to lose it?'

She tightened her grip on him. 'He will never know. This chamber is a separate place that has no part in the world beyond that door – ever. To each one, the other does not exist. I want to share this with you – now.'

273

He would have to move her aside in order to stumble down the stairs to freedom. The danger, the knowledge that this was wrong, warred with intoxicating desire stronger than he had ever known. In showing him this room, she had led him to more than just a secret chamber. And now she was asking him 'Do you dare to do this?'

He put his hand on her shoulder, whether to stave her off or draw her in he did not know, but just the act of touching her, the feel of the thin silk under his fingers, was like a shock of heavy lightning through his bones. She stepped into his body, curling one arm round his neck and stroking her other hand firmly down between them, knowing exactly what she was doing. William gasped and caught her wrist. She undulated her hips.

'So,' she whispered, her mouth a fraction from his, 'what lies beyond your deeds of prowess in the tourney and your fine words as a courtier? Are you my match, or are you unequal to the task, my fine English knight?'

She parted her thighs a little and pushed her hips forward. William closed his eyes for one last moment of resistance and then broke and gave way. 'Perhaps you are not my match,' he said hoarsely, and stepped off the edge into the maelstrom.

Without quarter given, the bed became a boil of activity, like a cauldron set over a hot fire. She was lithe and sinuous, experienced and highly skilled. She knew exactly what she wanted and he was determined that she would have it, but in his own time and not to her dictates but his. They were creatures of a kind, strong-willed, fierce, ravenous, each determined to have the mastery. Riding him, tight as the coils of a serpent, she demanded to know if he was ready to yield, and William, damp with sweat, laughed and rolled her over in a wrestler's move so that she was pinned under him. 'Are you?' He held her still, hips flattened to hers while the moment settled. Her pupils were dilated, her body glistening, and all her wild hair unleashed around them like a dark sea. He was near the edge, so near, but it couldn't end yet, not like this. She returned his laugh and he felt it ripple through his body.

'Why?' She licked her lips. 'Do you lack the stamina? We have barely begun.'

Withdrawing from the fray, he went to pour a cup of wine from the flagon on the plinth, giving himself a respite. 'I lack no more stamina than you,' he said, striving not to sound too breathless. He offered her the cup, keeping it in his hand, and they exchanged slow kisses for wine. He dribbled the last of the cup over her body and leaned over her to lick it off with the point of his tongue, delicate as a cat, until she cried out, head thrown back, and clutched him, digging her nails into his arm as her body spasmed.

Panting, flushed, slick with sweat, her lips parted in a wild smile. 'Oh yes,' she said. 'I was not wrong about you.' With a sudden move she was out from under him, straddling him again, and now moving with an inexorable rhythm like the waves of an incoming tide. Now slow, now fast. 'Do you yield?' she demanded.

'Never!' he gasped, on the brink, but determined to hold out. 'But I would settle for a truce.'

'A truce?' She slowed down, circling her hips. 'Well now, that is an interesting proposition.' She caught one side of her lower lip provocatively in her teeth and shook back her hair. 'It has merits, I admit.' She stopped moving for a moment and it was almost his undoing, because now there was only one point of focus. 'A truce while terms are negotiated to mutual satisfaction perhaps?'

He tightened his stomach, and reached to her, languidly stroking.

'Very well,' she laughed breathlessly. 'I accept . . . acceptance is better than yielding, isn't it?'

He was beyond reply except for a brusque nod, every muscle straining and rigid. He rolled her over again in a sudden flurry and buried his face against her shoulder, letting go with a muffled sob of relief and pure pleasure while she wrapped her legs around him and clung and cried out a second time.

Eventually he found the strength to flop over onto his back, and recover his breath. She followed him, nuzzling up under his armpit, and kissed his chest. William gazed at the jewelled light shining down through the top of the dome, and then angled his head to look at her. It had been a long time since he had lain with a woman, and that had perhaps sharpened the sensations, but even so, he had never experienced anything so intense. It was like being taken by a storm tide, pulled far out of his depth to the point of drowning, and then being flung back onto a damp seashore in a sparkle of air and spray. A new seashore, with a different landscape, and although it was beautiful, it was not a safe place to be. And he too was changed – his horizons expanded somehow.

She smiled up at him, glistening like a mermaid. 'Well,' she said, 'as truces go that was very closely negotiated – on both sides, although perhaps I was lenient.'

He laughed and wound a strand of her hair around his fore-finger. 'Ah but I was giving you leeway.'

'Is that so?' She curved her leg over his thigh. 'Now I have part of my answer to what lies beyond your tourney skills and courtesy.'

'And that is?'

'Shall I say that you have potential.'

He felt her smile against his chest. 'I shall take that as a compliment. What do you mean by "part" of your answer?'

She raised herself to look at him. 'Because there is more to know. More layers to reveal. You do not show yourself easily.'

William raised his brows. The image was erotic, but he was not sure that he wanted to be stripped down until he was raw. Layers worked together for a purpose. But then she too had more to reveal – should he wish to discover. She was accustomed to

276

reading people and part of the challenge was his resistance to her. Not that he had succeeded particularly well today, and she had not wasted any time. 'Neither do you, my lady, although I too have come to a better understanding.'

'Such as?' She tickled his chest with a strand of her hair.

'Such as how determined you are to have your way. Such as the risks you are willing to take – although I fully admit to taking risks myself. And such as the power you wield.'

'Ah, power.' She stretched lazily. 'That is more and less than you think. All my life I have had to live by my wits – I suppose you have too.'

He nodded. They were alike in several ways. They had risen by their own efforts, although it was more difficult for a woman. He used his weapons and she used hers. There was always that hunger, and uncertainty, the knowledge of how it all might be taken away.

'That is why we recognise each other, even if we do not know everything. We are kindred spirits.' She sat up and folded her arms around her raised knees. 'Heraclius is good to me. He is kind and generous – indeed he loves me. I live a privileged life and his position protects me, but I am not betraying him, and neither are you.'

William grimaced. He was not so sure about that; did not want to think about it.

Her gaze lost its wild tenderness and grew hard. 'I told you that he bought me and it is true. I was trained very young in the arts of pleasing men – when I was still a child in many ways. My husband and my family used me to sweeten their clients – rich silk merchants, traders in pearls and gems. They would come to our house in Nablus and I would have to entertain them so that my husband and my father made a profit on their goods.' Her lip curled with disdain. 'I came to Heraclius's attention when my husband sold cloth to his household. Heraclius would buy me for a night, a week, sometimes a whole month. My uncle

Zaccariah would broker the arrangement and take his share – he still does after a fashion. When Heraclius's duties called him away I was returned to my husband, who then sometimes sold me to other men if the asking price was right, and my uncle would finalise the deals.' Her gaze challenged him, fierce and defensive. 'You are not shocked?'

William grimaced. 'It was my father's duty to deal with the concubines at the court of King Henry's grandsire, and I heard some of their stories – many were similar to yours.'

Her eyes filled with bleak pain. 'When Giovanni died, Heraclius took me in and I became his official concubine. I have made a niche for myself. I serve him. I listen to him, rub his feet, lie with him when he wishes, comfort him, run his errands, spy through keyholes for him. I perform all the duties of a wife, and yet I am no wife and can never be.' She raised her head to look round the domed chamber, a bitter twist to her smile. 'Do you know how I came by this room?'

'You said it was your payment, my lady.'

'Heraclius wanted to have me to himself after Giovanni died, but I refused him. I said I wanted his recognition of my standing to him personally – something that was mine alone beyond the jewels and the silks. He gave me this chamber above his chapel, and only I have the keys. That is his covenant to me. He used to hold meetings here and store some of his robes, but now it is mine.' She left the bed to refresh the cup. 'Do you know why else I brought you to this chamber?'

William shook his head.

'Because while Heraclius is away, I may live my life as I choose, providing I am discreet.' She tapped her breast for emphasis. 'As I choose,' she repeated. 'Otherwise I have nothing. All the silk and finery in the world to make a gilded cage for my youth? Heraclius is forty years older than I am . . . and do not say I have a choice, because I do not, unless I want to starve or be murdered.'

He took her meaning but again it was a notion to avoid. As

to his own choice: he could have walked away. He could have left Jerusalem and gone to the Templar preceptory at Acre long before this moment – and at the back of his mind, unacknowledged until now, he had known for a long time that it would come to this.

She began to dress, and he admired her supple body and the lustrous dark hair that she gathered in handfuls and wove with swift expertise into a plait. The delicacy of her neck. Her breasts. He remembered them in his hands, round and soft, but firm. And the rest of her. He wanted to draw her against him and do what they had done all over again.

She smiled and, leaning forward, drew aside the sheet to expose his body. 'It is time to go,' she said, but her eyes lingered upon him, assessing, and William opened himself to her study, making no move to cover himself. Her lips twitched. 'You are like a big, relaxed lion,' she teased. 'Do you know, I saw lions mating once in the Judaean desert. It is a sight to behold for sure and you tempt me greatly, but we must be gone from here. People will miss us soon.'

William slowly reached for his own clothes. He had recovered enough to think that he might be persuaded into another battle for mastery, but he supposed she was right. 'Who else comes in here?'

'Only me,' she replied. 'And Zoraya, but she is discreet. No one else.'

'But surely people know it exists?'

'Yes, but they do not come here – none has the right, not even my uncle. It is my private concern.' She unfastened the silk cord from around her neck and dangled the key. 'People can hold you to ransom even if you trust them. They can be bribed, or they can speak out of turn and give you away. The less they know – apart from what you want to tell them – the better.' She stood on tip-toe to fasten the ties on his shirt with swift fingers.

He put his hands on her waist and kissed her. She responded

with enthusiasm before pulling away and descending the stairs. At the foot, she unlocked the door but did not open it yet. Instead she pressed the key to her lips before slipping the cord around his neck. 'It is yours now. I have anointed it with my kiss and made you the custodian.' She tucked it down inside his shirt. 'Show it to no one. I shall find a way to let you know when to come here to me.' She gave him a melting look, her eyes dark and soft. 'You should know that I have never given this key to anyone else. I promise you that is true.'

William caressed her cheek. 'It is a great gift, my lady.'

Her lips curved into a mischievous smile. 'You do not know how great yet, but perhaps in time you will learn.' She raised the end of her belt and gently brushed his lips with the golden silk tassel on the end. 'Let me leave, and wait a while before you go. We must not be seen in the same vicinity because tongues wag at court and there are always people watching. We must be utterly discreet.'

'I know that.'

She stood on tip-toe to give him a long, last passionate kiss, then turned and opened the door a crack, peeped out, and made a swift, silent exit. William closed the door behind her and leaned against it, feeling as though he had been hit by a pole axe. Slowly he made his way back up the stairs and re-entered the chamber, trying to recapture that first memory of seeing it. The jewelled mosaic walls and the light pouring down through the aperture.

Going to the bed, he picked up one of the pillows and inhaled her scent on it. She had taken a place inside him and made it hers, and now he was hungry and hollow and had nothing by which to measure this feeling. There had been women in France and England, and even a mistress during his time on the tourney circuit, but nothing that had prepared him for the storm that was Paschia de Riveri. He did not know if it was love, but it was fierceness and fire; it was lust tempered by a desire to protect and an exquisite, tender pain that nevertheless made him smile.

He knew he had crossed a line and that if he delved too deeply he would find guilt and shame. It was one thing to say that this domed room was a place out of time, another to embrace the temptation. It was wrong, and yet it felt holy too – a sacred thing to be held in wonder and grace. And surely somewhere between the two there must be a point of balance.

When he considered that a long enough time had passed, he descended the stairs, going down from light into shadow, although there was still enough illumination to see the door. He took the key from around his neck and his smile was a grimace, for it was as though by giving him this she had set a halter upon him. If he was honest with himself, this was not a truce at all. Had this been a joust he would have been bowled from the saddle and tumbled in the dust.

As he turned the key and locked the door his heart turned and moved within him too. He drew the curtain across, tucked the key back down inside his shirt and left the chapel. Paschia was kneeling before a small altar with lit candles, her head bowed in prayer. Knowing he was being tested, he acknowledged her with a slight bow of deference, his face the bland mask of a courtier, and continued on his way as if everything was ordinary and normal. Although desperately tempted to look over his shoulder to see if she was watching him, he resisted and walked straight ahead and out into the blinding sunlight.

Throughout the rest of July and August, as the Outremer sun burned to white heat, William and Paschia continued to meet in the dome above the Patriarch's chapel when time and chance permitted. William's patrols often took him away for several days at a time and he had other matters to occupy him. Customers came to him for help and advice with their horses and their harness. He developed a reputation for being able to turn his hand to practical matters both military and equine and his advice was sought. Since the King of England might be the next ruler of Jerusalem, people were eager to cultivate him. The lady Paschia, although she did not have Heraclius to care for, spent much of her time in the Countess of Jaffa's household. It was not always easy to make an assignation under the ever-watchful eyes of the numerous spies working for Paschia's uncle.

They made the arrangement that Paschia would touch a single plain gold ring on her middle finger when usually she wore many. She would come down to the stable yard with her servants in order to ride Rakkas and she would touch the ring as she spoke to him. He would respond by putting his hand to his heart, over the key, in a gesture that seemed no more than a courtly salute, although whenever William responded to the summons his stomach would churn with anticipation, and the heavy feeling of need became almost unbearable.

His men were accustomed to his coming and going. They knew he had business to conduct with all manner of folk and saw nothing untoward in his absences. As often as not those absences occurred in the middle of the day when everyone was taking shelter from the heat. Ancel would be visiting his woman and the others would be dozing or playing chess or working indoors on their equipment.

For a few stolen moments, William and Paschia immersed themselves in each other. William would make his way to the domed chamber, his body tense with anticipation. The under-current of knowing he was committing a terrible sin was subsumed by the euphoria of the moment. He would gaze upon the jewelled light pouring on to the bed and wonder how on earth this could be a sin when it felt so holy.

He knew Paschia must come here alone, or Zoraya her maid, for clean bed sheets would appear, or a fresh dish of sweetmeats. Sometimes he would arrive and find incense burning in a latticed brass bowl. He did not ask about the appearance of these things, sensing it would break the mood she wanted to create, and he would wait for her to come to him, listening for her soft footfalls on the stairs. As she rounded the last twist and faced him, their eyes would meet with mutual hunger.

Their lovemaking was often a passionate flurry because they had so little time, and the days between meetings built desire to an incandescent pitch. But there were treasured moments when they had more leisure and would lie entwined, hands stroking, feeding each other sweetmeats and grapes. Once she brought a yellow fruit of paradise, its shape extremely suggestive of the male member, and ate it lasciviously, while riding upon him until his body arched like a bow with the pure pain-pleasure of the sensations. Another occasion he came to the chamber straight from patrol, still in his armour, and they had taken each other in the heat of the moment, with blistering, erotic savagery.

Each time they came to the dome they agreed a new truce until the next occasion, and William found himself living for those moments, tense, on edge, sick with desire, knowing that the more deeply he became involved the harder it would be to extricate himself, and the further he fell the more uneasy his buried conscience became.

'How long do you think Heraclius will be away?' he asked one day as they lay entwined in a haze of sated desire.

She painted his chest with the soft golden tassel of her belt. 'Who knows? We should just make the most of the moment . . . I told you.'

William gazed up at the glittering mosaics on the walls of the dome. He could lie here for ever, but his time in this place with this woman was finite, even if the world beyond did disappear inside this jewelled bubble. 'Yes, you did, but I don't want it to end.'

She was quiet, and for a moment a cloud shadowed their refuge. She ran her hand over his forearm and touched the pink scar of the wound he had received in Constantinople. 'How did you come by this?'

William grimaced. In seeking to distract him she had driven his mind into darker corners still. 'It is naught. We encountered trouble on our road to Jerusalem and I received it during a fight.'

'But it disturbs you.'

He shook his head. 'It is not that.'

'Then what? You can tell me, my English warrior lord.' She spoke the last words with a teasing smile and whisked the tassel over his flat stomach.

'I let someone down and myself into the bargain.'

She said nothing, encouraging him with silence.

'My King and liege lord,' he said after a long pause. 'I was sworn to keep him safe but he died under my protection and I could not save him. Had I been firmer or wiser, or had the wits to find a way out of our dilemma, he might not have come to such an end. I have offered my own life up to God over and over in atonement, but he has not taken it, so I assume I am meant to live. I vowed to come to Jerusalem to pray for Harry and purge my soul. It is a year to the day since I set out with my men bearing his cloak to lay at the Sepulchre.'

She leaned over and kissed him gently. 'I am sure all will be well and you will make everything right. Anything is possible in Jerusalem.'

William returned her kiss and said ruefully, 'A year ago, I never imagined any of this was possible . . . and now I am wondering how long it will last, and I know it is a sin.'

'Hush.' She pulled back to look at him. 'No more brooding. I have told you, this is a place separate from the world. Let there be no talk of sin. I am to blame for many things that only God will ever know, but if I brooded upon them . . .' She broke off with a small shiver. 'My family . . . you have seen how my uncle is – how he conducts business?'

'Indeed so,' William replied darkly.

'He is valuable to Heraclius, and his web extends everywhere. There is no place where he does not spin his thread. He is not a man to cross. Those who tangle with him are either silenced, or ruined – or they die.'

'Like your musician?'

Her eyes widened. 'What do you mean?'

'Whatever the reason, your uncle was having him watched and intimidated. Perhaps Ptolemy knew too much and had a loose tongue. Perchance he was helped from this world, who can say?'

She bit her lip and looked away. 'I do not know; indeed, I do not think about it.'

'Perhaps you should.' He felt a dull heaviness that she had dismissed his suggestion rather than repudiated it.

'No!' She turned to him, eyes full of fear and denial. 'I refuse to let them intrude in this place, and you should too. It is the only way – that is what I am trying to tell you.' She kissed him passionately, and they made love again with fierce intensity.

Afterwards, as they cuddled together, William stroked her smooth flat belly. 'What if you get with child?' he asked. 'I know that the women of the court have ways of protecting themselves but . . .'

She gently traced her forefinger round the whorls of his ear. 'Do not let it bother you. I have the matter in hand. The Church says that to couple without procreating is a sin, and I obey that teaching, but if I desire to keep myself clean with sponges and preparations, then it is no sin.'

William was relieved because the matter had been much on his mind. With Heraclius away and time passing, a pregnancy would begin to look suspicious.

As they dressed, he imagined how it would be if she was his woman, his wife. It was not as though she was married to Heraclius; she was a widow, and free to wed. He had money lodged with the Templars from his tourney winnings and the rents from two houses in St Omer on which they could live, and then it would not matter if she got with child. Indeed, he would welcome it. But such ideas were like this room: a moment out of time; the wanderings of a foolish dreamer who did not want to wake up and face a different reality.

'You are still quiet,' she said.

'I was thinking that I must go and pray for my young lord since it is a year since we set out.'

She stood on tip-toe to kiss him. 'I admire your loyalty.'

He almost told her what he had been thinking, but held back. He did not want to break the moment and he knew how mercurial she was. One moment an imperious lady of the court, politically astute and powerful, then an experienced concubine, knowing every ruse and trick to bring a man to ecstasy, the next a loving, vivacious young woman with an impish sense of humour. If he told her what was in his mind, she could either melt in his arms or scorn him out of hand, and he was not ready to be that vulnerable before her.

She left then, slipping quietly down the stairs and letting herself out. William waited a brief while, straightening the bed, continuing to imagine the idyll, a smile on his lips and an unconscious frown between his eyes. Eventually he went downstairs and let himself into the chapel, glancing round to make sure all was clear. Then he made his way swiftly outside, the key tucked safely inside his shirt.

As he stepped into the hot mid-afternoon sunlight, Paschia's uncle came walking toward him. And William affected an air of relaxed nonchalance.

'You have business in the palace?' Zaccariah asked with suspicious belligerence.

'No business that concerns you, sire,' William replied. 'Since you ask, I was seeking a scribe to ask him to write a note for me.' He bowed and moved on, but was strongly aware of the other man's scrutiny and knew he and Paschia would have to be especially careful.

*   *   *

As the afternoon shadows lengthened, William gathered his small entourage and went to attend evening mass at the Sepulchre, the service conducted by the Bishop of Lydda in Heraclius's absence. Afterwards, William and his men remained in further prayer and lit candles for their young lord's soul. William took the small square of fabric that had been cut from the hem of Harry's cloak, together with his cross, and passed the items along the row for each man to kiss and honour.

Later, they shared a remembrance meal and composed speeches and toasts to honour the Young King – the ghost in the empty seat at their table. William had had one of Heraclius's scribes write out the tale of their lord's life, glossing over the difficult moments and making much of the deeds he had performed, recalling with affection the liveliness of his court, and Harry's vibrant, mischievous wit.

'He once held a feast where only men named William were allowed to attend,' William said with a chuckle. 'He told those who were resentful at being excluded that they should be glad not to be among so many commoners.'

'I was one of them,' Ancel said. He fed a sliver of chicken to Pilgrim, waiting expectantly at his feet.

'I brought you out a cloth full of food and a jug of wine,' William said. 'As I recall you'd had a good night at the dice, so it was worth your while.'

Ancel shrugged. 'I still wasn't part of the golden circle.'

The smile dropped from William's face. 'It wasn't always golden.'

'He loved you though. Why else would he have chosen your name?'

There was a taut silence. 'Yes,' William said eventually. 'And for that love, we are here now.'

They raised toasts again and told stories long into the night before retiring to their pallets, full of gratitude to be alive and sadness that Harry wasn't. For a while William stood alone in the starry darkness and reflected. He was at a crossroads and he

287

did not know which path to take, for none of them was straight to the horizon and he did not know what lay around the corners.

Ancel joined him, Pilgrim nudging his heels. 'I am going to visit Asmaria. I know it's late, but she won't mind.'

William clasped his brother's shoulder. 'Then you had best make haste and I shall see you in the morning. Give her my greeting and tell her to send a pie.'

Ancel grinned. 'I'll do that.' He hesitated, and gave William a hard look. 'Is all well with you?'

'Yes.' William rubbed the back of his neck. 'It is a day for remembering and evaluating – we are changed men from the ones who set out from Rouen that is certain. Whether we are redeemed or not . . .' He shrugged, because for him the matter was currently in doubt.

'Gwim?'

William sighed. 'I love you, I want you to know that. Never doubt it.'

Ancel eyed him almost suspiciously. 'And I love you, brother, and have never been in doubt of it, even if I have doubted you.'

It was a complex statement for Ancel to make, and perhaps more than anything showed William how much his clumsy, naive brother had grown in the year since they had set out. Perhaps more than he had.

'Go on,' he said. 'Do not keep Asmaria waiting.'

The brothers shared a fond bearhug until Pilgrim joined in with a spot of ankle nipping and they broke apart, cursing and laughing. Ancel picked up the growling dog and tucked him under his arm. William playfully tousled Ancel's curls and watched him walk away into the dark.

For himself, he could not sleep, and he went to the stables to check on the horses, and from there to the small chapel set up for the Patriarch's servants, there to spend the rest of the night in vigil for Harry.

*   *   *

288

On a burning morning at the end of August, William had just finished shoeing Chazur, a task he always performed himself because the act built trust and bonding between him and the horse. Besides, he enjoyed the forging and hammering, the smell of hot metal and horn, the closeness to his horse as he worked. Some other knights eyed him askance for undertaking tasks that could be left to an underling, but William had been taught by his father, who had been taught by his, and it was a matter of pride and practicality, although with the sun nearing its zenith it was time to retire to the shade.

He was running his hand down Chazur's leg when Eustace, who had been delivering a mended bridle to one of the King's hearth knights, came running into the Patriarch's yard. 'Sire! Sire!' he gasped, his face flushed and sweat-streaked. 'Saladin has returned to Kerak and is laying siege! They have just heard news at the palace!'

William set down Chazur's hoof and wiped his brow with the back of his sleeve. The other men left their tasks and gathered round anxiously.

'They say he is filling in the ditches and has brought up his siege machines,' Eustace continued.

'So it was all for nothing last time,' muttered Robert of London.

'He was always bound to return.' William removed his leather apron. 'A fly doesn't leave your plate alone just because you brush it away. And he will have learned from his first attempt. I said he would fill in the ditches, and he's clearly better prepared than before. It will be a harder fight, and we dare not let Kerak fall because his next target will be Jerusalem.'

The men exchanged glances, all knowing the danger in which they stood. The King's illness had worsened recently and he had been resting a great deal. Whether he was capable of leading an army to Kerak was debatable, and the leaders of the two military orders were absent on the mission to Europe, all of which Saladin would know from his spies.

'Better make sure every horse is well shod, and check the weapons,' William said. 'No doubt a call to muster will go out in short order. We cannot afford to delay.'

'I heard someone say the King has already ordered the beacons to be lit on the watch towers,' Eustace said.

As he was speaking, Paschia's uncle Zaccariah entered the yard with the soldier Mahzun of Tyre, several of the latter's mercenaries, and the handful of household serjeants that Heraclius had left behind.

'There's been news,' Zaccariah announced, marching over to William. 'We'll need every horse in the stables and every fighting man. See to it.'

William raised his brows at the man's peremptory tone. In England, Zaccariah of Nablus as a doorkeeper would have been subordinate to William in both rank and role, but in Jerusalem it was a different matter.

'Indeed,' William replied smoothly, 'it is in hand. My squire has already informed me of the details.'

Zaccariah scowled, clearly disgruntled at being pre-empted. 'If you have heard, then you will understand the need for haste. Every man capable of riding a horse and bearing weapons must go to Kerak's aid. There will be no shirkers.' He stamped off, treading heavily like a bull. Mahzun of Tyre gave William and his men a superior glance and followed Zaccariah.

Robert of London muttered under his breath and William said sharply, 'Best keep your thoughts to yourself.'

'But he implied—'

'I know what he implied. He was baiting us because we received the news first, and he hates to be bested. He is dangerous, and whatever you think in private, treat him with caution. He will be riding with us, and we shall have enough ado with Saladin without troubles on our own side. Come, we must sort out weapons and arrange provisions. Eustace, fetch the water flasks.'

* * *

William sat on the edge of the bed and slowly donned his tunic. Outside the sun was melting into the west and the domed room was cast in shadow save for a jewelled segment where light that was deeper than gold enhanced the mosaic with a richer gleam.

The look in Paschia's eyes was close to grief. Her dark hair was still loose and hung in a lustrous tumble to her waist, over the ruby silk of her gown. 'What if I never see you again?' she said. 'I cannot bear it.'

Her anguish surprised him because he had thought her inured to such realities and he had no experience by which to measure it. Whenever his father had ridden off to war, his mother had always made her farewells with a smile, and a promise that she would be waiting with open arms to welcome him home. She might have wept in private but never in front of her lord. 'I will return to you if I can, I promise. And if not, then you have God to thank for my life. Light a candle for me.'

'Do you think that comforts me?' she demanded. 'Shall I sit here and gaze at a stick of wax in your stead and have solace from my grief? I think not!' Tears filled her eyes and she began to weep.

He pulled her into his arms, his own throat suddenly tight with emotion, and tipped up her chin. 'Trust me, and trust in God. I will come back to you, I promise.'

She drew away and wiped her face with the palm of her hand. 'I have not told you but I had a brother,' she said. 'He rode off to war when I was twelve years old and never returned. We do not know what happened to him save that his bones lie bleaching somewhere in the Judaean Desert.' Her face contorted. 'People go out and they do not come back. I do not want that to happen to you – I could not bear it.'

Feeling a surge of protective tenderness he kissed her salty cheeks and lips. He understood now why she had bidden Heraclius farewell and then turned immediately, almost desperately, to him as her succour and security. It was as much need as lust. 'I am not your brother, and his fate is not mine. I must go, I have no choice – as you yourself once spoke of choices. God willing, I shall return.' He certainly hoped God was willing because if he died now he would not be in a state of grace; but he was not going to say that to Paschia. Instead he kissed her passionately, then again, gently, on the forehead. 'Pray for me and watch for me, and I will come.'

Leaving her standing in the last of the westering light, he followed the thin, almost blood-red shadow of the sun down the stairs to the doorway.

In the cool, grey dawn before the sun broke over the horizon, William knelt within the round of the Sepulchre and gave his personal oath to King Baldwin, to the Bishop of Lydda, and to Gerard de Ridefort, acting Grand Master of the Templars, bestowing his body, his life and his worldly goods to this campaign to deliver Kerak from Saladin in the name of Jesus Christ. Alongside him each recruited knight took the same oath on his bended knees and de Ridefort sprinkled each man with holy water. 'Now let any man who has not done so make his farewells for you may not see each other again.' The Templar's lined face was tight and keen. 'I want no man in my service who is not prepared to go into this with full commitment.'

William was still undecided about de Ridefort. Rumour said he had joined the Templars after the woman he had sought in marriage had been given elsewhere by her overlord Raymond of Tripoli and thus he harboured a grudge against the lord of Tiberius. Whether or not that was true, he was certainly a driven individual full of grim purpose.

In a pensive mood, William went to the patriarchal palace to collect his horses and equipment, and Ancel's too, for his brother had gone to take his leave of Asmaria and the children.

Zaccariah of Nablus was in the stable yard with his own mount, and Paschia was bidding him a dutiful public farewell. Noticing William, she gave him a courteous nod. 'Godspeed, messire. I shall pray for you and your men and hope you return safely.' Her tone was that of an encouraging but detached patron.

Her acting was flawless, and he strove to match it. 'Madam, we shall do our best, and thank you for your prayers.'

For a fleeting instant their eyes met, and then she lowered hers and walked swiftly in the direction of her dwelling. Her uncle gazed after her suspiciously and William turned to his own business, his shoulder blades prickling at the danger.

The army of Jerusalem set out on its second journey to Kerak in less than a year, a force united in gritty determination to deal with Saladin and drive him off once and for all, this time without the complication of wedding guests to consider. For King Baldwin it was probably the final time he would lead the army behind the True Cross. For Gerard de Ridefort it was his first command as leader of the Templars and the additional knights of Jerusalem. For Guy de Lusignan it was an opportunity to prove himself to possible allies and sceptical enemies alike, with the full backing of the Templars.

They rode around the north tip of the Sea of Salt and once again camped near its shores, ready to ride on to Kerak at dawn. Scouts were sent out to reconnoitre and numerous guards posted lest the Saracens should have skirmishers out seeking opportunities to raid.

William and Ancel were returning to their camp after seeing to their horses when they noticed a circle of men had gathered to make an impromptu arena around the mercenary knight Mahzun of Tyre and another warrior. The men were sparring with swords and shields; Mahzun was methodical and hefty with his blows and the other man swift and light. Puffs of gritty dust rose from the ground as they shifted and stepped.

Zaccariah of Nablus was watching the exchange with folded arms and his customary scowl and glanced over his shoulder as William and Ancel joined the circle.

'What's happening?' William asked.

Zaccariah shrugged. 'Nothing. A test of skill and weapons for a wager. Mahzun will win. The other's like a fart without the shit. I wouldn't employ him. Too many of his kind among our knights these days – untried soft swords.'

William arched his brows but otherwise ignored the remark, taking it as a cheap barb.

The men circled each other, launching blows, parrying and feinting. Mahzun almost cornered his opponent but the other knight managed to dodge the blow and weave back to the middle. Mahzun came after him again, arm rising and falling, speed increasing. His opponent blocked every attack all but stumbled on his back foot, and with a roar Mahzun crashed a shattering blow onto his shield. His sword sheared off close to the grip, leaving him with a hilt in his hand attached to a jagged stump of blade. Mahzun stepped back with a shout of rage and hurled the broken hilt to the ground. He turned to the circle of watchers, hands outspread, the hem of his mail shirt flicking out. 'A sword!' he bellowed. 'Someone give me a decent sword!'

No one moved. Swords were too precious to give up to someone as brutal in his approach as Mahzun of Tyre. Ancel reached to the short sheath at his waist. 'Here, you can have my knife!' he cried, pitching his voice high, so that it sounded more like a young squire's than a grown man's, and he ran out into the middle of the circle waggling the weapon. The audience hooted with laughter and nudged each other. Mahzun's opponent grinned as he clambered to his feet.

Enraged, Mahzun snatched the dagger from Ancel and, seizing him in a stranglehold, laid the blade against his throat. 'You will not make a fool of me before all these men, you halfwit cur!'

'It was a jest!' Ancel wheezed.

William started forward, his hand to his sword hilt. 'Let him go.'

Mahzun eyed William speculatively and his corded forearm continued to grip Ancel in a choke hold. The audience stirred restlessly, men unfolding their arms, tensing. Mahzun's gaze flicked round the gathering. 'No one makes a fool of me and lives,' he spat. 'Try that again and I will cut your throat!' He hurled Ancel to the ground, tossed the knife across the circle – not caring if he struck anyone – and, shouldering aside the gathering, stalked off toward his tent.

Zaccariah, who had been brokering the wager, was furious because he now had to return people's money. He cast a murderous gaze in Ancel's direction. Mahzun's opponent took the opportunity to beat a hasty retreat. Rubbing his bruised throat, Ancel staggered to his feet.

'You fool!' William remonstrated. 'What in God's name possessed you to do such a thing?'

Ancel coughed. 'How was I to know he would take it that way? Everyone else laughed. It was obvious no one was going to give him a sword.'

William rolled his eyes. 'So you just ran in on the spur of the moment and made yourself an enemy for life. You should have considered how he would react, rather than performing for the audience. I thought you'd learned some common sense since we've been here, but plainly you haven't.'

Ancel flushed. 'I made a mistake,' he said defensively. 'You make them too.'

William swallowed and gritted his teeth. He had been about to say 'Not like this' but considering his own follies in Jerusalem he had no right to take Ancel to task. His mistakes were sins, and potentially much worse. He retrieved the knife Mahzun had thrown on the ground and gave it to Ancel. 'Enough,' he said. 'We should eat, and check the weapons.' And then he pulled

Ancel close and knuckled the top of his head. 'You fool,' he said gruffly.

'I was taught by the best,' Ancel retorted, pushing him off.

Later, Onri joined William at his campfire. The punishing heat of the day had softened and diminished as the sun sank below the Judaean hills and the air now bore enough of a chill that William had draped a blanket around his shoulders. The nuggets of camel dung fuel gave off a strong heat and twirled pungent smoke into the darkness, lit here and there by oil lamps and lanterns. The horses snorted and stamped, and the soldiers hunched around their fires, playing dice, singing songs, and praying. Distantly, during lulls in the conversation, William could hear the sea lapping against the shoreline.

'You should be wary of Mahzun of Tyre,' Onri warned, prodding the fire with a poker, releasing a new wave of heat.

William grimaced. 'I am. When he comes to the Patriarch's palace I avoid him. He works for Zaccariah of Nablus and their dealings are often of the night. They put business each other's way.' He gave Onri a meaningful look.

'That is what I know of him also,' Onri said. 'But men hire him because he is a good fighter and always carries his task through to the end no matter what. That part is his honour, even if he lacks it elsewhere. You should keep Ancel out of his way for a while.'

'I intend to,' William said, 'but thank you for the warning.'

They sat in companionable silence for a little while. Onri brought out his dagger and set about sharpening it with a small whetstone.

'What do you think of de Ridefort?' William asked.

Onri's expression closed in. 'He has his own methods of rule. When he gives an order, he expects it to be carried out, and he is not a man to be crossed. Once he has committed himself, nothing will turn him back, and he is forceful in his decisions. More than that I cannot say.'

Or would not, William thought. Onri was a loyal Templar knight and orders were orders.

'Saladin will not stay to fight,' Onri continued. 'It is too great a risk to face a pitched battle before the walls of Kerak when we have a strong advantage. But he will have probed at our responses to see how we answer when our Grand Masters are absent and our King's illness is progressing. That is the reason the King has forced himself to come to Kerak rather than send out the army and remain in Jerusalem. He defeated Saladin once and drove him off last winter. His name is a talisman to us, and a fear to the Turks. What it will be like when we do not have him, I do not wish to think – unless perhaps the Patriarch is successful and brings a new king on his return.'

William said nothing. Onri had dwelt in England and they were both realists and knew the likely outcome.

Onri put the knife away and looked at William across the fire. 'What do you long for the most?' he asked. 'Settlement with a wife and lands to call your own, or continuing along this path you have made for yourself?'

'Now you ask a deep question.' William rubbed his neck. He could not tell Onri that his ideal would be to bring Paschia back to Normandy with him and make a new life with her, and yet Onri had posed a pertinent query that was one of the routes leading from William's present crossroads. 'All I can answer is that I do not know.'

'I still see you joining our order at some point,' Onri said. 'You have that quality within you. Perhaps you will stay in the Kingdom of Jerusalem?'

William shook his head. 'I said before, I am not worthy, and that still pertains. There are things you do not know about me.' He lifted his cup and finished the sour watered wine. 'I have much to think about and my path is not straight and winds beyond my vision.'

Onri's gaze remained unperturbed. 'Even so that does not

change what I see.' He rose to his feet. 'But I will bid you good night and go to my prayers. Think on it.' He gripped William's shoulder and walked away toward the Templar campfires.

William watched him and felt unsettled. Onri was a good man, a spiritual man, and a close friend, and William did not want to let him down. He tried to envisage himself wearing the cloak of a Templar, a celibate warrior monk, but the image refused to fix in his mind and faded into one of himself and Paschia embracing within the domed chamber. He knew which he wanted more, sin though it was.

27

Manor of Caversham, April 1219

It was dark, only a single light burning at his bedside, but William did not need the light, he could see perfectly well. In his mind, he left his bed and walked silently across the room, past his eldest son, nodding on his stool, past Henry FitzGerold, who was keeping Will company in light slumber, and the silver gazehound lying at their feet, nose tucked against tail, until he came to the wardrobe chamber. A coffer holding cloaks and robes stood against the wall and he saw himself push back the lid, remove the first winter cloak on top of the contents, then take out a white woollen robe with a red cross stitched over the heart, and then a cloak of the same cloth, almost as heavy as a hauberk. He had no strength in his arms, he could not even hold his own cup, but in his vision he was a man in his prime and it was no difficulty to hold the garments up and look at them.

'See?' he heard Onri say. 'You did know your path after all.'

28

The Road to Kerak, Outremer, September 1184

As they rode toward Kerak the next day at speed, Mahzun took the opportunity to intimidate Ancel. Under the guise of riding with the Patriarch's party in order to speak with Zaccariah, Mahzun rode up close to Ancel's horse and hemmed him in, making it clear that he had not forgotten or forgiven the previous evening's occurrence with the knife. When William trotted up to intercept, Mahzun reined back and made a false apology, but his eyes remained hard with threat.

As on their previous journey to Kerak, skirmishers from Saladin's army harried and threatened them. Archers swooped in like flocks of birds, shot their arrows into the midst of the advancing Franks, and then raced away uttering high, ululating cries. Some of the young bloods rode close enough to hurl spears before whirling round and galloping off, making high sport of the Frankish army. Several knights had to remove quilled Turkish arrows from their shields and mail. Some horses were struck too, although none wounded beyond piercings that made them buck and kick.

'Hold!' William commanded his own small contingent as he heard the oaths and anger behind him. 'They are trying to goad us into making a charge.'

Uttering a growl, Mahzun reined his horse out of the line and, seizing a spear, galloped toward one particularly persistent group who had been teasing them. They held until he was almost upon them, and then broke away, whooping and taunting; but

Mahzun was wise to their ruse and not tempted too far from the main army, and reined back. Instead he made his stallion caracole and, with a mighty effort, cast his spear down before the enemy so that it landed in the dust, point down and quivering. Then he returned to the Frankish troops at a prancing canter, to cheers and accolades. As he settled back into line, he cast a glittering look at William that was almost contempt.

Eustace was beside himself. 'Sire, we should do something!'

William shook his head at his squire. 'All he has done is to give a spear to the enemy and encourage young hotheads like yourself to follow his example and perhaps be killed by misjudgement. But still,' he added, because he too was goaded by Mahzun's deed, 'there is nothing to stop us from a little tourney training as we ride along.' He gestured to Eustace. 'The standing saddle perhaps?'

Eustace's crestfallen expression changed instantly and he kicked his horse to a canter, then slid off its back to the ground behind before leaping over its rump and back into the saddle. He reversed to face backwards, then scissored round to the front once more, and stood up, dropped down, leaped on, leaped off.

Several of William's men followed suit with similar tricks, showing off their horsemanship. Then William took a lance and performed several skilled manoeuvres with Ancel at a canter, riding on the edge, swirling and turning in precision but still keeping in line with the column. William deliberately chose Ancel from the men because he wanted to show Mahzun that his brother was accomplished and capable of defending himself. Ancel might not have Eustace's lithe skills on a horse, nor William's natural talent with sword and lance, but he was dogged and thorough, and once a technique was learned, it was mastered for life. Of them all, Ancel was the one who needed to practise least to maintain his edge.

Mahzun made a deliberate show of ignoring their performance, but William knew he had seen it, and the point had been made.

*   *   *

Kerak rose before them in great golden blocks of stone, the walls battered and pock-marked from the pounding meted out by Saladin's siege machines, which were now ablaze around the base of the fortifications. Some had clearly been demolished and transported away with the Saracen army, but many had been set on fire as time ran out. The ditch protecting the inner defences had been heavily filled in and it was clear that their arrival was timely, for Saladin had made far deeper inroads than his previous assault and had been on his way to victory.

The garrison, commanded by Reynald of Châtillon, welcomed the army from Jerusalem with relief, but there was no celebrating. After thanksgiving prayers had been said, the horses seen to and food eaten, repairs to the fortress were immediately set in hand and the ditches cleared and deepened. King Baldwin had his litter carried around the walls to inspect the damage and discuss the repairs required. Once again Saladin had retreated rather than engage in a pitched battle and William could see that the ailing young King was frustrated. Both Gerard de Ridefort and Guy de Lusignan opined that they should give chase, but Baldwin shook his head when they suggested it in counsel on that first evening.

'We would have to push the men and horses hard to catch up. Kerak must be fortified. I too am disappointed, but I will not allow that disappointment to breed recklessness. We must make this place secure first.'

William realised he was right. De Lusignan and de Ridefort were exasperated, especially Guy, who was spoiling for a fight. Others were more philosophical, and Baldwin was still trusted enough by the majority to hold all together.

Two days later, William was toiling with the other men, helping to clear the ditch of the rubble and detritus that the Saracens had thrown down in order to fill it, when he saw a messenger arriving in a cloud of red dust.

Ancel blotted his brow on his forearm, and pushed back the brim of the straw hat protecting him from the sun. 'Trouble,' he said.

'Certainly urgency,' William replied.

The King was unwell and intended retiring to Acre to attend his mother, who was seriously ill herself, and to recuperate in the care of the Hospitallers in a place where the sea breezes would be kinder to his condition. A detail of men was being left to fill in the ditch, and the rest were to return to Jerusalem with Gerard de Ridefort and the Bishop of Lydda. William and his knights had volunteered to stay a few extra days with the ditch diggers before returning to Jerusalem. While William longed to be with Paschia, this hard physical activity was both penance and abstinence. He was putting distance between himself and a temptation he could not resist.

The news swiftly emerged that Saladin was making his way toward Damascus, raiding as he went, and that he had sacked Nablus, although its population was safe within the citadel, defended by Maria Comnena, Balian of Ibelin's wife.

A contingent was organised to pursue the raiders and chase them off. It had to be swift, and the King was in no condition to command whatever the pace. William volunteered to go; so did Zaccariah, because Nablus was his native city and he still had important business interests there, and he took Mahzun as his personal bodyguard. Balian of Ibelin, lord of Nablus, whose wife was conducting the defence, was also riding north, and although Gerard de Ridefort was accompanying the King to Acre, Onri was to lead a conroi of Templars.

William and his men swiftly collected supplies from the stores, donned their armour, saddled their horses and rode out of Kerak, heading north on the tail of Saladin's army.

'Of course, again, it will only be to chase him away,' Onri said to William as they rode side by side at a trot. 'We do not have enough men for a pitched battle, and Saladin will not stand

and fight either. He is just raiding and attacking to bite us as he returns to Damascus. But at least people will see that we have come to their relief, and we are marking our boundaries.'

'The same happens on the borders between France and Normandy,' William responded. 'There are always threats and skirmishes, but seldom full battles, because neither king will risk all.'

Nablus had been burned, looted and sacked. Paschia's uncle was enraged to find his family premises in smoking ruins, although his mood improved when he discovered that his relatives had survived by retreating into the citadel, bringing with them most of their rich silk cloth, so at least their livelihood and his share in its profits had been saved.

Saladin had sacked the town and moved on, and as at Kerak, there was no fighting to do, only sifting through the ashes, tallying the losses and damage and clearing up. The lord Balian remained in Nablus to see to the city repairs and reassure the people that Saladin would not be returning. Onri, however, had to ride on to the border to ensure that the latter was true, and to check up on the small Templar castle and farming settlement at Petit Garin, on the road to the Hospitaller fortress at Belvoir and William and his men rode with him.

As they left the ruins of Nablus behind, William dreamed of Paschia with longing, and wondered how she would react to hearing that her birthplace had been burned to the ground. He imagined her running around the town as a little girl with long dark plaits. And then a young woman, and wished he had known her then. He wanted to fold her in his arms and protect her from everything that had ever hurt or damaged her, and promise it would never happen again.

Onri and his troop struck out along the road in the direction of the Hospitaller castle of Belvoir, which stood at the eastern edge of a plateau high above the Jordan valley, guarding two fords that led into the Turkish-held interior, controlled by Saladin.

Along the way, the knights came upon destroyed Samaritan villages plundered with swift efficiency, the livestock taken and the people slaughtered if they had not been swift enough to flee. As in Nablus, the houses had been ransacked and fired, and the water courses were polluted with the corpses of pigs and sheep.

The men rode on from these places having garnered what information they could. There was nothing they could do for the villagers, and nothing the villagers could do for them. William had seen such sights regularly when serving his young lord in the Limousin. Sometimes he had even been the cause of such devastation. Destroying the enemy's lands and resources took away his means of livelihood and stamped mark upon his territory like a dog pissing up a wall.

The Templar settlement of Petit Garin lay close to the River Jordan, and like the other villages had been raided and destroyed, the crops and vines burned in the fields and the animals slaughtered or driven off. A few villagers who had made their escape before the attack were stumbling around the ruins of their homes, dousing the flames, salvaging what they could, wailing over the dead and the missing. The small fortified castle had not withstood the Saracen assault; the door to the fortress had been burned and then smashed open by a ram and the Templar knight and serjeants defending the place had been decapitated, their heads thrust on spears at the edge of the village. In the strong September sun, the flies had already begun their work and the bodies were swarming. The Templars' weapons had been taken, as had their horses and the strong box.

William was a soldier accustomed to chevauchée, but this was on a greater level than he had experienced before. His gorge rose and he had to swallow hard. Eustace had given up the struggle and was kneeling on the ground vomiting.

Onri knelt and bowed his head to honour his fallen brethren, then stood straight and looked at William, his expression set and hard. 'We must bury them decently,' he said bleakly. 'We are

Templars, and that means we are afforded no mercy, nor do we ask for it. Our order began as knights dedicated to protecting ordinary folk on the pilgrim roads, but we could not protect these people from the might of Saladin's army, although they relied on us to do so.'

William laid his hand on Onri's shoulder in support. 'There was nothing anyone could have done. They stood in the path of the Saracen army, and the numbers were too great.'

'Yes,' Onri said grimly, 'and that does not sit well with me either.'

The soldiers set to and began digging graves for the dead Templars and all the villagers who had been killed. Another man had suffered a severe sword cut to the shoulder and was unlikely to survive, although he was able to tell them how the Saracens had come down on them like a swarm of locusts out of a dust cloud. Many of the villagers had been taken as slaves – the younger women, the older children, and the strong youths; the rest had been slaughtered. Unless settlers were found to repopulate Petit Garin it would become yet another derelict settlement.

Ancel worked beside William as they dug. His stocky strength and pragmatism suited the task and the brothers drew sustenance from each other in the rhythmic toil, the sudden touching of a shoulder, an exchanged glance. Eustace dug beside them, his movements jerky.

'Steady lad.' William put a hand on his arm and handed him the water flask. 'Rinse your mouth.'

Eustace gave a wordless nod and did as William bade him. Then he spat to one side of the trench, and wiped his hand across his face. 'I am all right,' he said hoarsely.

William nodded in a brusque man-to-man fashion. 'Yes, I know.'

There were no shrouds and the bodies had to be laid to rest as they were. William held a small child in his arms, a little boy no more than three years old, and set him gently down beside his fly-blown grandmother with grief, with tenderness, with a heartsick burning anger that went too deep for the swift fire of rage. This belonged to everyone – not just the men who had committed the atrocity, but as part of a longer chain in which each and every one of them was a link all the way back to Cain.

The Templars were buried side by side, their heads removed from the spikes and restored to their bodies. Onri had insisted on performing the terrible task himself and, grey-faced, saw to the burial service over the long dusty mound of heaped earth. And then he entered the church to pray and prostrated himself before the altar and wept.

After a while William followed him and knelt at his side, saying nothing, quietly sending his own prayers to God for the souls of the people they had just committed to the earth. The long silence forged the bond between the men into a stronger link of shared experience, and William remembered the moment on their pilgrimage when Onri had come to him and undertaken a vigil at his side in a wayside village church.

The silence of the chapel was suddenly riven by a shout and the clatter of hooves and jingle of harness. William and Onri hurried outside ready to draw their swords, and were met by a group of Hospitallers from Belvoir, also intent on discovering how Petit Garin had fared as the Saracen army came through.

'Saladin crossed the Jordan at the ford below the castle yesterday at dusk,' said the knight leading the contingent as he looked at the grave mound and crossed himself. 'He was moving swiftly even with the spoils of his raids. We sent out knights and archers to harry his flanks and we picked off a few of his warriors, but he kept his distance from us. We knew from his direction that Petit Garin must have lain in his path.' He grimaced. 'We'll succour the survivors at Belvoir until we hear from your order what is to be done – whether you will put in a new garrison?'

Onri shook his head. 'That will be for our Grand Master to decide. We drove Saladin off from Kerak but he has sacked Nablus and every village between here and the Jordan crossing.'

307

'But since he has crossed the river, it seems that the danger has passed.'

'Probably,' Onri agreed, and wearily pinched the bridge of his nose. 'We have a moment to recuperate and prepare for the next assault.'

The Hospitallers made ready to return to Belvoir, taking with them the surviving villagers, and Onri's party took the road to Jerusalem, leaving the remains of Petit Garin to its ghosts.

'We build settlements,' Onri said, riding beside William, 'but it is a constant struggle to keep them occupied and productive. We have to provide men to guard the villages and convince people to settle in the first place. The larger fortresses can hold out for years and to an extent protect the smaller ones against Saracen raids, but when an army comes through, then the small links break and the big links can do nothing. And Saladin knows this. To him, these raids are but small fish in his net. Kerak was the big one, and he will be back to challenge for it.'

'But not yet,' William said.

'No, not yet,' Onri said dourly. 'He has to share out his plunder and deal with whatever he must at home. His men will have their own business to attend – wives and families, crops and trade. But it will not be for long – not without a miracle, and miracles are in short supply these days.'

They had been riding for less than half a day when they came upon a Saracen camel train bearing sacks of frankincense, coloured leathers and woven woollen rugs. The two groups considered each other warily. The caravan was sufficiently well armed to see off ordinary brigands but not a troop of seasoned knights on warhorses.

Onri contemplated the train with a taut jaw while fingering his sword hilt. 'There is always temptation,' he said, 'but every day I pray to God to give me the strength to resist it.'

William gave him a questioning look. The men were restive,

and by the clink of armour and harness and the stamping of the horses William could tell they were eager to be unleashed. Just one word . . . just one move.

'If we attack them, then we make ourselves outlaws and jeopardise the entire kingdom,' Onri said. 'They journey under King Baldwin's protection and ours and they have the right to camp and trade along their designated routes.' He gave William a look both cynical and resigned. 'Towns might burn, people might be slaughtered and enslaved, but the exchange of goods continues, because where else would the riches come from in order to build the towns and assemble armies in the first place? Under the King's orders, we leave them in peace, and in turn, although they may burn our villages in war, our own merchants may ride through Saracen territory unhindered. That is the nature of balance. It is not a delicate thing in itself; indeed, it is very crude, but all it takes is a single stroke to begin Armageddon.' He eased his hand off his sword hilt and made a horizontal gesture with his hand, palm flat, indicating to the soldiers that they should keep their weapons sheathed. The moment passed, and the camel train moved on, slow-stepping along the well-worn track.

Perspiration cooling on his body as he recovered, William lay on his back and gazed up at the dome where the moonlight streamed in upon him and Paschia lying together in their haven from the world. They had come here at sunset and now it was close on midnight, and all they had done was make love and sleep and make love again. The intensity of the sensations still flickered through his body like the last of a storm rolling away to the horizon. He wasn't sure he had the strength to move, but knew he ought to.

'Stay,' she said as he gathered himself, and she pressed him gently back down before leaning over and lightly biting his chest. 'My uncle is not here, and neither is most of the household. No one will know. Even if people notice your absence, they will think you have gone to one of the places in the city.'

He resisted for an instant and then lay back, capitulating. It would be very pleasant to spend the night here and the opportunity might not arise again. But it was a risk. He had ridden in with his men just ahead of the twilight and seen to the stabling of the horses. Ancel had gone to visit Asmaria and would not be back until the morning, and the other men had their own business to attend now they had returned.

She kissed him again and moved lower, sweeping her hair over his body. William was amused and rueful. If she continued on her path he would have to cry quarter rather than agree a truce. But she stopped when she reached his stomach and, laughing, raised her head. 'I think you are indeed a lion,' she said. 'Or else you have swallowed one because I have never heard such ferocious growling before! When did you last eat?'

'Saddle rations about two hours before we arrived.' He stroked her face. 'Food was not the first thing on my mind.'

'And now it is?'

'Not entirely,' he conceded, 'but more than it was.'

'And you need to keep up your strength.'

He raised his brows, and with a laugh she leaned toward the plinth running around the edge of the dome and lifted from it a flagon, a platter of dates, bread and honey.

William pushed himself upright against the pillows. She lit the candles, and as the moonlight bathed the room they fed each other, nibbling and touching, making a playful jest of each mouthful.

Eventually, the edge taken off his appetite, although he was still hungry, William washed his face and hands in the brass bowl that also stood on the ledge. 'After Kerak we went to Nablus.' He knew he had to tell her before they slept or made love again; otherwise it would seem like an afterthought.

She had been washing her own hands, and briefly paused. 'Oh?' she said with forced indifference.

William gestured for her to come back to bed. She did so, but eyed him warily.

'Saladin had sacked the town,' he said as he curled his arm around her. 'The people escaped into the citadel with such goods as they could carry and they resisted attack, but the rest has been looted and burned. That is why your uncle has not returned – he is still there, setting matters to rights. Your relatives are all safe, and for the most part so are their livelihoods.'

She said nothing. He squinted down at her but it was difficult to read her expression for her face was partly covered by her hair.

'Have I upset you? What is wrong?'

She pushed out of his arms and sat up, hugging herself. 'No.' She turned her face away. 'I care not. I am glad it has burned to the ground – I hope it is all gone. I would never go back there.' She refilled her goblet and drank swiftly. 'You look at me askance. You look at me and you do not know what to say. How could you?'

He watched the expressions flit across her face. Anger and grief, desolation and bitterness. She was right: he did not understand, and he knew little of her past, save what she had told him on the day she brought him to the dome.

'Nablus was where I was bought and sold to sweeten my family's dealings,' she said with a shudder. 'It was where I realised my true worth. I learned that money and power counted for everything, and love for nothing. They would make a deal and expect me to open my legs or my mouth to seal it. If the home where I grew up has gone, then I am glad.' The cup trembled and she put it down and pressed her hands over her face.

William took her in his arms. 'I love you, let that count for all.'

'You fool!' she replied in a breaking voice, and clenched her fists against his bare chest. 'Did you not hear what I have just said?'

'Yes, and I answered you with truth. What is all the money and power in the world worth without love?' Tilting up her chin, he stroked his thumb over her tears.

'Compensation,' she said bitterly. 'And I have made sure that I have been well compensated.' She ran her hand down his body, over his hip and thigh, and then inwards. 'See how very skilled I am?'

William caught her wrist and brought it up to his lips. 'But it is not enough, is it? It will never be enough.'

Her eyes were wide and dark and lost. 'No,' she said, 'but it is sufficient to survive.'

She kissed him with passionate desperation and he took her back to bed. They had already made love twice and this time they did so with a slow, lingering gentleness that drew to a tender, exquisite climax. William buried his face in her neck, in her luxuriant silky black hair. He had said that love counted for all, but knew he was ignoring the cost.

'I see that Zaccariah of Nablus is back,' Onri remarked as the men paused between bouts of sparring with each other on the grounds to the west of the Temple Mount. 'I saw him ride in yesterday evening with his baggage train.'

The burning summer heat had yielded in early October to temperatures slightly less fierce, although William's shirt and quilted aketon were still soaked with sweat. He drank down two cups of spring water that barely quenched his thirst. He and Onri were well matched and it had been a constant dance of swift feints and strong blows, testing for weakness, perfecting technique.

William wiped a cloth over his face and then cleaned his damp hands and sword grip. 'I am afraid so. If I have missed him, it is only because he has not been constantly goading me and trying to extort money.'

Onri raised his brows. 'Extort money?'

'He says we owe rent for dwelling in the Patriarch's quarters and for the stabling of our horses.'

'Why should he think that?' Onri sent him a keen look as he cleaned his own sword.

'I made an agreement with the Patriarch for board and lodging in return for services, and indeed, the Patriarch had little interest in the terms.' William sat down on a bench and rested his cup on his thigh. 'It was mutually useful, and having extra men to guard the place was an increased incentive for him. I have paid my dues over and above, especially since my brother often lodges elsewhere. Zaccariah has an inflated sense of his own importance. He insists he is responsible for collecting rents, but he is lining his own coffers, not the Patriarch's. I had hoped he would stay longer in Nablus. Now I suppose he will be pestering us all again like a louse in the braies and doing his best to suck our blood.'

Onri snorted at the analogy with sour amusement. 'He is odious, I agree. The Patriarch overlooks his behaviour because he is useful at times and also because he is kin to Madame la Patriarchess.'

'Yes.' William looked away. He did not want the conversation to veer anywhere near Paschia, and this talk of her uncle was skimming a little too close. William had been dismayed when Zaccariah returned, and wished with his whole being that he had remained in Nablus.

'You could always move back into one of our houses,' Onri offered.

'Indeed, and I will think on it,' William said, and knew he would not – could not, because of Paschia. Onri believed far better of him than he deserved. 'I—'

He ceased speaking as Geoffrey FitzRobert arrived, out of breath. He had been at the Patriarch's palace checking a horse with a leg injury and William's first thought was that Saladin had ridden back over the border again.

'Sire, a messenger came to the stables looking to hire a fresh horse.' Geoffrey clapped his hand to his side and fought to recover his breath. 'He told me that Guy de Lusignan has destroyed the Bedouin camp at Dofar, killed or taken for ransom the nomads and their flocks and camels.'

William stared at Geoffrey, stunned.

Onri asked him to repeat what he had said, and as he listened his expression grew hard and grim. 'This is too dangerous.' He looked round to see who else had heard, but for the moment the news was confined to their corner of the training ground.

William sheathed his sword, realising that real warfare might end up on their doorstep, and from their own faction. Baldwin was going to be incandescent.

'That man has to be the greatest idiot in Christendom,' Onri muttered, and then pressed his lips together as though he had already said too much.

'I am not surprised,' William said. 'It accords with his behaviour before he came to Outremer. When the blood lust is upon him he is wild and cares nothing for the consequences. I must go.' He clapped Onri's shoulder. 'We'll talk later.'

Ancel sat at Asmaria's table, Pilgrim standing on his lap. Ever the opportunist, the dog was leaning over to lick the meaty sauce from Ancel's finished meal, polishing the platter with his tongue. Asmaria was busy putting the children to bed. Ancel raised his cup and looked at William over the rim. 'Why did he do it?' he asked.

William shrugged. 'Is it not obvious?'

'Because of what happened at Nablus and Petit Garin?'

'I am sure that is part of it, but it is also a challenge to the King. He is kicking him and the Saracens at the same time – punishing one for the damage wrought on Nablus and the other for not doing anything about it.' William refreshed his drink. 'He is flouting the law of the land. The Bedouin have the right to pasture their flocks where they choose by right of the King's writ, and they are valuable allies. They watch and report. In raiding their camp, Guy has destroyed that relationship and broken the rules. Moreover, he has clearly demonstrated he lacks the judgement, common sense and intelligence to be a king, even while challenging for that kingship.'

Asmaria walked past to fetch a blanket. Ancel squeezed her hand as she passed and she reciprocated by placing a kiss on the top of his head.

'What will happen now?'

'That depends on what the King decides to do.'

Ancel stroked the dog. 'What would you do if you were Baldwin?'

Privately, William thought it would be a good idea to send the assassins out after Guy and put an end to him, but held back from saying so aloud. 'I would isolate Guy from power, and I would harness his wife to control him. The Countess of Jaffa is the one with the true authority, not Guy, and if anyone can rein him in, it will be her. She is the mother of the heir to the throne and a princess in her own right. People will support her bloodline even if they do not support Guy. She will not want to see a civil war between her brother and her husband, so I suspect she will do all she can to keep the peace. What Baldwin must not do is take an army to Guy's doorstep, because that is exactly what Guy wants him to do. He will claim Baldwin is incompetent and will do his utmost to make it a fait accompli. If Baldwin ignores him, and the Countess of Jaffa plays peacemaker, there may yet be a chance. Unlike de Lusignan, the King is not a fool and he uses due consideration and reason rather than acting on the spur of the moment.'

He finished his wine and rose to go. 'Whatever happens, I think it best that we be prepared, and that means having our horses and baggage ready to leave at a moment's notice. Don't lend out any of the mounts we might need, and be on your guard.'

Ancel's eyes widened. 'You mean that?'

William nodded grimly. 'If war does break out between the factions, we will be caught up in it, and since we are caring for the Patriarch's yard and the Patriarch's support is for de Lusignan, we shall immediately be suspected of treason by King Baldwin's supporters.'

Ancel chewed his lip as the implications sank in. He glanced over his shoulder to the curtain behind which Asmaria was settling the children. 'What about them?'

'You must talk to her and decide what to do.'

'What if she wants to come with us?'

William knew what Asmaria had come to mean to Ancel, but how practical that relationship would be in another time and place was uncertain. Perhaps about as practical as that between himself and Paschia. 'If we left in haste it would be in a military capacity, but you could send for her.'

'And if I decided to stay?' Ancel asked on a note of challenge.

'I would not force you to come with me, but you would have to think carefully on the consequences. How would you cope without your companions? Who would be your lord and provide for you – de Lusignan? The Patriarch? Bohemond, if you went to Antioch?'

Asmaria returned and they fell silent, although the looks they cast at each other were tense and worried.

'Think about it,' William said, and took his leave. He thanked Asmaria for the food. She smiled, but looked anxiously between him and Ancel, and he wondered how much she had overheard.

'What is this I hear about you leaving?' Paschia demanded. William was ostensibly reporting to her on the progress of her mare and foal and they were standing in the stable yard in full view of the grooms and servants. Paschia's gaze was dark with anxiety and anger. 'Is it true? You would desert your post?'

It was astonishing how swiftly rumours spread. In Outremer,

even thoughts were unsafe. 'Madam, I do not know where you have heard such a thing.'

'That does not matter.' She gestured brusquely. 'However, that I have heard it is my concern.'

'Then you should know I have merely taken precautions. The news of the attack on the Bedouin camp at Dofar has caused great unrest.'

She arched her brows. 'That is as maybe, but it is no reason for you to leave. The King has always been too lenient on the nomads and after what happened to Nablus and those villages, who can blame a strong warrior for retaliating? The King should have pursued Saladin with more vigour.'

'But King Baldwin had a pact with the nomads,' William pointed out. 'Moreover, the Count of Jaffa has committed an act of defiance. If everyone broke the pacts and laws of the land, where would we be?'

She tossed her head. 'You are making a mountain out of a grain of sand. It will all pass over, you will see.' She regarded him with exasperated affection. 'Now is not the time to talk, but I shall see you later, and perhaps we can discuss the matter in more detail.'

William bowed, and put his hand on his heart. 'As you wish, madam,' he said, looking forward to the one and not the other.

'Why do you dislike Guy de Lusignan so much?' Sitting up in bed, Paschia tucked her hair behind her ears. 'Whenever his name is mentioned you get that look on your face, but you will never say.'

'Why do you like him so much?' William countered, pillowing his hands behind his head. 'Why do you think he will make a good king?'

'Because he is decisive, because he is in his prime and strong and has links with the Christian lands beyond the kingdom and will bring in fresh blood. And because he is Sybilla's husband

and stepfather to our young king Baldwin. It is his right to be the hand behind the throne. Sybilla is no weakling. She knows what needs to be done and Guy will see to her mandate.'

William snorted. 'If Sybilla endorsed the attack on the Bedouin then she is politically naive. If she did not, then who says that Guy will obey her mandate, or that she can control him, because clearly she cannot.'

Her eyes flashed with irritation. 'You speak of things you do not understand. Sybilla will smooth everything over with King Baldwin. It will not come to open war, I promise you.'

'But even so, Guy's action was imprudent.' Stung by the scorn in her voice, he added, 'I had to assess men when I served my King, and I know the game of politics. I understand how matters work.'

'Do you indeed?' She tossed her head, but then rolled over into his arms. 'You still have not told me why you do not like Guy de Lusignan.'

'But I have! Is it not obvious to you that the man has no judgement? It matters not if his wife does, because he clearly cannot govern his own actions and the best she can do is set them to right.'

'But you barely know him,' she objected. 'How can you decide on him from the few times you have been in his company?'

'Because I knew him before, in Poitou. He and his family tried to ambush my lady Queen Alienor. Guy murdered my uncle before my eyes – speared him in the back, which was either the act of a coward or a man without control. I was taken for ransom and treated no better than a dog until the Queen secured my release by paying a ransom to the Lusignans. During my time as their hostage I came to know Guy very well indeed, and I have no wish to become reacquainted.'

She arched over him and bit his lower lip, gently. 'People change as they grow older. Guy must have been no more than a youth at that ambush. You cannot hold it against him all your life, surely, or blame a boy for the way he acted in the heat of battle.'

'Since it was my uncle he murdered, you can understand why I might not forgive him easily,' William retorted. 'His attack on the Bedouin tells me he has neither learned nor changed. There are far better men in the world than Guy de Lusignan.' He suspected she found de Lusignan attractive. He was tall and golden and had a charismatic way with women, even if the barons of the kingdom were impervious.

She sat up, straddling him. 'You are as stubborn as an ox,' she said with exasperation. 'And pig-headed with it.'

William laughed, and she struck him, not altogether in play. They tussled and fought, tangling the bedclothes, until she suddenly yielded to him, parting her legs, wrapping them around his waist, and making soft cries of need and surrender that ultimately vanquished him; yet as she clung in her crisis and he surged to his own, he knew that it all came to the same thing in the end: she had taken him, but he had taken her, and it was not a truce, but a stand-off.

She slept after that, and William drowsed, his mind pondering their relationship. She was like no woman he had ever known. The closest he could come was Queen Alienor, but Alienor was steadier than Paschia, older and wiser, less likely to change on a whim, and of course they had never indulged in a physical relationship. It had always been Queen and royal servant.

He had hoped that when he came to make a match it would be with a woman who would be a gentle, tender helpmate, one who would not fight him at every turn, sometimes for the sheer excitement of the fight. This was a woman he should not want and with whom he should never have crossed that line. One moment she was a feral thing, biting and clawing, and the next she was as soft as a kitten in his arms, kissing the scratches she had inflicted, and snuggling up to him. He did not know where he was with her and that in itself was addictive, because he could lose himself and not know where he was either, save that it was like falling into a feather bed, and experiencing that moment of high sweetness before oblivion. He could almost thank God for it, except that it was very wrong; and yet he could not regret the sublime wonder of the experience.

He looked at her hands, folded over, vulnerable, imagined his ring on her finger and knew that had to make their union honourable. To have her lie beside him as his wife, sanctioned by a priest, and not to have to come to this place in secrecy, always watching for spies, always knowing that it could be no more than a few snatched and guilty moments. To have her as his alone, to protect her and keep her safe for the rest of their lives – and decently, without shame.

He turned her round to face him, all sleepy and warm. 'What would you say if I asked you to come away with me? To Normandy, or England. What would you say if I asked you to marry me?'

All the looseness left her body. She buried her head against him so that all he could see was her heavy dark hair.

'I would keep you safe, and cherished. You would never be bought and sold again.'

She raised her head, her expression one of stunned surprise with an undercurrent of wariness. 'You ask a great deal – of yourself I mean. I do not think you realise the consequences.'

'I do, and I am willing. When I set myself to a task or a vow, I never go back on my word.'

She sat up and the setting sun illuminated her body in red-gold light. 'You offer me yourself, and I know you would honour me because you set your honour highest of all.' She looked at him, her eyes quenched in shadow. You ask me what would I say? 'Perhaps you should not ask.'

'Is that a refusal?'

She shook her head and reached out to tenderly brush his hair from his eyes. 'No, my fine English warrior lord. But it is a warning.'

'So, if it is not a refusal, then you consent?'

'You said "if" you asked,' she replied. 'And I am warning you not to ask. You know whatever I answer now is like the spin of a gambler's coin. Whichever way it lands is the answer for now, but it is not the answer for another day and another spin of the coin. I do love you. I care deeply if unwisely, but what you ask—'

'If I do leave, will you at least consider coming with me?'

She frowned. 'I will consider it, and that is all I can say for now, save that you have offered me a truly priceless jewel.' She kissed him gently, and then, turning away from him, sought her clothes. 'I do not think it will be necessary for you to leave. Sybilla will sort this out. Truly a mountain has been made from a grain of sand and you have only seen the mountain because it is so much bigger, even though it is an illusion.' She braided her hair and efficiently tidied it away under her veil. 'I counsel you to think again about Guy de Lusignan, because he is fit and strong, and the King is not.'

William opened his mouth to answer and changed his mind. In this matter they were not as one; she did not understand the nuances, nor the loathing he had for de Lusignan – perhaps never would.

'You will see.' She kissed him a final time and, tapping the end of his nose with her fingertip, left the chamber.

As he dressed, William felt as if he was in limbo with a hollow longing inside him that could never be assuaged.

29

Manor of Caversham, April 1219

William thought he was awake, but was not sure that he could be, because Paschia was sitting at the bedside holding a jewel casket with blue and gold enamelling and riffling through the contents. Gold ribbons adorned her lustrous black hair and she was wearing the dress of flame-coloured silk that had been his favourite. Her skin was taut and young and her eyes were like dark gems.

Becoming aware of his scrutiny, she looked up and, meeting his gaze, held up an oval of clear, polished rock crystal set in gold. 'Your offer to me was like this jewel,' she said, 'priceless and pure, and I cherished it with all my heart.' She tilted the box toward him so that he could see inside, see it was full of numerous other jewels and gemstones in multiple colours: a chain of rubies, ropes of pearls, cuffs of gold and amethyst, sapphires as blue as a moonlit sky. 'You see,' she said, 'I could not have given up all of these in order just to have one. It was impossible.' She held the rubies to the light. 'Who can find a virtuous woman? She is more precious than rubies.' She shot him one of the smiles he remembered and her eyes sparkled with tears. 'Heraclius gave these to me.'

He stretched his hand toward her and a plain gold ring glinted on his little finger.

'Ah, William,' she said. 'My English lion.'

'I have always kept it.' He tried to smile. 'You often called me a fool.'

Closing the casket, she rose to her feet, her gown shimmering. 'Your only folly was me.'

'Yes, I still have the scars.'

'And the truce?'

He paused to think, to draw breath and sustenance. 'I stopped fighting many years ago, because I no longer had that need.' He looked to the door as a young woman entered, her hair falling to her waist in a skein of rippling gold. She was holding a small boy and she was heavy with child. 'I have my own box of jewels,' he said, 'and they have rendered me full compensation.'

The vision of Paschia faded and so did the one of his wife as a young woman. He watched an older Isabelle cross the room to the bedside. Her waist was thickened from the bearing of ten children, her belly softly rounded. She was carrying their youngest grandson, Ralph, in her arms, just six months old. The baby, free of his swaddling and clad in a linen smock, was joyously waving his little arms and legs about.

'You were talking?' Isabelle said as she sat down at the bedside.

'Was I?'

'You said something about jewels.'

'I was thinking of you and our children and grandchildren and how I have a treasure chest full beyond any reckoning known to man.'

She forced a smile. 'Mahelt has gone riding with her brothers, and I thought if you were awake, you might like to see this little one for a moment.' Very gently she placed the baby in his arms.

Grandfather and grandson regarded each other solemnly. 'Blue eyes,' William said. 'Like yours, like the sea.'

Ralph laughed at him, showing two small teeth, and when William gently tickled him, he gurgled with delight. The sound filled William with painful joy and made him chuckle. He was not going to see this one begin to crawl, let alone walk, but his blood ran in the baby's veins, and who knew what he would make of his life, which was all gloriously before him? William derived great comfort from knowing that life continued and he had been given the privilege of seeing his grandchildren, as many had not. 'I have much for which to be thankful,' he said softly. 'And I am well reminded.'

After a while she took Ralph from him and jogged him on her knee, and William saw the worry lines etched into her face, but she was radiant too as she played with their grandson and forgot her cares for a moment. He remembered watching her as a young mother, playing similarly with Will at Longueville and flashing him a glance so full of joy and pride that his emotions had magnified until he thought he would burst.

He thought about love and how it could be like a sheet of fire or the silky shine on a blade, or the tinkle of bracelets as a woman clasped her ankles around your waist, her nails as sharp as daggers. Or it could be the wide, deep ocean, more fathomless than a man could understand; or the harbour that brought the ship home to safe anchorage. And now he had to leave that ship and even that ocean, for something more profound and deeper still.

30

Toward Tiberius, February 1185

William rode into the nomad camp swathed in dark robes and mounted on Ancel's donkey, Lucky. He was certain he had developed saddle sores. His feet almost trailed on the ground and he had to constantly tap the animal's rump with a stick to make him move forward. But at least, even if one-paced, Lucky was tireless and more economical in terms of fodder and water.

Onri had chuckled at the sight of him thus mounted, his light armour swathed in robes such as the Arabs wore. 'No one would believe such a sight if they saw you in Rouen or London!'

William had rolled his eyes at Onri. 'I am not sure I believe such a sight myself.'

'You are doing us a great service,' Onri said. 'We won't forget.'

'I am not sure how to take that remark,' William had retorted and, with a click of his tongue and a tap on the donkey's rump, had set out on his mission.

He was to visit the Bedouin camp where he had sometimes bought horses and he was to ask their leaders to graze their flocks near an area that was constantly being raided by the Saracens. They would then report on what they saw and the Templars would utilise the information. Since William was on unofficial business and not riding with his men, lest the nomads in their turn were being watched, he had disguised himself as a common traveller with his shabby donkey. Following Guy de Lusignan's raid on the Bedouin of Dofar, the tribesmen were wary, and a single man entering their camp in native garb was likely to have more success than a troop armed to the teeth in Frankish war gear.

Finding the group was the first issue: it took him several days and a couple of false trails before he discovered them grazing their flocks in a sparsely wooded valley to the north between Jerusalem and Acre. News of his approach had already flown through the camp and the men were waiting for him, prepared either to welcome or repulse depending on the impression he made. A crouching woman ceased scooping nuggets of camel dung into a basket and watched him suspiciously. Another grabbed her playing child off the ground and hastened into a tent.

Dismounting from Lucky, William wondered if his backside would ever feel the same again.

He was greeted by the head man, Abdul, and invited to take refreshment in his tent. Lucky was led away to join the rest of the tribe's animals, and William handed his knife and sword to an attendant.

William removed his turban, his voluminous outer swathings, and divested himself of his light mail shirt and short gambeson. A male attendant brought water to wash William's feet and another provided a platter of sweetmeats and a syrup drink made from lemons and sugar, served in a cup of exquisite Tyrian glass.

William played out the game of social etiquette. Nothing could be hurried and all must be done with due reverence and purpose. Quietly the other senior men of the tribe arrived at Abdul's tent and took their places, and William greeted each one with a 'Salaam' and a bowed head.

Once the formalities had been observed, William presented Abdul with a silk pouch dimpled with jewels, gemstones, pearls and gold. William had not seen its contents until now and he was astonished, although his expression remained neutral. He and Paschia could have lived on the value of that pouch for the rest of their lives.

The Bedouin were clearly impressed by the gift but their faces grew serious when William told them about the border area that the Templars wanted them to watch and drew a diagram in the dirt with a stick.

'It will not be easy, but it shall be done,' Abdul eventually said with dignity. Against his sun-darkened skin his irises were almost tawny-yellow. 'Tell your lords that all shall be arranged; we shall keep watch and report.'

More of the lemon drink was passed around and a young man produced an oudh and began to play.

'We hear that the Templars have a new Grand Master,' Abdul said.

'That is so,' William replied, 'but he has been in that position ever since Grand Master Torroja departed with the other envoys, so there is little change for the moment.' He marvelled again at how effective the Bedouin were in trapping information – as if they had great fishing nets sweeping in news from miles around. Arnold de Torroja had died in Verona and the news had returned via a Templar galley that had braved the winter seas to bring the tidings. The Patriarch and Roger de Moulins were continuing on their mission as best they could.

'We also hear that the King has appointed a regent while he recovers from his illness – may he do so *inshallah*.' Abdul bowed his head and sent William a probing look.

'God willing,' William responded, touching his heart. 'But the kingdom is in good hands while the lord of Tiberius holds the reins.'

On hearing of the raid upon the Bedouin, King Baldwin had returned to Jerusalem from Acre. He had done his utmost to smooth the situation, sending reparations of camels, food and money to the survivors and castigating Guy de Lusignan in scathing terms. He had considered going to war against Guy, but following exhortations from Sybilla, backed up by de Ridefort, he had agreed to drop the matter, especially since he and Sybilla were in mourning for their mother who had died of her own long illness while he was at Acre.

Frail and sick, Baldwin had convened the High Court of Jerusalem and appointed Raymond of Tripoli as his regent, making it clear to all, including Sybilla, that he considered Guy de Lusignan unfit to rule. She had not responded, but William did not believe that it signalled acceptance, rather that she was biding her time, and treating Guy's behaviour as the tantrum of a frustrated small child.

'Indeed, the lord of Tiberius is deeply respected,' Abdul said. 'He is a man who has the wisdom to listen beyond that which he hears, and that is a good thing.'

William spent the night with the Bedouin, sitting round their fire, listening to their tales and in his turn recounting stories of his own life in lands that these people would never see. They were keen to hear about the abundant rainfall where for most of the year the grass was as green as the emeralds in the pouch of jewels he had given them. He was not sure that they believed him.

Later, lying on his rug near the tent entrance, he gazed at the stars, listened to the huff of camels, and thought of home. He wondered what Paschia would make of England and Normandy. How would she respond to a green country of mists and rainfall and golden-leaved autumn forests? The tart taste of an apple, and the blaze of a proper log fire? He closed his eyes to better imagine the scene but it faded and all he could feel was cold northern rain falling on his face like tears.

In the morning, William straddled Lucky and left the camp, provisioned with camel's milk and dried dates for his journey. The Bedouin were already preparing to move their flocks to keep watch and report. He could not remember his dreams beyond a sensation of wistful longing and the steady soft patter of rain.

* * *

After returning to Jerusalem, William took Lucky to Asmaria's house where Ancel kept him stabled. Asmaria used him to carry her wares, and Ancel paid for his upkeep.

'You have just missed your brother,' she said cheerfully, giving William a drink while he made a fuss of Pilgrim. 'He has gone to the bath house.' She eyed him askance. He had unwound his turban and now wore it as a scarf wrapped several times round his neck over his old quilted tunic. His hose was threadbare and his beard needed a good trim. A pungent aroma of donkey clung to him. 'Perhaps you might see him there,' she added with an impish smile.

'I think you are right,' William said with a grin.

She was clearly curious as to what he had been doing, but asked no questions. He finished the watered wine, thanked her and departed for the bath house, having paid her eldest boy to run to the patriarchal palace with a message for Eustace to bring him fresh clothes. He could have gone himself, but he did not want Paschia to see him and start asking questions, for she would have none of Asmaria's restraint. He did not want to think that perhaps he did not quite trust her and banished the thought because it was too painful to explore.

William found Ancel in the Patriarch's bath house near the Hospital. He was lying on a table being simultaneously washed and pummelled by Salim, one of the bath attendants.

'I have returned Lucky to his stable and fed and watered him,' William said. 'Asmaria told me you were here.'

Ancel turned his head on his folded hands and cocked one eye at his brother. 'I trust your journey was successful?' He did not ask what William had been doing.

'Yes,' William said, without elaborating, and began to remove his clothes.

'Have you been to the palace yet?'

William shook his head. 'I'll make my report as soon as I'm presentable. I've sent Asmaria's lad to tell Eustace to bring me clothes.'

Ancel hissed through his teeth as the bath attendant began to rub him powerfully with his soapy cloth. 'There is news,' he said in a choked voice. 'The King's condition has worsened while you've been gone. The Countess of Jaffa arrived from Ascalon yesterday.'

William looked sharply at Ancel. 'What is wrong with him?'

'A persistent fever – it abates and then returns and each time he grows weaker. I do not know any more than that, but Zaccariah has been stamping around with ants in his braies.'

Freshly bathed, wearing clean raiment, William left Ancel at the bath house and walked the short distance to the royal palace. The late winter day was cold and clear, the afternoon sky a pale, insipid blue without a shred of cloud. There had been very little winter rain so far – a few flakes of snow just after Christmas, and one day's solid downpour in late January, but nothing to speak of since early December. People were muttering that if it did not rain soon, there would be a famine in the autumn.

He was passed through to the King's day chamber by the ushers who knew him well and as he entered the room he was assailed by the scent of lemons and incense that did not quite mask an underlying fetid aroma of sickness. Baldwin was in bed, propped up with pillows and cushions. He wore a white headcloth and a loose linen chemise over his heavily bandaged arms. His face was gaunt and sunken beneath the ruins of leprosy and it was like looking upon a living corpse. He was all that held the Kingdom of Jerusalem together. A single indomitable will, a rotting body, and a stuttering heart.

A multitude of barons and magnates were gathered in the main part of the room and around the bed while a physician helped the King to drink a tisane. Some women sat to one side, and William saw the Countess of Jaffa among them. Little King Baldwin was playing at his mother's knee with a pair of toy knights. Sitting at Sybilla's side, comforting her, was Paschia. William's heart leaped as he took in her lithe figure, clad in a blue gown and demure white wimple, but knowing the danger, he rationed himself to a single swift glance. She was busy with Sybilla and had not seen him, and he did not want to draw her gaze.

He returned his attention to the bed where Raymond of Tripoli was watching the physician spoon the tisane into Baldwin's mouth. Baldwin choked a little but managed to swallow some of the medicine. An attendant gently patted his face with a cloth and Baldwin gestured with one of his bandaged hands to another attendant who helped him to sit further upright on the bed.

'I am not dead yet,' he announced in a slurred, gravelly voice. 'My body may be failing but my will is still strong. If I am to die in my bed, not on the battlefield, then I must ensure that I leave this kingdom strong in its resistance to our enemies and not divided against itself.'

'Indeed, sire,' murmured Raymond of Tripoli. 'That is the wish of us all and may God grant that it be so – but we pray that you recover as you have done before.'

'Indeed, may God grant such mercy, but if He does not then I must make provision,' Baldwin said. 'We hear no news from the Patriarch and the Grand Master of the Hospitallers, and we cannot depend on any arriving for weeks or even months to come, and therefore we must act now.' He lay back against the pillows, exhausted, his chest rising and falling rapidly. The physician leaned over him and Baldwin waved him aside. 'We shall summon the High Court to meet in four days' time and the matter shall be decided. Let the scribes send out letters now.'

'Sire, I shall see that it is arranged immediately.' Raymond bowed and turned away to begin issuing commands.

The future King of Jerusalem galloped past William on his wooden hobby horse, golden hair flopping over his brow. Not looking where he was going, he tripped over his feet and landed hard on the tiled floor. Being nearest, William hastened to pick him up.

'Sire, let me assist you. You were riding so fast that your horse could not sustain the pace.'

The little boy gazed at William from round blue eyes. Even though he screwed up his face and his knees must have been smarting there were no tears. 'My horse is the fastest in the kingdom, faster even than my papa's.'

By his 'papa' he meant Guy de Lusignan.

'I am sure that is so, sire,' William replied neutrally.

'Mama says he is coming to Jerusalem because my uncle the King is unwell and wants to see him.'

'Indeed.' William suppressed a grimace. The pigeons would be flying to Ascalon and Guy would be here on his own fast horse for the King was clearly dying. A proxy would have to be appointed, because Baldwin's named successor was this little boy. Raymond of Tripoli was acting regent, but it was clear from Sybilla's presence in the chamber and the child's comment that his stepfather was on his way that there might be a challenge.

'Mama wants to see him too, but I don't know why because they are always fighting under the bedclothes.'

William almost choked. At that moment Paschia arrived, her hand held out to take the young king and lead him back to his mother. 'Come,' she said, 'you must not run around in your uncle's council chamber; it is unseemly.' She looked at William. 'Messire Marshal, thank you for coming to the King's rescue; I am glad we can count on you.' Her eyes were filled with amusement, speculation and a glint of lust.

'You can always count on me, my lady,' William said with a bow.

'I am glad to hear it. I shall no doubt speak to you later.' She touched the plain gold ring on her finger and William placed his hand on his heart.

Paschia returned the boy to his mother, and William departed the royal palace for his lodging, feeling unsettled and disturbed.

* * *

332

William gazed up at the light pouring down through the apex of the dome while he recovered his breath. There had been no talking when he and Paschia came together, only frantic divesting of clothes and a white-hot all-consuming need for each other's bodies.

'Where did you go?' she asked him, one thigh curled over his and her hand across his chest. 'None of your men could tell me – or wanted to tell me. You did not take your horse.'

'I had duties,' he answered with a shrug. 'To do with protecting the roads.'

She narrowed her eyes. 'Duties you are not going to tell me about.'

William smiled. 'I do not think you tell me all of your business, my lady.'

She made a face at him. 'I will find out you know.'

'Perhaps, and perhaps not.'

She pinched him hard enough to make him flinch, and then rose to pour them each a cup of wine. He admired the heavy silk of her blue-black hair, her narrow waist and the curve of her buttocks.

'You know the King is dying,' she said as she returned to bed.

William took a swallow of wine and sighed. 'Yes. It seems to me that there is no balance in the world when the King of Jerusalem is soon to pass away and be succeeded by a child of six years who runs about the chamber on a pretend horse, while in England, King Henry has three grown sons all fighting each other for the crown.' He looked at Paschia. 'That little boy is going to be a minor for a very long time. He has much growing to do and his education has barely started. It will be ten years before he is capable of taking the reins. The Kingdom of Jerusalem has a sick king and a very small child to succeed him, and that is a powerless position indeed.'

'Yes,' Paschia agreed sombrely. 'All will depend on the regent – whoever is chosen.'

He arched his brows. 'I would hope Raymond of Tripoli prevails. He has the most experience and the barons will follow him.'

'But he is not the only one, and not everyone trusts him, including the Countess Sybilla, and she is the mother of the heir. Her say is paramount.'

'Not if she speaks for her husband, surely,' William said. 'No one will accept Guy de Lusignan. You know that.'

'No, I do not,' Paschia answered, her eyes flashing. 'He has supporters too and he is young Baldwin's stepfather. The Templars back him. Gerard de Ridefort will never stand shoulder to shoulder with Raymond of Tripoli. If you have any sense you will cultivate Guy, because sooner or later he is going to become King of Jerusalem. That is the truth of the matter whether you like it or not.'

They had gone from the ecstasy of a shared intense physical experience to a different tension bordering on argument like the charged edge of a thunderstorm.

'If King Henry agrees to come to Outremer, there will be no place for Guy de Lusignan. He was banished from court for my uncle's murder.'

'And if your King Henry does not come?' Paschia retorted. 'What is there to lose in being amenable?'

William shook his head. 'You do not understand.'

'Then make me understand.'

He dug his hands through his hair in exasperation. 'When I was at court, I answered to a king. It was my duty to say who came before him and who did not. It was my judgement to assess who was suitable and who should be turned away. I was on watch for any kind of threat. My service was my honour and my lords were men I could respect and feel that honour in serving. That is why I will not seek service with Guy de Lusignan, for I have neither of those things to sustain me. Now do you understand?'

She stared at him, and he stared back and saw something

flicker in her expression. Respect, or perhaps a reassessment of her opponent. 'I think you are being foolish.' She tossed her head. 'You should think again.'

'If I do, it will only be to come to the same conclusion.' He finished his wine, set the goblet aside and reached for her. 'If Guy de Lusignan becomes the power behind the throne, I shall return home. I cannot remain here and serve under such a man.'

She resisted the pull of his arms.

'Have you thought any more about my offer? That you could come with me in honour as my wife?'

Her eyelashes flickered down. 'I am still thinking,' she said. 'I do not know if I can.'

'But why stay here in a dead kingdom when we could have the world at our feet? You would be free of all that.'

She sighed and shook her head. 'I am the mistress of the Patriarch of Jerusalem – I have jewels and riches and a position, even if I am not his wife. How will I live if I am wed to an itinerant warrior, even if he is employed by kings? How will the people in England look on me? Can you protect me from their thoughts? When they know who I am, they will shun us both.'

William wrapped his arms around her. 'That will not happen,' he soothed. 'You shall want for nothing, I swear. I want our union to be honourable. I do not want you to go in fear of men such as your uncle, or to be endangered by what is happening here. I want you to be safe and I do not want to come creeping to your chamber like a thief in the night.'

Her resistance suddenly slackened, and she softened in his arms. 'When we are lying together like this, I believe you could protect me from anything and that we could make a life together.'

'Then believe all the time and say yes.'

She raised herself on one elbow and looked down at him, and instead of giving him a spoken reply kissed him tenderly on the eyelids, the points of his cheekbones, the end of his nose. 'My English lion,' she said, and then claimed his lips.

The kiss was meltingly sweet. William considered pushing her to answer him, but he took her physical demonstration as her line of truth and kissed her in return. He made love to her as if she were a fragile, precious vessel, each touch as soft as a breath, and each breath a feather of air over sensitive skin. So often their lovemaking was wild and elemental – a battle to take each other to the point where the only way out was to agree an exhausted truce. But now, with the first lust burned off and dreams in the air, a wistful tenderness permeated their union. This could be for ever, if only. Even when their bodies joined together there was no urgency, no will to dominate, but rather a wish to move slowly and smoothly, like waves undulating to shore in ripples of sensation that built with a powerful, slow intensity.

When the final surge crested, she wrapped her legs around him and clung to him for dear life, gripping his shoulders, legs clasped high around his waist as his breath locked in his throat and he let go. After that they slept, twined around each other like two swimmers washed up on an empty golden shore.

It was late when Paschia left. As she moved to the door, William swept her back into his arms like an undertow and kissed her again.

She responded with enthusiasm. 'I do love you, whatever happens, remember that,' she said. And then she was gone.

Standing alone, William wondered if there had been a note of regret, almost apology in her tone. He was still drugged with lassitude and the sensations engendered by their lovemaking. He knew in the moment and in the dome she was his, but beyond that it was a different reality, and on a whim, assent could change to denial.

He listened but heard nothing below. He went down the stairs and, having locked the door, entered the chapel. Fresh prayer candles burned to one side of the altar, and the painted frescoes were deeply shadowed as the light faded into dusk. As William crossed the room, his spine tingled and he looked round, alert for danger, but saw nothing, although the shadows were deep and could have concealed half a dozen people. He quickened his pace and left the building, but then lingered a while in the courtyard to see if anyone emerged behind him. No one did, and he decided that his heightened sense of danger was the result of an uneasy conscience. He retired to his chamber, flopped across his bed, and almost immediately fell into a deep slumber, his arm bent across his eyes.

William sat on a bench in the ante room of King Baldwin's chamber and watched the open doors which had been thrown wide to grant the King's soul an easy departure. Although Baldwin still breathed, those breaths were measured in hours rather than days. The waiting had begun the previous night and it would be night again soon and still the King clung to life and the court waited.

It was three weeks since he had summoned the High Court of Jerusalem in order to nominate a regent and execute a plan to deal with the administration of the country in the immediate aftermath of his death before Heraclius's mission returned from the French and English courts. Raymond of Tripoli, as expected, had been declared regent during little Baldwin's minority, but restrictions had been placed on his rule. The major castles were to be put in the hands of the Templars and Hospitallers and the little king was to be given into the custody of his great uncle Joscelin de Courtenay rather than being cared for by Raymond of Tripoli. However, that same ruling meant his stepfather would not be his guardian. If the child died before he attained his majority, then the matter of who wore the crown of Jerusalem was to be adjudicated by the rulers of France and England. It was a workable compromise.

A great crown-wearing ceremony had been held in the church of the Holy Sepulchre and everyone had sworn to uphold the young king's reign. He had been borne from the church on the shoulders of Balian, lord of Ibelin. Men said it was because Balian was the tallest man there and thus the young king could be seen by all, but in truth it was to satisfy the honour of all factions.

Messengers had already set out to Heraclius with the news of the court's decision, which meant they would probably try and speed the embassy's return. They were needed, and their reply was needed too, but William knew he must either leave with Paschia before Heraclius returned, which would take skilful and clandestine planning, or else make an end of it. Both options caused him turmoil not least because he knew he would not be in this situation had he not embarked on the affair in the first place.

He rose to pace the room, no longer able to contain the energy of his thoughts.

Paschia joined him, standing formally apart from him as he made his obeisance.

'There is no change, my lady,' William said.

Her face wore a look of strain and she fiddled with the plain gold ring that she used to summon him to the dome and that she had told him had belonged to her mother, and her mother before that. 'It has reached the stage where it makes no difference. Whether we wait an hour or a day or two days, the outcome is the same.' She moved away from him, brushing his hand as if by accident, and went to sit on a bench on the other side of the room.

There was a sudden commotion in the chamber beyond and Princess Sybilla emerged at a brisk walk, one hand clutching her midriff. Her pace quickened as she approached the turret stairs leading to her chamber. Paschia immediately hastened to her side, putting one arm solicitously around her waist. Moments later, Guy de Lusignan emerged, his expression set and grim as he followed his wife and Paschia.

The Bishop of Lydda came to the doorway to announce the death of the King to the gathered courtiers, but even before he spoke, everyone dropped to their knees and bowed their heads. William felt the rise and fall of breath in his own chest, the strength in his muscles. Another suffering young man gone too soon from the world, leaving a hole at the centre of everything that could never be filled by a small boy backed by an uneasy coalition of barons, many of whom would not choose to associate with each other. For now, Raymond of Tripoli was regent, but everyone would be looking to the return of the envoys from their mission and praying that a new king was on his way.

'How is the Countess of Jaffa?' William asked Paschia.

He was visiting her apartments, to report on her horses and deal with other minor business. The doors were open to public scrutiny and servants moved about their duties in the background. Zoraya was busy folding some of Paschia's clothes and putting them in a small coffer.

She stroked her cat. 'I am going to sleep in her chamber for a while,' she replied. 'She is deeply upset.'

'That is to be expected,' William said. 'She had her differences with the King, but they were still brother and sister and I know she loved him.'

'Yes, she did,' Paschia said, 'and he betrayed her. That is what grieves her most of all.'

William was astonished. 'How has he betrayed her?'

Paschia gave him a stony look, almost as though it was his fault. 'By trying to have her marriage annulled. By undermining her and ensuring that the regency has gone to Raymond of Tripoli. Her son is a king, but she will be allowed no say in his life, in how he grows to manhood, because she and Guy have been cut out of the plans. That is why she was weeping; that is why she was distraught. She told me that when he died, she ran out of the room before she kicked his corpse.'

339

'Dear God.' William struggled to assimilate what she was saying.

Paschia's voice shook with passion and her eyes blazed with tears. 'She is my friend. She has always accepted me, and acknowledged me for who I truly am. She sees me – she has always seen me, and valued my loyalty and my skills when others have dismissed me as nothing but the Patriarch's whore. And as she has been loyal to me, so I shall be loyal to her. You often speak of oaths and loyalty; well that is mine – and if it means loyalty to Guy de Lusignan, then so be it. I am sorry that King Baldwin is dead, and doubtless my lady Sybilla will be too, but for the moment her greatest sorrow is that she is not queen-regent.'

William drew a breath and held it. Now he knew where he stood, and why she was so keen to bring him into the Lusignan camp. He shot a glance at the maid.

'Zoraya will say nothing,' Paschia said with a dismissive wave. 'She is loyal to me unto death, and I trust her more than anyone.' She gave him a pointed look and then covered her face with her hands. 'You do not know,' she said through her fingers. 'You will never understand.'

'But I do know; I understand very well!' he replied. 'I have dwelt at the courts of kings and those who have agendas since I was the same age as the little King. Indeed, I have been a powerless hostage myself as a small boy. I was a squire in one of the greatest houses in Normandy and a hearth knight to Queen Alienor.'

She lowered her hands and looked at him with blank composure. 'Who is now her husband's hostage for the good behaviour of her sons, one of whom is now dead. Is that what you "understand", messire?'

'Yes,' he said tersely. 'I know how dangerous it is. Perhaps it is you who does not have any idea.'

She sighed, and rubbed the space between her brows with the tip of her index finger. 'I am weary of this. I wish you to escort me to the palace. Zoraya, have you finished?'

'Yes, madam.' The maid curtseyed and picked up a large silk-wrapped bundle and a leather satchel. She sent William a quick glance from dark hazel eyes and then dropped her lids. He hoped Paschia was right about her loyalty.

Paschia donned her cloak, fastened it across her breast and went out with Zoraya following a pace behind, and William bringing up the rear. As they were walking toward the gate, Zaccariah emerged from the palace and observed them with his hands on his hips and his eyes narrowed. Paschia ignored him, save to put her head in the air and sweep majestically through the gate.

William walked at her side, keeping a proper distance and ensuring that her path was unimpeded, his hand on his sword hilt as he inhabited the role of the stern knightly guard.

The soldiers on duty at the royal complex passed them through the doors. William would have turned back then but Paschia gave him an imperious look. 'You will not leave me until I have reached the chamber,' she said. 'You told me that you understood, and I gave you the benefit of the doubt.'

'As my lady wishes,' William replied, tight-lipped, and accompanied her to Sybilla's chambers.

He had been there once before, on the day that Baldwin had discovered his sister had absconded to Ascalon rather than see her marriage annulled. Then the room had been in disarray, the furniture overturned and filled with the evidence of a hasty retreat. Now Sybilla was pacing up and down, hands pressed together at her lips. A trestle of food and drink had been set up along one wall and various nobles were present, none of them belonging to Raymond of Tripoli's faction.

Paschia went straight up to Sybilla and curtseyed. Sybilla raised Paschia to her feet, kissed her on the cheek and led her away, speaking in a low voice.

Guy de Lusignan bore down on him, goblet in hand.

'Sire,' William said stiffly.

De Lusignan's expression filled with amused curiosity and a little contempt. 'Yours is not a face I would have expected to see here, but then I suppose if you are detailed to escort duties you have small choice. Or perhaps you are information gathering?'

'As you say, sire, I have my duties,' William answered blandly.

De Lusignan smiled, his eyes a vivid, sea-shallow blue. 'Of course, but since you are here, you are welcome to my table.' He extended his arm toward the board. 'Please, be my guest.'

William considered refusing, but it was a long time since he had eaten and he was ravenous. As Guy had observed, he could use the opportunity to garner information. He had once said he would rather starve than dine at Guy de Lusignan's board, but since he was trapped, he might as well make the most of the food and watch and listen – and try not to remember that extended right hand of Guy's thrusting a spear into his uncle Patrick's unguarded spine.

He heaped a platter with meat-filled spicy wafers and small salty strips of fish wrapped in vine leaves. There was plentiful bread and good wine. Once equipped with sustenance, William sat down on a bench facing the room and set to with a will; since he did not have to speak when his mouth was full, he could watch instead.

He noted the hangers-on and fixed them clearly in his mind. He was not necessarily going to go running to Raymond of Tripoli with tittle-tattle – Raymond had his own informers – but he was making himself aware for his own sake. Paschia might be scheming how to bring him further into the fold, but he was determined to stay out of it.

As William ate his way steadily through his meal, he watched Guy pile a different sort of platter to the rafters by telling expansive, bold stories to his friends and sycophants – the parody of a king. And his companions laughed or agreed with him, outdoing each other to praise him and gain approval. William was reminded of occasions at Harry's court when everyone had been jostling for position, smiles on their faces and knives behind their backs. Guy encouraged them, his gestures becoming ever more expansive.

Sybilla, attracted by the noise level, approached him and took his arm. 'Sire, there are matters that I must discuss with you urgently.'

William noted that she pinched him. The face she made to Guy and his cronies was that of a wife in need of succour, but to William it was plain that her husband was in danger of making a fool of himself and she was reining him in. His admiration for Sybilla increased, and his opinion of Guy was reinforced.

Having finished eating, he rose to take his leave.

'You must visit again,' Guy said as Sybilla prepared to lead him away. 'I could use your talent in my household rather than letting it go to waste. Your men too. You will find me generous.'

'Sire, I hope that whatever I do, I shall not waste my talent,' William replied, with a bow.

Sybilla steered Guy away, her hand on his arm like a mother guiding a recalcitrant child. William met Paschia's gaze and inclined his head to her, one eyebrow raised in irony. She ignored him.

He had much to think upon, but unless the envoys returned from their mission with King Henry or one of his sons in tow, he knew he would not be remaining. Paschia desired his compliance – he suspected she had told Guy and Sybilla that she could win him over to their cause. But he could not do that, even for love.

And then there were the Templars. Onri kept dropping strong hints that he should become a Templar knight, and William sometimes thought it would be a way out of his various dilemmas, but he considered himself unworthy of taking the vows that Onri, Augustine, and Aimery in England kept with such pure faith and sincerity. Nor did he approve of the new Grand Master, whose position was supposed to be neutral but who had a clear bias toward the Lusignan faction. While the country where Jesus Christ had been born, had walked and performed miracles, was the holiest on earth, it was ruled by men of dust.

When he returned to the Patriarch's palace, he went to the stables because it always settled him to spend time with his horses. Eustace was already there, sitting on an upturned bucket, cleaning harness. The sun had bleached the squire's brown hair to bronze-gold and he was lithe and muscular – a man now, not the boy who had cowered in God's shadow in the days following Rocamadour.

'Zaccariah of Nablus was asking if you were back from escorting Madame la Patriarchess,' Eustace said.

'Did he say what he wanted?'

Eustace shook his head. 'No, but he was asking questions about how many horses we had bought and sold and what we were being paid for escort duties, and poking his nose into our business.'

William grunted. Zaccariah was a great one for turning over every stone he came across in the hopes of finding something underneath he could devour or use for his own ends. 'What did you tell him?'

Eustace looked up from the tack and adopted the expression of a slow-witted oaf. 'I said I didn't know anything about my lord's business. My lord never tells me because I am only here to groom and polish and see to my lord's comfort.' Eustace touched his forelock for emphasis and rolled his eyes.

William grinned. 'Did he believe you?'

Eustace shrugged. 'He was not pleased, but he went away. I said I did not know how long you would be, and that you might have other business for all I knew.'

William nodded and dismissed the matter from his mind. He sent Eustace on an errand to fetch his working tunic from his chamber, and walked along the stalls talking to the horses and petting them until he came to Rakkas. The gelding whickered to William and stretched out his nose, seeking a titbit. William produced some dates that he had appropriated from de Lusignan's dining board and Rakkas whiffled them up, delicately spitting the stones out of the side of his mouth.

Hearing footsteps, he thought it was Eustace returning, but instead it was Paschia's uncle. A bunch of keys swung from his belt, and he was glowering as usual.

'I spoke to your squire earlier,' Zaccariah said. 'He played the fool, although I know he has his wits about him.'

'I spoke to my squire also,' William replied in a level voice, concealing his revulsion for this odious man. 'He told me you had been asking questions and I am as perplexed as he was, because I do not see that my business is your business.'

Zaccariah gave him a hard look. 'From what I have seen of late, you are doing very well for yourself.' He gestured around the stable yard. 'I think it is time you paid some rent.'

William shrugged. 'I think you will find that my arrangement on this matter is with the Patriarch.'

Zaccariah's own smile was a baring of teeth and he seized William roughly by the arm. 'And I think you will have to listen to me if you value your livelihood and your life. You dabble too deeply in the Patriarch's affairs – I think you know what I mean – and if you do not pay me a commission, I will let it be known where it will do you the most harm.'

Shock surged through William for Zaccariah's words and insinuations made it plain that he knew about him and Paschia. This man was no more than a common pimp trying to extort money. 'I do not know what you are talking about,' he said.

In an instant Zaccariah had slammed William round, pinned him by the throat and had a dagger at his ribs. Rakkas whinnied and plunged, tail swishing. 'By God you will know what I am talking about when the Patriarch returns and I tell him you have been interfering with my niece. Then you will know very well indeed. You might think it's worth paying me then.' Zaccariah seized William's purse and used the dagger to cut the strings. 'This will do as a down payment.'

'My lord, here is—' Eustace stopped in the doorway, and then dropped the bundle of clothes, hands flashing to his own knife.

'Step aside, oaf,' Zaccariah spat, 'or I will gut you like a fish before you draw your next and last breath.'

'Do as he says, Eustace,' William said.

Wide-eyed, breathing hard, Eustace moved to let Zaccariah shoulder past. The latter gave William a triumphant glare over his shoulder as he stalked off.

'He just robbed you, sire,' Eustace said in shock, eyes wide that William was not going after Zaccariah and doing something about it.

William sat down on a stool in the corner of the stall and dug his hands through his hair. His heart was thundering and he felt sick, the large meal he had eaten earlier lying like lead in his stomach. 'It was my own fault. I am always telling you to be on your guard and never to underestimate your opponent and I did not practise what I preached. Let it be. Let him have the money – he will not get any more.' He recovered enough to give Eustace a rueful smile. 'If my purse seemed full, it was because I had some tokens in there for a breast band I was making for Madam's horse. When he tips out the contents he is going to be sorely vexed to find harness decorations.' His smile faded. It was no laughing matter that Zaccariah of Nablus knew about him and Paschia. At the least he would continue to demand money with menaces, and at the worst he would lay the evidence before Heraclius and bring William down. However, since such a course of action also had the potential to bring Paschia down, and threaten Zaccariah's livelihood, he suspected he was bluffing on that score. The main danger was to himself.

'Why was he demanding money?'

'Because he wants part of the proceeds from our earnings and claims we owe him rent.'

'But we're saving that to see us on the road home and pay our way!' Eustace said indignantly.

'That does not matter to him. He only cares about lining his own coffers and keeping us intimidated and under his control.' William shrugged. 'I store the bulk of our money with the Templars, but I will warn the men to hide their purses and only carry as much as they need for a day.'

'I thought when we came to Outremer, to the places where Jesus walked, that it would be a place of great holiness and light,' Eustace said with disgust. 'Indeed, when I entered the Sepulchre and knelt at Christ's tomb, I felt that way; but when I saw the court and the lords and knights who dwelt there, I realised that it's not a holy land at all.'

William nodded grimly. 'You are right there, lad.' He patted Eustace's shoulder. 'Time that we made a decision about going home.'

'What about the Patriarch?' Eustace looked at him askance. 'Are we not to wait for his return?'

'I have some decisions to make about that too,' William said. 'But whether we go or stay, we should make preparations.'

31

Manor of Caversham, April 1219

William listened to the downpour pattering on the new leaves of the oak tree beyond his chamber window. He could smell the fresh spring air on the rain that was blowing into the room and spattering the window-seat cushions. Isabelle would mind, but he did not. Indeed, he wished he could leave his bed and go and sit there and feel the cool drops on his hands and face one last time.

He hoped that the roads on the Welsh borders were not too wet and muddy, for Jean should be on his way back by now if all was well.

His gaze wandered across the room to the garderobe chamber where all the clothes were stored and cared for – the dirt brushed from the fabric, and the moths kept at bay. Last year while in London before he had begun to be unwell, but with a premonition that he might need it soon, he had commissioned his tailor to make him a Templar mantle. The oath he had sworn to the order in the Holy Land had been a weight on his mind for a while. Just a little longer, he had told himself. Enough time to see his youngest children grow sturdy and strong and to ensure his family was protected when he was no longer there to shelter them.

He had been circumspect and no one save his tailor and almoner knew the cloak was in his wardrobe – especially not Isabelle or his children. They would know when the time was right. It was close now, but not quite yet. A few more days while Jean travelled from the rough roads of Netherwent to the green fields of the Thames Valley with his precious package.

Eustace entered the room and looked askance at the open windows. 'The rain is coming in, sire!' He reached to close the shutters.

'No,' William commanded, 'leave them. If the women complain, I take full responsibility. The cushions can be dried.'

'Don't you mean "when" the women complain, sire?'

William found a weak chuckle. 'Tell them that I am fully in my wits and I wanted to see and smell the rain. They will understand.'

'I will take your word for it, sire,' Eustace said dubiously. He was still slim and upright, although his rich brown hair was well frosted with grey now and his face seamed with the lines of middle age. 'I came to tell you that the grey mare has foaled – a chestnut colt with a white star – a fine little stallion.' He grinned. 'On his feet and suckling straight away. He's a beauty.'

William brightened. 'That is good to hear.' One of the benefits of being so ill was that no one brought him bad news for fear of weakening his constitution, and in the little time remaining, there were still moments of poignant delight.

'The lady Mahelt says to tell you he should be given the same nickname as your grandson – Turbeillon.'

William chuckled. 'Why not?' Little Roger was a whirlwind, and by the time he was old enough to sit a warhorse, this foal would be in his powerful maturity. 'Tell her I approve, and mark the foal for his use.'

'Sire, I shall.'

'Before you arrived, I was remembering the horses and the stables we had in Jerusalem.'

Eustace's face lit up with enthusiasm. 'There were some truly fine animals there. If only we could have brought a herd of them back with us – they would have been a sight to behold!' He sobered and flicked William a questioning glance. 'Do you wish we had never gone there, sire?'

William shrugged. 'Sometimes, but I tell myself everything happens for a reason. Even if I am not proud of happenings there in which I had a part, I am glad I fulfilled my oath to lay my young lord's cloak on the tomb of the Sepulchre and atone for what we did at Rocamadour. I have great and humble gratitude for that opportunity. To have walked the same paths as our Saviour has been a great comfort and blessing.' He gazed at the curtain dragging in the breeze. 'But some paths I trod there were not as positive and have lain on my heart and my conscience. I have made confession and been absolved many times. I have done penance and atoned, and dwelt in God's favour, but I still know that those things took place. A sin may be expunged by confession but it does not expunge the memory of that sin.'

Eustace frowned. 'I know there are matters from that time which have disturbed you, and it is not my place to ask, but I wish you to have peace.'

'You have a good heart. Do not let it be troubled on my account.' He patted the coverlet. 'Sit with me a while. If we are to speak of memories, do you recall how I came to employ you?'

Eustace immediately brightened again. 'I was at my father's forge when you came through on your way to a tourney. You had a piece of harness that needed repair, and when I saw you, and your armour and horses – the way you walked as though you owned the world – I knew I had one chance and I seized it.'

William pictured the slight brown-haired lad working the bellows. Eustace had been the fourth son and little required, but drafted in to work while the third brother was elsewhere. He had begged and pleaded to join William's entourage – to work for nothing but food and bedstraw. 'I had no squire at the time, and I was headed to a tourney where an extra pair of hands was essential.' William smiled. 'To be honest I was not sure I had done the right thing. It was like throwing a crust to a stray dog that then follows you around for the rest of its days. You don't know if you will be able to feed it, but it repays you with the utmost loyalty and devotion. And in truth, you were quick to learn and knew exactly which piece of equipment I needed right at the moment, and you always had the remount saddled and the lance ready.'

Eustace shrugged, feigning nonchalance, although his gaze sparkled with pleasure. 'I knew I had to make myself invaluable to you – that if I had been given a chance, I must not squander it.'

'And you didn't,' William said. 'We have been through thick and thin together. You're a grown man, but it is a privilege of my heart to still call you lad, because in spite of all, you have kept your innocence.'

'I don't know about that, sire,' Eustace said gruffly.

'In here.' William touched his heart. 'That is what I mean.'

Eustace blinked hard and pinched his inner eye corners between forefinger and thumb. 'Sire, I do not know about that either.'

'But I do. Come, do not grow maudlin on me. Do you remember all the horse races you used to win?'

He was rewarded with a grin, and once more Eustace was away like a hare, chasing stories of the old times and the joys of the tourneys and fairs they had attended. Tiring, William was still able to interject comments and take pleasure in the moment. Other, more spiritual times and reflection would come, but for now he was happy to dwell in the lightness of memory and bestow it as a final gift upon his squire.

By the time Eustace departed, the rain had stopped. William dozed, and was lightly aware of Roger, one of the chaplains speaking to him, and the comfort of prayers. He mumbled a response, an Amen, and followed his dreams into another time and place.

32

Jerusalem, May 1185

Sitting on the bed in the domed chamber, William waited for Paschia. He had been absent on a horse trading deal all week and she had been attending the lady Sybilla and only now had she sent him a message via her Nubian boy. William had done his utmost to be discreet, but was still on edge that he might have been seen. A part of him thought he should end these assignations, even while another part said he might as well continue, because he was as good as dead anyway. But he still had a responsibility to his men . . .

Hearing light footsteps on the stairs he reached for his knife. Of late he had not been sleeping well, and jumping at shadows. Paschia arrived and, seeing the blade in his hand, she stared. 'What are you doing?'

William let out the breath he had been holding and sheathed the weapon. 'I don't know any more,' he said. 'I was not sure it was you on the stairs.'

'Who else would it be?' She gave him a look that suggested he was being foolish.

'Your uncle, or one of his men . . . He knows.'

Alarm flitted across her face. 'What do you mean "he knows"?'

'About us.' He told her what had happened in the stables. 'He says unless I pay him "rent" he will tell Heraclius everything.'

'He will not do that,' Paschia scoffed. 'It would weaken his position and without me he is nothing. I know things about him that are just as damning. He is trying to intimidate you into giving him money because he will do anything to claw it into his coffers. But I agree that it is not good because now he has leverage.' She stroked his eyebrow with her forefinger. 'Do not worry, we will manage this. Offer him a percentage of what you make on the horses. He might even put more clients your way.'

William curled his lip.

'Or do as he asks and pay him.' She gave an indifferent shrug. 'There are many ways round.' She kissed him gently – tender nipping kisses that became more passionate until they were breathless and tumbled onto the bed together. She trailed her silk sleeves over his body until he thought he would go mad, and she held him on the edge until he was desperate but still enduring because he did not want it to end and he was determined not to yield while she straddled him and took her own fierce pleasure. The sight of her with arched spine and head thrown back, lustrous hair spilling to her hips, almost undid him, but he clenched his teeth and held onto his control until she gasped and fell forward upon him, and at last he could take his release.

Afterwards she wiped them both with a cooling rosewater lotion. Enjoying the long, smooth strokes, the sensual reward even in the return to reality, he touched her cheek. 'If I pay your uncle, I am letting him make a whore of you, and I will not do that.'

'But that is all he understands.' She drew back to look at him. 'You are only of use to him while there is profit in it. He tolerates you for the moment because of your standing with the King of England, who might come here to rule in Jerusalem, but he is weighing up the odds, and if your King chooses not to come, then you lose your influence and you become worthless to him unless you have something else with which to bargain.'

'I am not afraid of him,' William said, but his mind filled with the image of the dagger in the corner of the stable, and those hard, narrow eyes.

'You should be.'

William gently tucked her hair behind her ears, his knuckles brushing the filigreed gold at her lobes. 'Then if I am to pay him, let it be a bride price; let me make this proper between us. You are a widow, I am unwed. In law, there is nothing to stop us, and we do not have to stay here. We could go anywhere in the world.' Taking her hand, he kissed her palm, tasting salt and inhaling the scent of sandalwood.

She tugged free of him and, turning away, began to plait her hair, her movements jerky. 'I told you before that you should not ask.'

'Perhaps, but still I am doing so – for better not worse.'

She shook her head. 'You cannot spring such words upon me and expect an immediate answer. I will have to think on it.'

She was like a cat that had suddenly had its fur ruffled the wrong way when it had been enjoying being petted. 'Then do not think for too long. I am making preparations to leave and I want you to come with me as my woman and my wife, and then all will be honourable.'

Without reply she continued to dress. He leaned round and tilted her face to, and he saw the fear in her gaze. 'I love you. I will look after you and protect you, I promise.'

She rose to her feet without responding to his words. 'I have to go, and so should you.'

'But you will think about what I have said?'

'Yes, of course,' she replied, but he sensed her withdrawal.

When she had gone, he sat on the bed where they had just made love, scooped his hands through his hair and wondered how it had ever come to this.

William did not see Paschia after that for almost three weeks. She spent much of her time in the Lusignan household and he was absent on patrol and engaged in horse dealing outside Jerusalem. Her uncle had not been near him since their confrontation in the stable, but William knew it was only a matter of time before more demands were made. Zaccariah had set a watch on the Patriarch's chapel and it was no longer as easy for William and Paschia to make assignations. The domed chamber was now a flawed sanctuary for the world had intruded and burst the bubble. Sometimes William would receive a summons and set out, only to turn back or pretend to be doing something else because Zaccariah or his squire would be in the chapel.

Eventually, however, Zaccariah left on business, taking his most trusted men with him, and William and Paschia were finally able to snatch an afternoon together.

As they lay entwined and sated, Paschia gently tickled his nose with a strand of her hair. 'What would it be like if we had a baby?' she asked with a musing smile. 'A little boy with your eyes, or a girl with my hair?'

Her words shook him out of his lethargy like a splash of cold water in the face and he was immediately alert, wondering whether this was yet another of her playful games aimed at enhancing desire, or something else. He knew how much she enjoyed feeding on his responses. 'It won't ever be mine,' he said warily. 'Not unless you came away with me and agreed to be my wife, and who am I but a penniless knight?' She had told him not to worry, and like Adam in the Garden of Eden, he had taken her word at face value that all would be well. Now he gently pushed her up and away from him with his arms. 'Really? Are you with child?'

'What if I were?' she said with a note of defensive challenge.

He drew her back down against him. 'If you were, you would be my bride in all ways.' He eyed her warily and stroked her flat belly. 'Is it true? Are you?'

She looked down and fiddled with the plain gold ring on her index finger. 'I do not know. My flux is late.'

William conned over his rather patchy knowledge of women's matters. 'You cannot stay here if this is truth. You will have to come with me.'

She gnawed her lower lip. 'My flux may yet come.'

'But we should make plans.'

'Yes.' Her voice was wan and her earlier air of intimate teasing had dissipated as swiftly as smoke in the wind.

With no small effort, William tugged a gold ring of his own from his little finger, and slipped it onto one of hers. 'I want to make this right and honourable between us. 'Love me or leave me, I give you my ring. It was my mother's and now it is yours. If you will come with me, I will be a happy man and I hope you will be a happy mother to this child we have made between us. I ask you again: marry me and come with me.'

She wiped her eyes with the heel of her hand. 'You are honourable and good. I love you and I love your honesty, but I cannot follow you barefoot in my shift.'

'I would provide for you and the child,' William said. 'You would never go wanting and you would never be beholden again to your uncle or forced to play political games to survive.'

'But I would be dependent on you,' she said. 'Even if you love and honour me, you are not in a position of a man like Heraclius with great power at his command. I do love you,' she added in a subdued tone, and stroked his arm. 'I never expected it to happen. I took you to ease my lust and be my comfort while Heraclius was away, but it has become much more than that and now I must decide what to do.' A bleak look entered her eyes. 'I have lived my whole life with uncertainty with only my wits between death and survival.'

'Then we are alike,' William said, 'for I too have had to live like that. I do understand.'

'You do not,' she said. 'I could not follow you around with a small child. I would be little better than one of the baggage whores in an army's tail.'

William tightened his mouth at her words and she swiftly touched his face. 'I am not trampling your offer in the mud, my love, but I must be practical.'

'I have money,' he said tautly. 'Enough for us to be comfortable.'

'And when men learn who I am? Who I have been? Will they then give you employment, or will they turn from you in contempt? What will my status be? You say you have money but can you afford to keep me as Heraclius does?'

'You will be my wife.' A stone lodged in his belly. 'You cannot stay here, that much is obvious – you cannot conceal a child in the same way as a lover. I have offered you my worldly goods, my heart and my honour. If that is not enough, then it is not, and there is no more to be said.'

She pulled out of his arms and, leaving the bed, went to the window. He stared at the long dark hair spilling down her back and felt an overwhelming mingling of love and pain.

She gazed at the ring he had given her and at length she sighed. 'Very well, I will try, but it is not a promise.'

William's heart turned over. 'But what if you decide you cannot? What of Heraclius? You cannot stay in Jerusalem.'

'I have contacts. If it came to the worst, I could go to them for a time and I would be helped.'

'But do you have more trust in them than you do me?' he demanded. 'If it is more than lust, why will you not come with me?'

'Because there is more to it than that,' she whirled round with an exasperation the match of his own. 'We have to have the means to love. It is not just about you and me. I have people beholden to me in the palace and you have your men.' She gave a defensive shrug. 'It is not certain yet. We should wait until I am sure.'

'Then why tell me if you are not sure?' He suspected she had wanted to play with him and test his reaction. Perhaps appeal to his virility and add an extra fillip to their lovemaking, because that was her nature.

'Because it is preying on my mind and who else can I tell?'

she snapped. 'My uncle?' She shuddered, and for an instant covered her face with her hands. He reached for her but she avoided him and went to her clothes. 'We should go; we have been here too long already.'

'I will protect you, I swear I will.'

She gave him an enigmatic look. 'I know you think that,' she said, 'but I have learned not to rely on anyone. The only person who can protect me is myself.'

When she had gone, William donned his own clothes and thought about what Paschia had told him, and how he was going to manage to take her to safety as his wife. He looked down at his little finger, at the pale band of skin where his mother's ring had lain, and, feeling the loss, wondered if he had given it in vain. He knew that the contacts of whom she spoke would involve Sybilla which meant she would be beholden to the Countess of Jaffa and, by association, to Guy de Lusignan, and that made him feel sick. He had to make her see that leaving with him was their best future, although how he would do that he did not know. They were in a bind, and one way or another they would have to deal with it. For now, he had a great amount of thinking and organising to do, but circumspectly. He wanted to make everything honourable and right, but to do so would expose a festering murk of lies and deceit of which he was deeply ashamed and, once in the light, the repercussions might destroy them both anyway.

William sat on a bench in the hall of the King's council chamber, thankful for the cool stone wall at his back that gave shelter from the beating eye of the sun. Outside, Jerusalem baked in a furnace. Dogs and beggars panted in the shade, every plant wilted, and each day was clear, hard blue and gold like the colours in the city's blazon. The sky and the kingdom. Hot, dry, burning.

The spring had not been wet enough for seed to grow and the scanty rainfall had done nothing to green the grass or fill the cisterns. New wells had been dug in the valley of Hinnon but with patchy results, and the water was brackish and unpleasant to drink. Famine threatened and grain would have to be imported at inflated prices from overseas neighbours less seriously afflicted by the lack of water.

William observed the little King, who sat on a miniature padded throne beside Raymond of Tripoli as the business of the kingdom went forward. The child's attention was wandering. His paternal great uncle Conrad de Montferrat had arrived from Europe to be his guardian alongside Joscelin de Courtenay, who was the same from his mother's side. Guy de Lusignan was present too, and as restless as a hungry lion. He wore a gold silk tunic and his impatience showed in the way his fingers plucked at the embroidery on the sleeves. He folded his arms, unfolded them, and leaned back, puffing out his cheeks. The court had confirmed Guy's position as Count of Jaffa, and although Raymond thoroughly disliked him, he was being the consummate diplomat and treating Guy with neutral courtesy, his air that of a parent ignoring a tiresome adolescent.

Saladin had agreed a truce because he had his own difficulties in his territories. For now, the sere Kingdom of Jerusalem was ostensibly at peace with its Saracen neighbours while droughts and internal politics took their toll on both, but the reality was less smooth. Bands of brigands and thieves abounded on the roads and among the hills, waiting their opportunity to rob pilgrims and merchants, and hot-headed young men on both sides continued to skirmish, raid and break the truces. A convoy of merchants with a cargo of precious sandalwood had recently been robbed and slaughtered to the north of Jerusalem and Raymond had promised to send out extra patrols and be vigilant.

'I ask my lord de Ridefort to see to the matter,' he said, addressing the Templar Grand Master who was sitting close to his right-hand side. 'I realise that these were not pilgrims, but these brigands are as likely to target them on another occasion and we must hunt these people down before they grow stronger.'

De Ridefort inclined his head. 'I shall see that it is done.' His reply was neutral even if his posture was stiff with his dislike of the Regent.

William suspected that he and his men would be recruited to the task, for it was ideally suited to the secular knights in the city.

The next supplicant was ushered into the hall to kneel before the Regent and William saw with shock that it was Augustine de Labaro, whom he had last seen setting out with the deputation to England and France. Even in the heat he wore his heavy white mantle with the red cross of the order on his breast. Although lean and hard-travelled, he was immaculate as he knelt to Raymond, little Baldwin and the senior advisers occupying the dais. Raymond gestured for him to rise, and Augustine bowed again before handing over the wallet of letters he had been holding. William's chest was tight with anxiety, for if Augustine was here, then Heraclius would not be far behind.

'I left the Patriarch and the Master of the Hospitallers at the French court with King Henry and King Philippe,' Augustine said. 'The kings are still debating what to do, but neither is prepared to come to Jerusalem at this stage, although both have pledged their support.'

A muscle flickered in Raymond's jaw, and a murmur rippled around the chamber.

'The kings have given permission for the Church to preach to the people and encourage them to support Outremer in any way they can, especially the knights, and many have undertaken to come as soon as they may.' Augustine hesitated. 'When I left, we were unaware that King Baldwin had yielded up his mortal soul to God, although the news will surely have reached the Patriarch and Grand Master de Moulins by now.'

'When do they expect to be back?' Guy de Lusignan demanded, his expression intent.

Augustine bowed in his direction but turned to address

Raymond and the child-king again. 'By the end of August,' he said.

William bit at a loose strip of skin against his thumb nail. So, he had about eight weeks left if he was going to depart with Paschia, which was a fine margin. Matters would need to be set in motion immediately.

Once the court session had broken up, William sought out Augustine to speak with him, and they clasped each other like brothers.

'I am sorry King Henry would not agree to come to Jerusalem,' Augustine said, 'for he is a man who well knows the business of ruling a kingdom.'

William shrugged. 'I gave the Patriarch all the help I could, but in truth I knew it would be a miracle if he succeeded.'

Augustine's mouth twisted. 'It was bound to fail from the moment they met. The English barons thought our envoys too richly dressed and scented for the land of Christ and could not understand why they were seeking aid when they were wearing gold and pearls and drenching themselves in perfumes that only earls and kings could afford.'

William winced. 'I warned the Patriarch that King Henry would not appreciate such an approach.'

'Well perhaps it was an excuse too for the English barons to sneer at men with different ways, and also perhaps it roused their envy. But you know how much Heraclius sets store by his garments and his person – how worldly he is.'

'Yes,' William said.

'He should have gone to the King of England in ashes and rags, tearing out his hair, not in gold and riches. Why should people give their silver to Outremer when we clad ourselves in more wealth than their kings?' Augustine rolled his eyes. 'But the King still offered him money and Heraclius answered what we really needed was someone to govern the kingdom. Henry agreed to come, but only if his barons consented, but of course he

361

directed them in private to refuse. We were blocked at every turn.'

'I am not surprised,' William said, 'but you were right to try. Again, I am sorry it did not come to fruition.'

'I told King Henry you had succeeded in your mission to lay his son's cloak on the Sepulchre and I said you had done him great service. I spoke with Aimery too and we prayed for you and gave thanks.'

William's stomach clenched. 'I am not deserving of your prayers and accolades,' he said, 'for I am not in a state of grace.'

Augustine gave him a serious look. 'Well that is all the more reason to strive to attain it. If you cannot find a state of grace in Jerusalem, then where else can you?'

'Yes,' William agreed with a touch of despair. 'And the same for the falling. It comes twice as hard.'

'If there is anything I can do . . . any matter you wish to discuss . . .'

William shook his head. 'No, but I thank you for the offer, and the news. I will talk to you later.'

'You have to come away with me.' William drew Paschia into his arms the moment she arrived at their assignation in the dome. 'Now, soon, before Heraclius returns.' He buried his face against her throat, inhaling her scent. 'I have told you I will protect you and our child and I mean it – to the last drop of blood in my body and the last beat of my heart.'

She pushed herself away from him. 'You say you will give me everything, but you ask me in return to abandon my security. Love might enrich our lives, but it does not give us the wherewithal by which to live. Believe me, I have seen love go begging because it does not have the means to flourish.' Reaching up to her hair, she began unpinning the elaborate coils. Concealed among the lustrous tresses were small pouches of money and gemstones. 'I have been sewing the same into the linings of my cloaks and gowns,' she said. 'I must bring as much wealth as I can muster without others suspecting.' Unpredictable as ever, she flashed him a sudden smile, inviting him to admire her ingenuity.

A spark of optimism kindled in William. If she had taken the time and trouble to find ways of transporting her jewels, it was a step forward. 'That is indeed resourceful. I have done the same with my cloak and my belt lining, but I don't have time to grow my hair!'

She laughed. 'You could always wear a wig, or stuff your braies – although they are already well occupied!' She angled her gaze downward, and then set her arms around his neck and kissed him until they were both breathless. She pulled him onto the bed, eager to the point of being voracious, and it was almost like their first time together. Each time he made to draw back, she urged him on, arching, biting, gasping her pleasure. Even when she climaxed, she did not rest, but began building again, to the next one, feverish almost to the point of desperation.

Eventually William held her still and calmed her with long, smooth strokes of his hand. 'Enough. I dissolve the truce and cry quarter. You have won.'

Her breathing gradually calmed and she lay in his arms, rosily flushed, sweat glistening, while he caressed her belly.

'I did not think you would yield the contest so easily,' she said with a smile.

'That was not easily.' He returned her smile but he was preoccupied, suspecting that she had been trying to lose herself in physical sensation to avoid the moment when she had to make hard decisions. 'Nothing has ever been easy with you.' He laced his fingers through hers, and added softly, 'We shall make a good life together. We can settle in St Omer and raise our children and breed the finest horses in Christendom.'

She stroked his face. 'It is a beautiful dream, William,' she said wistfully.

'It is more than a dream,' he replied with fierce conviction. 'It is real.'

'And when I am with you, you make me believe it is real.'

'Then cast aside your doubts and believe. I shall organise our route. Start packing what you need.'

She kissed him, and turned away to dress. As she coiled the jewels back into her hair, she changed the subject. 'I need your escort tonight to visit the Count and Countess of Jaffa. I have promised Sybilla that I will attend her and Guy wants to talk to you about horses.'

William grimaced. The last thing he wanted to do was socialise with Guy de Lusignan.

'I ask you to do it for me,' she said, jutting her chin. 'Look at what I am giving up for you.'

William swallowed his irritation. After all, it would not be for much longer and for her sake he would bear it. 'As my lady wishes,' he said, but without enthusiasm.

'I do wish it.' She kissed him again, swiftly, and was gone.

William's mood was pensive as he left the room. The chapel was empty and he kept to the shadows as he made his way outside. Crossing the courtyard, he noticed Mahzun of Tyre deep in conversation with Paschia's uncle, and was immediately on his guard. Zaccariah eyed William narrowly. Mahzun glanced once and then looked away. Ignoring them, William departed the palace and made his way swiftly to Asmaria's house to find Ancel.

His brother was sitting cross-legged on the floor in the main room, eating a pie and playing dice for spills of wood with the children. He grinned on seeing William and spread his hands in welcome. 'Will you join us?'

William shook his head. 'I have to escort Madame la Patriarchess to a gathering organised by the Count and Countess of Jaffa.'

Ancel snorted. 'I wish you good fortune of that.'

'I doubt any will come,' William replied, making a face. 'I want a word.'

Ancel pushed the last morsel of pie into his mouth, dusted off his hands and, telling the children he would return in a moment, followed William out into the hot, still air.

William watched a brown lizard with copper-jewel eyes basking on the wall. 'I've just seen Augustine at the palace. He's here ahead of the envoys and he says that King Henry is not coming.'

Ancel shrugged. 'We always knew that in our hearts.'

'Perhaps it is time to go home while the pilgrim ships are still sailing.'

Ancel eyed him sharply. 'And not wait for the Patriarch's return?'

William stared at the lizard and did not meet his brother's gaze. 'Whether we stay or go, the situation will not improve. You see how it is with all the factions fighting for control and the drought worsening.'

Ancel pursed his lips. 'What if I want to stay?'

Imagining what would happen to Ancel if he did, William shook his head. 'How would you make your way in the world without an affinity?' He gave Ancel a concerned look. 'Do you really wish to do that?'

'No, I want to go home, but I was thinking about Asmaria and the children. They have become part of my life and it will be difficult to tear myself away from them.'

'Then ask her if she will come.'

Ancel chewed his lip. 'I do not know if she would. She has made her life here and has her own livelihood.' He eyed William curiously. 'I thought you would say leave her behind.'

'No,' William replied in a subdued tone. 'I would not ask you to do that.' He experienced an upwelling of love for his brother who possessed all the innocence and integrity that he lacked. Whatever he did, he was going to let someone down. If only he could unravel what was woven, but that was impossible; he had to make the best of the cloth he had. When he thought about telling Ancel about Paschia, the words jammed in his throat.

'I will see what she says,' Ancel replied.

William hugged him fiercely with a mingling of affection and guilt. Ancel returned the embrace and drew away, looking bemused. Turning to go back inside to his dice game, he paused with his hand on the door. 'Asmaria heard in the market today that there has been another raid on the pilgrim route near Tiberius.'

'Yes,' William said. 'Onri is taking out a Templar patrol tomorrow and we are to ride with him, although I do not know how well we will fare. The raiders know when to attack and when to lie low. I shall see you at dawn.'

That evening William escorted Paschia to the gathering at the Count of Jaffa's hall where Sybilla immediately summoned her to join the women. By moving around the edges of the room making sure that someone was always in front of him, William managed to avoid Guy de Lusignan.

Gerard de Ridefort, Grand Master of the Templars, was present and spoke briefly to William about the following day's patrol. 'The raids have been escalating,' he said with displeasure. 'These men must be stopped and pilgrims and merchants protected. It does not reflect well on the order or on the kingdom that their activities continue and make fools of us all.'

'Indeed, sire,' William replied. 'But it is difficult when they slip away into the hills and the desert, or cross into territory we do not control.'

'Then perhaps we should control it,' de Ridefort said, his mouth downturned.

Guy joined them and William had no choice but to make his obeisance to a man whose notion of setting an example was to plunder merchant trains himself and ignore the boundaries.

'You are elusive, messire Marshal,' Guy said, his look calculating.

'I have many duties, sire, as you can appreciate,' William answered neutrally.

'Indeed, but perhaps you should curtail the least important in favour of the most pressing.'

'That is what I already do, sire.'

Guy raised a gilded eyebrow. 'Then you should think again. Times change swiftly in Outremer, and what is true one day may be false the next.'

'I have observed that too, sire.'

Guy's blue eyes sharpened. 'Actually, I was hoping you might look at my dun stallion. He's gone lame on the nearside forehoof.'

William had no time to deal with such trivia, but to keep Guy from pestering him said diplomatically, 'If you wish to bring him, I will look, sire.'

'Good, I shall do so, and we shall talk some more. You still owe me that saddle.' He pressed William's arm and turned to de Ridefort. 'A word if you will, my lord.'

The two men moved away, Guy smiling and clearly pleased with himself.

William grimaced. He intended to make very sure that he was not available when Guy came visiting.

Paschia joined him for a moment, and her own expression was smug, like a cat that had just licked cream off its whiskers. 'There, it is not so difficult after all to have a rapport with the Count of Jaffa, is it?'

William suspected she had manoeuvred him into attending this gathering for that very purpose and that Guy had been briefed to pounce. 'Indeed not,' he said, 'but sadly I cannot stay longer. I have to talk to the men about tomorrow – with your permission of course, madam.'

She gave him an amused if exasperated sigh, and hooked her little finger around his in a brief intimate gesture. 'If you must, but first the Countess of Jaffa wishes to speak with you. I want you to return when you have finished your business with your knights, for I shall require an escort to my quarters.'

'As my lady desires,' he said.

'And you know all about my desires,' she replied flirtatiously.

Ill at ease, William donned the mask of a courtier and went to present himself to the Countess of Jaffa. Sybilla smiled and bade him sit by her side, signalling a squire to pour him wine and offer him a platter of coloured almond paste flavoured with rosewater. She enquired how he was faring with genuine warmth and interest. William matched his tone to hers and replied with courteous, conversational platitudes.

After a brief lull Sybilla faced him directly, still with a smile on her lips. 'The Kingdom of Jerusalem needs more men like you,' she said. 'We have so few who are truly reliable and trustworthy.'

'I am honoured, madam.' It was more of the same thing, but he was constrained by the circumstances to sit and listen.

'If you chose to stay and swear fealty to me, I could give you wealth and lands beyond anything waiting for you in England. Instead of a handful of knights you would have a considerable affinity and you would be able to equip them with the finest of everything and be a man of high standing.' She gestured with her hand palm upwards to illustrate her largesse.

William inclined his head. She was a skilful player, for it was an excellent inducement and he might have seriously considered it were it not for her husband. 'Madam, again you honour me. I shall certainly think on the matter.'

Sybilla gave him a meaningful look. 'Do not think about it too long, messire. He who waits loses. You have already proven your worth and we shall gladly welcome you, and grant you a place in all of our counsels.' Her words subtly emphasised the point that he would have the increased political weight that came with a higher status. And that too was an enticement.

'Indeed, madam, I shall think on it, and thank you.' He bowed and, as he took his leave, wondered if he could overcome his antipathy. If he could sit at their council table then perhaps he could have an influence from within. He glanced toward Guy and imagined saluting him, taking orders from the man. It was like exploring an aching tooth to see if it still hurt, and discovering that yes it did, and no amount of sweetness would dull the discomfort.

He was making his way out of the palace when Zaccariah joined him. 'Do not return for my niece,' he growled. 'I shall escort her myself.' He set his hand to his dagger hilt in emphasis. 'You will stay away from her if you know what is good for you.'

William eyed him with contempt. 'Since my lady requested me as escort, I shall do her bidding unless she commands me otherwise.'

Zaccariah grabbed William's arm. 'You have trespassed on ground that is not yours, and that trespass will end!' he hissed.

William wrenched free and walked off, but was disturbed, because the threat from Zaccariah was more than just bluff.

He dealt with his men, giving them orders for the morning, warning them not to stay up late carousing, for they had to be on the road at dawn. He double-checked the horses, the harness and equipment, and while his practical mind was busy with the task, he pondered what Sybilla had said and placed it side by side with his intention to leave. To embroil himself with the Lusignans and gain wealth, prestige and power, or to depart with Paschia and face a less exalted but ultimately honourable future in his homeland. Either choice, could, of course, mean an early death.

Preoccupied, he returned to the palace to escort Paschia and her maid back to the patriarchal lodging. There was no sign of Zaccariah, no dark figures lurked in the shadows with a blade.

Paschia looked up at him and smiled expectantly. 'I trust that your meeting with the Countess of Jaffa was successful?'

'The Countess certainly gave me food for thought.'

'And have you decided what to do?'

She must know what had been asked. She and Sybilla had probably talked about it over one of their embroidery sessions, trying to find persuasions that would bind him here.

'Yes,' he said.

'And that is?'

'I am already sworn to the King of England and his Queen and I have promised to return to them. I cannot in good conscience give my oath to the Countess of Jaffa.'

'In "good conscience"?' Her voice rose in disbelief mingled with scorn. 'It seems to me that you only have a conscience when it suits you, messire. Do you know what you are throwing away for you and your men?'

'Yes,' he said. 'And also, what I am not losing.'

'Is that so?'

She pressed her lips together and they walked the short distance to the Patriarch's palace in strained silence. Unspoken words hung between them and the longer the silence lasted, the fuller it became and the smaller the aperture grew for the words to be expressed. All too soon, yet with a feeling of dull relief, William brought Paschia to her door.

'I will bid you good night, madam,' he said formally, all too aware of the maid and the torchbearers. Zoraya might be trustworthy, but any one of the others would carry tales for a fee.

'I wish you Godspeed and success on the morrow,' she said stiltedly. 'Visit me on your return and we shall talk.' She gave him a brief assessing look, one that William had seen often before when matters had not gone to plan but she was pondering ways of pushing them until they did.

He bowed, and put his hand over his heart where the key to the dome lay against his skin. Pain twisted inside him as he watched her enter the house and firmly close the door.

William returned from patrol three days later. They had seen no sign of the brigands but the band was experienced at evading armed patrols and only materialised to take on weaker targets. Having made his report, William went to eat with his men at the Patriarch's palace and begin a discussion about plans for

370

their return to Normandy, although made no mention of Paschia because he needed to think about how to broach the subject and now was not the time. No one raised objections to the general notion of leaving which was thought to be a good decision since King Henry had declined to take up the mantle of kingship in Jerusalem. The country was riven by drought just as the leadership was riven by factions, and by the time they returned home they would have been gone for more than two years.

Paschia was absent from the palace. Her red door was closed and none of her servants to be seen. William was not unduly concerned. She was probably attending on Sybilla and doubtless they were still discussing how to persuade him to join Guy's faction. Zaccariah was absent too, and although William was relieved, he did not relax his vigilance, for his gatekeepers were still present and watchful.

Over the next week, William continued to make preparations to leave and assemble items to go into his saddlebags and onto the pack-horse. Paschia remained elusive, and by the seventh day, he began to feel anxious, for she should have sent a message by now. Forcing himself to focus on the task in hand, he opened a small wooden chest to check its contents. There were several phials of water from the River Jordan; the pouch of salt stones from the Dead Sea that he had privately named Lot's Wife's Necklace; a scraping of mortar from the walls of the church of the Holy Sepulchre; a cross of olive wood from a tree in the Garden of Gethsemane; and the small, square patch of brown wool and the pilgrim cross taken from Harry's cloak. The sight pierced him with grief and he began to shake. 'Christ help me, Harry,' he whispered, swallowing tears.

He was not in a state of grace; should he die now he was going straight to hell – the very thing he had come to Jerusalem to avoid. Before he left, he had to make things right in the sight of God.

Folding the small square of cloth, he replaced it in the box, wiped his eyes and, leaving his chamber, set out with renewed determination to Paschia's dwelling house.

It was still locked up and his answer was a hollow echo when he pounded on the red door with his fist.

'Madame la Patriarchess is not here,' said a voice behind him.

William turned to face a groom from the stable, one of the unskilled men employed to sweep and barrow the dung. William had always suspected that he was one of Zaccariah's spies but had made a point of being amenable to him and paying him tips, because one side could always be played off against the other. Just now the man was shifting tensely from foot to foot.

'Do you know where she is, or when she will return?'

The groom shook his head and brushed away a fly. 'No, sire, but she left the day after you rode out, with her maid – borne in a litter she was.'

William clenched his fists and felt as if he was on the edge of dissolution. There were many reasons she might have gone on a journey. 'What of her uncle? Where is he?' He paid the groom a coin from his purse.

The man tucked the money away and shrugged. 'Gone to Nablus on business.'

'And did Madame la Patriarchess accompany him?'

'I do not know, sire – couldn't say where she was going – she didn't tell anyone.'

William paid him another coin. 'If you hear anything more come and tell me.'

The man took the money, saying he would do so, leaving William to stand in the courtyard, as baffled and anxious as before.

Three more days passed without word. William snapped at the men and he had no appetite, nor could he settle to any task. On the afternoon of the third day, having just finished some lance training with Eustace, he was dismounting in the stable yard when he saw Zoraya coming toward him, her air her customary one of quiet composure. 'Thank God!' He strode to meet her, his heart pounding. 'Where is your mistress?'

Eustace stared and then looked away. Zoraya did not answer. Her dark eyes were inscrutable as she put her hand on her heart to indicate that William should go to the domed chamber.

William handed Flambur's reins to Eustace. 'Stable him,' he commanded. 'I have urgent business.'

Eustace said nothing, his expression taut and closed.

His heart thundering, William took off at a near run toward the palace. Paschia's uncle was still absent and few servants were around in the heat of the day, but he checked himself as he reached the cool darkness of the Patriarch's chapel with its dappled puddles of light from lamps and candles. Taking a deep breath, forcing control on himself, he crossed the room, slipped through the door, and climbed the stairs.

Paschia was already in the domed chamber, sitting on the bed waiting for him, her head down and her hands folded. She had no smile for him, no fire to light her eyes. Indeed, she avoided his gaze altogether.

'Thank God,' he said. 'I have been worried about you. What has happened?' Sitting down beside her, he tilted her chin toward him.

Her eyes were shadowed with exhaustion and a faint sheen of sweat dewed her forehead. 'I cannot come with you, William,' she said in a choked voice. 'While you were away I . . .' Her voice faltered. 'While you were away I miscarried the child, so you may trust you have done your duty by me.'

Her words came at him as if from a distance. 'I don't . . . what do you mean? You were in full good spirits when I left to my duty.'

She turned her face away. 'I began to bleed and I lost the child. Zoraya has been tending to me at the Convent of St Anne.

God saw fit to punish us. I will never lie with you again because the sin is too great. That cup is empty.'

'No,' William said. 'No.' A huge chasm opened under his feet.

'You were planning to go and you still should.' She clasped her hands, knuckles whitening. 'I love you; my heart is not my own any more,' she said almost bitterly. 'I never thought to fall so hard or so far, and now I am counting the cost of my foolishness – and my lust. Do not lead me into further talk or ask questions, for I shall not answer. Just accept it is over between us.' Taking his hand, she placed in it a single iron nail, the metal glinting with dull light. 'I want you to have this and keep it safely, for it will always protect you. It represents the holy blood of Jesus and you will never have another such because it comes from a mould taken from a nail of the True Cross.'

William stared numbly at the metal spike lying across his hot palm with a total lack of comprehension.

She stood up and moved away from him. 'I cannot come with you. Do not ask it of me, but know that I wish your life to be fruitful and joyous and good.' Her voice cracked. Two tears rolled down her face and she wiped them away on the side of her hand like a child.

William gazed at her in numb shock and clenched his fist around the nail. 'Is it because I refused to agree to swear fealty to Guy de Lusignan? Is that your price?' He stood up and tried to pull her into his arms, but she wrenched away with fire in her eyes.

'No, it is not because of your attitude to Guy de Lusignan, even though I think you the world's greatest idiot for turning down such an offer.'

'Then why? Your uncle?'

She swallowed, then shook her head. 'It is over, William. I have no reason now to go with you. My place is here in Jerusalem with Heraclius and I must prepare for his return. I would not thrive anywhere else.'

374

'"No reason now",' William repeated, feeling sick. 'Oh, indeed, my lady. You show me my true value to you whatever pretty words you use.'

Her voice caught and cracked and tears ran down her face. 'They are not pretty, William, and this is not a pretty situation. It was always a dream, and now we must return to reality.'

He rose unsteadily to his feet, still holding the nail. 'For me, our future is the reality. It is what we can make it, yet you are not prepared to take that step.'

She wiped her eyes, looked down. 'I cannot.'

'You mean you will not.' William drew himself up to his full height and looked at her standing in front of him, so haunted, so delicate, so vulnerable, but filled with the terrible strength to bring him to this. He could not think clearly; he had to escape, but to leave was to accede to her dictate of finality.

'The key.' She held out her hand. 'Give me the key and then go.'

In silence, he removed the cord from around his neck and handed it to her. She took it, looping it around her hand, tightening her fist, and still she did not look at him.

Somehow, he forced himself to walk out of the room and down the stairs, his spine straight, his head carried high. Crossing the chapel, he was no longer furtive but strode out, not caring who saw him. He passed people and did not speak, seeking only the sanctuary of his chamber, and once within he sat on his bed with his head in his hands, still unable to believe it had come to this. He had offered her everything and it was not enough, and if it was not enough to change her mind, it meant that he was not enough, and it was a desolate feeling. His heart had been wide open to her and she had hit the target. On the battlefield, he would have been dead. He lay down on the bed and curled up, a raw ache in the pit of his stomach.

Eustace put his head round the door and looked at William, his eyes widening in consternation. 'Sire, what is wrong?'

'Nothing,' William said dully. 'I will be all right by and by. I will call if I have need. Tell the others I am not to be disturbed, and close the door.'

Eustace went out again and William lay folded on his bed as the day dimmed to darkness. Everything in his life for the past year had revolved around Paschia and now there was nothing. How did he go on from here? Tell himself it had never happened? Had she truly played him for a fool and just used him as a comfort and diversion during Heraclius's absence? Her mutable nature was part of her allure because he had never known where he truly stood with her and it had been a challenge.

Perhaps it had all been a ruse to try and bring him into de Lusignan's camp, with the added benefit to her of sexual gratification – until she got with child and had to face the consequences. Possibly she had indeed fallen for him against her intention. Clearly she did not think he could keep her in the manner she desired. He was not some great prelate with jewels and prestige at his command, but a knight of modest means by comparison. The reality that killed the dream.

Some hours later, Eustace returned and looked at him with troubled eyes. 'Sire, you are not well; you are shivering.' He came to lay his hand on William's forehead. 'You have a fever and you are sweating.'

William brushed him off with irritation. 'It is nothing,' he growled. 'Go away.'

Eustace unfolded the blanket from the foot of the bed and draped it over William. 'Sire, if you are not any better by Compline, I shall send for a physician.'

William dragged the blanket up around his ears. 'I said go away,' he snapped. 'I do not want to see you or anyone else and I do not need a physician!'

Eustace gave him a wounded look. 'I will be outside the door. You can shout if you need me, sire, and I shall keep guard.' Head high, very much on his dignity, he went out.

William groaned into the blanket. Rolling over, he faced the wall and made a concerted effort to draw himself together. He did feel shivery and hot at the same time and a dull headache beat through his skull like a fist on a drum. He was still gripping the nail and a red welt striped his palm. Sitting up, he threw off the blanket and, falling to his knees at the side of his bed, prayed to God to sustain him and help him through this morass. Surely if something was worth fighting for, it should not be yielded at the first battle. If he gave up now, he would always wonder and always think less of himself.

Several hours later, he staggered to his feet. He was light-headed and nauseous, but determined. He washed his face and hands at the laver and changed his stale garments for a clean shirt and rumple-free tunic.

Opening the door, he almost tripped over Eustace who had been sitting on a stool, leaning his spine against the wall, but who immediately sprang to his feet.

'Are you feeling better, sire?'

'I am not ill,' William snapped. He stared at the spoon Eustace had been carving. 'Have you nothing better to do? Go and polish the harness instead of wasting your time.'

Eustace gave him an aggrieved look, but compressed his lips and went to do William's bidding. William followed him to the stable yard and looked around, hands on hips, picking fault with everything – the way some stray wisps of bedding had not been swept up, the untidiness of the dung heap, even the manner in which a horse's mane had been braided. The surprised and resentful looks from the men made him feel worse because he knew he was being unfair. Flinging on his heel, he stalked from the yard and headed to the palace.

Paschia was in the Patriarch's chamber, sitting in Heraclius's chair, surrounded by her household and dictating letters to a scribe. Her face was powdered and made up with cosmetics. Red cheeks, ruby lips, dark-lined eyes. She dripped like an icon with

377

pearls, jewels and silks, and her glorious hair was concealed by an ornate gold turban wound round her head and fastened with a huge ruby.

William clenched his fists and strode forward as though he had business of great weight. Reaching the dais, he turned around to the gathered messengers and servants. 'I have important news for Madame la Patriarchess for her ears alone. Please, if you would all leave.'

Paschia's head jerked up and she shot him a look of furious indignation. The servants had all frozen, aghast. 'Leave us,' she commanded with an imperious gesture of dismissal, 'but remain within call and do not close the door. Zoraya, stay.'

Her people departed, several looking over their shoulders, and the scribe was clearly annoyed at having to abandon his parchment half-written.

When all had gone but the maid, whom Paschia sent to stand by the partially open door, Paschia narrowed her eyes at him. 'Do not ever do that to me again,' she hissed. 'You compromise me and set tongues wagging by such arrogant and foolish behaviour.' Her hands clenched on the arms of the chair. 'Who do you think you are to walk into my chamber and make such demands? I will not tolerate it. You are fortunate that my uncle is not here.'

Dismayed at her fury, William nevertheless held his ground. 'I have come to reason with you. I have come to find the woman who told me I owned her heart and took me for her soul mate. I want you to reconsider and come with me, whether there is a child or no child. It is still not too late.'

She drew herself up, her features set in harsh lines. 'If I ever agreed to come with you it was because you pressured me and because it was a dream to while away an afternoon and bring a different piquancy to our meetings. I told you at the outset that what happened in that chamber was a moment out of time, but you have chosen to ignore my warning.' Her lip curled. 'I could never go with you.'

'My offer was true and open,' William said grimly. 'Do you tell me that all this time you were trifling with me?'

She made a throwing gesture with her hand as though casting something away. 'It is not my doing but your own in being so naive as to think we could just ride away together and make a new life. It was a dream, William, a dream! Do you not understand? What do I have to do to make you see?' Her voice had been rising, but she recalled herself and lowered it; but although the volume decreased, the vitriol did not. 'Now you have put us in a situation that could throw us both into public disgrace and exposure. How dare you!'

William stared at her. Although they had often argued, he had never been on the receiving end of her political rage, a ruthless, excoriating fire; a fight for control and survival.

She rose and faced him. 'You are never again to come to me unless I specifically command your presence,' she said icily. 'If you do, I shall set the guards on you and I shall have you hunted down like a sewer rat. I can do it. You know I can, and I will, I swear it. Now do you understand?' She pointed at the open door. 'Get out, get out now!'

William was shocked into silence. It was as if she had taken his being, burned it to ash and then blown it away with a single puff. There was nothing left. He was dust. He gave her a blank look, turned on his heel and walked out, his steps steady and his shoulders back. Her servants and supplicants were clustered outside the chamber and he passed them as though they did not exist, and he did not feel their stares because everything was blank.

33

Manor of Caversham, April 1219

William was dreaming, his slumber too deep to awaken, but close enough to the surface to feel the excruciating pain in his body and it was like being unmade from the inside by an assassin's dagger. He could see Paschia rolling on the floor, clutching her belly, in a chamber lit by a single lamp that yielded a grainy, unwholesome light in otherwise pitch darkness.

Her uncle stood over her, his lips curled back in disgust. 'You slut, you whore!' he spat. 'I am sick of clearing up your messes. You shall not leave and you shall not bring this disgrace on your family and ruin all our work by your rutting with every brazen knight and troubadour who takes your fancy.' He drew back his foot and kicked her in the belly. 'You shall bear no bastards while I am keeping guard.' The candle extinguished in a sudden puff of air as though blown out, and the darkness was complete, but he could hear Paschia screaming and the pain continued to surge, until it was so great that there was no room for breath.

And then he was fighting to the surface and someone was putting a cup to his lips. Too weak to struggle, he tasted the bitter brew on his tongue and choked. He could hear prayers being chanted and there were whispered, agitated voices around his bed. Someone gripped his hand. Behind his eyes the darkness was suddenly dazzled with brilliant light and he was certain that this must be the end, but how could it be when Jean had not yet returned with his shrouds? The pain stabbed him like knives, but he forced himself to accept and embrace it because it was the only way through.

'He has never been this bad before,' he heard Isabelle say, her voice tremulous with distress. 'I cannot bear it, Will; I wish I could take his pain.'

'Hush, Mama, I know,' their eldest son replied in a comforting murmur. 'So do we all. The physician's nostrum will help in a short while.'

The brightness diminished and William was able to open his eyes and see his chamber, as if lit by dusty sunlight. 'It is not my pain, and I bear it gladly,' he whispered. He could not tell if they had heard him. The terrible tearing sensation had diminished to a biting ache. He was drained and exhausted but he could focus now and he had more understanding. It was like being torn open, but only so that a missing piece could be restored in order to heal the entirety. 'Tell your mother not to be concerned,' he said hoarsely. 'Tell her to pray for me and then take some rest.'

'As you wish, sire,' Will said, 'but I will stay with you. Do not say there is no need, because my will is as stubborn as yours.'

William managed a smile. 'How could it not be when you have it from both parents?'

His son gave him a wry look before turning to put his arm around his mother and murmur words of reassurance. William heard her draw a deep breath, gathering herself before she came to stoop over the bed, kiss his cheek and press his hand. 'I will offer up prayers for you and come back later, my love.'

'I am depending on it.'

She left the room and he knew she would weep outside the door and he felt guilty and sad, but soaring above that was enormous pride in his woman. In their thirty years together she had never once shown weakness or let him down.

'Make sure your mother eats and drinks and takes some rest,' he said.

'I will do my best,' Will replied, 'although as you have said, she is stubborn when set upon her path.' He raised the goblet. 'You should drink some more tisane, I can tell you are in pain.'

William started to shake his head, but changed his mind and succumbed to the inevitable and took small sips of bitterness from the cup. Will's hand was as steady as a rock and William's was weak and shaking.

'As once you cared for and protected me, so I honour you the same, my father,' Will said, and then added curiously, 'What did you mean when you said it was not your pain?'

William swallowed but still some tisane dribbled from the side of his mouth, and Will dabbed it away on a napkin. 'I was dreaming,' he said. 'I was not in this time and place.'

'Then where were you? What had happened to cause you such distress?'

'It wasn't my distress,' William said, 'but it was of my making, and it was long ago, in Outremer.'

'You never speak of that time,' Will said, 'or if you do, it is only to tell a tale to amuse an audience. It is like rain running down a sheet of glass. What remains protected behind that glass is unknown to all.'

William closed his eyes and felt Will tuck the covers around him. He heard the squeak of the lantern hinge as someone inserted a fresh candle. 'Yes, but in my dreams I am on the other side of that glass and standing in the rain.' He shifted his head on the pillow. 'Has there been any news from Jean?'

'No, sire, but I do not think he will be long now. Three days perhaps.'

William closed his eyes. Three days. So much could happen in three days.

He woke up curled on his side facing the wall, fists clenched, and for a moment all he saw was blank whiteness. Was it daylight? Had he lost his sight? Perhaps he was dead. Rolling over with

382

great difficulty, he realised he was still in his bed at Caversham, although superimposed upon the walls and rafters was a vision of the domed room in Jerusalem. He could clearly see the mosaics even though they were transparent, and as he watched, the pieces of tesserae came flaking down around him in a jewelled and jagged rain.

The image shimmered and faded, leaving him in the solid reality of his chamber; indeed, more solid than usual in a strange way. His gaze was drawn to a pair of banners propped against the wall in the corner. The pied flag of the Templars and the white cross of the Hospitallers were draped against each other in unison. Light from the window sparkled on the spear point and another vision pierced him, stealing current reality. He saw himself kneeling, arms outspread, and felt the stinging triple ends of a knotted lash striking his shoulders and back. The pain was fiery but he welcomed it because he deserved it, and each blow was an acknowledgement and purging of sin. He clenched his teeth, took the blow, and the next one, and it was very real.

'Father?'

The shimmer left the air and the vision dissolved, but the pain was still with him in a fan of fire across his spine and the back of his rib cage. His youngest son Ancel, eleven years old, was looking at him with consternation in his dark hazel eyes.

William motioned that he wanted a drink, and Ancel was swiftly attentive. The cold rock crystal touched his lips, and as he swallowed, the sweet, pure spring water assuaged some of the pain. 'I am glad to see you.' He winced to hear the weakness in his voice. 'Plump the pillows for me, there's a good boy.'

Ancel obliged, and William gazed at the bloom on his skin and saw his youth and strength. His younger sons were often present in the background in the sickroom, helping out, acting as squires, but he knew the constraints that his illness set upon them and the rest of the household. They were unable to roam far because they might instantly be recalled.

'Are you well, Papa?' Ancel asked – a polite question with lurking concern.

William nodded reassurance. 'Yes, now I have seen you.'

'Shall I sit with you?'

William gestured assent. 'But you do not need to talk to me. It will be enough to know you are here.' He held out his hand and Ancel took it, and as William gazed, the child's hand in his became a man's.

34

Jerusalem, July 1185

William was curled up on his bed facing the wall when the door opened on an aroma of bread and savoury broth. The smell almost made him retch. He heard the tray being set on the floor and then felt a touch on his shoulder. Turning, he faced his brother.

'Asmaria sends you soup and bread and her good wishes,' Ancel said.

'Thank her for them, but I am not hungry.' His belly was full with grief.

Ancel frowned. 'You must eat, Gwim. You cannot go any longer without nourishment. We are all worried about you and we don't know what to do.' His tone bore a note of aggrieved exasperation. 'You tell us when we must go on patrol or pilgrim escort. You are the one who goes to the palace and talks to the officials and barons. A few days ago you were organising to leave, and now you take to your bed and won't speak. It's like having an empty space where you ought to be. You have never been like this before – never, and I do not understand.' Ancel drew up a stool close to the bed and put his palm to William's brow. 'You had a high fever for a couple of days but that's gone. You should be recovering by now. What is wrong?'

Guilt twisted inside William, and remorse, for he was indeed their leader and he had let them down. 'I cannot tell you, except that I have committed the greatest folly of my life and I do not deserve your concern.'

Ancel eyed him sidelong. 'Just what have you been doing, Gwim?' He sat down on the bed and gestured to the food. 'Asmaria's broth will grow cold and she has gone to the trouble of making it for you. I will be in serious trouble unless I tell her that you drank it all.'

Ancel's use of the childhood diminutive softened William's resistance and allowed a crack of light into the darkness. He sat up, took the tray onto his knee and regarded the steaming bowl. The scent cramped his stomach and he almost heaved. For Ancel's sake he took a few swallows but it was all he could manage. 'I am sorry, you will have to drink it yourself and lie to her.'

Ancel removed the tray and set it aside. 'Tell me what is wrong,' he urged. 'You say you do not need a physician, but I am going to bring someone from the Hospital.' His voice was suddenly ragged and angry. 'If you die, Gwim, then where does it leave the rest of us? If you are a leader, then in Christ's name be one!'

The words, the anguish in his brother's voice, forced William back from the edge of the abyss. 'Perhaps you are better off without me – choose another leader.'

'We don't want another. We want you, and it's because of you that we are here at all and that we have come this far.'

William rubbed his hand over his face. 'If I tell you, I could get my throat cut, and you would risk yours too.'

'Have I ever let you down? I can keep my mouth shut.'

'On our family's honour,' William said intensely.

'On our family's honour,' Ancel repeated, crossing himself. 'On God's honour too.'

William flinched. 'Not on God's honour. What I have done is not in line with God's holy law.'

Ancel stared at him, fear dawning alongside the astonishment. Nevertheless he reached out and grasped William's hands. 'If you cannot tell your own brother, then what does it say about the way you think of him?'

William struggled to speak. The words reached his mouth, but lodged there, unuttered. At last he forced them out like shards. 'I have done a heinous thing,' he said. 'For many months I have been conducting a liaison with a lady of the court.'

Ancel's mouth dropped open. And then anger sparked. 'You tell me this and then will go no further? What of the rest? Who is she?' A look of sheer horror crossed his face. 'Dear God, do not tell me you have been fornicating with the wife of Guy de Lusignan.'

William stiffened. 'No,' he said tersely, 'not the Lady Sybilla.' The guilt twisted inside him. 'You really do not know, do you?'

Ancel mutely shook his head, and William struggled with his words. Even to speak her name was painful. 'The lady Paschia de Riveri,' he said. 'I have offered her my hand in honourable marriage.'

Ancel's jaw dropped in astonishment. 'Sweet God on the cross. Are you mad? The Patriarch's concubine!'

William grimaced. 'All offers have been refused in no uncertain terms – it is over between us. Indeed, the lady has turned against me and warned me not to approach her on pain of death. You speak of playing with fire, well for my sins I am in that fire, and I am damned.'

'Ah no, Gwim, do not say that. It is not true!' Ancel put his arm around William's shoulder and gave him a fierce hug and then said with a valiant effort at lightening the moment: 'I understand . . . hah, I am living with a widow myself!'

William gave a humourless smile. 'But she does not have a prior arrangement with the Patriarch, nor does she have an uncle who wants to kill you.'

Ancel shrugged as if the difference between their situations was a trifling thing. 'I will not breathe a word of this to anyone, I swear to you on my life. It is as safe with me as a sealed casket.'

William was humbled by Ancel's response. All their lives until recently he had been Ancel's place of safety, but now their roles had reversed and he knew he was unworthy to receive such grace. 'I have failed you, and the men.'

'You cannot be a God all the time, Gwim. I used to think you were, and I was angry whenever you fell off the pedestal I'd given you, but I've learned since then. You have feet of clay like the rest of us and I welcome that and take you as you are – sins and all.' He picked up the bowl and began spooning the broth into his mouth. 'You really should have some. It is not right that a man nicknamed Greedy-guts should be ignoring his food.'

Tears pricked William's eyes. 'You are by far the wiser and purer man for staying out of this bind, brother. Everything I did on the way to Jerusalem, all the effort to bring our young lord's cloak to the tomb of Christ, all the atonement and prayers to put everything right – I have made it all pointless because of this.'

Ancel twitched his shoulders. 'Everyone is a sinner. Many have committed far worse than you. You should confess and have done.'

'I do not think I will ever "have done",' William said bleakly. 'My burden is a heavy weight. But you are right about the confession. We should leave as I had planned, but if I am to wash away my sins then it must be in Jerusalem because there is no holier place on earth. If I cannot make my penance here, then where else shall I go?' He bent his head. 'Had she agreed to come with me, we could have been married, and our union would have become an honourable thing, but now, it stands as the sin of fornication.'

'But how would you have lived?' Ancel asked practically.

'That is what she said too – that it was a dream. If so, then I am now in the nightmare.'

Ancel scraped up the last of the broth and set his bowl aside. 'You'll feel better when you have eaten and slept. Yes, you lay with a woman of the court, a concubine – you should not have done it, but it is over. Seek absolution and be done.'

William wished it was as simple as that, but he said nothing. Revealing his affair had been difficult enough.

Neither of them spoke again for a while. As twilight darkened the room, Ancel lit the candles and stayed at William's side. He broke the loaf that Asmaria had sent with the broth, and William ate some this time, and drank a cup of wine. When his men Guyon and Guillaume came to enquire how William was faring, Ancel opened the door a crack and reported that William was recovering from a bout of fever and sleeping but would soon be well and speak to them on the morrow.

Returning to the bed, he poured more wine for both of them. 'Do you remember when we were children? You were a lot older, but you still played with me. You used to pull me on a sled on the frozen pond at Hamstead – I thought you were as strong as an ox.'

William found a smile. 'I certainly felt like one pulling you!' The fierce cold burning his breath; the laughter; the kinship; their sisters throwing snowballs.

'And I remember you at the forge, making a perfect horse shoe. I can still see you striking that bar of red iron as clear as day. I thought how miraculous it was and how I wanted to be just like that.'

William nodded. He had been ten years old, proud of his precocious natural ability, and he had enjoyed showing off to his wide-eyed little brother.

'And carrying me on your back when we all went mushroom picking with Mama. Do you remember that?'

William's mind filled with the image of an autumn day, sunlight filtering through the trees in dusty rays. Himself and his siblings dancing along the path with the leaves turning to copper on the branches and underfoot. Their mother with a foraging basket over her arm, teaching them which fungi were safe to pick and which to avoid. A golden day with King Henry recently come to the throne, and the future secure after the depredations of war. He could feel Ancel's arms clinging around his neck as he ran with him down the path, Ancel pretending that he was a knight and William his sturdy destrier. And then tumbling in the leaves and play-wrestling. A time of joy, and even if the war had taken their innocence, those days of foraging in the woods were a memory of incorruptible sustenance.

'Yes, I remember.'

'Then it is enough. Go to sleep. I will keep watch.'

William was jerked awake some hours later by the sound of loud banging on the door and Zaccariah of Nablus shouting, 'Come out here, you brazen son of a whore. I want words with you!'

Ancel sprang to his feet and William rolled over on the bed and sat up, heart racing.

Fists pounded again and the door shook. 'Open up!'

Ancel looked over his shoulder at William and, swallowing, drew his knife. 'Go away!' he shouted back. 'My brother is ill. I will not have you disturbing him while he rages with fever. For God's love leave him be!'

'I will cool his blood for him,' Zaccariah yelled, his words slurred with drink, 'for I shall spill it in the air! Do not think I will let this rest. I will return and he shall face me and account for what he owes – he knows full well what I mean!' He gave another mighty crash on the door and then they heard him stumbling away down the stairs, cursing to himself.

Breathing harshly, Ancel sheathed his knife. 'Dear Christ,' he said, and almost retched. 'Gwim, you cannot stay here.'

William rose unsteadily from his bed, weak as a lamb. 'Have the men take themselves to the Templar compound as soon as it is light, and we should go there now. Onri and Augustine will vouch for us.'

Ancel nodded brusquely. 'Jesu.' He let out his tension on a hard breath. 'What would Mother say?'

In the middle of all William's darkness and desperation, a sudden glimmer of dark humour kindled unbidden. The remark was always Ancel's greatest rebuke, higher even than God's disapproval.

'I never want to know,' he said, and the laughter died as swiftly as it had arisen.

Over the next few days William gradually recovered, going to ground in a groom's chamber in a corner of the vast underground Templar stable complex where he was able to sleep. Ancel kept watch over him, and Onri made sure they were not disturbed. His men were given quarters on the west side of the compound where there were dwellings for secular knights and employees.

When William was awake, his mind was often as dark as the darkness of sleep, but within its deepest recesses he was examining the ruins of what had gone before and levelling the ground in order to rebuild his life. The debris had to be swept aside and what remained must be purged and cleansed.

By the third morning he felt slightly better, and even had an appetite for the chicken pasties that Ancel presented to him from Asmaria's kitchen.

Ancel watched him eat for a moment to make sure he was truly on the mend and then said, 'I have something to tell you: the lady Paschia's uncle returned to your room yesterday morning.'

William almost choked and had to take a swift swallow of wine. 'How do you know?'

'I went to collect your clothes and was on my way out when I saw him coming and I hid behind a pillar. He went up to your chamber and I heard him force the door.' Ancel took the cup from William's hand and drank. 'He was shouting and swearing to find you gone, and vowing he would find you and deal with you as you deserved. Then the lady Paschia arrived . . .'

'Go on,' William said hoarsely.

'He wanted to know where you were – called her a slut and a whore and said he was sick of clearing up the mess every time she ran after men like a bitch in season.'

William compressed his lips.

'She said she did not know where you were and she would

391

not tell him even if she knew. And then he called her a traitor to her own kin and said she must be here when Heraclius returned. He swore that if a single word of your affair with her got out, he would kill both of you.'

William's heart lurched. Even now he found himself thinking of the danger to Paschia – and to his men. The danger to himself did not matter.

'She called him a fool and said that his own behaviour had already compromised her – that people would be asking why he was searching for you with such rage.' Ancel flicked William a worried look. 'He said he would tell them it was because you had been thieving the Patriarch's most precious possessions. She warned him that if anything happened to you, she would kill him with her own hands. "You have done enough already, you will not harm him," she said.'

William's throat constricted.

'He told her that he would see about that, and then he left.'

'And Paschia?' William could hardly say her name.

'She was crying, but then she saw me. She did not ask what I had heard – she must have known it was most of it – but she said to tell you she was sorry, she would do what she could, and for the rest you must save yourself.'

William was silent, digesting the details.

'What if Zaccariah of Nablus reports you to the Patriarch?'

'He won't. His own position depends on hers. Heraclius will turn a blind eye providing it is kept from full sight. He will only see what he wishes to see – like all of us.' How many men had there been before, he wondered, and how many of them dead? Ptolemy for certain, and Zaccariah spoke as if there had been many others.

'Now I know why you wanted to leave before the Patriarch returned,' Ancel said. 'Are we still going to do that?'

William stared bleakly at the wall and eventually shook his head. 'No, or at least I cannot, for I must atone for my sins. You may leave as you wish, I do not hold it on you or any of the men to remain against your will.'

Two deep vertical furrows appeared between Ancel's brows. 'We will not leave without you. How could we? If we are all one body, it would be like cutting off our head. If you stay, then I stay, and the others will say the same, even without knowing the reason.' His voice grew fierce. 'If you command us to leave, you will be defied.'

'I am not worthy of such loyalty,' William said wretchedly.

Ancel shrugged. 'But you have it, and so you must be worthy, or why else would we still be at your side? Does that mean you think us all fools for staying? It is what you taught us.'

Ancel's comment made William feel worse, but at the same time uplifted. It gave him a reason to go on, a reason to strive and to put things right.

William found Onri busy in the armoury sorting through a new consignment of spears and examining them for flaws. 'I need to speak with you,' he said.

Onri set aside the spear he had been studying, dusted off his hands and looked William up and down with a critical and concerned eye. 'I knew you had been unwell with a fever but I had not realised how seriously – your brother was a regular guard dog and would not let anyone near. You're as gaunt as a cadaver!'

'I am recovering well enough,' William replied with a shrug, 'although I am grateful for Ancel's care and I hope with the help of the Templars to make a better recovery still.'

Onri raised his brows. 'That is an ambiguous statement. Do I take it that you intend to join the order?'

William sent him a pained look. 'I am unworthy to do so, but I desire to serve and atone for my sins.' He took a deep breath. 'I want to serve not just for my term in Outremer, but all my days as a secular knight if the order will accept me.'

Onri's brows remained raised. 'Is this connected with your hasty departure from the Patriarch's palace?'

'It was not appropriate to remain there for various reasons,' William said flatly.

Onri pursed his lips. 'I cannot grant you acceptance as you must know. Only the Grand Master has that right.'

'I understand, but I am asking you to speak for me.'

Onri gave him the same concentrated look that had been fixed on the spears he had been examining for signs of weakness. 'Certainly, but I suspect that some grave circumstance has led you to make this request – I wish you had come to us before it happened.'

'I wish it too, but hindsight always makes us wise,' William replied, wondering how much Onri knew or suspected.

Onri grunted. 'Help me finish these spears, and I will see what I can do.'

Onri brought William to a chamber on the west side of the church and bade him wait. William gazed at a mural depicting Templar knights fighting the infidel on horseback with lances. A statue of the Virgin holding the Christ child stood in a niche, surrounded by candles, and although the image was fair to look upon, he was taken back to his sin at Rocamadour and felt smaller than nothing.

Glass lamps suspended on chains hung from the ceiling. Rolled-up parchments were piled on a table beside a chess set and a locked ivory casket. A white cloak hung on a wall peg with an ebony staff propped beneath it against a solid weapon chest. There was little to indicate the personality of Gerard de Ridefort beyond that of being a conventional man. William did not know him well save for his dislike of Raymond of Tripoli and his leanings toward de Lusignan. It was not the politics that brought him here now and de Ridefort was but the gatekeeper, the man he had to go through in order to make his atonement.

The shaft of sunlight gilding the floor had illuminated several more squares before Onri returned with Grand Master de Ridefort. William immediately knelt on the sun-warmed flags and lowered his gaze.

'Look up,' de Ridefort commanded, and William raised his head to meet a pair of flint-grey eyes set under bushy silver brows. 'Brother Onri tells me you ask to join us as a secular knight of the House of God.'

'Yes, sire,' William said. 'I wish to give my service to God and his Holy Mother in order to atone for my sins and I desire to perform that service for the term of my life.'

Gerard's thin lips disappeared as he pressed them together. Then he said, 'Brother Onri commends you to me and indeed you have served us on the pilgrim roads and at Kerak with valour, but I would know what sins you have on your conscience before we go further in this.'

William strove not to break contact with that piercing gaze. 'Sins of the flesh, sire,' he said. 'Fornication.'

A look of distaste twisted de Ridefort's lips and he made a sound in his throat that might have been contempt. 'A common failing of many. I say to you what I say to all – that flesh must in that case pay recompense.'

'Sire, I am willing to render whatever recompense is required,' William replied with determination. 'Even unto my life.'

De Ridefort grunted again, as if William's reply fell short of the mark. 'Do not say that lightly, messire, for you may indeed be called to render that sacrifice.'

William set his jaw. 'I am ready, sire.'

'So be it.' De Ridefort gestured for him to rise. 'Brother Onri will explain your entitlements. You shall remain here at the Temple unless you have permission to be elsewhere, or you are praying at the Sepulchre. And you will be as subject to the rule as any of the men under oath, even if you have not given yours in full and even if you are not entitled to wear the white mantle of the order.'

'Sire,' William said in acknowledgement and relief. He experienced a sensation of letting go, of having a broom sweep across the floor, sending all the dirt, detritus and broken dreams into the gutter.

'Go now,' de Ridefort said. 'Make your preparations and return at Compline.'

William bowed and left. He was light-headed, empty, staggering. One burden had been lifted from him, but now he must prepare himself to shoulder another for the rest of his life, however long or short that might be.

35

Manor of Caversham, April 1219

William shifted restlessly, close to consciousness but not awake. He could hear people around him talking softly as they kept watch, but the past still had him in its grip and the sound of their voices mingled with the chanting of the Templar brethren. The sharp pangs of his current mortal illness were superimposed upon his dream where the blows of a knotted triple scourge thudded like stones upon his naked back.

He knew if he opened his eyes he would see his room at Caversham and his loved ones gathered around his bed to comfort and sustain him, but in his vision he was prostrate before an altar in a cavern beneath the Dome of the Rock. He had confessed to the sins of lust and fornication and now he was being purged. This was his penance, and he knew with bleak resolution that after this there were no more chances for him.

Candle light danced around the rock walls of the cavern, creating jagged shadows, and around him the Templar brethren stood witness to the blows thudding across his back, a dozen in all. It was not enough, he wanted more, but he had to be in a condition to work and fight. Onri administered the punishment, grim-faced, and he was not gentle, but neither did he strike to incapacitate, and after the twelfth blow he stood back, breathing hard.

De Ridefort gestured for William to stand up. 'Now you owe your life to God. Even if you have not taken vows in full, even though you may serve other masters when you leave this land, you are still bound in the service of the Templars while you live.'

William bowed his head in acceptance and did not think it an onerous commitment. As he donned his shirt and the cool linen settled against the bruises and abrasions, he already felt cleansed and lighter, although he knew it would be a long road to consolidate his redemption.

He joined the knights in prayer and was eventually ushered out into the courtyard where he stood blinking in the bright light and felt that he was gazing upon the world with new eyes and a fresh sense of purpose. Looking back on his affair with Paschia and all that had led up to it, he realised how much he had gone against his own principles. Standing on the open ground before the Templar church of the Holy of Holies, he vowed that from this day forth he would hold to his honour whatever the cost. He would go on from here and make peace with himself and keep his own truth.

He woke up fully to his chamber in Caversham to find his son Gilbert holding his hand. Obviously it was his turn to keep vigil. The youth wore a tunic of soft green wool clasped by a round gold brooch. His hair was like Isabelle's, thick and fair, the colour of sun-ripened barley streaked with gold, and his eyes were a deep slate-blue. He was intended for the Church and was a studious youth, but still being trained in military matters because being versatile was never a disadvantage.

Although very tired, William was comforted by his presence.

'You are awake, sire,' Gilbert said. 'Do you wish to drink?'

William shook his head.

'I was remembering the time when I was a child and we were ducking for apples in the autumn.'

William strove to concentrate. It was difficult to come back from something as profound as that moment on the Temple Mount. 'Tell me.'

Gilbert looked at their joined hands. 'You were always teaching us lessons even when we were playing. You pushed my head under the water with my hands tied behind my back and I was supposed to retrieve an apple with my mouth, but I breathed in and choked. Once I had recovered, you made me do it again and concentrate on the task, and when I came up with an apple, you said I must always have my wits about me, whatever the distraction, and never lose sight of the main goal. I want you to know that I never have – and I have always loved you for that lesson.'

Warm affection glowed through William. 'And I love you for taking in that lesson and reminding me of that day. It will stand you in good stead throughout your life.'

Gilbert kissed William's hand. 'I will always honour you, Papa.'

'And I will always be proud of you,' William reciprocated, knowing that this was Gilbert's personal farewell even if there would be other official times before the end. 'I am glad to have this moment with you, and to see the promise of the man you will become. I have a task for you – just a small one. Bring Father Geoffrey to me if you will.'

'Of course.' Gilbert stood up. 'Is there anything else I can bring you?'

William smiled and shook his head. 'Nothing beyond your prayers – and eat an apple for me when they ripen in October, and remember me.'

'I shall plant an entire orchard in your honour,' Gilbert replied, his throat working.

William drifted back into dreams for a short while and behind his closed lids saw himself and his men riding out, passing messages to various Templar fortresses along their route. He could smell the dry, stony scent of Outremer, and feel a scarf blowing across his nose and mouth as they rode into a grit-laden wind. The surge of the horse under him and the oven-heat of the sun on armour. The dust of a burning summer where the rains had failed and the crops were sparse.

That first mission had taken them several weeks to accomplish, bearing messages between strongholds. Although a truce had been made with Saladin, the roads were still plagued by brigands and raiders, and there were sporadic but constant outbreaks of fighting. No one attacked William's group, but they came across burned-out small settlements, and often passed robbed corpses at the wayside, and knew they themselves were being watched from a distance.

'You wished to see me, sire?'

William opened his eyes and regarded his almoner Brother Geoffrey, a Templar monk who sometimes acted as his scribe. He had pleasant cherubic features and a halo of fluffy white hair. William directed him to the chair at his bedside. 'I have been dreaming of Outremer of late and how I came to give my promise to the Templars,' William said to him with a tired smile.

Geoffrey clasped his hands and gave him a questioning look.

'Few people know of my time there,' William said. 'I have kept it to myself for more than thirty years. Men say I performed great deeds, but in truth they know nothing. Some things that I did there do not tell a worthy tale. It no longer matters, save for one thing.' He hesitated then said, 'I told you many years ago that I gave my oath to the Templars that I would serve them all my life and become one of them when I died, so that my soul would serve in the next world.'

Brother Geoffrey dipped his head. 'It is a great thing that you have so sworn, sire.'

'No, it is a just due, and the time is now close when I must render payment. I want you to send for Grand Master Aimery in London, and ask him to come to me.'

Brother Geoffrey bowed and rose to his feet. 'It shall be done, sire. Will you be wanting your cloak?'

'Not until Jean returns with the shrouds,' William said. 'Let all progress in its rightful course.'

36

Jerusalem, August 1185

William was grooming Flambur in the underground stalls on the Temple Mount when Onri came to find him. 'The Patriarch has returned,' he told him. 'He will be back in Jerusalem by noon. The Grand Master wants us to form a guard of honour at the Gate of David as soon as we may.' He gave William a long look in which much was said without words, then moved further into the stable to find his mount.

Once Onri had gone, Ancel, who had been rubbing down Byrnie, joined William. 'What will you do?'

William resumed his task. 'I shall do as commanded. I can hardly skulk in the stables, can I? Heraclius will want to talk to me about King Henry, and will want to know why I have moved out of his palace.'

'But what about . . .'

William worked on the stallion's hide in grim silence, then paused the curry comb and sighed. 'All that is behind me. I have confessed and been purged. There is no reason to tell Heraclius and every reason to keep silent.' He swallowed bitterness. 'We have been courtiers for a long time. If we cannot come through this, then we have learned nothing. If I feel guilt it is because I have failed myself and God by not living up to higher standards. But guilt about Heraclius? No. I would have made her my wife, not kept her as my concubine.'

*   *   *

Clad in full armour, William rode through the streets of Jerusalem with the knights of the Temple and Hospital forming a guard and escort of honour for Heraclius as he processed toward his palace. People lined the streets and cheered, glad to have their Patriarch back, and he had staged his return as a triumphal entry. His silk robes were encrusted with silver and gems and there was not a part of him that did not shine, for, beneath his mitre, his face was bright red and glistening with sweat in the summer heat.

Raymond of Tripoli rode at his side with King Baldwin, and behind them processed a gilded train of courtiers, all robed in finery. All the knights of the military orders too, Templars and Hospitallers, were resplendent and austere in the red-crossed black and white of their holy orders. William rode at the rear with the other secular knights and his manner was subdued. Heraclius was home and he must live with the fact that Paschia had made her choice to stay with him. This ageing, sweating, worldly prelate with the power of the cross at his fingertips was her compass, and it turned his own desire from gold to dross.

In the courtyard of the patriarchal palace, Paschia was waiting for Heraclius with the household, including Zaccariah of Nablus. She wore a loose flowing robe in the Greek style, embroidered down the centre line, and her hair was concealed by a spotless white wimple.

She approached Heraclius as he dismounted and, kneeling to him in the dust, bowed her head, concealing her face by pulling one of the ends of the wimple across her nose and mouth, so that she appeared shy and almost virginal.

Even from the rear of the escort William saw the joy on Heraclius's face and felt his heart tear and bleed again, and knew with bitter clarity that Paschia had been right. It was a dream. She would never have given this up to go with him; he had not stood a chance.

*　*　*

402

Later, William attended prayers in the Templar chapel and was scourged once more in penitence for his sins, again administered by Onri. Emerging from the service stiff and sore but in a relieved and calmer frame of mind, he found Augustine waiting for him, his expression carefully neutral. 'The Patriarch wants to see you.'

'I have been expecting the summons,' William replied. Dreading them too – but he was prepared.

'Make a good accounting of yourself.' Onri set his hand to William's shoulder in a gesture of support that at the same time pressed on the tenderness left by the scourging and made William wince at the reminder of his sin and the penance.

'I will walk with you,' Augustine said and fell into step beside him.

They left the Templar precinct and walked toward the Patriarch's palace. The sun beat down from a bleached sky and the streets were mostly empty as the citizens hid from the heat and waited for the shadows to lengthen. Approaching the palace, William remembered the afternoons he had spent with Paschia in the domed room while others rested. They had embraced the fire, and the burn had been glorious. Now there were only ashes.

Augustine did not speak on their walk, but as they approached the palace he turned to William. 'I hope you have found your path,' he said quietly. 'And I am sorry for what has happened. I want you to know, that is all.'

William's chest tightened. 'I am sorry too. I do not know if I have found my path, but I know now that which is not my path and I am forever in the debt of the Templars for reaching down a ladder to let me climb out of the pit.'

Augustine nodded gravely. 'I would clap you on the back but I have more compassion than Onri.'

Arriving at the Patriarch's palace, William was ushered through into Heraclius's chamber which, from being almost devoid of people for a year, now bustled with activity. Scribes and secretaries were already toiling over their lecterns and servants were dealing

403

with the patriarchal baggage. Paschia was absent, and William was mightily relieved.

'Ah,' said Heraclius as William was announced, 'come in, my boy.' Gesturing expansively, he smiled at William, but the expression did not reach his eyes. 'I hear you have taken a secular oath to the Templars and moved to the Dome of the Rock.'

William swiftly assessed the Patriarch's expression but detected nothing beyond ordinary curiosity. However, clearly someone had told him of the decision.

'Yes, sire. When I heard that King Henry would not be coming to Jerusalem I wanted to make a commitment for the sake of my soul before I returned to his court.'

Heraclius gave a short nod. He was greyer and thinner, more honed and sinewy after his journey, with a harder polish about him. The heat flush had diminished, leaving a slight mottling on his throat. 'That is between you and God, and I would not stand between a man and his commitment.' He stretched his spine, placing his hands in the small of his back with a grimace. 'That King of yours. I am afraid you fell woefully short in preparing us to meet him.'

'I am sorry, sire, I gave of my best.' If Heraclius and his advisers had listened harder to the clues in his narratives rather than hearing what they wanted to hear, they might have had more success.

'He is like a hard beam of wood, and hammer as we tried, we made no impression at all.' Heraclius shot William a look filled with exasperation, almost as if he believed that William had been colluding with Henry.

'Indeed, that is so, sire,' William said neutrally. 'I tried to tell you that he has a strong will and I am sorry if I failed and you misunderstood me. I would also say that the last High Churchman who disputed with King Henry became a martyr, for he is fierce when challenged. There is nothing more you could have done.'

Heraclius sighed and threw up his arms. 'Indeed. I told him

404

that more than money and promises we needed a ruler, but that was another part of hammering in vain. He was most hospitable and we lacked for nothing save his support. He played with us and vacillated.' Heraclius's voice warmed with anger. 'He told us he had to consult his barons before he could agree, but that only meant consulting them to provide him with a way out. They very conveniently reminded him of the "sacred" oath he had taken on his coronation to defend his realm. And then he said he must regretfully decline. His youngest son offered to come but he would not let any of his offspring take up the mantle.'

'I am sorry for that, sire,' William said diplomatically, 'but knights will come to swell the ranks and surely you have raised the awareness of the difficulties here.'

'Yes,' Heraclius said curtly, 'and in the meantime we walk a slippery rope across a chasm of crocodiles.' He waved his hand in dismissal. 'Enough. You may go.'

With relief, William bowed and took his leave. Walking down the corridor, he was tense, hoping not to meet Paschia and at the same time vividly remembering how he had once collided with her in this very place. He could still see her looking up at him, her cat in her arms, her eyes dark pools of admiring innocence. If only he had heeded the danger and resisted temptation.

He heard sudden footsteps behind him and, as he turned, was shoved hard and slammed up against the wall. A dagger pricked his throat.

'Just one word from you about the lady Paschia,' hissed Zaccariah of Nablus. 'Just one word or look out of place to the Patriarch, and I will spill your blood. Do you understand?'

William felt the hot trickle on his flesh, but this time he was ready. 'Yes, perfectly.' As he spoke he made a lunge and a twist just as sudden as Zaccariah's pounce. And now the dagger was in his hand, and he set it under the other man's ribs and in his turn drew blood. 'And I say to you that if you dare to pursue me or lay a finger on Paschia, you will die. Do you think you are the only one with access to nets and spies?' He shoved Zaccariah hard, making him stagger, and kept hold of the knife. 'Stay away – do *you* understand?' Then he stalked off, the weapon gripped at the ready, thinking he should have made a killing blow, even if it would have caused grave complications.

Two days later, William was summoned from weapons practice on the Templar tilt ground and commanded to attend Raymond of Tripoli at the palace.

'The Regent needs experienced knights to hunt out a persistent group of brigands and the Grand Master suggested your name,' Onri said as he delivered the message.

Eagerness surged through William, for here was a chance to use his skills that would consolidate his atonement and take him out of Jerusalem. The Grand Master and Regent heartily disliked each other as men, but this was business upon which they both agreed.

Arriving at the palace, he was ushered into Raymond's chamber. Guy de Lusignan was present, as were Heraclius and the lords of Ibelin and Ramlah. The child king sat among the gathering with his mother, wearing a gold circlet over his fine blond hair. He appeared pale and delicate beside the gruff, bearded men, but William went first to him and knelt in obeisance. The boy looked to Raymond of Tripoli who gestured for William to rise with the palm of his hand. Baldwin copied it.

'Sire,' William said, and bowed, before turning to acknowledge the Regent. 'You sent for me, my lord?'

Raymond leaned forward on his great chair. 'There has been another raid on a sugar caravan bound for Jerusalem from Tiberius. A particular group of thieves are making the attacks and then escaping into lands controlled by Saladin.' He looked round the gathering, resting his gaze pointedly on Guy de Lusignan. 'I do not want to damage the truce – it would be inadvisable at this time. I need a deputation to go north, seek

406

them out and deal with them. It would not matter if it was a few stinging flies but this is a whole wasps' nest and must be destroyed before the danger escalates. I need more patrols and I am recruiting knights who have the experience to deal with the matter.'

'Sire, it would be my honour and that of my men to assist in this mission,' William said eagerly.

'So be it.' Raymond of Tripoli nodded. 'Let it be done as soon as you may.'

Pink rags of cloud tattered the eastern skyline as dawn broke over Jerusalem. For now it was pleasantly cool, but once the sun began its climb, the day would develop its usual punishing burn. William wore a linen tunic over his mail as he waited outside the Templar stables for everyone to assemble for the mission to deal with the raiders. As the rising sun spread fingers of warm gold across the Dome of the Rock, he was serious and composed and mostly at peace with himself.

A contingent of twelve Templar knights formed part of the group, including Onri and Augustine. There were four Hospitallers and a party of mercenaries and Turcopole warriors. Ancel appeared, leading Byrnie with one hand and taking devouring bites from a piece of folded flat bread with the other, melted cheese oozing out of the sides. Digging in his saddle pack, he produced a bulging linen cloth and handed it to William. 'From Asmaria,' he said.

The delicious aroma rising from the cloth made William's mouth water as he unfolded it. As he continued to recover from his affair with Paschia and set his feet on a different path, his appetite had returned full measure. 'That woman is a marvel,' he declared once he had swallowed the first mouthful. 'No banquet food could equal this.'

Ancel looked smugly pleased. 'She sends her prayers and hopes for a safe return.' He wiped his hands on his own cloth as he finished, and placed it in his saddle pack. 'I have been talking to her about when we do leave. I asked her if she would come back with me to Normandy.'

The raw place inside William twinged as he thought of his own failed future with Paschia, but he quickly put it aside and pretended it wasn't there. 'What did she say?'

'That she would think about it and tell me when I return.' Ancel grimaced. 'She says she has a secure place in Jerusalem and she must think of her children too. I said I would provide for all of them, but she still said she wanted to think.'

'At least she was honest with you.'

'Yes,' he said. 'I believe she will agree, but she is like me. She needs to know the ground in front of her is solid before she will take the next step.'

William smiled a little because Ancel had clearly come to understand himself on this journey. Paschia had needed to know too. She had chosen to stay rather than face the unknown. He realised now that Paschia might be politically astute and a player who moved across the board like a queen with a scythe, but it was an illusion. She was just a vulnerable girl wearing the gown of a greater being. If Asmaria decided to come, then Ancel would have something far more solid and true in the end. The satisfying meal rather than a gilded subtlety that melted away to nothing and left the stomach hollow. 'You have a good woman,' he said, returning his cloth to Ancel.

Ancel gave a broad smile. 'I know.'

The grin faded, and Ancel cursed under his breath. Turning to look, William saw Mahzun of Tyre arriving at the rendezvous with half a dozen men. He was riding his raw-boned chestnut, and sat tall in the saddle, his black hair bound in two oily plaits under the Turkish helmet he wore by preference. His dark gaze skimmed flatly over William and his contingent without acknowledgement, except a slight curl of his lip, as though he was looking at flies on meat in the marketplace.

William shrugged. 'It was always a likelihood. We shall make our camp away from his and not bother him unless he bothers us.' He gave Ancel a warning look.

'Don't worry, I'm not going anywhere near him.' Ancel looked sidelong at Mahzun. 'I saw him speaking with Zaccariah of Nablus yesterday when I was passing the Patriarch's palace. He was either being hired or paid, because he was tucking a pouch of money inside his shirt.'

William absorbed the news with unease. 'Let us just be wary and keep our distance,' he said. 'It won't be for much longer.'

The party rode north-east for three days beneath a scorching late summer sun. There was no breeze; banners hung limp on staves and sweat dripped relentlessly from men and horses. Scouts went out and returned with nothing to report, and the news from the watch towers where they paused to replenish their supplies was as empty as the landscape.

On the third evening they camped by a small oasis of good water surrounded by date palms and sat round their fires cooking flat bread and eating dried meat and fruit plumped up in a little wine. The horses were hobbled and guarded.

Two Bedouin informers slipped into the camp, swift, dark shadows, and whispered their report in return for gold bezants: the enemy they sought planned to raid a Frankish village three miles to the north, close to the border with the Saracens. The Bedouin scouts indicated that the group was large and well organised, and that perhaps several separate groups had joined forces to carry out the raids.

Ancel looked at William across their fire. 'We'll be fighting tomorrow then.'

'More than likely,' William agreed.

Ancel looked away into the night. 'All the time we have dwelt here I have been preparing for battle and expecting to fight. We have faced many dangers and skirmishes but mostly it has been like a cloudy sky that does not rain. Now it feels as though a storm is coming.'

'Yes, it does.' William drew his sword and set about polishing it with an oiled rag. 'Does it trouble you, brother?'

'A little,' Ancel said. 'We are so close to going home. To have weathered everything and then not to make it through this stage would seem like the cruellest trick ever played.'

Ancel's remark made William uncomfortable because his own mood was what did it matter if he died here in the service of God? But then, if he died, so too did his men and his brother, and he could not take them down with him. He had a responsibility to see them safely through. 'It will be all right.' He touched Ancel's shoulder. 'Whatever happens.'

'Yes.' Ancel shrugged and smiled. 'I am glad to have had you for a brother should it come to death.'

William's affectionate touch on the shoulder became a thump. 'None of that,' he said gruffly. 'Come. We will protect each other and pray to God to keep us safe.'

Even before first light the men were awake and about their final preparations – filling water flasks and helping one another don gambesons and mail. The horses were harnessed for battle with leather barding and padded chamfrons over the neck area. The destriers stamped and pawed, knowing what the activity presaged.

William went to pray with his men and was confessed and shriven by a Templar chaplain. And then he in his turn addressed his men as they returned from their prayers to mount their restless horses. 'You have trained for this all your lives. You are experienced and battle-hardened. I trust you with my life and I hope you trust me with yours. This task must be done; the settlers are depending on us to protect their homes, their lives and livelihoods. It is why you took your knightly oaths. You know your duty. God will watch over us and protect us. We have his blessing.'

The men crossed themselves and embraced each other, and

William did his best to ensure that the atmosphere was one of brotherhood and unity and that any hint of farewell was pragmatic. They knew their business and what was at stake and were ready for whatever happened.

William saw Mahzun of Tyre patting his horse and feeding it dates, and despite his dislike of the man he experienced a brief moment of empathy for a fellow warrior. Mahzun glanced across, caught William's eye, and sent him a strange look – a mingling of speculation and challenge, woven with grudging respect – before turning away.

The last stars had barely faded from the sky as they departed the oasis. By the time they approached the village, flat-roofed save for the crenellated church tower and surrounded by olive groves, the gold had stretched across the eastern horizon like yolk spilling from a broken eggshell. The dogs were already barking frantically at the far end of the village and, as the knights arrived, dark smoke was rising from that direction. The raiders had wasted no time.

Onri swiftly organised the men, although everyone knew his part and was eager to join battle and accomplish what they had set out to do. William signalled to his own group, and while the Templars and Hospitallers rode through the front gate, he swept his troop round to the back to cut off escape from that direction.

He was fierce and exultant, but calm too. His armour and that of his men was more than just the protection of mail and good horses. It was the skill and training of decades; it was determination and belief.

The raiders were lightly armed and riding their smaller, swift-turning horses, but they had nowhere to flee when hit before and behind by the solid force of the Frankish knights. Those who tried to take refuge in the dwellings were turned upon by the villagers, made bold by the arrival of heavy support, and even if they did not engage, they cried out, alerting their saviours to the whereabouts of the enemy.

It was a swift and complete rout with no survivors. A couple of injured raiders were kept for questioning, but Mahzun of Tyre strode up to them, cut their throats and kicked their corpses. When Augustine remonstrated with him, Mahzun shrugged at the Templar as he sheathed his knife. 'No point in letting vermin live. They knew they were dead men anyway; they would not have talked.'

As the bodies were picked over for loot, William noted that several of the raiders appeared to be Franks. One was red-haired, another fair with a blond beard. Others were native in appearance. Brigandry, it seemed, was the preserve of all factions. Their clothes had seen better days and their mounts and equipment were mediocre.

Onri studied them with his hands on his hips and a frown between his brows.

'So few and easily overcome to have caused so much mayhem and damage,' William remarked. 'Sufficient I suppose to raid and terrorise a small settlement, but I cannot imagine them plundering a sugar caravan.'

Onri nodded agreement. 'At least we have cleared up this particular nest, but I would wager there are others. These are scavengers – the kind that exist on the outskirts of bigger kills.'

The bodies were piled into a cart by the villagers and taken away to be dumped into a ravine, there to be picked over by jackals and vultures. The knights made camp that night in the settlement and tended to their wounded, although there were no serious injuries and the worst only required a few stitches. Augustine had orders to take the Templars on to the fortress at Belvoir, carrying out a reconnaissance patrol along the way, but the rest of the men including the Hospitallers and Onri were to return to Jerusalem to report and receive further instruction.

During the night, Mahzun of Tyre became unwell with vomiting and belly gripes. Unable to sit his horse, he promised to follow when he could.

Ancel shook his head to William as they rode from the village. 'For all his claim to be such a great warrior, none of us would stop behind for the gripes,' he said scornfully. 'If you ask me, he drank too much last night and because he's a mercenary he thinks he can do as he pleases.'

William shrugged. 'You are probably right, but I will not miss his company.'

The first night on the return journey to Jerusalem, William and his men once more camped under the stars at the watering place. A small trade caravan was already there, on its way to the coast with a cargo of coloured leathers, and William bargained for a supple piece of red that would make a fine binding for a sword grip. The merchants were wary at first and then amenable: trade was trade, and since the knights showed no inclination to murder them and plunder their goods, they were glad of armed company.

The second night was to be spent at a Templar watch tower on the Jordan pilgrim road. The mood was jovial as they moved at a steady pace toward their destination. The fight had been much easier than everyone had expected and they were pleased to be returning to make a positive report and collect their pay. William, however, was still on edge because there had been fewer raiders than expected, and not as formidable as they had been led to believe. Glancing around, he frowned to see the men so strung out. 'Eustace!' he commanded. 'Bang the drum!'

The squire broke off jesting with Geoffrey FitzRobert, and with immediate understanding reached for the skin drum strapped behind his saddle. Settling it before him, he began to beat out a steady rhythm using a large cauldron spoon. 'A long way to go! A long way to go! But we'll be there by nightfall if we're not too slow!'

The pace picked up; the men closed ranks and straightened in their saddles. William gestured for them to join in the chant and after a few moments pointed to Ancel. 'Now you.' Eustace

413

tossed the drum and spoon across and Ancel took up the beat. 'A long way to ride, a long way to ride! It's a good thing I have a stout backside!'

Loud guffaws greeted Ancel's verse. The drum was passed on again and more verses sung, growing increasingly ribald, but the men were together now and compact. At the front, the four Hospitaller knights grinned, but kept aloof.

A mile further on they came to an area with boulders either side of the path. The Hospitallers drew rein and their horses sidled. William held up his hand to silence the drumming, and as the sound died away he heard a scraping sound from the rocks and a jingle of harness. An arrow suddenly tipped off the rim of one of the Hospitaller's shields with a metallic clang, then another and another until the shafts were plummeting like rain. A Hospitaller horse was struck in the shoulder and went mad, plunging and rearing. Guyon de Culturo swore as he broke off a shaft that had struck his saddle, narrowly missing his thigh. As the knights raised their shields, a band of armed riders came flying from the road between the boulders like a swarm of hornets and attacked them with mad ferocity. William barely had time to draw his sword and within seconds was engaged in close, hard fighting.

Some of their attackers were Turks to judge by their armour, but others were clearly Franks, and William realised this must be the main group they had missed and the better fighters, armed for business. The others had been expendable decoys.

William's arm rose and fell. He unhorsed a Turk, and Flambur trampled the man underfoot. He struck a hefty backhand blow at another adversary and felt the man's arm bone snap. It was difficult to look round in his helmet and work out what was happening. Ancel had been separated from him by the press but he was aware of him fighting hard in front and to the right. A powerful Turkish warrior was belabouring a wooden club to the right and left, creating mayhem. William saw a blow connect with Ancel's ribs and spurred Flambur forward to try and reach him, his breath burning in his throat, all around him the clash and thud of close and desperate hand-to-hand battle.

Ancel managed to extricate himself but that spiked club was still rising and smashing down. William tried to force further forward but faced a solid knot of battling men. Redoubling his efforts, he cleared enough room to draw breath and saw Mahzun of Tyre fighting beside the Turk with the club, a reddened sword in his fist.

'Traitor!' William bellowed.

The fight boiled over him again and everything grew too desperate and bloody for William to have any chance of going to Ancel's aid. Flambur jostled breast to breast with another horse and William struck down its rider. Swords, axes, short spears flashed and turned. Shields took gouges and blows as each man tried to avoid his enemy's blade and stay in the saddle. Another brief space, and William saw Ancel hurl himself into the fray and lunge at the warrior wielding the mace, cutting savagely into his right side. The Turk raised the weapon to strike again but at its zenith it lost impetus and he crashed from the saddle as Ancel jerked his sword free.

The fighting redoubled. Mahzun forced his chestnut between William and Ancel, his sword flashing. William was already fighting off a determined attack on his left, and as Mahzun plunged forward to make a killing blow, he was trapped. Ancel intercepted the downward chop of the sword and knocked the blow away. Teeth gritted with effort, William struck down his opponent and pivoted to help Ancel but another horse barged into Flambur, catching the stallion in mid-turn, and he went down, pitching William from the saddle. William hit the ground, tasting blood as he bit his tongue, the air jarring from his lungs. He was dead if he stayed down so forced himself to his feet, his breath tearing in his chest and his vision a blur.

Ancel held firm between William and the opposition, taking

a terrible battering on his shield and hauberk. Flambur had struggled up from his fall and William caught the reins and hauled himself back into the saddle. His knights were making valiant efforts to reach him, but no one was within striking distance as Mahzun changed his grip and brought his sword down, breaking through Ancel's guard and cutting deep into his left thigh. As Mahzun drew back to strike again, William made a desperate counter effort and succeeded in hacking open a row of rivets on Mahzun's mail, smashing through to the gambeson. It was not a killing blow but enough to crack ribs and hamper Mahzun's assault. Robert of London and Geoffrey FitzRobert pressed forward and Mahzun, after one more flurry, reined away, for his group had broken under the spirited defence of those they had attacked and were scattering and fleeing.

Ancel swayed in the saddle, blood flooding from his wound. William dismounted from Flambur, leaped up behind him and grabbed the reins. Onri was signalling for their troop to ride for the safety of the watch tower two miles away. 'Take up the wounded!' he roared. 'There is no telling if they will regroup!'

William signed to his own men and they retreated in formation as fast as their horses could gallop with Eustace bringing Flambur alongside his own mount. Dust clouded around them, misting the debris of shattered lances and the broken corpses of horses and men they left behind. William was churning with shock as Ancel slumped against him. Byrnie was sturdy, but his burden was double, and he hoped the horse would hold out.

'Do not for God's love let go, you fool!' William shouted to Ancel over the galloping hooves and the wind of their speed. 'Hold on!'

Ancel groaned a reply. He tightened his grip on the reins, but his head flopped and he was close to losing awareness.

They thundered into the tower's small courtyard. William dismounted, covered in blood and staggering. Several people rushed to help. 'No,' William panted, 'not me, tend my brother!'

He turned to Ancel, who was barely conscious but still clinging to the reins for dear life. Carefully easing him from the blowing horse, William bore Ancel inside and laid him on the chamber floor. Ancel's face was dirty white like raw dough as William removed his helmet.

'Help him someone!' William cried, looking around in urgency. 'For God's mercy, someone help him now!'

A man went running and returned a moment later leading a dark-robed Hospitaller chirurgeon with a silver beard and a lined brown face. He was swiftly donning a leather apron, and a youth hurried after him bearing a satchel of instruments and rolls of bandage.

Kneeling stiffly at Ancel's side, he gestured for William to unlace Ancel's chausses so that he could examine the wound. The mail had split under Mahzun's blow and there was blood everywhere. Ancel arched his spine and squeezed his eyes tight shut, gritting his teeth in agony as William removed the mail, his fingers reddening rapidly.

The chirurgeon probed the wound, frowning in concentration, and Ancel writhed, a scream lodging in his throat. Clucking his tongue, the chirurgeon took a small glass phial from his satchel. He measured several drops into a cup of water and made Ancel drink it. Then he delved in his satchel again, brought out a small wooden wedge and pushed it between Ancel's teeth before probing the injury again with a pair of tweezers and removing a thin shard of bone.

'The leg is broken,' he said. 'It must be packed to control the bleeding and then splinted before we can move him. After that he must lie as still as a stone – do you understand?' He beckoned to his assistant.

William swallowed and nodded. Gazing at the extent of the wound, which seemed to be a deep cut that had broken the bone, he was horrified. He had seen men with lesser wounds die or lose their leg, and if the latter, he knew of no one who had survived such surgery, although he had heard tales at second hand. The wound was so deep and bloody that fever was going to be as big a danger as blood loss. He hoped desperately that the chirurgeon knew what he was doing and prayed to God to send the man a steady hand.

'You are going to be all right,' he told Ancel, gripping his hand. 'I am here, I will stay with you.' He turned to the chirurgeon. 'I beg you to use all the skills you have at your command to heal him. Do not let him lose his leg.'

The man gave William a sharp look. 'Amputation might be for the best, messire.'

'No!'

The chirurgeon's wiry silver brows drew together. 'It would go against my better judgement.'

William set his jaw. 'No. He cannot lose his leg.'

The Hospitaller shrugged. 'I shall do my best, but I make no promises.'

William nodded stiffly. 'Do what you can.'

The chirurgeon and his assistant set to work. They cleaned the wound and aligned the bone as best they could, then packed the slash with gauze and cotton, smeared with unguent. William sat with Ancel, pillowing his head, speaking in his ear, telling him all was well, and wondering in despair how his brother was ever going to come back from this.

'You are not putting in stitches?' William asked as the Hospitaller covered the wound with a light linen dressing smeared with more unguent.

The man shook his head. 'The cut must be washed out daily with salt water and watched for signs of blackening because that means the limb is dying and must be removed. Keep him as still as you can. He has lost a great deal of blood and he will surely die if it begins again – and he may do so anyway. He must drink – as much as you can get into him of honey and water – and watch for when he pisses, for that will be a good sign. If he does not, then . . .' He made another shrug serve for the rest.

More injured men were awaiting the chirurgeon's attention and he went to deal with them. William laid a light blanket over Ancel and tucked a pillow under his head. He was battered, cut and bruised himself, but it was all as nothing. The other men stood around, their expressions full of shock and grief.

'Mahzun of Tyre,' said Geoffrey FitzRobert, rubbing his brow and then quickly dashing tears from his eyes. 'He betrayed us. Some men will sell their souls for money.'

'He has no soul.' William bowed his head, remembering Ancel telling him about Paschia's uncle giving the mercenary a bag of coins.

'He won't dare show his face in Jerusalem again now,' Geoffrey continued. 'He's an outcast and a marked man.'

Eustace returned from seeing to the horses. A cut striped his left cheek from ear to chin and he had another across the back of his hand. 'Is he going to be all right?'

'Yes,' William said with gritty conviction. 'The chirurgeon has stopped the bleeding but says the leg must be held straight. As soon as he is well enough, we'll get him to the Hospital in Jerusalem. They will know how best to care for him.'

'We were played for fools,' Robert of London said grimly. 'The group that hit the village were expendable – a softener to draw our teeth.'

Ancel's eyelids fluttered, and he opened his eyes. His pupils against the dark hazel irises were pinpricks.

'Gwim?' he croaked. 'Are we saved?'

William nodded. 'Yes, you are safe now.'

Ancel squinted, and licked his lips. 'But it's dark and I always imagined the heavenly realm would be light. Where are we?'

William swallowed and struggled to find a firm, reassuring voice when all he wanted to do was weep. 'Ancel, we are not dead.'

'Then where are we?'

'In a watch tower on the Jerusalem road, and safe. You took a sword blow to your leg while you were defending me. No, stay still. You have lost a lot of blood and your leg is broken. The chirurgeon has tended to you, but says you must not move on pain of the life you still possess.'

Ancel lifted his head and looked down at himself, then let his head drop back onto the pillow. 'Dear God,' he whispered. 'I remember the sword and I remember Mahzun of Tyre – that whoreson betrayed us all.' The last word ended on a gasp of pain.

'You saved my life, but I would rather have died than see you wounded like this.'

Ancel closed his eyes. 'I am sorry not to have given you your wish, but I could not do that.'

William almost choked on his guilt and grief. 'You shall have the best treatment and care. You have the strength to come through this. Your sacrifice will have been pointless if you do not live, because it will destroy me.'

Ancel's eyes remained closed and he did not answer.

That night William kept vigil at Ancel's side, his head in his hands, his mind on the Young King and how he had failed in his duty to him, and now he had not protected his own brother when it mattered.

Onri sat down beside him to keep him company.

'All I keep thinking is what shall I tell our mother if he dies?' William said. 'But our mother is already with Jesus.' He swallowed hard. 'Ancel would always threaten me with her disapproval if he thought I was doing wrong or had failed in my duty – as now. I am the older one, I am the leader. I should have protected him, not the other way around. I should have taken the blow because it was intended for me.'

'That blow fell where it did,' Onri said firmly. 'I know you would have taken it had the timing been different, but you cannot let that cloud your vision. You are better than that, and this is the moment of your forging. You are in the fire and if you are true steel, you will not warp or break. If you go down the path of blame and self-recrimination, you will be of no use to anyone, including yourself. You will be as wounded as your brother, and that is not what he would want.' He poured wine from the jug by the bed into an earthenware cup. 'When we set out for the Holy Land, Aimery entrusted me with your welfare and I swore to him I would see you safe, so if we are talking of blame, then I have a burden too because I have clearly failed to do mine many times along the road.'

William grimaced. 'I would not set any of this on you.'

'You do not,' Onri replied. 'Whatever I take upon myself is my burden, not yours.'

William looked at Ancel as he muttered in his slumber. 'The man who gave him this wound was often employed by Zaccariah of Nablus and was probably paid to kill us because of my dealings with the Patriarchess.'

'But he has turned against everyone else too,' Onri said. 'If he was paid to remove you and your brother, it was but a small part of a much greater whole. He is a mercenary who has always lived on the edge and this would have happened anyway. He must have been playing a double game for a long time.' Onri gripped William's shoulder. 'Do your penance and move on from this. You must.'

William compressed his lips. It was easier to say than do; however, his men were depending on him and he had to be strong and focused to get them out of this bind.

He spent the rest of the night in prayer and vigil at Ancel's side. Ancel had to be woken in order to drink and he was kept drugged by carefully measured doses of poppy syrup – enough to keep the edge from his pain. Too much and he would fall asleep and not wake up.

'I will not let you die, do you hear me?' William said, holding his hand. 'I will get you to Jerusalem and you will be healed, do you hear me?'

A couple of times Ancel responded by squeezing William's hand, and once he opened his eyes and smiled and said, 'Gwim'. William took it as a hopeful sign, but the very mention of his name filled his eyes with tears, although he did not weep in full until somewhere near dawn, when Ancel finally pissed dark urine into a wadded-up cloth.

Each day the chirurgeon came to check Ancel's wound – sniffing it, cleaning it out with salt water and smearing it with unguent – and each day the news remained cautiously optimistic. The flesh stayed clean without sign of darkening and the rest of Ancel's leg remained a healthy colour. William fed his brother nourishing meat broth and gradually he improved and grew stronger.

Onri rode off to Jerusalem, returning ten days later accompanied by a contingent of well-armed Templars and Hospitallers. The wounded were loaded onto carts and brought to Jerusalem by slow stages. Ancel, heavily dosed with poppy syrup, was carried out to one of the carts in a litter, his leg kept as straight as possible by splints of board. He was insensible for much of the journey and clearly in great pain when he was awake, but he bore it with stoicism.

'We sent out patrols in search of the raiders,' Onri told William, who was concerned about being attacked again on the road despite their strong escort. 'We found some deserted camps with shallow graves at one of them, but there was no sign of Mahzun of Tyre and the remnants have scattered like dust in the wind. They will be hunted down eventually but they are not in any condition to challenge us a second time.'

William was reassured, but some anxiety remained. He would have felt less uneasy had Mahzun been among the casualties.

* * *

William saw Ancel settled in the great Hospital in Jerusalem, where they had lodged when they first arrived in the city. Capable of housing over a thousand patients in its vaulted precincts, it was divided into aisles and courts with eleven wards each served by nine serjeant brethren day and night. Ancel was given a bed in a quiet area, and was visited by Brother Jakob, a native Christian chirurgeon, although the treatment was largely more of the same. He was to remain lying flat to give the break a chance to knit, and for the wound to continue to heal.

One of William's first errands was to visit Asmaria. She welcomed him with a pensive look, but bade him with quiet dignity sit at her table where she poured him wine and set a dish of bread and olive oil before him.

William stared at the food. He did not feel like eating but it would be an insult if he did not so he forced himself to take a bite of bread and wash it down with the wine.

'I have some difficult news for you about Ancel,' he said.

Her expression sharpened with fear. 'I knew when I saw you without him. What has happened? Do not tell me he is dead!'

William shook his head. 'No, not that. He has been injured in battle though – a wound to the thigh that has broken the bone. The Hospitallers are caring for him.'

Asmaria slumped down at the table and put her face in her hands for a moment, then looked up at him with tears in her eyes and determination in the set of her lips. 'Oh, the poor man. What can I do to help him?'

'Pray for him,' William said.

She looked at William unflinchingly. 'How badly is he wounded?'

William grimaced. 'The wound will mend, but he will no longer be a fighting man and it remains to be seen how well he will walk.'

She rose jerkily, and busied herself around her room, folding and unfolding a cloth but plainly without purpose. Pilgrim danced round her legs, wagging his tail, and she picked him up and hugged him to her ample bosom. He squirmed, straining to lick her face. 'I will care for his dog and donkey for as long as he has need,' she said, and then buried her face in the dog's fur.

Riddled by guilt, William put a pouch of coins on the table. 'This is for you from Ancel, and I will bring more. I know my brother paid his keep and I promised him I would support you while he cannot.'

She gave a distracted nod. 'Thank him for his generosity, but I am able to support myself. I will send him one of my pies if you will take it to him when I have baked.'

'Certainly,' William said. 'That will lift his spirits. And keep the coin. He desires to think he is providing for you.'

She nodded understanding. 'I would visit him, but I know the monks forbid women in the men's part of the Hospital. But give him all my love and tell him to recover swiftly because I am waiting for him. Promise you will tell him that.'

'Indeed I shall, and that too will increase his determination.' William rose to his feet to take his leave and kissed her cheek, inhaling a faint scent of cooking spices and smoke. He experienced a rush of affection for this homely, honest woman. Ancel had chosen well – better than him.

Ancel's expression was guilty, almost furtive, on William's return, and as William drew a breath he detected a familiar perfume that sent a surge through his body. He recognised too the intricate glass phial of rosewater on the shelf at Ancel's bedside because last time he had seen it had been in the dome. There was also some fresh bread in a cloth and a bowl of dates that had not been there earlier.

'I see you have had a visitor,' William said, short of breath.

Ancel cleared his throat. 'She has only just left.'

A pang twisted William's heart. Had he not lingered at Asmaria's he might have arrived to find Paschia at the bedside, or leaving the Hospital. Her scent was utterly disconcerting. Plainly, while ordinary street women were discouraged, no one was going to refuse the Patriarch's concubine.

Ancel looked at him warily. 'She said she had heard of my injury and wanted to know how I was faring.'

William raised his brows.

'She said she knew I must have fought well and that God would not let me die.' Ancel screwed up his face. 'I told her I was unsure if that was a mercy, and she answered that you needed me and I must live. And then she held my hand and told me about her brother who had died . . .'

William wondered if she felt as guilty as he did about Ancel. Had she known about the treachery of Mahzun of Tyre? Was she involved in it?

'She told me if I needed anything, I had but to name it and she would see that it was provided, and she promised to return and make sure I was receiving the best of care.' Ancel looked at William sidelong. 'And then she kissed my brow.'

William sat down at Ancel's side, feeling slightly sick.

'What else could I do?' Ancel demanded indignantly. 'I could hardly spurn her or refuse to speak. I did not ask for her to come, and she was kind.'

William forced himself to be pragmatic. 'At least if she is visiting you then you have the goodwill of the Patriarch.'

'I think she deliberately came when you were not here.'

'And no surprise. Doubtless my every move is being watched.' He would not think about that. 'As it happens, I too have received a kiss, but from your woman.'

'Indeed?'

Ancel's face revealed he was not entirely sure about that, and William was wryly amused. 'You need not worry about her taking a fancy to me. Her concern was all for you. She says she will send you a fresh pie as soon as she has baked.'

425

A spark kindled in Ancel's eyes. 'Is she still buxom and rosy-cheeked?'

William nodded. 'Although not as flushed as she is when she has you to make her red in the face.'

Ancel smiled, but then looked down. 'But will she still want me when she sees how I am?'

'Of course she will. Asmaria is a determined woman. You are her man and nothing else matters to her. Besides,' he said heartily, 'you are not going to be lying there for ever.'

'It feels like for ever.'

William looked at Ancel. 'You have greater strength than anyone I know to come this far,' he said. 'It's just a little further.'

A little of Ancel's brightness returned. 'I wish I had a pie now,' he said.

Over the next two weeks, William continued to tend to Ancel, although he had to undertake another pilgrim patrol with the men. It was strange not to have his brother riding at his side; there was a cold space where Ancel's presence should have been. He tried to focus on his duty but it was mundane and he kept going back over the attack in his mind and trying to make it end differently. He kept seeing the moment when Mahzun of Tyre's sword had bitten into Ancel's leg, and each time he relived it, his own body reacted with a jolt, for the blow had been meant for him.

As William returned to Jerusalem from his latest patrol, the storm clouds that had been gathering throughout the day broke over the hills and for the first time in months it rained. Lifting his face to the sky he embraced the droplets dappling his face, and thought of England with longing.

By the time he had stabled his horse, washed and prayed, the rain had stopped, but the streets were still damply steaming as he made his way from the Temple to the Hospital.

Ancel was in a buoyant mood. The leg was healing well and

although he was weak from bed-rest, he had a good appetite and he was alert. William was telling him about the patrol when a little brown-and-white dog dashed up to them, his tail wagging so fast that it was a blur, his mouth wide open, tongue lolling as he panted with joy. Launching himself upon Ancel, he commenced licking him with vigorous enthusiasm. Ancel laughed and spluttered and put his arms around the dog, exclaiming. And then he looked up and saw Asmaria advancing toward him with her familiar round-hipped sway, her basket over her arm. As their eyes met she cried his name and ran the last few steps, then stooped to him, kissing his face, making almost as much fuss as the dog.

William grinned. Clearly Asmaria had found a sympathetic ear and been given permission to visit. He made to leave and give them a moment alone, but had barely taken a step before he saw Paschia walking toward Ancel's bed and everything inside him stopped. She was utterly poised and beautiful, clad in fluid grey-blue silk, a white wimple framing her face. Since only Ancel knew the full story of their relationship, he had to bow and look pleased and meet her gaze, but it was almost more than he could bear, as all the memories and emotions struck against the wall he had built and battered to break through.

'It is good of you to bring my brother what he needs,' he said stiffly.

'It was the least I could do,' she murmured, eyes downcast.

'The least?' William swallowed the bitter words that she had done more than enough and she flashed him a hard, swift look that dared him to say anything else.

Asmaria looked round over her shoulder, her face flushed and tear-streaked. 'Thank you, my lady, thank you for what you have done!'

'I am glad to bring comfort,' Paschia replied warmly. 'Everyone shall know that you are here with the Patriarch's express sanction and goodwill.' She turned again to William, and he thought

427

about what could have been and how this was its ghosted shadow. 'My own brother was on my mind,' she said. 'I like to think someone would have cared for him the same . . . and because he is your brother too.'

'And it does you no harm to be beneficent in public.'

She lifted her chin. 'Yes,' she said bitterly, 'Madame la Patriarchess and her good works.'

'Do you know who gave my brother his wound?'

Her face was blank, her stance rigid. She too had her wall, he thought.

'Mahzun of Tyre,' he said when she did not answer. 'He has affiliations with the bands raiding the pilgrim roads, and since he also has connections with your uncle . . .' He let the words hang and gather weight.

She lifted her chin. 'What concern is that of mine?'

'You told me you would hunt me down like a sewer rat. What am I to think, my lady?'

Her composure slipped and a look of complete shock crossed her face before she rallied. 'This is none of my doing. I swear to you I have no knowledge of it.'

'Did you also have no knowledge of what happened to Ptolemy? Do you put your fingers in your ears and look the other way and say you do not go to those places where such things lurk?'

Her voice shook. 'Believe what you will, but it is the truth. I would not be here otherwise.'

William was not in a merciful mood. 'You might in order to salve a bleeding conscience,' he said with contempt. 'But if I take what you say at face value – and I have no reason to do that – it still leaves your uncle connected to a man who has turned traitor to his fellow soldiers and almost crippled my brother. I have no doubt that the blow Ancel took was intended for me. Is that how you wish to live?'

She stared him out. 'You use what dice you have at your command. This is none of my work, and whether you believe that or not is your choice.' Going to Ancel again, she stooped to him. 'I must leave, but I will keep watch on your progress and pray for you, and so will the Patriarch.' She squeezed his hand, touched Asmaria's shoulder, and without looking at William walked swiftly away.

He gazed after her with a mixture of longing and bereavement, exacerbated by the perfume lingering in her wake, and could not decide whether he trusted her or not.

Leaving Ancel and Asmaria to each other's company, he returned to the Temple and, as he entered the precincts, saw Heraclius standing in the forecourt talking to Gerard de Ridefort. William started to avoid them, but he had been seen, and the Patriarch beckoned him over.

'How is your brother faring?' Heraclius enquired. 'He has been much in my thoughts and prayers.'

'He is slowly mending, sire. The wound is healing well but will take some time.'

'Indeed,' Heraclius said with mendacious sympathy, and changed the subject. 'The Count of Jaffa is hosting a banquet in honour of his wife in a week's time. I shall expect your presence there, and bring your men. The Grand Master shall be attending too.'

The words alarmed William, because at worst there could be talk and plotting against the Regent, and at best he had no intention of spending time in the company of Guy de Lusignan. However, he could not refuse the orders of the Patriarch and a Grand Master he was sworn to serve. Since Guy and Sybilla wanted him in their household and under their control, de Ridefort might well send him there.

Heraclius bade farewell to de Ridefort and drew William to one side. 'I know you are troubled by this, but you are highly valued, I want you to know that. It would be better for all concerned if you were to find common ground with the Count of Jaffa. The banquet will provide you with that opportunity – one that will reap great reward.'

'Will the Regent be there?' William asked pointedly.

Heraclius gave him a hard look. 'That is not your concern. We shall expect your presence. Do I make myself clear?'

'Perfectly, my lord,' William replied stiffly, knowing he would have to go and somehow find a way around pledging any kind of allegiance.

'Excellent,' Heraclius said, and the steely glint in his eyes was replaced by a kindly smile. 'It is for your own good, my boy.' He patted William's arm and went on his way.

William did not believe that for a moment.

The day of the gathering, Heraclius summoned William to his private chamber at his palace. As William was ushered into the room by a guard, he caught a trace of Paschia's scent and hesitated, for it was like striking a physical barrier. Thankfully she was not present in the chamber, but he would not put it past her to be listening behind a curtain. Her cat was purring in Heraclius's lap, and the Patriarch was stroking it with a gentle hand.

'Sit.' Heraclius indicated the chair opposite him.

Warily, William did so.

'I have been talking to Grand Master de Ridefort,' Heraclius said, his words as slow as the motion of his hand upon the cat's fur.

William raised his brows and waited. The silence extended while Heraclius studied him, as though making his mind up about something. Then he said, 'Is there anything you want to tell me about your time here while I was away on my mission?'

Shock struck William like a bolt of lightning. Had Paschia rendered the ultimate betrayal and spoken to Heraclius? Or perhaps her uncle, or a servant? 'My lord?' He managed to keep his voice neutral. 'Is there something wrong? All my accounts were in order and I did not spend all the money you left for my use.'

'I have no complaints on that score,' Heraclius said, 'but I was wondering if you had had some dealings with my gatekeeper. My lady seems to think that you and her uncle had some serious differences of opinion.'

William hesitated, trying to decide what to answer that would reveal nothing even while he did not know what had been said. 'We had some disagreements of opinion over rent,' he said at length. 'And on where duties ended and began, and how to deal with certain situations.'

'Did you do anything to earn his enmity?'

William felt his face start to burn. 'The rent issue was enough, your eminence. I stood up to him and he saw me as a threat to his business. I also observed dealings he had with men I considered disreputable – such as Mahzun of Tyre, who betrayed us and wounded my brother.'

'Ah yes. Was that the reason you left my employ and went to the Templars?'

'Yes, sire – and to purge my soul. I came to Jerusalem to be cleansed of sin, but realised I was travelling in the opposite direction.'

Heraclius leaned back, still stroking the cat, his expression thoughtful. 'From what I have heard thus far, it might be best for you to return to your King.'

William was taken aback, if relieved that his affair with Paschia remained unknown – or at least unspoken. 'Sire, I have not completed my penance and I am sworn to serve the Templars.'

'Yes, indeed, and that means obedience to their rule. If their Grand Master ordered you to go, you would have to obey.'

William tightened his lips. 'Yes, sire, but my brother cannot be moved yet.'

Heraclius stopped stroking the cat and it leaped from his lap. 'Let me put this bluntly, so that we may both understand. While Madam de Riveri remains in my household, I am bound to keep her relatives provided for and employed. Whatever Zaccariah of Nablus has done, or may do in future, he is valuable to me and has served me well. One does not have to like a guard dog in order to find it useful. I can tell him to drop his grudge against you, but it would have as much effect as standing on the shore and ordering the tide to retreat because he would smile to my face and still find a way to do you damage. I cannot guarantee your safety, and so it is better that you leave. Penances for the health of your soul can be arranged and I think you will find my lord Gerard amenable to your departure.'

'Have you spoken to him on the matter?'

'No, but I shall do so tonight – he has letters to send to the Templars in Normandy and requires a trustworthy envoy, and you are ideally suited to the task. However, if you do decide to stay, then he and I will both expect you to acknowledge Guy de Lusignan as your liege lord. I am sure he will find suitable lands where you can settle as his vassal.'

William managed not to recoil, but his body stiffened. He knew Heraclius would never seriously expect him to swear to de Lusignan, and if he stayed, he would still be a target for Paschia's uncle, and so would Ancel. Heraclius was plainly not prepared to do anything about Zaccariah of Nablus. Indeed, William harboured an uneasy suspicion that Heraclius knew a great deal more than he was saying.

'Make your choice,' Heraclius said, 'and choose wisely.'

'Ah,' said Guy de Lusignan, smiling, as William bowed to him. 'I see that the Patriarch has finally managed to get you here. Do not worry, you are among friends.'

'I am not worried, sire,' William replied. Just sick at heart and humiliated. He could see others watching him and de Lusignan together. The latter's smile was a smirk. It was like being a fish caught in a net, a fine silver fish that had long been hunted. He was the one who had always been aloof and above the morass, but now he had been landed in the same boat and he was no different to the rest, indeed worse off, for had he chosen to join de Lusignan earlier he could have held an elevated position. Now he was one of the many. He was accustomed to people taking him as a serious opponent, not a powerless victim.

Making his excuses as soon as he could, William left the chamber and climbed to the crenellated walkway at the top of the building. Drawing deep breaths of untainted air, he looked out over the city as the last red streak of the sun dipped below the horizon and night closed over Jerusalem. Lights from fire and lamp glimmered here and there like stars.

It was time to leave, too dangerous to stay. Staying meant becoming an ally of a regime for which he had no respect. Guy was the kind of man to get everyone killed; he suspected the same of de Ridefort. However, something about the urgency with which he was being asked to make his decision aroused his suspicions.

Returning to the festivities, his mood was pensive and his feeling was of instinctive unease now rather than social discomfort. He took his place among the men, and was smiling and affable for their benefit and his own, and when it was time to go, he sought Heraclius.

'My choice is to leave,' he said.

Heraclius adjusted his cloak. 'You have made the right decision, my boy,' he said. 'I shall make arrangements, and you had best make yours.'

William bade farewell to Guy de Lusignan, who remained under the impression that he had finally fished William into his net. Thanking him for his hospitality, William did not disabuse him of the notion. Guy would find out how matters stood soon enough and that his catch had slipped through his hands.

In the underground cavern on the Temple Mount, clad only in shirt and braies, William prostrated himself in the centre of the star mosaic on the floor, surrounded by the Templar brethren of Jerusalem, including Onri, Augustine and Grand Master de

Ridefort. Outside the sun was setting over the city, but the underground chapel was entirely dependent on candle light. The smell of incense was heavy, and layers of gauzy, aromatic smoke wove across the cavern.

'Do you request the company of this house?' de Ridefort asked.

'I do,' William replied in a firm, strong voice, as he made a sacred commitment to God and the Virgin Mary to serve the Templar order as a secular knight for the rest of his life, however long or short that might be.

'Will you take on the role of serf and servant to this house and abdicate your will?'

'I will.'

'And will you ever do as you are bidden and serve the Templars as they deem fit?'

'I will.'

His voice rang around the chapel. Onri stepped forward holding two lengths of folded silk cloth. Other brethren including Augustine helped Onri open out the silks, each man taking a corner and wafting the fabric through the incense smoke again and again like billowing sails while de Ridefort blessed the cloths and spoke of what it was to die and be reborn in service to God and the Virgin through the Templars.

The silks were floated over William's prone body, light as air, bearing the fragrance of sanctity. He heard the voices chanting and felt the vibration of the sound become a power that coursed through him, connecting him to all things as he lay with his arms outspread. The silks settled upon him lighter than a sigh, and the brethren departed on soft feet, still chanting, extinguishing the candles as they went, leaving him in the darkness and silence of the tomb.

At first, it felt like flying, and time ceased to exist. If the bubble of the dome with Paschia had been a physical, sensual time out of mind, this was the opposite moment. Seeing nothing, feeling nothing, covered in diaphanous silk, but as a mantle of silence for aeons, instead of the whisper of a transient lust.

And eventually he felt the lightest touch through the shrouds as the silks were lifted from him, filling each breath he took with the holy scent of incense. He was being raised up and the light was too sharp for his eyes, even though it was only of candles. He was gently escorted, a Templar on either side, to take communion, and his hair was shorn at the nape with silver shears in token of his sacrifice, his penitence and rebirth cleansed of sin.

Exhausted, swallowing tears, he was helped up the stairs and brought to another room where the daylight dazzled him. A simple meal had been prepared of bread, honey and wine and it was eaten in silence by the brethren while Onri read from the Gospel of St John. At the end of the meal, Gerard de Ridefort presented William with the shrouds, now folded and wrapped in a bundle of plain cloth.

'Keep these safely with you in preparation for your dying day,' he said. 'Let them be draped over your body as surety for your resurrection and you shall be safe. You have been shown what it is to die. They are the symbol of the commitment you have made to the order. Now go and prepare yourself for your journey, but first you must sleep.'

Still in a daze, William stumbled back to his lodging on the far side of the compound. Carefully he put the shrouds on a shelf above a small, carved statue of the Virgin before falling on his bed and sinking into slumber. Unlike his experience in the cave, covered by the shrouds, it was not a dark sleep of noth-ingness, but one filled with images that came swiftly, one after another. A beautiful young woman with thick golden hair to her hips and blue eyes that held all the colours of the ocean. For a moment he thought she was an angel, but then he saw that she was with child and there were other children with her too. Boys and girls, dark and fair, that looked like her and looked like him. And then another bed in a well-appointed chamber with three window spaces open to the sky where an old man lay asleep, his hands clasped on his breast, and he knew the man was waiting, and he knew who he was.

William found Ancel in a communal area for the Hospital patients, playing dice. His broken leg was still held straight by two boards and supported on a long bench but he was able to hop around on a crutch and was limitedly mobile.

He was in a good mood, and a modest pile of winnings was stacked at his side. 'See,' he said to William, 'I can still earn my keep.'

'Indeed, you have great skill,' William said with a preoccupied smile.

He watched Ancel game, and when they had finished, he helped him back to his bed. Ancel busied himself, putting his winnings in his pouch. 'I shall give half to Asmaria when she comes tomorrow.' He glanced curiously at the bundle William had in his hands. 'What's that?'

William sat down at his side and unfolded the wrappings, exposing the lengths of silk. 'It's a gift. This is what I want to be wrapped in when I die, just so that you know.'

Ancel gave him a wide look and touched the silk with its pattern of peacocks and foliage gleaming in the weave, its chevroned border and embroidered cross on the larger piece. His eye caught the smaller Templar crosses embroidered in the corners. 'Very rare and costly.' His expression became wary. 'What did you do to warrant such a "gift"?'

William replied quietly, 'I have sworn myself to the service of the Templars without taking the full vows and this is the covenant of that oath. But you are my only kin should I die before we arrive home, and what you say and do at my wake speaks for me to all men.'

Ancel eyed him sharply. 'Very well, I shall see to it as best I can, should it come to that, but what makes you think it will?'

'I don't, it is a precaution.' Which was not entirely true. William

436

drew a deep breath. 'We have to leave within the week. I am working on a padded cart for you so you will be able to travel in comfort and we'll go by sea where we can so you can rest your leg.'

Ancel's eyes rounded with shock. 'Why?' he demanded. 'I thought we would stay until after the Christmas feast. It is too soon!'

'I have important letters to bear for the Patriarch and for the Templars, and their need is immediate. I cannot leave you here in Jerusalem because it would not be safe.'

'And you think travelling like this will be any safer?'

'I cannot leave you here with Zaccariah of Nablus at large to do his worst and you with no means of income.'

Ancel was silent for a while. 'I do want to go home,' he said eventually. 'I have always wanted to go home, but not like this.' His mouth twisted. 'It doesn't seem as though I have a choice, does it? What of Asmaria?'

William shook his head. 'The travelling will not be easy and we have documents to carry, but send for her once you are home and she can come to you on the pilgrim ships in the spring.'

'Yes,' Ancel said, but not as though he believed it.

'I mean it, truly.'

'I am sure she can find better bargains than a cripple she has to cross oceans to be with.'

'You are wrong,' William said vehemently. 'She sees you as you are and you see her the same. She might be asking herself why a man of your rank should ask someone like her to cross oceans and come to him. Think on that.'

Ancel grimaced. 'I will . . . if I survive. You should find some shrouds for me also, Gwim.'

'We are going to win through, I promise you.'

Ancel raised his brows and looked sceptical.

37

Manor of Caversham, April 1219

William watched the sunlight move slowly across his bedclothes, bringing gold to the plain brown coverlet. It had rained last night, but the dawn had been clear and the air was fresh and green. The last couple of days he had been unwell and in great pain, but this morning he felt better. It was as though the morning sun had warmed him through to his bones and given him a life-enhancing surge of energy. He had made his confession earlier and arranged for his almoner Geoffrey to distribute alms to the poor. He had even eaten some bread and broth from a spoon without feeling sick and had felt regret for the hope he had seen in Isabelle's eyes as she tended to him. He was not coming back from this, he was just sustaining himself for a little longer, for the time it took to complete what he had to do.

'I dreamed of you last night,' he murmured to her where she sat holding his hand. 'And our children.'

'Did you? What did you dream?'

'Of the years we have had. Of seeing you lying on our marriage bed with your golden hair unbound and thinking that I had wed an angel. I was not wrong.'

A small sound escaped her throat and her fingers entwined with his.

'I never quite believed I deserved you, Isabelle.'

'You were the answer to my prayers too.' She looked down at their joined hands. 'I saw you walking across the courtyard toward me at the Tower of London, so straight and purposeful, and I thought here is a man who knows what he is about, and that if you were kind, it might be all right . . . but you were so much more than that, and I could not believe that God had been so generous. Although He is not being generous now.' Her chin trembled. 'I would not trade one moment with you, except for these past few months.' She leaned over and kissed his brow and then his lips, and after saying something about her household duties made a swift exit.

He knew she had taken leave before she cried in front of him, and he was deeply saddened, but it did not detract from his own sense of accepting what must be.

She was only gone a short while, however, before she returned, her eyes pink-rimmed but her expression sternly composed. 'Jean is back,' she said.

He strove to sit up. 'That is excellent news. Make sure he takes the time to eat and recover and then send him to me. Another hour will not matter and I know that unless strictly ordered, he will not bother. Tell him to bring Will and Henry with him when he comes.' William's heart quickened with anticipation and even a little fear. Waiting for the shrouds had been a burden even though he had been certain that Jean would bring them in time.

'I have already seen to it.' She managed a smile. 'He would have come to you immediately as you say, but he was mired from his journey and in need of a drink at least.'

As she left, William listened to the sound of his grandchildren playing on the sward outside his window and his mind drifted for a little while, imagining what the spring day was like outside. The lush grass that would make the cows fat and sleek. The fine grazing in the water meadows by the Thames had been the first thing he had noticed when he came to Caversham, and the swans, white wings curved as they sailed upon their reflections in sky-mirrored water. It was his lot to be buried with the Templars, but a part of him, some small spark of soul, would linger here.

The door opened and Jean entered. He walked straight to the

bedside and knelt and, taking William's hand, kissed it. 'I came as swiftly as I could, sire.' His brown eyes filled with chagrin. 'My horse cast a shoe on the road yesterday and that lost me a few miles of daylight.'

'No matter,' William said with warm affection. 'I told you I would be here and so I am, and you have still made good time and done well. I trust you have refreshed yourself as ordered.'

Jean nodded ruefully. 'Your lady was insistent. She said you were still strong enough to refuse to see me if I did not.'

'And so I am.'

'I am pleased to hear it, sire.'

William knew very well from the worry in Jean's eyes what he was seeing when he looked at him, but they played the game of diplomatic tact.

'I have brought your lengths of silk, sire,' Jean said, and placed a large leather satchel on the bed, which he unfastened and from it removed a package wrapped in linen and tied with silk cords.

Beyond Jean, William saw Will, Isabelle and Henry FitzGerold enter the room and he beckoned them to his bedside. 'Come,' he said to Jean, 'bring out the cloths and let us see what we have.'

Jean fumbled with the cords and William's body leaped with impatience. It was like the excitement of waiting to see old friends, and it had been so long . . .

The ties finally unfastened, Jean unfolded the protective linen outer packaging and drew out two pieces of folded white silk, very fine and light in his hands. A scent of incense rose on the air in an invisible smoky thread.

'Open them out,' William commanded.

A joyful, tender pain flashed in his solar plexus as Jean handed a corner of one length of the silks to Henry and they unfolded and draped it over the bed, softly gleaming. And then the second one. The larger piece bore a pattern of peacocks woven into the fabric that showed up in subtle intricacy as the light shone upon the silk. A thin border of interlacing ran around the edges between lines of purple and gold, and a cross made up of smaller crosses shimmered gold and purple on the white.

Setting his eyes on these magnificent pieces took William back thirty years and filled him with an emotion that almost stopped his breath. He imagined them being wrapped with sacred care around his body to take him forth from the world even as they had brought him back into it after the maelstrom that had been Paschia. Setting his hand on the cloth, he experienced a qualm, not of the unknown, but of the finality. Once he was dead, unlike the first time of lying under these shrouds, he could never come back. Never know again the loving physical touch of those around him or take part in the life he had been so privileged to live.

'What is this, Papa?' Will said, gazing at the silks with questioning eyes.

Behind him William saw Isabelle put her hand across her mouth, her eyes filling with grief that was almost horror. He could understand what a shock it was, especially to see them draped over his bed as if already covering his corpse. He wanted to comfort her, to say that it was all right, that it was all part of life even though it was about death, but knew it would not be her experience.

'I have had these two pieces of silk for thirty years,' he told those gathered around his bed, having from somewhere found the strength to raise his voice. 'I brought them back with me from Outremer and since that time it has always been my intention to have them draped over my body when I am laid in the earth.'

Will shook his head in wonder. 'I have never seen these before. You never told us.' His tone was gentle but raw with sadness, not quite reproach.

'No, I did not,' William replied. 'It was a private matter between me and God. I have always known where they were, but never needed them, until now.'

Isabelle made a tiny sound and then stifled it against the back of her hand.

Will cleared his throat and said gruffly, 'They are truly beautiful, my father. It is strange that you would think so far ahead when you were in Outremer.'

'Death was very close there. Indeed, I did not know if I would survive, but I did, and there was no holier place on earth.' He looked at his son and those gathered around his shrouded bed. 'When I was in Jerusalem, at the time that I obtained these silks, I made an oath to the Templars to serve them as a secular brother all my life and to give them my oath and my body when it came my time to die. These cloths are part of the covenant I made. I shall be laid to rest at the Temple in London – all that was decided long ago.' He turned his head to Jean D'Earley. 'Jean, of your love for me, when I am dead, I want you to cover me with them and surround the bier in which I am carried to the Temple. If there is bad weather, then buy cloth to shield them so they will not become damp or dirtied. Once I am buried, give that cloth to the brothers and tell them they may do with it as they will.'

'As you wish, my lord.' Jean swallowed hard.

Seeing the grief and tears around him, William was brought close to the edge himself, but he was vastly relieved to have the silk shrouds, his deep comfort and symbol of life beyond the tomb.

'What shall I do with them for now, sire?' Jean asked hoarsely.

'Take them to my chapel and have Father Nicholas bless them and wash them in incense. Then return them to me and put them under the bed so that I have the comfort of knowing they are close to hand. Jean, my thanks, you have done well.'

Jean bowed and touched his heart. 'My duty and my honour, sire.' With great reverence and care he folded up the silks, and returned them to their protective covering.

William looked at Isabelle. 'Now,' he said, 'I would like a little time alone with my wife. There are things I have to say to her, and she to me.'

Slowly everyone trooped from the room, stunned, wiping their eyes. Will was the last to leave, closing the door behind him.

Isabelle moved to his bedside. 'In all our years of marriage you never told me,' she said, with tears in her eyes, her voice grieving and hurt.

'I told no one. They were part of a personal vow and no one else's concern. When I was in Outremer, I had much on my conscience. I was burdened with sins I had committed and bad decisions I had made. Those silks were a covenant of a life that started afresh – my final chance. You have always known of my links with the Templars.'

'Yes, but not this. It is one thing to conceal yourself from others, but not from me . . . you have had all of me, my wholeness, but I have not had all of you.'

It was difficult to find breath to speak, but he strove nevertheless because it was important. 'I have shared more with you, Isabelle, than anyone in my life. When we were wed, I told you some parts were mine alone to me and you accepted it then, so why can you not accept it now?'

'I do accept it, but I still wish I had known, or that you had trusted me enough to tell me.'

'I trust you most of all – and to understand.'

'Then you ask a great deal.'

'Yes,' he said simply. 'But not too much.'

She bit her lip, her eyes shimmering with tears. 'I wish I could be wrapped up with you too. I will find it so hard to go on without you. We have always been each other's strength.'

'Indeed, while we have had that privilege,' he replied, 'but you must go forward on your own account without me, and I am relying on you to find that strength and courage as I have relied on you throughout our marriage. I know you full capable.' He had to pause again to gather his breath and compose his own

443

emotion for what he needed to say. 'I love you for what you are, who you are and what you have been to me. Many times circumstances have parted us and this will be just another of those times. We are one whether separated or not.'

'I have no words,' Isabelle said in a choked voice. 'You have said them all for me. Whatever I add would be grief as well as comfort.'

'We have always known without words, but while it is time for truths, let us have it all out. If I am to die a Templar, I must take the full vows.'

She nodded tremulously.

'I want you to go into the clothing store and bring out the cloak you will find in the third coffer along.'

She left the bedside and went to the garderobe chamber beyond, but before entering she hesitated, and he saw her brace her shoulders and raise her head as if to face and withstand a blow. And then she moved forward. He heard the chest lid being thrown back, and then a long, long silence, but filled with a tension that no word or sound could convey.

She returned with her arms full of a white woollen Templar cloak, so thick and heavy that it was an effort for her to carry. She laid it on the bed, her expression a smooth mask, but now and then her face gave a betraying twitch.

'When did you have this done?' she asked.

He tried to draw a deep breath but could not; his lungs were empty. 'Last May, before we set out to tour our lands. It was part of setting matters in order. Once it was done, I did not have to think on it again. I had been letting it pass me by, but I wanted to be prepared.'

She sat down on the bed and put her hand on the cloak. 'When we went to Paris, three years ago, I wore my court shoes to attend the King of France – do you remember? I walked and danced until the soles were worn through. I did not tell you then, but I intended them to be for my own burial – but I changed my mind and wore them out instead. And now you show me shrouds you have kept for thirty years, and this cloak. I cannot . . .' She stopped speaking and sat down, tears rolling down her cheeks.

'I knew if I told you, you would not take it well. You have always known I would take Templar vows at my death. It gave me peace of mind to have this cloak made while I was still in good health. Like those shrouds, it is part of my own preparation – private to me. I wish I could make you understand.'

'I do understand, but it still hurts.'

He touched the cloak, remembering when he had ordered it to be made – the feeling of relief that he had set the thing in motion, and once it was done, it would be ready for a time of his choosing and would no longer disturb his mind. But he had always known it would be difficult for Isabelle. 'I have been trying to find the right moment to tell you, but I have never found it. But time has forced my hand because it has run out, and very soon I shall be making this formal and public.'

She stared at him in dismay.

'Once I take the full vows of a Templar, I may no longer embrace you, nor you me. It is forbidden by the rule.'

'This is what you want?' More tears brimmed over and spilled down her cheeks.

'I made my vow to the Templars more than thirty years ago, and the time has come to fulfil that promise. For my honour, for my soul, this is the way it must be.'

She sat very still for a long time, gathering her composure, and then she gave him a direct look. 'It is your choice, and I must abide by it,' she said. 'I have loved you ever since our marriage, and for that love, I will let you go.' She rose to her feet, removed her wimple, and took down her hair. Her once lustrous golden-blonde locks were almost all silver now, but still thick and rippled with waves from being plaited. She stepped out of her shoes, took off her belt, and climbed onto the bed beside him. 'I know you are in pain, and that all things carnal

445

and of the body have had their time, but I want to lie beside you just once more, as your wife. If I have this, then I can face the rest.'

He moved to one side to allow her to lie down, and set his arm around her shoulders even though it hurt. 'What I would give to reverse the wheel of time and have this a different spring season with you a young wife in my arms and myself whole and strong.'

She touched his cheek with her fingertips. 'I wish it too.'

'This bed,' he said with a smile in his voice. 'Do you remember I had it made by a carpenter in London?'

'Yes, I remember . . . from an oak felled at Hamstead. Its pieces have travelled wherever we have dwelt.'

Their marriage bed, the heart of their home, William thought. Where they had slept, made love, talked and quarrelled and mended such quarrels in the time-honoured fashion. Their ten children had been begotten and born within its hangings. Draped with different covers, it had served as a day couch and witnessed the daily traffic of the chamber: the scratching of the scribes' quills, the robust discussions of knights and vassals, the gossip and laughter of informal assemblies, the closeted intimacy of private discussion. Now it waited to render the final service.

'The tales it could tell,' William remarked.

'Then perhaps for decency's sake it is a good thing that beds do not have voices.'

He laughed, but the laughter brought on a coughing fit and pain like knives. Isabelle hastily left the bed and fetched him a cup of the syrup of poppy mixture. He was in too much discomfort to refuse it.

'I never thought to say this, but I am ready for the end of my path,' he said as she took the cup back from him. 'I grieve to leave you behind, but each mile is a burden and I would have done.'

'I know,' she said softly. 'And I would not have you carry it further than your will takes you, but bidding you farewell is the most difficult thing.' She lay down again at his side and put her arm across him, protectively, as he had once protected her, and he was awed and humbled by her courage and strength.

At some point he felt a soft kiss on his brow and heard a sound that might have been a stifled sob. He was aware then of Isabelle leaving the bed and tip-toeing away to her prayers. The pain returned, but before it could rage someone gave him more poppy syrup, and as he closed his eyes, the colours swirled and turned against his lids, and he found himself again in Jerusalem.

38

Jerusalem, October 1185

Slowly William rose from his knees. He had been at prayer for so long that he was as stiff as an effigy, and cold and hollow with hunger. On the morrow he would set out on the long journey home and he had been praying for God's forgiveness and help on his way. He had letters for King Henry and also from the Templars to their brethren in Normandy and London and he was under orders not to ask questions. That was part of the bargain he had made in exchange for his shrouds and his soul.

Breathing in the sacred atmosphere, he gazed at the arches of stone, the gilding and magnificence where once had existed no more than a simple tomb hewn from the rock. Now it was the centre of the Christian world, and when he walked away from it he would never be here again. 'Amen.' He crossed himself and went outside to the courtyard where the candle sellers were doing the same brisk business that had occupied him on the day he arrived.

A young man who had been examining the wares at one of the candle stalls approached him. William recognised Zaccariah's squire and stiffened.

'I have a message for you from a certain lady,' the youth said.

William could not prevent his upper lip from curling. 'Do you indeed?'

The young man's eyes were knowing and cynical beyond their years. 'She says to meet her by the draper's stall in the Covered Market and to tell you that it is important.' His attitude said that he knew exactly what kind of important.

'And why should I trust you?' William asked.

The youth had the utter self-assurance not to be perturbed. 'Because my lady paid me enough.' His dark eyes were as hard as Zaccariah's, whose place he would one day take.

His words held the ring of truth, and William nodded curtly. The youth flourished an elaborate salute and swaggered off as if he owned the street, his hand on his dagger hilt.

William did not immediately turn in the direction of the market, but stood deliberating. He had emerged from the Sepulchre purged and cleansed, ready to leave all this behind. He was very tempted not to go, but knew if he did not, he would always wonder. While nothing she could say would ever make it right, a last meeting might close the book and lock the clasp. Of course, it might also be a trap . . .

Fastening his cloak against the evening chill, he walked the short distance from the Sepulchre to the Covered Market running parallel with Malquisnet Street. Most of the booths occupying the arches were closed and only a few lamps glimmered to light the way along the paved corridor. The draper's booths were all shut, but as he neared them he saw Zoraya swathed in her cloak, keeping watch, a lantern in her hand. She saw him and turned to signal, and Paschia stepped out from a shadowed archway. She wore a dark mantle with a glint of silver braid down the edge and her wimple was pulled forward, partially concealing her face. Her perfume whispered to him, and he gave an involuntary shiver.

'What is it that you want of me, my lady?' he asked.

She stepped closer to him. 'I am glad you have come – I did not know if you would. I wanted to wish you Godspeed and I want you to be safe on your journey.'

'If that is all, then there is no point in this meeting: you could have said these things in public.' He looked round, still more than half suspecting a trap.

'I want you to take Heraclius's two fastest horses,' she said.

'Take Rakkas. I will vouchsafe that you have my permission. Only be swift about it – as swift as you can.'

The urgency in her words disturbed him. 'Why is it necessary for me to leave so quickly that you would give me the best horses from the stables?'

She bit her lip. 'It is too dangerous for you to stay.'

'If it is, then you have made it so. You told me you would hunt me down. The first time it did not work and Ancel paid the price, but now you have found another way. If I am caught with the Patriarch's horses, then I may be taken as a thief and executed.'

'No!' Her eyes widened. 'I would never do that! I finished our affair for your own good. It was always a dream, but you took it for reality. I warned you at the outset but you did not listen.'

She who had begun it, he thought, although he had played his own part in allowing himself to be led from the path and into darker alleys. 'And the child?' William curled his lip. 'Did you end that too?'

She dropped her gaze. 'My uncle found out and made sure I miscarried – he is capable of anything. While you remain here your life and the lives of your men are in danger. I say do not tarry any longer because he will finish you. You must go!'

He wondered of what she was capable too. He could not trust her, and yet she had taken a risk in meeting him and she had been very solicitous of Ancel, although that was probably guilt. 'He has told you this? Just how much of a party are you to his schemes and plans?'

'Of course he has not told me,' she said impatiently. 'But I hear and see things, and I can bribe squires just as easily as he can.'

William wondered whether that bribery was only in coin, but refrained from asking her if she had taken the dark-eyed young man to the dome too. He did not want to know.

'Yesterday evening my uncle received a message from Mahzun

of Tyre.' William looked at her sharply, and she shook her head. 'That is all I know. My informant only overheard part of what the messenger said, and had to leave before he was discovered. I cannot tell you Mahzun's whereabouts because I do not know, but he is not far away. If questioned, my uncle will deny everything, or find some excuse that will make everything plausible and smooth. He will not stop. He will bring you down any way he can while you are close enough to be harmed. If he has not done so, and the same for Ancel, it is because I have paid him to leave you alone, but I have no more money without asking Heraclius, and now Mahzun is back.'

William swallowed and shook his head, feeling sick. There were no words.

She made a small sound and gave him a little package wrapped in an exquisite green silk cloth. 'Take this, but do not look at it until you have left Jerusalem. I would not blame you if you hated me,' she added in a small voice, 'but it does not alter what I feel for you. I would have followed you if I could, but even for love, even though you offered me what no man had ever done before, it was impossible.'

William looked down at what she had given him. Through the layers of cloth he could feel that it was a ring. A swift glance at her right hand showed him that she no longer wore the plain band that had belonged to her mother, the one that had signalled their assignations, although the one he had given to her was still on her finger.

'You can be sure I will treasure it,' he said, 'as I once treasured you.' He bowed to her, then turned and walked away, and did not look back, although each step was pain.

The late October morning dawned bright and clear, perfect for a journey. A two-wheeled cart had been prepared for Ancel, the interior heavily padded, and he had been helped into it and settled among heaped cushions and furs with his broken leg well supported. In public he was open and smiling despite any misgivings he might harbour in private, and he made regal flourishes from the cart like a prince travelling in a silken litter. Pilgrim leaped in and out of the cart wagging his tail, ready for a great adventure.

Asmaria was among the group gathered to bid them farewell, wearing her best gown and fur-lined cloak. The children were scrubbed and shiny and she had brought a basket of her famous pies to see the men off on the journey, with a special one for Ancel. The sight brought a moment of welcome relief to William as he remembered Baldwin de Bethune bestowing similar fare on their outward journey. Somehow it completed the circle.

Asmaria and Ancel had said their serious farewells at the Hospital the previous evening where he had promised to send for her as soon as he was settled at home. He had given her the jewelled silk tunic and turban he had won at Kerak to sell in order to provision herself for the journey, and she had given him a small silver cross strung on a green silk cord.

Heraclius was present to wish the party Godspeed. He handed each man a small pouch of money and gave his blessing, and also parchments of safe conduct. To William he returned the map he had borrowed, worn in the creases, well travelled but still serviceable. 'God hold you in his keeping, my son,' he said. 'Remember us often in your prayers as we shall remember you. And greet your King for me and tell him I still hope to welcome him to Jerusalem one day.'

'I shall indeed do so, my lord,' William replied, his smile warm, giving nothing away of the price he was paying.

Paschia stood quietly beside Heraclius, her gaze downcast and modest, her garb that of a sombre matron. William made a determined effort not to look at her. Although the last tie between them was a frayed thread, it had tangled itself into a knot around his heart rather than being a straight line that could be easily severed.

Several knights of the royal household with whom William had ridden to Kerak were also present to make their farewells and give him messages to pass on to friends and family in Normandy and England. Onri and Augustine were riding with them for the first day of their journey, to honour the pilgrimage they had made with William to reach Jerusalem, but would turn back on the second morning.

Among the many who came to salute them on their way, Guy de Lusignan was something of a surprise.

'You could have been a great lord in Outremer,' Guy said with scorn, brushing a speck from his sleeve. 'Never forget when you are sleeping under a hedgerow with holes in your hose that I offered you that chance. All you had to do was wipe the slate clean as I did, and begin again.'

William stared into Guy's clear glass-blue eyes. He might have the looks of a hero, but that quality did not extend to the rest of him. However, he did not intend insulting him when he never had to see him again. Besides, Guy was right. If he had stayed and become Guy's man, he could have had an elevated position in Outremer – for as long as he lived, which he reckoned would be a short span indeed. 'I promised King Henry and Queen Alienor I would return and make my report to them, sire. What happens beyond that is my own clean slate. My time here is ended.'

Guy gave a scornful shrug. 'You throw it all away.'

'No, sire,' William replied. 'It is for others to decide what happens here. I shall still continue to serve Outremer when I am home – as I have vowed. Indeed, I can do more there than here being constrained by Jerusalem.' He thought it ironic that Guy was telling him he was throwing his future away when Guy had it in him to squander everything.

Zaccariah of Nablus stood watching them with folded arms. 'My advice is to take the main roads. You will be safer there with your burdens.' He flashed William a broad, false smile. 'You are in my prayers too.'

William forced a smile in return. 'As you are in mine,' he replied, knowing what they were both praying for.

'God speed you, William.' Paschia spoke for the first time, and sent her uncle a meaningful look. 'May your road be clear and safe – and may you reach home unscathed.'

William risked a glance at her. 'That is impossible, madam.' He inclined his head. 'But I shall certainly hope to arrive there a wiser man.'

She dropped her gaze again, and he turned his horse.

They left the Holy City by the Gate of David, and with each stride Chazur took away from the city the knot became a little tighter, turning the pain inside him to a hard ball. It was difficult enough to leave and draw away from where Paschia was to a place where she was not. As he threw a scatter of coins into the crowd, he wondered what his time here had been worth.

He had bound the silks around his body, making a thick padding like a gambeson, protecting him against the cold bite of the wind and affording him spiritual comfort and sustenance, almost in the same way that Harry's cloak had done on the way to Jerusalem. He had a reason to keep going and a duty to fulfil, but he was also well aware that he had been given the shrouds in the expectation that he might soon die, and it was all the more reason to keep them close to his body.

Ancel had departed the Holy City making grand flourishes like royalty and calling out gaily to all, but as they travelled along the road, without an expectant audience, he became quiet and introspective. Pilgrim curled up beside him and went to sleep, nose on tail.

That night they stopped in a pilgrim hostel and dined on mutton broth and flat bread. William sat down in a quiet corner and took out the package Paschia had given him and discovered it was indeed the plain gold ring that had belonged to her mother – her most treasured possession. He stared at it on the palm of his hand for a long time and then threaded it onto a leather cord and fastened it around his neck, tucking it down inside his shirt where the key to the dome had once lain against his heart. It carried a weight of sadness and experience about what could have been, but in its eternal circle, it also taught a lasting lesson. A man could only go forward on one path – for better or worse.

Feeling pensive, he returned to his men and sat down at Ancel's side. 'How are you finding the journey?'

Ancel shrugged. 'Not as comfortable as I was in Jerusalem, but it is tolerable, and it is good to be out of the Hospital and to see more than four walls.' He stroked Pilgrim's ears. 'It was the right thing to do, Gwim, even if I argued against it at the time.'

William forced a smile. 'I had little choice, but yes, it was.' He touched Ancel's sleeve. 'I am sorry for all you have suffered because of me. I may never be able to make it right, but I will do my best for you.'

Ancel looked at the wall. 'Even if I recover from this I can no longer make my way in the world as I once did. My livelihood has gone.'

William felt a flush of guilt. 'There are other things you can do. Our father always found places in his household for men who had been honourably injured and could no longer fight.'

'I do not want charity,' Ancel said tightly. 'How will I support Asmaria if I do not have the wherewithal?'

'It will not be charity,' William said.

'Will it not?'

'You have much to offer. I know our cousin Rotrou at Perche will be glad to have you. He offered you employment after the tourney at Lagny.'

'That was when I was whole,' Ancel said grimly.

'Yes, and I know you cannot serve him as a warrior now, but you have qualities that he will still value. You can read and write – which I cannot – and you can still train others to the warrior skills even if you can no longer perform them. It will be all right, I swear.'

Ancel shrugged. 'We shall see,' he said.

In the morning, they set out from the hostel and Onri and Augustine bade them farewell and prepared to return to Jerusalem. Onri clasped William's shoulder. 'I will pray for you and hope you win through.' He exchanged a look with William that said more than words. 'Whatever happens, I want to know.'

'I shall send word,' William promised. 'I would ask you, even though you are vowed to have no contact with women, to keep an eye on Ancel's lady, and to make sure she lacks for nothing and has safe passage when my brother sends for her.'

Onri dipped his head. 'It shall be done,' he promised, and if his tone was over-hearty, William paid no heed to that particular nuance. If they both pretended everything was all right, then it might be.

The weather continued cold and dry over the next few days as they made their way along the meandering course of the River Yarkon toward the coast road and the port of Caesarea in order to take ship for Cyprus. William was on constant guard and insisted that the men wear their mail and keep a lookout for anything untoward. The armour was heavy, but at least the sky was overcast and the weather cool. In summer heat it would have been unbearable.

Ancel was being cheerful as they rode along, banging the drum and singing marching songs. They had passed a field of sugar cane at the roadside and everyone was munching on short lengths of the fibrous stems to extract the sweet, sticky juice. The river reflected the grey early November sky and they could almost be winding alongside a riverbank in England, were it not for the lack of willow, alder and bramble. Instead there were cypresses, cedars and sparse Jericho oaks. But still the thought was of home and he was filled with nostalgia and longing and a need to be there.

The group approached yet another twist in the river where the movement of the water had created a shallow inlet bordered by a low muddy bank. William decided to call a halt and replenish the water bottles and change over the horse pulling Ancel's cart, before they pushed on to the coast. They had set out early and had made good time, but a rest would refresh everyone.

William produced a handful of dried dates for himself and Chazur from his saddle pack, pushing the horse away as he tried to grab more than his share.

Suddenly from the higher ground to the west, William saw a group of horsemen cresting the slope and bearing down on them at a canter. His heart kicked into a swift rhythm, for these were clearly not fellow travellers hoping to share a water hole.

'On guard!' he shouted.

Several of his men had noticed the danger too and were already drawing their weapons and mounting up. William scrambled into the saddle and issued rapid orders.

Within moments the group was upon them, weapons flashing, and William was unsurprised to see Mahzun of Tyre leading them. The horse drawing Ancel's cart, already half unharnessed, reared in panic and tried to escape, bucking and twisting until the cart overturned, tipping Ancel into the mud and water. William heard him cry out, but beset on all sides, striking and parrying, was helpless to go to his aid.

Sweeping aside Robert of London's sword, Mahzun of Tyre confronted William with teeth bared, his eyes a black glitter. He was totally focused on his effort to bring William down and kill him. William met him with similar intent and they were evenly matched, for Mahzun was bigger and stronger, a force of nature, but William was swifter, more flexible, and thus able to dodge or turn the blows. Mahzun hammered at him with single-minded concentration. When William blocked a high blow, he immediately went low in an effort to control the fight. Parrying, turning, dodging out of reach and then striking at Mahzun and being blocked, William knew he had to end it. Either he would kill Mahzun or Mahzun would kill him. If this was his time to die, so be it. He would go to God with his shrouds bound around his body and it would be an honourable end.

Mahzun raised his sword. William feinted left, then right, and for an instant opened himself to Mahzun's greedy blade, just enough for the mercenary to take the bait; and then he cut in under Mahzun's guard and with one tremendous effort struck a blow that severed Mahzun's head from his body. The mercenary tumbled from his saddle and his horse bolted, dragging the corpse through the dust, spouting blood. The head bounced on the path and rolled down the road a little way, coming to rest on the side of the helmet that was still attached by the chin lacings.

Seeing their leader brought down in such a dramatic and final manner, his men fled, leaving their dead in the road, but not before Eustace and Robert of London had captured Mahzun's servant.

William reined about and rushed to help Ancel who was clinging perilously to the cart wheel, half submerged in sticky, clinging mud. He had been striving to pull himself out of the water while the battle raged and had gripped a tent mallet in his fist to defend himself. He was white with pain and gasping as William and Geoffrey FitzRobert managed to drag him clear and lie him on the ground. His wound had opened again and was leaking slug-gishly.

'Give him some poppy syrup,' William snapped at Geoffrey, 'and bind his leg. Eustace, Guyon, see if you can make a litter from the cart.' He crouched beside Ancel. 'It's over. Mahzun of Tyre is dead.'

Ancel squeezed his eyes tightly shut. 'You should have left him for me,' he attempted to jest through gritted teeth.

'If I had known you were so eager, I would have done,' William responded, conspiring with his bravado. 'We'll see what we can do to fashion you a litter, but the cart's ruined.'

William left him to the ministrations of Geoffrey and Eustace and, rubbing his mired hands on his filthy surcoat, went to deal with the mercenary who had been taken prisoner. He dared not think of Ancel beyond the practicalities of dealing with a wounded man and moving on from this place lest there were other pursuers. They were utterly vulnerable if they were attacked again. If he thought about what the tumble had done to Ancel, he could not have functioned.

'Shall we slit his throat, sire?' Robert of London asked grimly.

William shook his head. 'Not yet.'

The soldier, who was an older man but the equivalent of Mahzun's squire and body servant, was spitting blood from a broken tooth but had suffered no worse damage than bruises.

'Tell me who sent you to do this and I will spare your life,' William said. 'On my honour, which is more than your master's.'

The man glowered. 'My master told me we had a job to do and I followed orders, that is all.'

'And who gave him that job?' William demanded. 'Who was his paymaster? I advise you to tell me because your life depends on how much you cooperate and I am not disposed to be merciful.' He forced the man to face Mahzun's headless corpse, lying some way down the road where the horse had dragged it before Mahzun's foot had finally untangled from the stirrup.

'The one who often paid us to do tasks, although he was never our master,' the mercenary replied, almost proudly. 'We only took the contracts my master chose.'

'And who would "the one" be?'

The soldier shrugged. 'The Patriarch's gatekeeper, Zaccariah of Nablus. He would often put work our way.'

William had expected to hear such a reply but his gut still churned. 'Including raiding the pilgrim roads, or was that your own work?'

The soldier tightened his lips and gave a small movement of his shoulders.

'Did the Patriarch know of this business?'

Another shrug. 'Eventually everything reaches the Patriarch's ears. What he does about it is up to him. But it was Zaccariah of Nablus who told us you were bearing important letters he would pay well to see for himself.'

'Did he indeed?' William turned and went to the head lying in the dust. He had done many things in battle but had never decapitated anyone before. However, it was a standard form of execution in Outremer. Any Templar captured by the enemy could expect to suffer that fate. Picking up the head by the helmet strap, he tied it to the saddlebag of Mahzun's retrieved bay stallion, and brought the horse to their prisoner. 'As you value your life and your honour,' he said, 'return this to Jerusalem and present it to Zaccariah of Nablus. Tell him it stops here. Tell him I cut off Mahzun of Tyre's head and I will do the same to him if he dares to come near me and mine again. Make sure you do tell him, because I will know if you do not – it would be the height of stupidity to trifle with the long arm of the Templars. After you have fulfilled your task, I suggest you make yourself very scarce. Understood?'

The man nodded to show that he did, his throat working as he swallowed.

'Go then.'

William handed him the horse's reins and the mercenary leaped into the saddle and spurred off down the road, Mahzun's head banging at his side.

'Do you think he will do as you bade him?' asked Robert of London dubiously.

William shrugged. 'Who can say? I hope the threat will be enough, but what will be will be.'

He returned to Ancel. Geoffrey had cleaned him up and managed to stop the bleeding and the poppy syrup was doing its job, which was a good thing, because now they had to transport him in a makeshift litter for the twenty miles to Caesarea and a ship bound for Cyprus.

'It is over,' William said as Ancel raised heavy lids. 'We are going home.'

39

Temple Church, London, April 1186

William dismounted from Bezant in the stable yard of the new Templar complex and gave his reins to a groom. The April morning was bright with birdsong and the trees in the orchards sweeping down to the Thames were fluffy with blossom, petals floating like snow in the strong breeze blowing off the river, but in his fur-lined cloak William was invigorated, not cold.

Walking up through the Temple grounds to the new church, he thought back on the previous few months and the place his life had come to now. He had returned to England with the court two days ago, and had taken leave of King Henry to come here and finish weaving another thread of his business.

He had arrived at his cousin Rotrou's castle of Perche in late January after making his return cautiously by sea and land. Rotrou had welcomed the party warmly and settled them by his fire to recuperate and bring him news of Jerusalem, where he had sworn to go himself.

As William had hoped, Rotrou had offered Ancel a permanent place in his household and a secure home in which he could make his long recuperation. He would walk again, but he would always limp. The unthinking, casual ease was gone. And he would never fight from the back of a horse again. But he had clerical skills, was good with youngsters, and would make a fine tutor to the squires at Perche. It still felt like crumbs and dregs from what had once been a feast, but it was more than survival. William had promised to visit when he could, and Ancel had been stoical as they embraced. 'I saved your life, Gwim,' he said. 'Do not waste it.'

Those final words in his mind, William had gone to King Henry and Queen Alienor at Lyons la Forêt and made his report, giving Henry the salient facts with a soldier's upright duty. Henry had remarked that he was deeply relieved that William had not returned smothered in perfume and posturing like the Patriarch, to which William maintained a diplomatic silence. He would gladly tell Henry everything he wanted to know about the state of the Kingdom of Jerusalem, but let the rest remain behind a curtain.

Henry had granted William a minor estate in the north of England together with several wardships and various privileges that would provide him with a living, albeit far from court. It would do for now, and Queen Alienor had promised her support. It was a time for evaluation and settlement before returning to the fray.

The gentle slope had brought him to the new Temple Church and William stopped to consider the harmonious round of soft tawny stone. The curves slightly echoed the old building in Holborn, but the new structure had a vibrancy and solid beauty that had been missing before.

Entering the porch, William gazed at the exquisitely rendered arches over the doors with their tight foliate and geometric patterns. And the doors themselves, stout and strong, decorated with wrought-iron bands in an intricate but graceful pattern that added a layer of artistry and strength. Tears pricked the back of his eyes. Swallowing, he laid his hand to the latch ring, opened the door and walked inside.

And then stopped, for he was standing inside a replica of the rotunda in Jerusalem.

Dark marbled columns, softly gleaming and trellised with gold, rose to support a lofty galleried dome. The air had the same aromatic smell of the incense that burned in the braziers of the

Holy Sepulchre, and took him straight back there. A stone plinth ran around the walls for the brethren to sit and conduct their business. A variety of carved and painted faces gazed out from arches of blind arcading behind the plinth. The sun poured down from the dome, illuminating the altar in a dazzle of light. It was perfect and complete; uplifting and filled with holy mystery. William fell to his knees, raised his eyes to the clear light pouring onto the pale flags of the floor, and gave thanks to God for his life and his deliverance, and although his heart was tender and sensitive, his emotions were of joy and relief, and reassurance. This was where he would be buried, he knew it inside his living bones.

At a light touch on his shoulder, he looked up to see Aimery standing beside him, dressed in his white woollen robes, a warm smile creasing his cheeks. 'I knew by God's grace you would come back to us,' he said, and as William rose to his feet he clasped him in a hard embrace.

William returned the hug and felt Aimery's solid strength, as firm and robust as these walls, but uplifting too. 'Indeed, it is by God's grace, certainly not by my own.'

Aimery's gaze was keen. 'By whatever means, you are here.' With his arm around William's shoulders, he brought him to sit on the plinth encircling the round.

'The church is a wonder and a great glory to God,' William said, following the shafts of light upwards, and marvelling.

'Indeed it is,' Aimery replied with a smile. 'And consecrated by the Patriarch himself.'

'Yes.' William did not particularly want to think of Heraclius because it inevitably led down other roads, but it was unavoidable. 'I have brought you letters from him.' He indicated his satchel.

'I thought him well meaning and a fine orator,' Aimery said.

William nodded again. 'He was disappointed not to have more success with King Henry, but I did not expect him to do so. Henry would never trade England and Normandy for Jerusalem.'

'No, indeed.' Aimery looked at William and folded his arms. 'I suppose you have many tales to tell of your time there, although perhaps not quite yet.'

William shook his head. 'No,' he said, 'not quite yet – although some I will gladly share with you later.' But never what had been between him and Paschia. That was a personal reliquary, and his cross to bear.

Aimery looked sidelong at William and said nothing, but folded his arms.

'I have come to render service to the Templars,' William said eventually. 'I took an oath in Jerusalem that I would honour the order and the Blessed Virgin as a secular knight for the rest of my days.'

'You chose not to take the full oath?'

It was a straightforward question without hint of reproach, and William shook his head. 'I did not deem myself worthy at the time, nor do so now. It is not my path for the moment, but perhaps in the future.'

Aimery patted his shoulder. 'You are among friends and allies. You are one of us and you will always have our support and protection even as you will bestow us yours.'

A sense of serenity and gravitas settled on William. 'Not all that I looked upon in Jerusalem was fair or honourable. Indeed, many of the dealings were murky and corrupt. Men of the cross were no exception – and neither to my shame was I. I swore when I took my vows that in future all my dealings would be right and honourable and for the good of all – a personal vow to myself.'

Aimery nodded with sombre understanding.

'The King has given me land in the north country and should I desire marriage, the wardship of Heloise of Lancaster.'

Aimery rubbed his chin. 'And do you desire marriage, Gwim?'

William shook his head and smiled a little at the use of the familiar name. 'I am not sure it is the right opportunity. I shall go north, and I shall do my best for my wards, but is this all there is? I have the skills to be of service in a wider arena.'

Aimery looked thoughtful. 'I agree, and we shall do everything we can to help you. As you say, there is no point in swearing you to service and then ignoring your talents. But I would advise you to visit your lands and use some time to rest and take stock of your life and let matters unfold. If there are wounds, let them heal. You can pick up your path as soon as you are ready, and by then all will be in alignment.'

'You always see through me and straight to the crux of the matter,' William said with a smile.

Aimery's eyes twinkled. 'Perhaps because we have known each other since our mothers sat side by side to gossip and watch us roll around on the floor like puppies. We have always been brothers, not of womb and seed, but in everything else.'

They sat in silence for a while, and William had to wipe his eyes. 'Speaking of brothers, there is one more thing I would ask of you,' he said when he was sure of his voice.

'You have but to name it.' Aimery rubbed the back of his neck. 'I know you acted as a decoy for certain letters and took your own life into your hands.'

William did not ask how Aimery knew. The Templar network functioned across all boundaries, in the same way that Zaccariah's did. The trick was in finding the safe strands that were bridges rather than the sticky threads of a web.

'Ancel was badly wounded in Outremer – broke his leg taking a blow intended for me – and it has limited what he can now do. He is settled at Perche with our cousin Rotrou and will dwell there the rest of his days in other employment. He left a woman in Jerusalem . . .' Here William faltered and looked down at the ring on his little finger. He too had left a woman in Jerusalem. When he raised his head, Aimery was looking at him narrowly. 'A good woman,' William said. 'Honest and strong and loving. We could not bring her with us, but it would gladden his life

466

and make it bearable if she could come to him. The arm of the Templars is long, as you say, and if you could help bring this about when the pilgrim ships sail . . . I can give you her name and where she lives. I have money with which to secure her passage. Onri has promised to help in Jerusalem, but I would have it secured from here also, because of the distance and uncertainty.'

'Leave it with me.' Aimery touched his sleeve. 'I will arrange it, I promise.'

To William, Aimery's promise meant that the thing was as good as done, and he experienced a lightening of blessed relief.

Riding from the Temple Church, the afternoon sun low in the sky, polishing Bezant's copper hide with gold, William felt that a great weight had finally lifted from his shoulders, and he was smiling. Never had the grass smelled sweeter or the air more fresh. He had his life, and even if a few shadows remained, they only gave more strength to the light.

40

Manor of Caversham, May 1219

'William?'

He turned his head on the pillow and looked at Aimery, who was leaning over him, holding his hand. His frame was a little stooped, like a weather-embattled tree, and his face heavily lined with the weight of years, but his eyes were bright with awareness and wisdom.

'Dear friend,' Aimery said, 'it grieves me to see you in such a plight.'

William gave a rueful half-smile. 'Grand Master,' he said, slightly teasing Aimery's exalted rank within the Templars. 'I trust in God to make all things right.'

'I had masses said for your soul at the Temple Church before I set out,' Aimery said. 'I know why you have summoned me.'

William squeezed his hand. 'We go back a long time you and I. Of course, you know.'

Aimery drew back to remove his hat and cloak, and having plumped William's pillows, settled down in a chair at William's side, as though paying a normal social visit. William recognised with a pang of affection that Aimery was trying to make things seem normal and as if time was unimportant – and in a way, it was.

William played along with the charade. 'Remember when we hid in the undercroft at Hamstead and drank wine from the barrel?' It was just before I left to train for knighthood at Tancarville.'

'And your father discovered us.' Aimery made a face but laughed.

'Ancel was there too, but we hid him behind a hogshead in the corner and saved him a whipping.' William's mind filled with a vision of Ancel crouched in the shadows, holding his breath, eyes wide with fear. 'I did not save him in later life.' He thought of Ancel limping around with the aid of a stick, in Rotrou's service, and then later with Rotrou's son Geoffrey. Ancel had trained the squires and undertaken many a supervisory and administrative task, but his future as a warrior had been curtailed.

Aimery took his hand. 'It was God's will, William. You cannot take all the blame on your own shoulders – although I know it has long been a pattern for you. Ancel made his own choices.'

'But because of my actions.'

'Which were made in turn by the actions of others. You have been absolved many times. Now you must forgive yourself because that chain still binds you to the ground – you cannot be free until you sever it.'

A sharp pang made William gasp, and Aimery helped him to drink from the cup of poppy syrup. William lay back, forcing his will through the pain.

At least Asmaria had come to Ancel, escaping a few weeks before Jerusalem had fallen to Saladin, and they had made a good life together at Perche, even if it was one constrained by Ancel's injury.

In Jerusalem, little King Baldwin had died aged just nine years old and his mother had claimed the throne and crowned her husband Guy de Lusignan as her king and consort, and all had come to disaster. Less than a year after his coronation, Guy, with Gerard de Ridefort at his side, had led out the army of Jerusalem against Saladin and in a terrible error of judgement brought almost the entire force to slaughter, including the majority of the Templars, among them Onri and Augustine, at the battle of Hattin. In returning when he did, William had avoided their fate, and although he had grieved for both men, he had concluded that God truly did intend him to live, and that Paschia had not only been a great threat to his life, but in a strange way his saving grace.

Paschia herself, with her ability to land on her feet even in dire circumstances, had survived the taking of Jerusalem and escaped with the Patriarch and their baby daughter. He felt no bitterness toward her now. All that had leached away with time, healed many years ago by his beautiful, golden Isabelle, who had stood by him through thick and thin without vacillation. His solace, his love, his helpmate, and mother to their ten children.

He had made his peace with the Virgin, endowing this chapel to her at Caversham, his priories at Cartmel and Tintern de Voto in Ireland, and St Mary's in Rospont. Had she forgiven him? He had always wondered if his change of fortune on his return from Jerusalem had been her doing, but like any queen, the Queen of Heaven expected service in return.

A drift of melancholy remained, like the last wisp of incense vanishing in church and the final leaf tugging from the tree as winter arrived. But beyond winter came spring. He had served in every season and would continue to do so.

'My heart is whole and free,' he said as the poppy syrup gradually eased the pain.

Aimery nodded comfortably. 'Well then, old friend, tell me what you have been seeing here.'

'The sky through the window,' William said. 'I have become an expert on the weather just from watching how the clouds move, and smelling the air while I still have breath.' He paused. 'And Jerusalem. I have been back to Jerusalem without walking a single pace from my bed, and now I know what I must do. It is time to fulfil what I vowed all those years ago. My next step will not be in this world and I need to don my armour and be firm in my intent and certainty.' He gave Aimery a wry smile. 'It is like resting a siege ladder against a castle wall. It must be solid, and to set one's foot on the rung and take that first step requires the ultimate courage and strength of purpose.'

Aimery nodded agreement. 'You have done that many times in your life.'

'Yes, but this will be the hardest one because it is final – there is no descending from this one. I ask you to be the scaffolding to hold me steady.'

Aimery gripped William's hand, pleating the loose skin over his knuckles, and William saw the tears shining in his eyes. 'You do not need me for that,' he said, 'but whatever I can do, I will.'

It was quiet. The sun was setting in a flush of gilded apricot and soft tawny and soon the first stars would prick out. Bats flitted in the early spring air, and he heard the 'weet-weet' of a female tawny owl in the oak trees beyond his window; the soft tick of logs as they settled in the hearth where his eldest son sat with Jean D'Earley playing chess, keeping watch, but leaving William to his own thoughts and slumber.

Aimery had departed two hours ago, taking the barge down the Thames back to London following a solemn meal held in William's chamber for all those who had witnessed William taking the full Templar vows and departing the secular life. Now all that remained was the waiting, but he was calm and unafraid.

He gazed at the seal Aimery had placed in his left hand bearing the image of two Templar knights astride the same horse. That was his shield. His empty right hand was for his sword when the time came. It lay sheathed with his Templar mantle at the foot of his bed. The silk shrouds had been washed in incense, blessed, and placed under his bed, close enough for him to touch if he wished. Soon they would be draped over and around him, even as they had in Jerusalem, protecting him until the resurrection. His body would rest but his spirit would be alert, awake and awakened.

He heard again Aimery's words, spoken softly following the

vows. 'Blessed be your life. Blessed be your passing beyond it. You were a worthy man in life, and a worthy man you leave it.'

The sunset faded, and the sky turned to the luminous dark teal of evening. Everything had a beginning as well as an end, and then a beginning again. Dawn to dusk, to dawn.

'It will not be long,' he said and, with a feeling of wholeness and fulfilment, closed his hand over the seal, sensing upon his face the delicate gossamer brush of silk.

Author Note

When I wrote my novel about the life of William Marshal up to 1194, *The Greatest Knight,* I knew that William had spent the years 1183 to 1186 on pilgrimage to the Holy Land fulfilling a pledge to his dying young lord that he would take his cloak to the tomb of the Holy Sepulchre in Jerusalem. What he did there (beyond obtaining his own burial silks) was a mystery. Sadly, because of time constraints, structure and word count on that novel, I was unable to cover that particular period of his life and so included a bridging chapter that worked well in the context of the story and was as much as I knew at the time.

I have always wanted to return to the question of what William Marshal might have done during those missing three years. Since writing *The Greatest Knight* I have continued to study William and his family for personal interest and that period of absence from 1183 to 1186 has continued to intrigue me.

A couple of years ago, while discussing future projects with my then editor, she asked if I would consider writing another novel about William Marshal. Since I had been thinking of just such a project myself, we were in complete accord, and I was delighted to be given the go-ahead to write the story of William's pilgrimage.

So, what do we know about his time in the Holy Land?

The answer is very little.

Shortly after he died, William's eldest son, also called William, commissioned a chronicler to write his father's life story as a poem. It has survived in its original Old French, has been translated into English, and runs to over nineteen thousand lines. It is known as the *Histoire de Guillaume le Mareschal*, or 'History of William Marshal'. In the Middle Ages, a 'histoire' was both a history and a story – a tale that blended truth and fiction, rather like a historical novel today. In the case of the *Histoire de Guillaume le Mareschal*, the truth forms a solid backbone, but tends to big up its hero and gloss over the moments that were perhaps not quite so heroic. However, it still gives us an insight into the world of the late twelfth and early thirteenth centuries and presents us with William Marshal as he desired to be seen for posterity – some of the edges smoothed, but nevertheless remaining vibrant and three-dimensional. When this portrait is added to the known material, including his charters and documents, a powerful overall picture of the man emerges . . . but not of his time in the Holy Land.

Of the 19,215 lines in the *Histoire*, only twenty-four of them concern his time in Outremer (a medieval term for the Holy Land, meaning 'the land beyond the sea'). The lines tell us nothing specific about what he did, and part of that narrative is historically inaccurate. The *Histoire* tells us that William took his leave of King Guy, his knights, the Templars and Hospitallers, who were all disappointed to see him go home because of his fine qualities. The problem is that when William left the Holy Land, Guy de Lusignan (who had been his enemy in Poitou) was not yet king. William was back in Normandy by February 1186, and Guy did not become King of Jerusalem until seven months later. So, there is some fudging going on – either because of lack of information or because what happened in the Holy Land stayed in the Holy Land. The writer of the *Histoire* confesses that although William performed 'many fine deeds' he does not know what they were because 'I was not there, and I did not witness them'. Nor can he find anyone who can tell him what they were.

The main thing we know about William's time in Outremer is that he obtained his own burial silks (the inspiration for this novel and its title), very possibly from the Templars. On his deathbed, William sent his dear friend and former squire Jean D'Earley to Wales, to retrieve the pieces of silk from storage and bring them to him. When Jean returned, William had the pieces laid out on his bed to show to his retainers and family. Only now did he tell them that he had had them for over thirty years and had always intended them to be draped over his body when he died. He also added that while in Outremer he had given his body to be buried by the Templars wherever and whenever he should die. Professor David Crouch, senior authority on the Marshals, believes that William must have felt that his life was in serious peril at some point during his time in Outremer and that he made his will and involved the Templars in it. I believe it is no coincidence that in the *Histoire* he reveals the pieces of silk to his eldest son and his inner circle of knights immediately preceding the information that he desires to be buried by the Templars. I suspect that the cloths were his covenant with the order – a symbol of the pledge he took to them in Outremer.

A year before William was ordained into the Templars on his deathbed, he had had a Templar mantle made and kept it just as well hidden as his silk cloths. The mantle symbolised his entry into the Templar order and a farewell to all things secular. The silk shrouds were his farewell to the world, to be displayed as he was borne to his grave (unless bad weather intervened in which case they were to be covered and protected by plain grey cloth). Even stored away for three decades those lengths of silk were highly important to William.

What did the silks look like?

Again, we don't know, only that they were very fine and of choice cloth sufficient to cover William's body and his bier. We don't know if they were patterned or coloured. There is a very famous white silk that was made in the city of Tyre. Known as *tafeth*, it was 'exported thence to all parts, being extremely fine and well woven beyond compare'. Some white silks were woven with a pattern and there are samples to be seen in the V&A collection of medieval textiles. From slightly later, textile historian Maria Hayward tells us about the medieval pall and that it was a rectangular cloth, often with a central cross of a different fabric, prominent from the thirteenth to fifteenth centuries. John Duke of Bedford had a pall of red velvet with a red satin cross and decorated with his badge. William Marshal's cloths could well have been a precursor to these later sumptuous decorations.

Templar Silks is itself a 'histoire' – a work of history and fiction. We know that William Marshal departed for the Holy Land on pilgrimage at some point in the high summer or autumn of 1183 following the death of his lord Henry the Young King from dysentery but we do not know his method of travel. Some historians state that he travelled by sea (which was becoming popular but hadn't reached its heyday), but that lies in the realms of conjecture; he could just as easily have taken the overland route, especially since this would allow him to rack up indulgences along the way (a sort of points system for entry into heaven: the more indulgences you had, the less time you had to spend in purgatory). I sent William overland, via the area controlled by the kingdom of Sicily, which included Apulia and the port of Brindisi, because Henry II's daughter, the Young King's sister, was Queen of those lands and I felt that William may well have taken that route and would have been assured of safe passage.

Constantinople in 1183 was in a state of turmoil. The previous year there had been a massacre of the Latin Christians, and although a new Latin church was being built in reparation and some mea culpa noises had been made, the situation was unstable. However, there was the attraction of the great church of Hagia Sophia with its magnificent mosaic of the Virgin Mary. Alienor of Aquitaine, the Young King's mother, had sojourned in Constantinople during the Second Crusade and may have filled her eldest son with visions of the wonders she had seen there, so I had my reasons for sending William by that road.

Further researching William's potential journey to Outremer, I reasoned that he must have been accompanied by a small entourage, including men who were known to have been in the Young King's affinity, or who were beholden to William and may have been on the witness list of some of his early charters. William would not have set out alone and by the circumstances of his vow must, I suspect, have travelled with others known to his young lord and seeking to redeem their souls. I have also sent William's brother Ancel with him. We know Ancel was with William at the tourney of Lagny sur Marne in 1179 and I think it likely that he would have accompanied William to the Holy Land. He was a younger son who would have had to make his way as best he could, and being a part of William's entourage after 1179 would seem a likely choice. The only other reference to Ancel in history, apart from Lagny, is in a charter he witnesses for the Count of Perche, a Marshal cousin, in 1189. In *The Greatest Knight* I sent him off to Perche after the tourney of Lagny, but I now believe he accompanied William to Jerusalem. What happened to him there is the speculative part of my 'histoire', based on my alternative researches with Akashic consultant Alison King, and at the end of his adventures he is back at Perche.

The situation William found on arriving in Jerusalem is as written in conventional history. King Baldwin IV, in his early twenties, was slowly dying of leprosy and the vultures were gathering. His sister Sybilla was married to Guy de Lusignan, a Poitevan incomer who one chronicler claims had been banished from court by Henry II for the murder of Patrick Earl of Salisbury, who was William Marshal's uncle. Whether Guy's was the hand on the spear is open to debate but certainly his family were responsible for Patrick's murder and there was no love lost between Guy and William even if they were not outright enemies.

Guy had been appointed regent of the Kingdom of Jerusalem, but the established colonists would not unite behind him and considered him arrogant and inept. His little stepson, Baldwin, was heir to the throne, and the main power struggle was over who was going to rule in the child's stead when King Baldwin died.

To this end, a deputation was sent to Europe seeking help and led by Heraclius, Patriarch of Jerusalem. The envoys set out in the summer of 1184 and I think it more than likely that William had a hand in the preparations because he had so recently come from Henry II's court and had served the Angevin hierarchy for at least fifteen years. He also had excellent contacts within the courts of northern Europe and was known to Philippe of France.

Patriarch Heraclius has often come in for a bad press from film, novel and historical writing. He's seen as a worldly prelate, too concerned with his perfumes, rich clothes and of course his mistress, Paschia de Riveri, to be spiritual. It has to be said that much of what is written about him comes from the pen of one of his main rivals, William of Tyre, so needs to be read judiciously. To me, he came across as an affable, urbane and reasonable sort of man, one who enjoyed his pleasures most certainly, but one with humanity and a concern both for Jerusalem and the welfare of his fellow man. He was responsible in consultation for helping to negotiate the surrender of Jerusalem to Saladin without a bloodbath in the aftermath of the disastrous battle of Hattin, after Guy de Lusignan led the Christian army of Jerusalem to its destruction. He was to die during the siege of Acre in the winter of 1190/91, as did Sybilla Queen of Jerusalem and her two daughters.

William's affair with Paschia de Riveri is conjectural on my behalf, but it's certainly not a wild flight of fantasy, and it's one of the reasons historical fiction exists – to explore the 'what if' and 'who knows'. William was once accused of having an affair with the Young King's wife Marguerite. I do not think he did, but he must have had a certain reputation with the ladies for that accusation to be given credence in the wider court, and the Marshal's department was responsible for policing the concubines and whores who populated that court. It has also been revealed recently that William may have had an illegitimate son. David Crouch in his revised edition of his biography explores that possibility, brought to light by evidence in the Marshal charters of a certain Gilbert Marshal of Mundham who Professor Crouch thinks likely to have been William's son, born out of wedlock. Add to that the ten legitimate children William and Isabelle de Clare had between them, and one finds a man who enjoyed the physical company of women.

What we know in history about Paschia de Riveri is that she was a draper's widow from Nablus. Heraclius was in the habit of buying her services from her husband whenever he wanted her company and would then hand her back to her family in the interim. After her husband died, she became Heraclius's full-time mistress. She is portrayed as parading around Jerusalem with her household, dressed in jewels and silks, and because of her influence on the Patriarch was known as 'La Patriarchess'. They had at least one daughter but we don't know her name or date of birth, only that Heraclius was in a meeting one day when an excited servant came flying in to shout the news to all and sundry that the 'Patriarchess' had borne him a daughter!

Given Paschia's circumstances and the convoluted dealings at the court of Jerusalem, I thought it not unlikely that Mafia-like business was the norm and sex, money and power were at the root of all scheming, even as they are today. If William became caught up in it, then I feel it taught him valuable lessons that would stand him in good stead in later life. He learned the worst so that he could be the best. Although we know Heraclius's end from history, we do not know what happened to Paschia de Riveri or their daughter. All we know about her is what I have reported in the paragraph above.

While researching the Marshal's role in the Kingdom of Jerusalem, it became clear that it was more concerned with horses, harness and stabling than in the Angevin realms. This was an integral part of the Marshal's duties in England and Normandy, but the position had a wider and more important role, whereas in the Holy Land the horse care and equipment element was still pivotal to the Marshal's position and duty, hence William's involvement at that level during his time there.

As a final note, I was fascinated by how powerful William's dedication to the Virgin Mary seems to have been. I suspect that robbing the shrine at Rocamadour had an enormous effect on him. As a medieval man he would truly have believed he was going to hell for what he had done, and perhaps his young lord too, who had died in agony before his eyes. In making his vow to the Templars, both as a secular knight and then a full brother in his last days, William would have been vowing himself to God and the Virgin. His foundation at Cartmel is dedicated to the warrior St Michael, and the Virgin. His chapel at Caversham is dedicated to the Virgin (it had a wonderful jewelled statue of the Virgin dating to this period which is now lost) as is Tintern de Voto in Ireland and the church of St Mary's in New Ross, among others. Devotion to the Virgin is an especially English phenomenon in the twelfth century, but William Marshal appears to have been particularly fervent. There is no overt indication of this in the *Histoire de Guillaume le Mareschal* but I consider it to be one of those personal things, so much a part of him that it went without saying, under our noses if we care to look.

Select Bibliography

For anyone wishing to read further on the subjects covered in the novel, here are just a few of the books I found useful during my research. For any readers interested in viewing my full research library it can be found here:

http://elizabethchadwick.com/my-reference-library/

Barber, Malcolm and Keith Bate, *The Templars: Selected Sources Translated and Annotated* (Manchester University Press, 2002), ISBN 9780719051104

Benvenisti, Meron, *The Crusaders in the Holy Land* (Macmillan, 1972), ISBN 39229752

Biddle, Martin, Gideon Avni, Jon Seligman and Tamar Winter, *The Church of the Holy Sepulchre* (Rizzoli, 2000), ISBN 0847822826

Boas, Adrian J., *Archaeology of the Military Orders* (Routledge, 2006), ISBN 0415 487234

Jerusalem in the Time of the Crusades (Routledge, 2001), ISBN 0415230004

Crouch, David, *The Acts and Letters of the Marshal Family: Marshals of England and Earls of Pembroke 1145-1248* (Cambridge University Press for the Royal Historical Society, 2015), ISBN 9781107130036

William Marshal, Third Edition (Routledge, 2016), ISBN 9781138939332

Drake Boehm, Barbara and Melanie Holcomb, *Jerusalem 1000-1400: Every People Under Heaven* (Metropolitan Museum of Art, 2016), ISBN 9781588395986

Hamilton, Bernard, *The Leper King and his Heirs: Baldwin IV and the Crusader Kingdom of Jerusalem* (Cambridge University Press, 2000), ISBN 0521017475

Hillenbrand, Carole, *The Crusades: Islamic Perspectives* (Edinburgh University Press, 1999), ISBN 0748606300

Hodgson, Natasha R., *Women, Crusading, and the Holy Land in Historical Narrative* (Boydell, 2007), ISBN 9781843833321

Holden, A. J. (ed), *History of William Marshal*, with English translation by S. Gregory and historical notes by D. Crouch, vols 1 and 2 (Anglo-Norman Text Society, 2002)

Kedar, Benjamin Z. et al (eds), *Crusades, Volume 12* (Ashgate, 2013), ISBN 9781472408990

Mitchell, Piers D., *Medicine in the Crusades and the Medieval Surgeon* (Cambridge University Press, 2004), ISBN 0521036607

Phillips, Jonathan, *The Crusades 1095-1204* (Routledge, 2014), ISBN 9781405872935

Richards, D. S. (tr.), *The Chronicle of Ibn al-Athir for the Crusading Period from al-Kamil fi'l-Ta'rikh Part 2* (Ashgate, 2007), ISBN 9780754669517

Riley-Smith, Jonathan (ed.), *The Atlas of the Crusades* (Guild Publishing, 1991), ISBN 9780723003618

Upton-Ward, J. M., *The Rule of the Templars* (Boydell Press, 1992), ISBN 0851157017

Wilkinson, John, Joyce Hill and W. F. Ryan (eds), *Jerusalem Pilgrimage 1099-1185* (Hakluyt Society, 1988), ISBN 0904180212

William of Tyre (Archbishop), *A History of Deeds Done Beyond the Sea* (originally published by Columbia University Press in 1943, republished as part of the Great

Library Collection by R. P. Pryne, Philadelphia, Pennsylvania, 2014) I also wish to thank my dear friend and colleague Alison King for helping me to access the peoples of the past via her extraordinary psychic talent.

Acknowledgements

This is the page where I express my gratitude to everyone who has been there for me while I have been writing *Templar Silks*.

My thanks to my former editor at Sphere, Rebecca Saunders, with whom I first discussed the idea of a novel about William Marshal's pilgrimage, and who then handed on to my current editor Maddie West who has the same passion and is brilliant to work with. My thanks, too, to the terrific team at Sphere: my publicist Stephanie Melrose and other colleagues, Amy Donegan, Jennie Rothwell, Cath Burke and Thalia Proctor. Also to my copy editor Dan Balado for a light hand, common sense, and an excellent eye for detail.

I also want to express my gratitude to everyone at the Blake Friedmann literary agency: my agent Isobel Dixon, also Julian Friedmann, Hattie Grunwald, and the other lovely people in the contracts department and behind the scenes who make sure all runs smoothly, especially Sam Hodder and Emanuela Anechoum who deal with my rants about overseas tax forms!

I need to thank Simon Hicks and Kimberley Gardner, people very dear to my heart, who also happen to be amazing emergency and critical care nurses. They were both extremely helpful in talking to me about the difficulties Ancel would have faced after receiving his injury and in detailing to me the best- and worst-case scenarios. Any errors of judgement and misinterpretation are mine alone.

Thank you to my husband Roger – for those who have read

my acknowledgements down the years, yes, he is still making me mugs of tea, doing the ironing and being my stalwart support ship and research assistant. And also huge appreciation to my dear friend Alison King for friendship, long conversations over all kinds of beverages, and for continuing wonderful adventures in time travel.

Thank you also to my many Facebook friends and readers. There are too many of you to mention without upping the word count to the point of giving my editor a heart attack, but you bring joy and normality to my day.

Special acknowledgement

While I was writing *Templar Silks*, Carole Blake, my beloved agent and dear friend of twenty-seven years, suddenly passed away. She plucked my first novel, *The Wild Hunt*, from the 'slush pile', began reading it in the office and very quickly got in touch to offer to represent me. I was a stay-at-home mother at the time, looking after two small children, but with a burning ambition to be a published novelist. Carole took me on, sold my books around the world in sixteen languages, and raised me up from an inexperienced hopeful to a fully-fledged internationally published writer. She was always there to further my interests, to fight my corner, to advise and to nurture. She believed passionately in my work – as she believed in all of her authors. I shall love and miss her always, and yet I have a suspicion she will always be around. A closed door was never an obstacle to Carole. When faced with dilemmas I often ask myself what she would do, and I find my solution.

If you enjoyed *Templar Silks*, find out where
William Marshal's journey began . . .

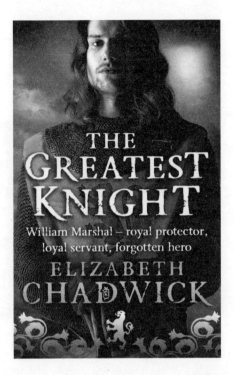

A penniless young knight with few prospects, William Marshal
is plucked from obscurity when he saves the life of Henry II's
formidable queen, Eleanor of Aquitaine. In gratitude, she
appoints him tutor to the heir to the throne. However, being a
royal favourite brings its share of conflict and envy as well as
fame and reward. William's influence over the volatile, fickle
Prince Henry and his young wife is resented by less favoured
courtiers who set about engineering his downfall.

Available now

Discover Elizabeth Chadwick's bestselling
Eleanor of Aquitaine trilogy

'An author who makes history come gloriously alive'
The Times

'Picking up an Elizabeth Chadwick novel you know you are
in for a sumptuous ride'
Daily Telegraph

Available now